Peter Watt has spent t... trawler deckhand, build... man, private investigat... Royal Papua New Gu... worked with Aborigine... Guineans, and he speak... ...... and pid-gin. He now lives at Finch Hatton in Queensland.

Good friends, fine fishing and the vast open spaces of out-back Queensland are his main interests in life. Peter Watt can be contacted at www.peterwatt.com

Excerpts from e-mails sent to Peter Watt since his first novel was published:

'. . . thank you for the hours of entertainment you have given me . . .'

'As much as it pains me as a Kiwi to praise an Aussie, your books are bloody marvellous . . . They say you're the next Wilbur Smith; you have already passed him. Can't wait to read more of your work.'

'I wanted more! . . . no superlative would be sufficient to describe your work.'

'Your books are marketed here [UK] as being as good as Wilbur Smith . . . or your money back. They certainly live up to that billing. Keep writing!!'

'I can honestly say in all my years of reading, your books have to be on my list of the best ever.'

'. . . *Cry of the Curlew* was a fantastic read. Never have I enjoyed a novel as much.'

'They are the most enjoyable books that I have read in a long time . . . I look forward to reading more of your books in the future.'

Also by Peter Watt

EDEN

PETER WATT

PAN

Pan Macmillan Australia

First published 2004 in Macmillan by Pan Macmillan Australia Pty Limited
This Pan edition published 2005 by Pan Macmillan Australia Pty Limited
1 Market Street, Sydney

Reprinted 2008

National Library of Australia
cataloguing-in-publication data:

Watt, Peter, 1949– .
Eden.

ISBN 9780330421881

1. World War, 1939–1945 – Fiction.
2. Male friendship – Fiction. I. Title.

A823.3

Set in 11.5/13 pt Bembo by Post Pre-press Group
Map by Laurie Whiddon
Printed in Australia by McPherson's Printing Group

Papers used by Pan Macmillan Australia Pty Ltd are natural,
recyclable products made from wood grown in sustainable forests.
The manufacturing processes conform to the environmental
regulations of the country of origin.

This book is dedicated to Naomi Howard-Smith, whose love and patience defies even an author's ability, to search for the words of gratitude.

ACKNOWLEDGMENTS

Foremost, I would like to thank the team that worked with me on the production of this novel: my publisher Cate Raterson, editor Julie Crisp and copy editor Jan Hutchinson. My many thanks to Jane Novak and her wonderful mum and dad, John and Jill Novak. And to all at Pan Macmillan Australia in Sydney, Melbourne or on the road somewhere in Australia selling books. Many thanks to my wonderful agent, Geoffrey Radford of Anthony Williams Management.

Since the release of my last novel I have discovered a real Eden. A little village called Finch Hatton, west of Mackay in Queensland and located in the scenic Pioneer Valley. As such I have had the fortune to meet many wonderful and hospitable people, whose friendship has indirectly or directly influenced the creative process of writing. So, my thanks go out to the following: Mel and Alice Lowth; the Camilleri family of Joe, Heather, David and Michelle; our two local police officers, Ian Galpin and Jamie McClean, and their respective wives, Dani and Tain; our ambulance officers, Steve and Carlin Eggleston, whose services have been used; Bob and Jeanette from the corner store; Barb from the second hand shop; Karl and Anne-Maree, from our local café; Heather and Errol from the post office; our local council representative Gary Parkinson and his lovely wife, Trudi. I should also mention Marg who looks after our injured wild life. A special thanks to the wonderfully helpful ladies from the Mirani Library whose assistance was invaluable.

An important place for an author to go and relax and meet friends and readers is the local pub. In this case my thanks go out to Carmel and Dave Blann from the Criterion Hotel who have quietly done so much for the community. To Michelle and Tony behind the bar, my many thanks also. A fellow writer, Blair Hunt, and Jack and Jan Bobbins. Around the bar I would like to recognise Les Thomas, Gary and young Jim, brothers Pat and Pike. Not to forget Heather, who sells the raffle tickets on Friday night.

My alternative place to meet friends is the Pioneer Valley Hotel, at Gargett, and my thanks go out to Lyn and Peter Goodale for their hospitality and cold beer. Also my thanks to Lisa and Jan behind the bar and Marg in the kitchen. And not to forget Ian Barnes, OAM, at the bar.

My continuing thanks go out to my old friends Robert Bozek and Nadine. And to Phil Murphy in Cairns, for his ongoing advice on military matters. A special thanks to Jenee Molyneux for her assistance with prewar aircraft information.

My continuing thanks also to my family for their

support. To Aunt Joan and Uncle John Payne in Tweed Heads, sister and brother in law, Kerry and Ty McKee, and my mother, Elinor Watt, who is cared for by the wonderful staff at the Pioneer Valley Retirement Centre, Mirani.

I would like to make a special mention of a true, great Australian who served both his country and community with distinction. Mr John Warby, OAM, ED passed away in 2004 but has left us with a story of courage and dedication to ideals we often forget are the basis of a just and stable society. A special welcome to the world of writers goes out to Dave Sabben, whose novel Through Enemy Eyes will be released soon.

Last but not least, my thanks go out to my old wantok, Lawrie Norgren, former member of the engineers who served his country in South Vietnam, for his critiques on the novel and the hours spent discussing the life known to former soldiers and residents of Papua New Guinea.

EDEN

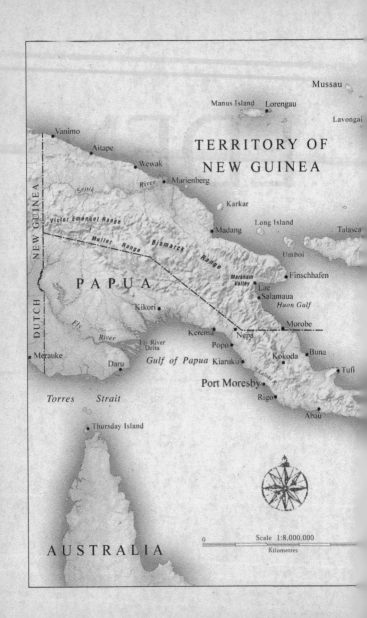

TERRITORY OF
NEW GUINEA
and
PAPUA

ieng

Tabar Islands

Tanga

Namatanai • **New Ireland**

Rabaul

Feni Island

Nissan Island

Wide Bay

Buka

Buka Passage

New Britain

Bougainville

Kieta

Buin

Choiseul Island

S o l o m o n

I s l a n d s

S o l o m o n

Yeka Vekalla

Kulambangra

Ysabel

New Georgia

Malaita

iriwina Island

suia

Kulumadau

S e a

Yaugunn

Nggela

sson Island

Woodlark Island

Normanby Island

i

Guadalcanal

Misima Island

Adele Island

Tagula Island

C o r a l   S e a

PALESTINE

July 1941

PROLOGUE

Only the woman's dark eyes showed from behind the heavily veiled face. She stood with the crowd that had gathered in the marketplace to gaze with curiosity at the strangers who now walked the streets of Old Jerusalem. They were uniformed men wearing khaki and their demeanour had a cockiness about it that spoke of self-assuredness.

'They are the English,' a woman, similarly dressed in the voluminous, traditional chador of the good Moslem, muttered in Arabic.

Fatima strained to hear the words of the woman standing beside her. Arabic was not Fatima's native tongue. It was a language she had learned when her husband, a French citizen from Corsica, had moved from North Africa to avoid the war raging between the Allied and the Axis forces in the deserts of his adopted country.

Two of the soldiers moved closer as they picked their way through the marketplace like the tourists that they temporarily were. As curious as children, the two men examined all that was on display. Fatima could clearly hear them. With a start she realised that not only were the two soldiers speaking English, a language she was fluent in, but they had a distinctive accent she was all too familiar with.

'They are not English,' she said to her female companion. 'They are Australians.'

The other woman glanced sideways at her. 'I have heard of the Australians from my father who said they were here many years ago when the Ottomans were fighting the British. Why have they returned?'

Fatima did not reply. For now she felt a joy she had almost forgotten existed. She was reaching the fortieth year of her hard life. She had not always been known as Fatima. It was a name she took when she chose to follow the way of the Koran. The product of a European father and Chinese mother, once she had been known by the name of Iris. But that seemed a lifetime ago when she had been young and beautiful.

Captured, sold into a form of slavery to the man who was her husband, Iris had lived to experience many cultures from China to Papua. From Papua to North Africa and now to Palestine.

Her immediate reaction was to step forward and address the two soldiers. She would proclaim who she was and ask for their protection. But the thought died as it had come. She was no longer Iris, the young woman who once loved an Englishman in a faraway place. She was Fatima, a follower of Allah.

Iris watched from behind her veil as the two soldiers idled away. What use was it now to seek her old identity? For all she knew, those who had once loved her probably thought she was dead.

Part One

KARL'S WAR

July 1941

ONE

The township of Port Moresby was little changed, Leading Seaman Fuji Komine of the Imperial Japanese Navy thought as he gazed at the approaching shoreline of Ela Beach and the protruding wharf where a Burns Philp steamer was unloading its cargo. The bare hills were brown under the hot tropical sun and the capital of Papua still retained a frontier appearance.

But Fuji was not wearing his uniform and to all intents and purposes he blended with the Asian crew of the small coastal steamer as nothing more than a deckhand. He wore a loin cloth and at twenty-five years of age his slight body was defined by muscle. Only his dark eyes gave any hint of his high intelligence and behind them burned the fanaticism of a man on a sacred mission for God – or, in the case of the Japanese sailor, the Emperor.

'You savvy you all come back tonight,' the

European skipper bawled from the bridge at his motley crew as they gathered to disembark to explore the streets and shops of Port Moresby. 'No givee trouble whiteman,' he added by way of warning to his predominantly Filipino and Chinese deckhands. 'You givee trouble and white fella lock you all up, you hear?' The crew nodded, mumbling their understanding. They were very aware that once ashore they would be considered less than human by the Australian authorities who had an inbred contempt for Asians.

Fuji scowled at the skipper's attempt at pidgin English, never letting on that his own grasp of the language was probably more fluent than the burly, red-faced captain's. For Leading Seaman Fuji Komine was born in Papua and even now thought about meeting his father, Isokihi the Boat Builder as he was known to the barbarians of Papua and New Guinea.

Fuji left the deck to go below and change into clothes that marked him as a Chinese coolie: cotton pants and shirt. To many Europeans his switch in nationality made little difference – one Asian was like any other in appearance.

The steamer docked, the gangplank rattled down and Fuji stepped ashore for the first time in seven years after having fled Papua when his involvement with the criminal O'Leary was violently terminated. It had been four months since the beginning of his mission to covertly locate suitable sites in the islands surrounding Papua New Guinea and the Torres Strait to dump fuel and essential supplies for Japanese submarines prowling the southern waters. He had worked aboard an old but sturdy, low-slung Japanese

10

fishing boat with other members of the navy, all working under the guise of fishermen, not an uncommon sight in these tropical waters. They would be put ashore under cover of night. During the daylight hours Fuji would photograph and mark the sites on admiralty charts for future reference. When the targeted area reconnaissance had been completed he was left behind to assume the role of a nomadic sailor-cum-labourer, working the ports and plantations of the scattering of islands between Australia and Papua. He had befriended and eventually recruited a few local natives with vague promises of them being well rewarded should he call upon their services in the future. He exploited their resentment of the Europeans lording themselves over the natives in the islands but had to be extremely careful as much of the native population of the Torres Islands were loyal to their Australian bosses and his covert activities could easily be betrayed to the police.

Although a lowly, non-commissioned officer in the Japanese Navy, Fuji was a member of its elite naval intelligence and, if successful, the assignment promised recognition with its subsequent reward of promotion. To the dedicated Japanese military man, to fail left only one recourse to avoid interrogation – suicide. Such was the way of Bushido. His controllers had supplied him with a good supply of Australian currency and false papers describing him as a marine engineer, and these were the only weapons he carried in his precarious life as a spy. Both had been useful in gaining a job aboard a coastal steamer out of Thursday Island and heading for Port Moresby.

The Filipino second in command accepted the young Chinese sailor as part of the crew although he did not need another engineer. The money in the palm of the Filipino sailor's hand told a different story and he did not ask questions as to why a Chinese engineer would need to bribe his way aboard. With a shrug the Filipino had dismissed the gesture. Believing Fuji was probably on the run from one of those Chinese criminal gangs in Shanghai, he gave him a working passage.

Fuji was on the final leg of his mission and his meeting with a successful contact in Port Moresby would reward him with a place in the navy aboard one of the mighty battleships of the Pacific Fleet. But Fuji was feeling extremely nervous. Not for the upcoming contact with the Moresby-based agent but for the meeting with his father. Fuji might not fear death but he did fear his father's opinion of him. At least now he had returned to the land of his birth as a warrior of the greatest navy on the Pacific Ocean. Surely his father would be proud of him.

Fuji's father's house was a ramshackle arrangement of logs and thatch built just above the shoreline. Around the house were the framework slips for his small boats, highly prized by the Europeans for their tough sea-worthiness. Wood shavings and timber off-cuts lay scattered in the yard where hens wandered, pecking at the grubs and insects plentiful in the surrounding rainforests.

The walk to Isokihi the Boat Builder's premises

had taken Fuji all day and he arrived at dusk to see a tiny glimmer of light from the lowest window of the bungalow. His father's house had not changed in the seven years he had been away, Fuji thought with just a touch of relief. His memories of its crude but comfortable interior were pleasant. He remembered his mother as she silently went about tending to the house and his father, more with love than the subservience traditionally expected of a good Japanese wife.

Fuji took a deep breath. 'Honourable Father,' he called as he stood outside the hut, and after a silence that seemed to last forever his father emerged from the low door to stand before his son.

Fuji bowed respectfully but noticed that his father remained standing not fully recognising his son. The squat, solidly built, balding boat builder was a direct contrast to his slimmer son who had inherited his mother's family's physical characteristics. 'May I enter?' Fuji asked.

His father gave a slight nod of his head, turned his back and was followed inside by his son. The first sight Fuji had inside the house was of his mother and her poorly concealed expression of maternal joy at seeing her beloved son. Fuji bowed to his mother but she disregarded protocol to rush to her son and hold him, babbling words of love and concern. 'You are too thin, my son,' she said as he disengaged himself with some embarrassment at her lack of dignity.

'I am well,' he replied formally, glancing sideways at his father.

Ignoring his son, Isokihi lowered himself behind

13

a traditional, low-set table and picked up his chop-sticks. It was a difficult moment and Fuji sensed something was wrong. He felt awkward, as if he were once again a little boy in trouble.

'I know why you are here,' his father said as he raised a piece of food to his lips. 'You are spying.'

Fuji was stunned by his father's perceptiveness. How could he know? As if reading his son's thoughts, Isokihi continued. 'I have heard from the natives I trade with that a young Japanese man was travelling between the islands talking about one day rebelling against the Australians. They said he could speak fluent English when needed and that he was a Papuan like themselves.'

'I am a warrior for the Emperor,' Fuji answered passionately. 'My mission is to prepare the way for the conquest of the barbarians who have enslaved the black men and brought loss of face to our family in this country. I do not apologise for my task. I thought my return would bring joy to you. Or is it that you are no longer a true son of Japan?'

Isokihi slowly placed the chopsticks on his bowl and Fuji felt a stab of fear. Although he was younger and fitter he still had an instinctive dread of his father's anger. He stood tensely, wondering what his father would do.

'I saw war long before you were born,' Isokihi said quietly. 'As a very young sailor in the Emperor's navy fighting against the Russian fleet at Tsushima in 1905 I saw death in every form. And then I returned to a country dying from famine whilst we were fed because we had done the Emperor's will. That is why

I left my country to seek peace and prosperity for your mother and I here. Do you think war will make the world a better place?'

Fuji was stunned by his father's revelation. Never once in his life had he believed that his father was anything but completely loyal to the Emperor. His father's confession was akin to treason and brought dishonour to the family name. Looking to his mother Fuji saw only grief in her face and realised that, through her silence, she too must harbour the same treacherous sentiments as his father. 'I will leave your house,' Fuji said bitterly. 'And I will never return until I come as a conqueror to teach the barbarian Europeans respect for our empire.'

'I will not inform the Australians of your activities,' Isokihi said in a slightly conciliatory tone. 'Your mother will prepare some food for your journey – wherever it may take you.'

'I do not need your food,' Fuji spat as he turned to walk away. 'You are both dead to me,' he added, but he could not bear to look at the pain in his mother's face lest he break down and cry. This was not the way of Bushido. It seemed that his father had adopted the weak and effeminate sentimental ways of the barbarians and Fuji refused to be part of it. Slamming the door he stormed out into the night.

Isokihi hung his head, squeezing back the tears threatening to unleash themselves in his wife's presence. How could his son not see that this was their country now? Had he not been born on the very soil of the great island to the south of Japan? The boat builder still loved the land of his birth but he had been away for so long that he no longer felt its clutch on him. How ironic that he should side with Papua when his son, a native of the land, had chosen to serve a country he had not visited until seven years ago.

Fuji stumbled away from the house, past the boatyard on the beach. The tears could not be restrained and he was glad that no one could see him crying. But his tears were not for learning that his parents had sided with the barbarians as much as for losing a father who he so desperately had wanted to bring honour to. He had been rejected once again, and his enlistment in the navy six years earlier had not brought him the recognition he so desperately sought from his peers and superiors either. As he had not been born in Japan or one of her territories they had looked down upon him as almost a barbarian himself. He was a foreigner with Japanese blood and was forced to work his way up to his current lowly rank through being the best at everything he did. At least that had been recognised. This dangerous mission would enhance his prestige, and tonight he would sleep in the jungle, having been trained in the toughest military schools of Japan. On the morrow he would make contact with the most important agent in Papua – a man of considerable wealth and power, accepted without suspicion by the Australians.

Fuji found a stream and washed away the night. Insects had bitten him and the ever-present threat of malaria was in the Japanese sailor's mind. But it was a risk he knew he must take if he were to complete his mission before returning to Japan.

He trudged along a track he knew so well from his childhood and found the place where he would make contact with the agent. It was a bungalow-style home with wide verandahs and beautifully kept tropical gardens – a private, unobtrusive house to outside eyes but still one that, through its lack of unpretentiousness, betrayed obvious wealth.

Outside the house an old Papuan man, wearing only the traditional white cotton skirt known as a lap-lap, was tending the gardens. His black skin was criss-crossed with numerous scars, indicating a hard life. The gardener caught Fuji watching him and glared back, shouting in pidgin, '*Yu rausim.*'

Fuji ignored his demand and, striding forward, snarled, 'I have come to speak with Kwong Yu Sen, you ignorant black bastard.' The dishevelled young man's fluent English startled the gardener and he took a step backwards.

Before the Papuan gardener could react any further a slim, composed Chinese man, in his late middle age and wearing an immaculate white suit and matching hat, rose from a cane chair on the verandah to see what the commotion was about. He stopped when he saw Fuji and frowned. 'Is that you Fuji Komine?' he asked.

'It is, Mr Kwong,' Fuji replied. 'I have come to see you in private about matters of importance.'

Sen gestured for Fuji to follow him inside the house. 'I would never have guessed in a million years that it would be you who would make contact,' he said wearily as if the young man's visit had already tired him. 'It was rumoured when you disappeared from Papua all those years ago that you had been working for that murderer, O'Leary. But your meeting with me has to be more than coincidental in light of the news I have received from my German masters.'

Fuji glanced around to ensure that they were alone. The house was clean and comfortable, with expensive European furniture and adornments to make life pleasurable.

'You are to report to me from now on,' Fuji said less than politely having no reason to make the Chinese merchant feel comfortable. 'I doubt that there is any reason to elaborate on why it is me who you will be working for.'

Sen slumped into a chair. He had never wanted to return to Papua from Singapore a year earlier but his German controllers in the intelligence service had ordered him back. There was no choice in the matter. The Nazis controlling Europe would eventually win the war and hunt him down if he were to finally confess to the Australian authorities his role in spying on them in the Great War. Either way he was a doomed man. Had it only concerned himself he may have considered telling all he knew, but he had a family now and to do so would put their lives in dire jeopardy. 'Do you not fear being recognised in Papua?' he asked.

Fuji broke into a rare smile. 'It is a risk I must take if I am to complete my mission for the Emperor.'

18

'We are not at war with Japan,' Sen countered. 'Why would the Germans want me to work for you, when it is they who are at war with the Australians?'

'I am not here to indulge in strategic politics with you,' Fuji replied. 'Your country is at war with Japan and yet you live in the safe haven of Australian territory. Does not that concern you?'

Sen rubbed his face with a clean handkerchief. He felt physically ill at the young Japanese man's presence and at what it meant for his future. It meant that the time had come to once again betray those who trusted him. The hardest part of this betrayal was having to work with an enemy that was really an enemy of his own people, the Chinese. Sen had heard of the terrible atrocities committed by the Japanese troops in Manchuria, Nanking and other places on the Chinese mainland which they had conquered and occupied. His German controllers had ensured that Sen's family remained in Singapore with veiled threats of violence to them if he did not fully cooperate. To see this arrogant young Japanese standing in his house directing him to obey orders was almost more than he could bear. But bear it he must, if he were to retain all that he had achieved for his family.

'What am I to do?' he asked Fuji.

'You will receive a cargo very soon from Hong Kong. In that cargo will be a crate marked as dried ginger. In the crate will be a radio and instructions on how to operate it. Your code name will be Krait.' Sen winced. The krait was a small but highly venomous snake found in Asia. 'The rest will be told to you when the time is right.'

'Is that all for now?' Sen asked, looking up at Fuji standing over him.

'No,' Fuji answered. 'I will take a wash and some food before I depart. Then you will not see me unless I request you to do so.'

Leading Seaman Fuji Komine had completed his mission and its success would be judged by his superiors. But he knew what he had done was not unique. All over the Pacific islands and Asia where the Europeans and Americans had strategic interests, other young Japanese men were quietly going about similar tasks of espionage. The secondary stages of sabotage and subversion would be activated when Japan went to war with the Pacific powers. Although Fuji did not know when this would be, he did know it was as inevitable as the sun rising each day and he knew from his own intelligence department that even the Americans were aware of this, although they wondered not only when but where war would come to them.

TWO

Europe had fallen. Only Britain held out in its island fortress. The war to end all wars had failed and the armistice that had been signed in 1918 had only sown the seeds for future conflict. Its inevitability was apparent to the tall aristocratic man who stared out over the tranquil, tropical waters of the Papuan bay. Why had the Allied powers not realised that they could not destroy a nation as proud as Germany with their crushing demands of the Versailles Treaty, Paul Mann brooded.

So much had occurred in his life since that dreadful third day of September 1939 when the Australian government had declared war on Paul's homeland. Within half a day the local sergeant of police had come to the plantation with his revolver drawn and had demanded uncomfortably that Paul, his wife Karin and sixteen-year-old daughter Angelika go with him in a truck to Port Moresby to be interned as possible enemy aliens. Sergeant Ian Groves had appeared uncomfortable with his duty as over the years that Paul had lived in Papua, they had become friends. 'Just in case you try to escape,' he had said sheepishly when Paul had asked disdainfully if the firearm was necessary.

'Paul?' The voice of his wife called to him from above the beach where he stood watching the gently hissing Coral Sea sweep the sand to the edge of his boots. 'Are you ready to come inside for dinner?'

Paul Mann turned to gaze up to her. 'I will come soon,' he replied and resumed his solitary staring across the Papuan Gulf. Germany was conquering Europe with an unimaginable speed when Paul compared it to his own experience in the stalemate of trench warfare. Now a new generation had taken over and his very own son was wearing the uniform of the men he had once fought. Karl had resigned his job as a *kiap* – a patrol officer in Papua – to enlist in the Australian Army only weeks after the outbreak of hostilities. There had been a terrible argument between father and son in the house that had seen so many good times for the family who had sailed from Germany over twenty years earlier to take up residence on this tropical frontier. Paul had raged at Karl that he could not possibly consider enlisting in an army that might confront the men of his birthplace on the battlefield. To do so was akin to treachery.

'I have lived longer in Papua and Australia than I ever did in Germany,' Karl had responded calmly.

'This land is my country now – not a Germany under that lunatic, Adolf Hitler.'

Paul had turned away from his son who stood like a young giant on the front verandah of their house behind the beach. The fronds of tall coconut trees waved in a gentle breeze. 'You are German,' he had reiterated stubbornly. 'You are forever linked to where your roots are.'

'But my friends are Australian. Your very best friend, Uncle Jack, is an Australian. I know you two are as inseparable as brothers despite everything that happened up until 1918. Can't you see, Papa, that it is where our hearts may be that counts more than where we may have been born. We have no choice in where we may be born but can choose where we want to live. I love this country. Angelika was born here and for that alone I am prepared to fight anyone who may want to take it all from us. Hitler is out to conquer the world and he will not stop with Europe. He may even decide that New Guinea be returned to Germany in an attempt to resurrect the old empire of the Kaisers.'

Secretly, Paul had to concede what his son had said had merit. But over-riding all his son's arguments was Paul's self-identification as a German. It was something he had spent four horrific years in the trenches of the Great War fighting for, losing his best friends, and taking to the grave the faces and memories of a generation squandered on Europe's mud-and-barbed-wire landscape.

'I am asking you one last time if you will remain in Papua in your present job,' Paul had begged his son. 'It is not your war.'

'I'm sorry, Father,' Karl answered with pain visibly etched in his handsome face. 'Uncle Jack has said he can get me into the army with a commission.'

'Jack Kelly,' Paul had exploded. 'Your Uncle Jack has been putting these wild ideas in your head?'

Karl had hung his head at his father's wrath. 'Uncle Jack signed up in the last war – even though *his* mother was German,' the young man had offered feebly. 'He must have had to think hard about that decision then.'

Paul had felt betrayed by his best friend. Jack knew the horror of war and yet he was obviously encouraging Karl to join up, which made the man no real friend if he was playing God with Karl's life. 'Damn Jack Kelly to hell,' he had sworn. 'He will never step foot in my house again.'

That had been almost a year earlier and Paul still felt the distant echo of regret at his anger but in his stubbornness he refused to make contact with the man who was as close as his brother. He knew that his wife and daughter did not agree with him. Jack was a part of their lives in ways only women could understand. He was family, as was his son Lukas, and Karin had loved the boy as her own. She had been his surrogate mother and did not discriminate against him because he was not of their blood. Paul had come to realise her stance in the matter from her cold silences when they were together. But he had his pride and had made his statement. Much as he missed his friend, Jack Kelly was damned to hell for helping Karl enlist in an army destined to confront Germany. The brief Mann family internment had not prejudiced Karl's enlistment and subsequent commission into an infantry battalion. Even now Paul's son was somewhere overseas – his whereabouts undisclosed by the censorship his son was forced to impose on himself in his letters home. About all Paul could ascertain was that his son was possibly in the Middle East.

Paul sighed and started to the house where he could see a welcoming flicker of light through the windows. It had been Jack Kelly's personal intervention with the principal administrator of Papua and New Guinea that had ensured that Paul and his family were released to return to their home. Jack had passionately vouched for Paul not being a threat to any war aims after he had spoken to his friend and Paul had coldly given his written agreement to remain neutral in the conflict, for the sake of his wife and daughter if not for himself.

Paul walked slowly to the house where Karin was waiting for him on the verandah with a pot of coffee and two mugs. This evening ritual of taking coffee as the sun set over the rows of coconut palms had become an established quiet time for them both. Paul smiled. Why was it that Karin was just as beautiful as the day they had met so long ago in Munich? Her long tresses of blonde hair were shot with grey but nothing else seemed to have aged about her. Her skin was still smooth, like that of a young girl, despite living in the tropics. And her eyes still danced with mirth at his feeble attempts at humour. Time had rounded her body with a natural softness that he loved when they lay in bed at night listening to the sweet, soft sounds of the bush around them. Love was a strange thing only made stronger when two people shared both hardship and the good times together.

'Is it the letter that bothers, my husband?' Karin asked, pouring a mug of thick black coffee. She had been with her man through a long war, a troubled post-war Germany and finally in the intervening years between the wars, in her earthly paradise of the plantation.

Paul slumped into a cane chair, accepting the coffee mug with both hands. The evening air was warm and still, suffused with a balmy peace that was just a small part of what made Papua paradise.

'It has been years,' Paul sighed, sipping from his mug. 'And I may have been wrong not to tell Jack about the first letter. But I still feel that I did the right thing considering how his life had changed.'

Karin had come to learn of the letter written and posted by Paul's brother-in-law, Gerhardt Stahl. It made mention of Gerhardt's daughter, Ilsa, who in fact had been unknowingly fathered by Jack Kelly to Paul's sister, Erika. The first letter had arrived just after Jack married Victoria and, fearing that its contents would disturb the happiness of his best friend, Paul chose not to answer the letter.

Years later, a second letter had arrived, this time from Ilsa Stahl in America informing the Manns of Gerhardt's death and requesting information about Jack Kelly. Once again Paul concealed its contents from Jack. Why? Paul was not sure himself but he still chose to keep the past locked in secrecy. Maybe it was just a feeling that the past should not intrude on the present. For whatever reason, Paul realised that the arrival of this second letter weeks earlier might compound his possible mistake of the past. Had it been a mistake to hide the existence of Jack's daughter from him? How ironic, Paul pondered, gazing across the well-kept tropical gardens at the beach below, that the daughter of Jack Kelly was his own niece, binding the two families by blood.

'Don't you think you should tell Jack?' Karin asked. 'I think your best friend has the right to know by now that he has a daughter who is almost twenty-one.'

Paul continued to stare at the sea. 'I have made my decision,' he responded. 'War is not a good time to learn of such things,' he said quietly. 'We all have enough to worry about.'

Karin fell silent and the pair sat in the dying sunlight while Paul continued to agonise over his decision not to tell his estranged best friend that his daughter had written to her Uncle Paul asking if he knew of a man called Jack Kelly. Ilsa Stahl was a ghost of the past and should remain there, Paul concluded.

Victoria Kelly had always liked the great island of Bougainville that lay to the north-east of Papua. Although the natives still had a reputation for cannibalism they also had a respect for the European settlers and Victoria attributed this respect to the German occupation of the land prior to the Great War. The Teutonic, iron-hard discipline had enforced law and order on a warrior people and its legacy was a proud people, not quite subservient but prepared to work with the Europeans of the newer Australian administration.

Victoria stood on the deck gripping one of the three mainmasts of the schooner, *Independence*. The schooner was a recent acquisition, purchased when Jack had sold the smaller lugger, *Erika Sarah*, to meet the growing demand for cargo shipping between the islands. The *Independence* had been built in Delaware in 1901 of oak and Georgia pine. She was 132 feet long, gaff-rigged with clean sharp lines. Jack had the schooner fitted with the most powerful inboard marine engine he could obtain, for motoring when the wind was down, and despite the fact that she was a working sailing boat he had also relatively comfortable captain and crew quarters installed. Victoria had christened their schooner the *Independence*, in honour of her country and the fact that it made them free to follow their mutual dream of being their own bosses. The schooner had put them both into debt but the busy trade between the islands was rapidly paying off the overdraft. It was both a floating home and main enterprise for the couple.

From the deck Victoria could see the jungle-covered shoreline disappear in the wake of the schooner as one of the native leading deckhands steered a course, south by south-east, back to the island of Papua and New Guinea. The sea was a gentle, blue-green swell with a clear blue horizon topped by white, powder puff clouds.

They had delivered their last cargo of tea, kerosene, powdered milk and precious books to a plantation on the western coast and it was time to lie back and read the package of mail that had been waiting for them at the final stop.

'I've sorted it and have a mug of coffee for you,' Victoria heard Jack call from below. 'As usual, most of it is yours – except for the bills which are, naturally, mine.'

Victoria smiled. The usual Jack Kelly dry humour, she thought. But that was just one of the many things she loved about the man she had married. Not that she ever let him forget when the important anniversary came around each year. 'I'm coming down,' she called back and made her way to the hatch.

Inside the spacious cabin she saw Jack sitting behind a table, reading a letter with just a little difficulty. His male pride would not allow him to have his eyes checked and, now approaching fifty years of age, his eyesight was becoming a bit blurry. He was frowning and Victoria wondered whether it was the contents of what he was reading or his trouble seeing the words. He glanced up at her with a beaming smile. 'Your coffee is in the pot.'

Victoria gazed for just a moment at her husband and felt a surge of love for him. He still had the hard body of a man half his age and the same face she had fallen in love with somewhere between Port Moresby and the Fly River years earlier. He was not a classically handsome man but one who had enchanting eyes and a beautiful smile. He was a man's man, yet with a gentle and romantic side which he displayed to her all the time – well, at least when his male friends were not around. But that was the way with Aussie men, she mused. Her Yankee upbringing made her used to men pandering to her needs with flowers and polite manners. She had been able to twist American men around her little finger with her beauty. But not Jack Kelly. His love and attentiveness just came naturally to him.

Victoria was in her late thirties now and worried about things like the little lines beginning to form at the corners of her eyes, even though she knew that with her exotic high cheekbones and long jet-black hair, men still considered her beautiful. She had once made a comment to Jack on the changes time had wrought to her appearance but he had just looked at her blankly and said he could not see them. In any other man she might have considered his response as male flattery but with Jack she accepted that he truly could not see her ageing.

'Is it from Lukas?' she asked as she poured herself a mug of coffee from the old blackened iron pot on the stove.

'Yes,' Jack frowned. 'It seems that he is planning to come back as soon as possible.'

'I hope not,' Victoria said, sitting down opposite Jack. 'He has a marvellous life in Hollywood, a life that most young men would kill for.'

'I keep telling him that,' Jack agreed with a pained expression in his face. 'He wants to come back and enlist, despite all I have said to him about staying out of it.'

Victoria took a long sip of the black coffee and grimaced. Being a tea drinker by choice, one thing

Jack could never do was make a decent brew of her favourite beverage. 'I can understand his desire to return and enlist,' she said. 'His country is at war and he is a young man very much like his father. Besides, you helped young Karl get his commission in the army.'

'If he had seen what we saw back in the last one he would not join up,' Jack muttered angrily. 'He could get himself killed in a war that we are fighting for the poms. Your country is smart in staying out of it altogether. Lukas has been in America for so long now that he even has one of your Yankee accents and as far as I am concerned the States is now his home – thanks to your friends, and Joe Oblachinski. And as for Karl, Karl was here and would have enlisted anyhow. All I did was make sure he got to be a boss – rather than a worker in the army – by getting his commission.'

'I am not sure if Mr Roosevelt will stay out of it,' Victoria said. 'Our navy is already engaging U boats in the Atlantic on convoy escort. That sort of thing could draw the States into the war and it seems that your Mr Churchill and my President are quite pally. There is a lot of sympathy for the English resistance to the Germans. Back in the States I know of some young men slipping over the border into Canada to join up. Anyway, does Lukas say when he will be returning?'

'He says he is catching a ship in June to return to Australia. At that rate we should see him up our way around August or September. Bloody fool.'

Despite her husband's concluding comment on

his son's intelligence Victoria could see the hidden happiness in Jack's demeanour. He missed his son, having not seen him in over four years, and she knew that Jack would be counting the days to Lukas' return. Victoria flipped through the small pile of envelopes addressed to her. Most were from the United States of America from friends who still found her life in the Pacific aboard a schooner something very romantic and exotic. Hollywood movies depicted such life as never having to work but merely lying under a coconut tree drinking fruity cocktails whilst being cooled by dusky maidens with big ostrich feather fans or palm fronds. The calluses on Victoria's hands contradicted that perception. Trading in the islands was hard – and sometimes downright dangerous.

She found the letter she was looking for, recognisable by the heavy but neat handwriting. It was a letter from her uncle, a high-ranking naval officer in Washington. He was a big, burly career sailor who, as a widower without children of his own, had a soft spot for his favourite niece. Victoria carefully opened the letter of thin aerogram paper and began to read the clipped sentences, so militarily precise. Jack watched his wife and wondered at the worried expression on her lightly tanned face. When she had finally read the four pages she looked up at Jack. 'How ironic,' she said as she reached over to take Jack's hands in her own. 'It seems that my Uncle Bernie will be in Australia next month. He wishes to meet me in Townsville. He writes that all my expenses will be reimbursed for the trip down to meet him.'

Jack knew of her Uncle Bernie, better known as Commander Bernard S Duvall, and the last he had known, from his wife's chatter about her esteemed relative, was that he had something to do with the Office of Naval Intelligence. Jack did not have to ask why she had been summoned to meet her uncle. His wife was a very remarkable woman with an interesting past. Some things were better not discussed, even between spouses.

'All going well we should be in Moresby in a couple of days,' Jack said, folding his son's letter. 'It will give you a chance to make contact with the general and see what is up.'

Victoria leaned forward to hug her husband. 'He is not a general, and you are the most wonderful man on earth,' she said, grateful that he had not asked any questions. 'I promise I will not be away too long.'

'Hope not,' Jack said gruffly. 'I can't afford to lose my best deckhand and captain's mate for very long.'

Naval Lieutenant Kenshu Chuma peered through the periscope of the Imperial Japanese submarine I–47 and focused on the schooner. He could read the name; it was called the *Independence* and she was sailing on a course that cut across his bow. Eleven hundred yards, he calculated. It was a good time to test his crew.

'Action stations! Prepare to engage enemy surface vessel,' he commanded on the bridge of the confined, dank Japanese submarine.

His crew reacted quickly and with skill. In seconds they were ready to engage an enemy surface vessel from below the sea. In the bow, all six torpedo tubes were loaded and the torpedo men waited for the order. They were cruising silently on the electric engines at around seven knots although the boat was capable of eight and a half knots submerged. The I–47 was a *Kaidai* Type 4 submarine and her keel had been laid at the Japanese shipyards in late 1929. On the surface, powered by her 6000 horsepower diesel engine, she was capable of a further two knots of speed to push her 320 feet of length through the water. And the I–47 could dive to 200 feet if threatened.

Kenshu was very proud of his crew. They were the best of the best of the best in the Japanese navy and, as such, each man strained to prove his worth. 'Nine hundred yards and closing . . . Stand down!'

The sweating crew relaxed. The passing schooner was simply an opportune target for honing their skills. But as they were not at war, they would not have wasted one of the valuable fourteen torpedoes the submarine carried in her belly on such a small and defenceless target. They would have surfaced and used the boat's deck gun to sink the Papuan registered schooner, but the *Independence* sailed on, blithely unaware of the Japanese sub's presence under the waves.

It was not in the Japanese captain's orders to be spotted by ships of any navies. His was a long range, covert operation to put ashore, and take off, intelligence personnel of the Imperial Japanese Navy and he was en route to pick up one leading seaman, Fuji Komine, from the Papuan mainland.

Lieutenant Chuma handed over the bridge to his executive officer and went to his tiny cabin to rest. There he could dream of bigger targets in the future. Maybe a British battleship or an American carrier to fire his new and deadly torpedoes at, he mused as he lay down on his bunk. The barbarians of the West had underestimated the ingenuity of Japanese scientists in developing this new torpedo. Propelled by oxygen, it delivered a 500 kilogram warhead up to 40 000 yards. It was far superior to anything the West possessed and would help win any war at sea. But the new torpedo had one other deadly secret: as it was propelled by oxygen the rising bubbles dissolved in the water, barely leaving a wake. How the Japanese submarine commander would have loved to fire one and watch the terrible results of its impact. All his crew – from the cook in the galley to the executive officer now on watch on the bridge – knew that it was only a matter of time before the drills turned to the real thing. And when the time came, these same waters would be theirs to control for the Emperor.

THREE

Lieutenant Karl Mann lay on his stomach on the rocky ground, blistered by a searing summer sun. He held the binoculars steady to compensate for the shimmering walls of the old fort. How ironic, he thought as the shimmer danced along the walls, that he was fighting Frenchmen in Syria rather than his father's relatives in North Africa or Crete. Maybe his father might have approved of his enlistment had he known that his estranged son would be killing his father's former enemies.

'Much going on, sir?' the young soldier at Karl's elbow asked.

'They have machine guns at each corner and substantial barbed wire all around, Private Bell,' Karl replied as he closed his eyes to reduce the debilitating effect of the heat glare that was magnified by the powerful glasses. 'It is not going to be easy.'

'Kind of strange us fighting the French Foreign Legion,' Bell mused. 'My old man fought alongside them during the last war and said they were bloody good soldiers. So it seems a bit stupid for us to fight them now.'

Karl grinned but did not let on that his own father might have been up against Private Bell's on the Western Front. It had been difficult for many of his men to comprehend that there were now two sides to France: the Free French side under the leadership of Charles de Gaulle, opposing the German occupation of his country; and the French under Petain, sworn to fight for Germany under the terms of the armistice signed in the French town of Vichy. The latter had occupied Syria and the Levant after the Great War under the terms of the Versailles Treaty. In fact, Karl had trouble understanding the strategic reasons for the Australians being committed as an expeditionary force to take on the Vichy French alongside the British Army. It was all a bit of a muddle.

Karl raised the glasses one more time and caught the fleeting glimpse of a white *kepi*. The Legionnaires were at home and waiting for the attack. Very carefully, he and Private Bell slithered from the slight rise around 600 yards out from the stone-walled fort to make their way back to company headquarters and report on the French positions. As he made his way back he had a fleeting thought: how different was this heat baked land of craggy and desolate hills to his own home in the wet jungles of Papua. It was like comparing Hell to Eden.

Company headquarters was a carefully camouflaged series of trenches dug into the hard and rocky ground. Karl located the company commander's shelter and found the major poring over a 1:200 000 scale map of the area. 'Should be bloody one in twenty thou maps,' he grumbled as Karl squatted down at the entrance of the covered trench. The company commander glanced up at Karl. 'How did it go?' he asked in an irritable tone. The men did not like each other. Major Jules was of French descent and had taken an instinctive dislike to Karl on account of his German blood. The animosity between superior and subordinate had dogged them ever since they had steamed from Australia to the Middle East.

'Private Bell did a good job of sketching the positions and terrain,' Karl said, handing over the pages of drawings. 'It is going to be a bit of a bastard.'

Major Jules took the papers. 'See any of your relatives out there?' he sneered.

Karl bridled at the provocation. 'We are up against the French, sir. Maybe some of your relatives might be more appropriate,' he replied calmly.

He saw the company commander's eyes darken with anger. 'Be careful, Mr Mann,' Jules spat. 'Your attitude verges on insolent.'

'My apologies, sir,' Karl answered. 'It was meant to be a joke, nothing more.'

The major glared at Karl for a moment with a smug expression. 'I have some news for you, Mr Mann,' he said. 'The CO has been asked to detach any officer who might have a good grasp of German back to Jerusalem and naturally I thought of you. You will

38

need to get your kit together and report to battalion HQ for movement orders.'

'But my platoon . . .' Karl attempted to protest.

'Sergeant Crane will take command of your platoon for the assault on the fort,' Jules said. 'In the meantime I thought you would be pleased to be out of the action.'

Karl felt the anger rise in his throat. He could have punched his superior for his underhand attack on his courage. As capable as his platoon sergeant was, it was he as the platoon commander who was ultimately responsible for the lives of his thirty men. The company commander's insult stung as hard as any punch to his face. But he calmed himself to deny his superior the pleasure of upsetting him. 'When do I report?' he asked.

'Now, Mr Mann,' Jules replied, avoiding Karl's glare by perusing the sketches and maps Private Bell had compiled on the reconnaissance mission.

Karl was pleased that he was not required to salute so close to the enemy's positions. Such a gesture could indicate to the enemy that an officer was present and a priority target for enemy snipers. He rose stiffly with the assistance of his Lee Enfield rifle and walked back to his platoon position. What the hell did the brass want with him in Jerusalem? Whatever it was it would be keeping him from his men and the action he both craved and dreaded.

Jerusalem felt a million miles from the harsh Syrian front. Karl had been intrigued by the ancient biblical city when he had first passed through a month earlier on his way to Syria with his battalion. They had spent only a short time in the city, not long enough to explore all its mysteries and delights. But now he was back with orders to report immediately to the King David Hotel where the British maintained a headquarter staff.

Karl was saluted by the British guards at the entrance of the hotel and entered the sumptuous building. Glancing around the clean, cool foyer, he noticed a table manned by a British military police sergeant in an immaculately starched uniform and blinding white broad belt. The sergeant glanced up at Karl who stood towering over him.

'I am Lieutenant Karl Mann and I am here to report to a Captain Featherstone.'

'Lieutenant Mann, is it sir,' the MP said, flipping through the pages on a clipboard. His tone left Karl aware that mere junior officers reporting to staff headquarters rated just one level above the Arab cleaning staff. 'I see your name is on the list to report to Captain Featherstone. You should have been here ten minutes ago.' Karl ignored the sergeant's insolence. He was no doubt appraised as a German colonial from Australia and a citizen soldier to boot. These were not endearing qualities to the regular British Army.

The MP gave Karl directions as to where to go in the hotel and to whom he should first report. The mention of the department smelled of dangerous intrigue.

He found the room and, considering the highly

classified and mysterious work of the British intelligence arm, was surprised to see that it did not have an anteroom with orderlies. There was just a number and no name on the solid timber door. He rapped and a voice called, 'Enter.'

Karl stepped inside the small room and was surprised to see two officers smoking cigarettes and a civilian wearing a white tropical suit and matching Panama-style hat. Karl saluted as he recognised the rank of the two military men as being that of colonels. One of the colonels returned the salute.

'Lieutenant Mann reporting to Captain Featherstone,' Karl said, standing to attention. The captain, wearing civilian clothing, thrust out his hand. 'I am Featherstone, old chap, pleased to meet you.' Karl was taken back by Featherstone's disarming smile and clear blue eyes. He was around five foot six, Karl guessed, and about his own age. His grip was firm and engaging. 'Take a seat, old chap, while I conclude some business.'

Coming from the civilian dressed army captain the request sounded more like an order, and Featherstone turned to one of the colonels concluding their business. 'I think that this Jewish chap, Moshe Dayan, will get on with our Aussie allies as their guide,' he said as if addressing equals rather than briefing superiors. 'Good chap and well respected in the Jewish community.'

Karl leapt to his feet when the senior officers were about to depart and snapped a salute. The two officers, having barely acknowledged his presence, left the room.

'As a captain you certainly know how to handle top brass,' Karl said when the door closed.

'Oh, I am not an army captain,' Featherstone smiled. 'I am a naval captain.'

Karl was taken off guard at the revelation. Naval captains were much higher in rank than army captains. There was no real comparison between the names in the order of seniority between the two services so it was no wonder the two army officers treated Featherstone with the respect due his rank. 'But don't let that hold you in awe, old chap. Like you, I have been pulled away from my unit to do a job, I hope you may be able to help us. I can see by the confusion you seem to be experiencing that you are wondering just why you are here.'

'I have been wondering but guess it has something to do with me being of German blood,' Karl answered.

'That is correct,' Featherstone replied in good German but with an accent. 'But before we get better acquainted I will need to verify a few things with you first,' he continued in German. 'So take a seat and make yourself comfortable. Smoke if you wish.'

Karl sat down on a leather settee whilst Captain Featherstone opened a satchel and removed a buff-coloured file. Karl could see his name and regimental details typed on the cover and shifted uncomfortably. It was like that whenever the military probed his life and links to Germany.

'Born in Munich and emigrated to Papua in 1920 with your mother, father and aunt. Your father was a major in the old Imperial army of the Kaiser and received decorations for his efforts on the Western Front.' Captain Featherstone read from the file in front of him without looking up at Karl. 'Your father, mother and sister interned in Papua in '39 but released on the recommendation of the senior Australian administrator acting on the advice of a close family friend, Jack Kelly. It seems that your father and this Captain Jack Kelly met at the battle for the Hindenburg Line back in 1918. An interesting story – so I have been told. You enlisted in officer training in Australia with the support of Jack Kelly who it seems had quite some pull in colonial politics.' He paused and looked directly at Karl. 'How do you feel about the Australians locking up your family for no other reason than they were German?' Featherstone asked abruptly.

'It was a procedure I think any country would apply under the circumstances,' Karl replied. 'After ascertaining that my parents were of no threat to our interests they were immediately released – with reasonable conditions applied.'

'I noticed that you said "our interests". What do you mean by that?'

'I mean my country's interests – Australia – I am an Australian in all ways. I worked for the Australian government as a patrol officer in Papua before the war and if I have to, will die for Australia. Does that answer your question?'

With a sigh Featherstone replaced the file in his satchel and sat down. 'Cigarette, Mr Mann?' he asked, offering a packet of Players brand to Karl who retrieved one from the packet. Featherstone leaned forward to light Karl's cigarette. 'You don't normally smoke,' he commented when Karl took a deep suck on the nicotine, smiling when Karl stiffened at his observation. 'I have to know a lot about anyone who might work for me,' he continued in an attempt to reassure the Australian. 'Little things like that are important for me to know. I believe that you are also a first grade rugby player – rowing for Cambridge was my thing.'

Karl wondered at the man who sat before him. He had the accent of a highly educated man, was fairly young to be a naval captain and said he once rowed for Cambridge University. He also spoke passable German and had a charisma that was unmistakable.

'I played in Papua but have had less opportunity in the army.'

'The tactics of rugby have a bit in common with what we do in my department,' Featherstone mused. 'Attack and defence, seeking a weak point to exploit to score a try – then convert the try.'

'It sounds like intelligence work to me. Not my background though,' Karl said, and watched for a reaction.

'That is exactly why you were singled out,' the naval captain said. 'I needed a face that is unknown in these parts. Yours fitted and I pride myself on choosing the right man for the right job.'

'Am I able to ask why I am here?'

'First, I have to have your assurance as an officer of the King that you are prepared to do what your country requires of you without ever divulging the nature of the mission. Do I have that?'

Karl knew he had little choice. He was a soldier sworn to follow orders to defend his country. It seemed obvious that he had somehow been singled out for whatever intrigues British intelligence had for him. Featherstone was merely attempting to let him think that he had a choice in the matter to cement his commitment to the mysterious task ahead. 'You do,' Karl answered. 'Do I have to swear on a Bible or something?' he continued with a note of wry sarcasm.

'Nothing like that, old chap,' the captain answered. 'Just do your sworn duty to King and country as you have been doing with some distinction to date. I think that you will find the job has its little benefits – like a comfortable room at the hotel, hot and cold running nubile native girls and food that does not come from a tin. And you also get to return to wearing a comfortable civvy suit.'

Featherstone continued to brief Karl on what was available whilst he was detached to work for a department or unit that did not identify itself to him. Not even why he was the one to be selected for whatever was ahead had been revealed to him, other than that he was an 'unknown face'. It also had to be something to do with his Germanic links – that much he guessed.

When the briefing was over Karl was escorted to a room which had been set aside for him by the chatty naval captain. He left Karl at his door and strode away. Karl stood for a moment looking down the hallway at the strange British officer's back. What the hell was he in for, he wondered as he turned the key in his door. It was like some bloody dream or a Hollywood movie with Humphrey Bogart. What the hell, Karl shrugged as he stepped inside his small but comfortable room. He would find out soon enough and have to be prepared to play his role. It was not every day that a simple infantry officer got to wear civilian clothes in a theatre of war.

The rain lashed the beach and the normally placid tropical waters crashed on the shoreline. The night was darkened even further by the heavy rain clouds and any light was sure to stand out. Fuji felt the full fury of the storm in his face as he kept his vigil from amongst the rocks just off the small headland and he huddled in the rain, trying not to shiver as he continued to stare into the inky blackness that was the Papuan Gulf.

There! There it was! Fuji felt his heart thud hard at the welcome sight he had so patiently waited for on this isolated piece of land outside Port Moresby. The submarine had surfaced and although it tossed about like a heavy cork, the signaller was attempting to make contact with a flashing light. With shaking hands numbed by the cold Fuji replied to the code with a battered hand torch procured from Sen. His own coded reply was accepted and Fuji strained to see the series of dots and dashes of the light-transmitted Morse code but with the heavy seas some of the signal was lost behind the waves as the sub wallowed in the deep troughs.

And then he felt his spirits plummet as the

message came through. He was not going home but was to remain in Papua until further contact. He was to continue gathering information for intelligence, to be transmitted by Sen, and wait until his superiors decided when he would be eventually picked up. Fuji acknowledged the message and the distant light from the sea disappeared as quickly as it had appeared.

So he was to remain in the country of his birth. For reasons of their own the high command of the Imperial Japanese Navy thought it was the right course to take. Fuji hugged himself and tried not to think of the discomfort he had endured in the storm as he had waited for his pick-up. He knew that he was trained to obey orders without question, but he wondered why his superiors considered his role of espionage in Papua so important that they would risk leaving him in a place that was to all intents and purposes enemy territory. He had been adjudged as a sailor of high initiative – granted through the legacy of not growing up in Japan itself, where such a quality was not deemed to be a high priority in a society dominated by the militarists. To blindly obey and not ask questions was the norm but Fuji had lived amongst a people who were forced to use initiative to survive in a frontier country.

Wet and hungry, Fuji trudged the native track back to Sen's residence which he reached just on sunrise. He was not a welcome sight to the Chinese trader.

• • •

The *Independence* docked at Port Moresby late afternoon after weathering the low in the Papuan Gulf. With the rising of the sun the weather had broken and the day proved to be clear and calm. The little township nestled in, and on, the low hills around Port Moresby had a clean sparkle as a result of the overnight storm and already a few spots of green could be seen on the bare hills, as seemingly dead grass made a temporary thrust for the sunlight now retreating behind the same hills.

'What will you do when I get to Townsville?' Victoria asked Jack as she joined him at the helm with a mug of sweet, dark tea.

'About time I put the old girl up on the slips for a bit of overdue scrape and anti-fouling,' Jack said, steering on the schooner's motor towards a place at the wharf. 'Give the crew a bit of leave to see their *meris* and *piccaninnies* and maybe catch up with a few old mates at the pub.'

Victoria was relieved at his answer, although she was still feeling just a little guilty about leaving her husband to answer the summons of her uncle. But she knew Jack understood the importance of military matters, having been a highly decorated officer in the Great War. He had learned of her role as a part-time collector of intelligence around the Pacific islands for her country and acknowledged it was a necessity. In a sense it might be called spying but Jack accepted that the Americans might be their most important allies should Japan decide to open hostilities in the region. England was preoccupied with its own survival in faraway Europe and Australia's defence was not a high priority to Churchill and his War Cabinet. Jack had long figured out that the Yanks really ruled the great Pacific Ocean, but had a competitor in Japan for total Pacific domination.

The Australian was aware of his wife's very detailed diary on just about every aspect of what she saw when they ferried supplies and personnel between the islands or took out the occasional charter of wealthy tourists – mostly from the United States. As a former infantry captain the entries reminded him of his own battle diary: of terrain and tactical points of interest. There was something comforting in the fact that the Yanks were at least keeping an eye on his corner of the world and thus he gave tacit support to Victoria's activities.

With the docking complete Jack and Victoria walked into town to seek out the relative comforts of civilisation at a hotel. Jack paid a visit to the post office and returned to sort the mail on one of the single beds the small but clean room contained along with a small wardrobe, mosquito net and overhead, fly-specked fan.

'Looks like your uncle is already in Australia,' Jack commented as he handed a post-marked letter from Australia. Victoria opened the letter and scanned the contents. 'Uncle Bernie has written that he has telegrammed money to our bank,' she said. 'He has instructions for me to steam down and meet him the week after next in Townsville. He says he is enjoying a holiday down our way and would like to finally meet you.'

'Admirals are a bit out of my league,' Jack said

with a grin. 'But he is welcome to head up Papua way anytime.'

'Thank you, darling,' Victoria said, leaning over the bed to kiss Jack with a resounding smack of lips. 'I am sure you two old warriors will get on like a house on fire.'

'Sure we will,' Jack answered with less conviction than his wife. 'When do you plan to leave?'

'Tomorrow, if that is possible,' she answered. 'I would like to go south and do some shopping for us. You need a whole new wardrobe.'

'No use for suits on the boat,' Jack grunted. 'But you spend as much as you like on yourself, you deserve it.'

The next day Victoria was able to obtain a berth on a ship going south and Jack watched from the wharf as the steamer pulled away. He waved to Victoria and waited until the ship was in the channel beyond the island. Sighing, he turned and walked back to the centre of the town. There was something on his mind he had not confided to his wife. He missed the company and conversation with his old friend Paul Mann and his family. Maybe he would attempt to see Paul and patch things up between them since their last meeting almost two years earlier. Jack knew only that young Karl was somewhere in the Middle East, and when he was settled in the bar of the hotel with the newspaper and a beer in front of him, the war news was not good. In Crete, he read, the German paratroopers had finally overcome fierce resistance from the poorly equipped force of Aussies, Kiwis and Brits. The defenders had inflicted savage casualties on Germany's most elite fighting men but a major airfield had fallen and the Germans were able to airlift in an overwhelming force. Jack prayed that Lukas had not been on Crete and, placing the paper on the bar, he took a swig from his glass. If only he had been young enough to join up again, he thought bitterly. He had considered attempting to enlist under a false name but was drawn back to his civilian status by the promise he had made to his wife – a promise he very much regretted making. She had told him that one war in a man's lifetime was enough and that she needed him, as did his son, Lukas.

But he had only promised not to try and join the fighting in Africa and Europe. He had promised nothing about enlisting again. It was a very thin line to walk and in a court of feminine laws his case would not really stand up.

Jack grinned and swallowed the remaining contents of his beer. He folded the newspaper under his arm and left the cool bar to make his way to see an old friend. He hoped the chief administrator of Papua and New Guinea would be in. He was a powerful friend with the ability to get things done and there was something called the New Guinea Volunteer Rifles, a local military unit of men drawn from the ranks of old Papua New Guinea hands – men like himself.

'You cannot stay here,' Sen said under his breath. 'You stand out as a foreigner in the Moresby district.'

Fuji glanced over his shoulder and could see the native gardener eyeing him with more than curiosity. Both men stood face to face in Sen's tropical garden of colourful frangipanis and bougainvillea. Fuji felt like laughing at Sen's statement. He had been born and lived most of his life in the Port Moresby district. Rather than being a foreigner, if anything he was too well known. He also knew of the local rumours that linked him to the infamous and murderous recruiter of native labour, O'Leary. 'You will explain to anyone that asks about me that I am a relative from China on a visit to you.'

Sen wiped his brow with the back of his hand. 'You look nothing like a Chinese man,' he replied in an exasperated tone.

'To you,' Fuji replied. 'But to the barbarian Europeans we Asians all look alike.'

Sen had to cede his point. He had experienced the contempt that Europeans displayed towards his own people, whose civilisation and history were far more sophisticated than they in their arrogant ignorance could comprehend. But Sen still held the ancient dislike and contempt for the Japanese race, of his own people. The terrible war raging in China only exacerbated Sen's dislike to hatred. 'That explanation will only work if you are not recognised by any of the old Papua hands – they know your father and will probably know you.'

'I have thought about that,' Fuji said. 'I will avoid any areas in town where the Australians gather. I will be discreet.'

Sen stared for a short time at the young Japanese

sailor. It did go through his mind to betray Fuji but he dismissed the thought when he contemplated the possible reaction by his new controllers, the Japanese. He was aware of how ruthless they were and did not doubt that they would seek revenge against not only himself but his family in Singapore. It was their way. 'You should come inside,' Sen gave in. 'I will find suitable clothing for you.'

Fuji instinctively knew that the gardener dressed in his lap-lap was still watching them – with more than curiosity.

FOUR

Standing side by side outside the tin shed that was also the airstrip's terminal, the two men made an impressive pair. One had a face known to millions whilst the other, younger by a decade, was hardly known at all. Yet the well-known actor of the silver screen cherished the company of the younger man who had been his pilot for the flight from Los Angeles to a tiny, formerly Spanish town in southern California that nestled on the coast.

'They're bloody late,' the actor snarled, flipping open a packet of cigarettes and offering one to his pilot who declined with a polite shake of his head. 'Jose was supposed to be here to pick us up.'

'No, Errol,' Lukas Kelly said with a yawn, kicking the fat tyres of the Lockheed Electra he had flown into the isolated desert airstrip. 'We're early. I picked up a tailwind.'

Errol Flynn lit his cigarette, inhaled and watched the exhaled smoke waft away on a gentle breeze. It was a magnificent day, the sun hot and still in the early morning sky, and the silence of the isolated airstrip a pleasant diversion from the noise and stress of the movie lots at Jack Warner's studios.

Errol glanced around and spotted a bench outside the tin shed. The airstrip was seemingly deserted except for an old man pottering amongst the forty-four gallon drums marked 'avgas'. He appeared to be the caretaker and took little notice of the two men who had stepped from the recently landed aircraft.

'How about we sit over in the shade and wait,' Errol said, walking towards a corrugated tin shelter. Lukas followed and they sat down and stared from the open-sided shed at the heat haze rising over the sunburnt airstrip. 'Not as bloody hot as Papua,' Errol said, and in this sentence he touched on the place that linked them in the common bond of true frontiersmen.

'Always gets me how the Yanks identify you as an Irishman,' Lukas said for no other reason than he knew it would take his friend's mind off the delay in hitching a ride into the little village.

Errol smiled and flicked his cigarette butt at a lizard basking on an empty oil drum. 'The Yanks don't even know where Australia is,' he replied. 'So it is easier to identify me as an Irishman.'

'They ought to be making a movie about your times in Papua and New Guinea rather than casting you in bullshit roles about cowboys,' Lukas said, leaning back against the tin wall behind them. 'Far more exciting stuff than some of the movies you have been in.'

Only from Lukas Kelly would the vain actor accept such a comment on the films he had starred in. It was not as if the young Australian who had trained to fly in the United States was criticising his acting abilities, only some of the scripts Errol had accepted to star in. 'The Yanks don't believe there is such a place where a man had to fight against Kuku warriors, be hunted by the Dutch in the jungles for poaching birds of paradise and end up nearly being hanged by the bloody Papuan authorities for a so-called murder I didn't commit. It is a bit beyond their comprehension when they live in a country without head-hunters, cannibals and any real frontier left to boast about anymore.'

Lukas knew that all Errol had told him of his time in Papua and New Guinea back in the late twenties and early thirties was true. It had been corroborated by friends and acquaintances of his father, Jack Kelly. Lukas also knew that there were many on the great tropical island to the north of Australia who would dearly love to see the now famous Hollywood actor return – not for his fame, but for the money that he owed them and the chance to settle scores over the women seduced by the former Tasmanian's animal charm and dashing good looks. Lukas grinned, wondering what could be better than to be the pilot assigned to flying stunts for movies and ferrying the great names of Hollywood around the country. He rubbed shoulders with the rich and famous who were forced to rely on his skills as a pilot to get them safely from one place to another in a time when aircraft had a habit of losing their way and landing heavily in many pieces on the ground when things went wrong. Young and beautiful would-be actresses found the Australian's sex appeal very much like that of the famous Errol Flynn, and Lukas was very rarely without a young lady on his arm at Hollywood parties.

But the smile on his face faded and the guilt was returning. His country across the Pacific Ocean was at war with Germany and Italy, and friends he had gone to school with were in uniform fighting in North Africa, Greece and Crete. He had read the newspaper accounts of the war which seemed so far from the tranquillity of California with its sunshine, orange trees and movie lots. War was an unreal event that did not touch him until he thought about his father in Papua and his best friend, Karl Mann in uniform somewhere overseas, possibly fighting his Germanic relatives. 'You think we might end up in the war?' Lukas asked unexpectedly.

Errol gave the pilot a sideways glance. 'You mean America?' he asked to clarify the common 'we' between fellow Australians.

'Yeah.'

'Hard to say,' Errol answered, drawing another cigarette from his packet. 'Roosevelt is a bit pro-British from what I have heard. And his lend lease program just seems a way to beat the neutrality bit with the voting public. But it is definitely a means of supporting the Poms against Germany. No, I think it will take another *Lusitania* sinking or something similar to get the Yanks mobilised against the Germans. They went in to help Europe in the last war and twenty years later the bloody Europeans start another one. The Yanks remember that it was their boys who died in Europe in a cause that was meant to bring stability to that part of the Old World. It seems that they figure they died in vain.'

'Good point,' Lukas conceded. 'Would you sign up if the Yanks went to war?'

The actor paused in lighting his cigarette and gazed into the distance. 'This country has given me everything. But . . .' he trailed away in contemplative thought.

'You don't strike me as a pacifist,' Lukas said quietly.

'I think that there are many ways to serve in wartime. I doubt that mine would be as a front-line soldier. I felt that my portrayal in *The Sea Hawk* of a British privateer for Elizabeth the First had a clear anti-Nazi message. That has to mean something towards helping the Brits' war effort,' Errol replied carefully.

Lukas did not pursue the subject. He had no doubts about the actor's physical courage. He was a man who would fight any other on the drop of a hat. 'How about you?' Errol asked.

'I made up my mind a while ago,' Lukas said, staring into the heat haze. 'I am going back to Australia to sign up with the Royal Australian Air Force as a pilot. I was just waiting until my contract was up with JL – and now it is. I leave next week on a ship bound for Sydney.'

'You're going to leave all this behind!' Errol exclaimed, staring hard at Lukas. 'You are a fool. Why don't you at least wait and see if the Yanks go to war?'

'I can't,' Lukas replied with a shake of his head. 'I have mates who are even now putting their lives on the line while I sit around getting fat off the land here. My dad did not hesitate to sign up in the last war and if I keep sitting around here it will look like I am a coward shirking danger. It hasn't been easy honouring the contract.'

'I know JL,' Errol said. 'I know that he would have released you if you had asked. He got himself into a bit of trouble when he released that film *Confessions of a Nazi Spy* in '39. He was even called up to appear before a Senate investigating committee to justify its release. They had it in for him because they saw the film as an incitement to bring America out of its isolationist stance on European matters. But old Jack beat them. He was able to provide evidence that he had his facts from a former FBI agent who had accumulated them in the course of his work. So you see, Jack would have been sympathetic to you breaking the contract and going off to fight the Nazis.'

Lukas already knew about the incident as it was well known in Hollywood circles. He felt guilty as he could not tell his friend that he had used the excuse of the contract to delay enlisting for service in Australia. His reluctance came from meeting one particular beauty. Her name was Veronica Laurents and Lukas was smitten by the nineteen-year-old, raven-haired beauty.

Lukas had met her a year earlier when he had been a guest at one of Errol's infamous parties held at his hill-top mansion Mulholland Farm. Prostitutes had been acquired to perform on beds where through two-way mirrors the actor's guests could watch from above the bodies writhing in sexual ecstasy below. The young would-be starlet had accompanied an ageing actor of the silent screen to the party and Lukas had bumped into her at a bar that was generous in its supply of hard liquor. Despite his seemingly loose ways with the available women of Hollywood, Lukas was at heart a man whose strict Catholic upbringing did not allow him to approve of such wanton excess. Or perhaps it was simply his almost forgotten belief in God that steered him away from the orgy of flesh. As a pilot he had seen the face of death once or twice when his flight had run into trouble. On these occasions Lukas had prayed for survival, promising, as he fought the controls in the cumulus nimbus thunderheads that threatened to tear him and his plane apart, to give up hard liquor and loose women. And he believed that these promises had helped put him back on a righteous path.

But such promises faded with time. On the evening of this particular party Lukas still had the promise ringing in his ears after a dangerous flight in the Sierra Nevada skies during which a violent sandstorm pummelled his flimsy aircraft. So he had adjourned to the bar and was struck by the big violet eyes that turned to him as he mixed a gin and tonic. The young woman was dressed in a silky red, body-hugging dress and her long dark hair flowed down her shoulders, shimmering in the half-light of the room. For a brief moment Lukas stood transfixed. 'I don't know you,' he blurted and immediately felt embarrassment at his clumsiness.

'And I don't know you,' the sweet voice purred in reply. 'Are you an actor friend of Errol's?'

'A friend, but not an actor,' Lukas had replied. 'I'm a flyer. I work for JL.' He was not sure what the flickering change in the young woman's expression meant when he announced this. Was it disappointment? He hoped not.

'I see,' the young woman said, turning towards him with a drink in her hand.

'My name is Lukas Kelly,' Lukas said, thrusting out his hand and immediately cursing himself for the male gesture.

The beauty hesitated and violet eyes barely concealed curiosity. 'You have a strange accent, Mr Kelly. Are you English?'

'Australian,' Lukas replied. 'Although my Aussie cobbers tell me that my accent is more Yankee than Aussie.'

'I am Veronica Laurents,' the girl said with a smile, extending her hand to curl softly in Lukas's own broad palm. 'I am actually here as a guest of Mr Arthur Jensen – you may have heard of him.'

Lukas frowned. 'Old bloke who did some movies back in the twenties,' he said, reluctant to let go of Veronica's warm hand. 'Never saw any of his pictures though. It was a bit hard to get them back in Papua.'

'What – or where – is Papua?' Veronica asked as

61

she slid her hand away. 'I don't know of any place around here by that name.'

'Papua is a big island north of Australia. It is a place of jungles inhabited by head-hunters and cannibals.'

'It sounds very exciting and dangerous,' Veronica said with just the trace of a little shudder. 'Have you ever met a real head-hunter or cannibal?'

'Dad and I had a couple working for us as deck hands on our schooner before I came here.'

'Really!'

Before either knew it they were deep in conversation and had drifted away from the mansion to sit under the stars. Veronica confessed that she had only come to the house because she thought she might meet some famous producer or director who might assist her in getting a foot through the door to an acting role. It was the way with Hollywood. She had travelled from New York months earlier and had been able to survive in Los Angeles on her wealthy parents' money without having to seek employment at one of the cafés or diners. Films had fascinated her and she was sure that they were the means to true immortality. Veronica did not elaborate on how she had spent her time between haunting agencies and Lukas did not ask. The fact that she had attended one of Errol's infamous parties said enough. But he did not care, he was bewitched by this stunning young woman who shared the starlit night with him.

Before dawn he was able to spirit her away to an airstrip, belt her into the co-pilot's seat and with a clearance take her on a flight over the sleeping city into the rising sun of the dawn. From that moment on Veronica had been his.

But it was a tempestuous relationship. His duties flying around the country for the movie industry kept him away from LA and often enough on his return she would not be in her expensive, comfortable apartment. When she did make contact with him she always had an excuse that she was at some party or other because of her attempts to establish a career. Lukas knew what she said was true; one did have to be seen around town to catch the eye of the right people. It made him uneasy but he continued to remain loyal to Veronica. However, he often asked himself if she was loyal to him.

But she had promised to be available to go out to dinner upon his return from this flight and Lukas was just as eager as his fellow Australian for Jose to turn up and convey Errol to the little village he was heading to for whatever reason. For when that was done Lukas could turn around and fly back to LA to the promise of Veronica's bed and body.

'Will you be doing the pick-up flight?' Errol asked, cutting across Lukas' thoughts.

'Ah, no. Harry will be bringing the old girl back for you,' he replied, referring to the aircraft in warm and familiar terms.

'So this might be the last time I see you, if you are heading back to the old country,' Errol said. 'I am going to miss our reminiscences of the wild times in Papua and New Guinea, old sport.'

With a start Lukas realised that the famous actor was reminding him that the good times in America were rapidly coming to an end. 'It seems you could be right,' Lukas replied as the distant sound of a car engine intruded into the silence of the tranquil countryside. Both men shaded their eyes to see the approaching Dodge sedan pluming a trail of dust on the unsealed road. 'Looks like Jose is on his way to pick you up,' Lukas added. 'No reason to hang around.'

'You head back now, you will be in time to take your lady out tonight,' Errol said, standing and stretching his well-toned body. He reached inside his trouser pocket and retrieved a small silver item. 'I just happened to have one of these spare,' he said passing Lukas a small lapel pin in the shape of a penis and testicles and inscribed 'FFF'. Lukas took the offered gift and broke into a broad smile. He was aware what it was and also what the inscription meant.

'Flynn's Flying Fornicators,' Lukas said with a chuckle.

'Or a word like fornicator,' the actor replied. 'You never earned it in the traditional way of my friends but it has the word flying in it so I think it should act as a talisman for a pilot. Keep it close when you go flying into the wild blue yonder in search of Nazis, young Lukas.'

Lukas thrust out his hand as the growl of the approaching car engine grew louder. 'Take it easy cobber, and watch out for those who have no appreciation of what an Aussie can do when let loose in Babylon.'

Errol took the hand and gripped it firmly. 'You take it easy over there. Give my regards to the pretty *meris* around Moresby. *Lukim you behain, wantok.*'

Lukas nodded and turned to stride back to the aeroplane waiting to return to LA. 'See ya, cobber,' he responded as the big black car arrived at the tin shed. A thin, nervous-looking man of Spanish appearance, in a sweat-stained white suit, stepped from the car to greet the famous actor.

Four hours later the heavens were taking on a beautiful mauve haze as Lukas climbed to a height above the rugged tree-covered mountains below his aircraft. He was fighting a headwind and wished that his co-pilot had been able to make the trip with him. But Billy had been taken sick and Lukas was forced to make the flight alone. Had Billy been at the controls it would have allowed Lukas a chance to catch up on some sleep before landing at the airstrip just outside LA.

Lukas had great faith in the aircraft. It was one of the new, all-metal passenger planes capable of transporting ten passengers and its silver skin reflected the night sky. Either side of him growled a big nine-cylinder Pratt & Whitney radial engine, each delivering 450 horsepower. A state of the art aircraft and it was no wonder the famed aviator Amelia Earhart and her co-pilot, Jim Noonan, had opted to use the same model for what became their ill-fated flight in 1937 when they disappeared somewhere in the Pacific. Lukas did not think that the plane had been at fault. More like weather or poor navigation, was his opinion, although a few pilots he knew complained that the long, broad design of the nose impaired forward vision. But Lukas did not agree with their opinion. He loved flying the Electra.

The Australian glanced routinely at the plane's control board and noted that all the dials were reading as they should. He was cruising at 10,000 feet on his slow descent to LA and maintained a good speed of 158 knots. Ten minutes north-west lay Hollywood and soon he would see the first bright lights on his horizon. Although it would be a night landing this did not concern Lukas as the skies were clear and the wind kind to those who travelled its currents.

He had time to pleasantly anticipate his meeting with Veronica tonight as it was going to be a very special rendezvous. He would be telling her that he was leaving the States to return to Australia where he would enlist in the RAAF for military service, and he pondered the meeting now with some trepidation. How would she react to his announcement? It was the only patriotic choice he had when his country was at war. But her country was not and his news may not be seen in the same light as his own good intentions.

Lukas glanced down once again at the glowing rows of gauges. It was time to commence his descent and radio the control tower at the airstrip. As he looked up to establish a landmark for the approach into LA airspace his whole world exploded. In a split second he saw a dark shape hit the perspex cabin window and then felt as if his head had also exploded. Immediately his aviator's mind registered a bird-strike. The wind howled through the blasted window and tore at anything loose in the cabin. Terrified, Lukas suddenly was aware that the mauve skies had turned black – completely black. With horror, he realised that he was blind. He touched his face and felt shards of the window as well as something wet – blood. The stinging throb in his head was overpowering his ability to think but he instinctively knew that his left wing had dropped. The aircraft commenced to roll over and spin down. Blind or not he forced back on the controls and rudder to level out before the descent became an uncontrolled spiral into the earth below.

Miraculously, Lukas could just see the faint shimmer of stars through the smashed window. He was regaining his sight – at least partially in the right eye. His training caused him to take control of his terror, forcing it to subside. The gauges registered that the aircraft was still functioning and it seemed the worst damage was to the smashed windscreen and himself. He reached for the radio and broadcast a mayday. It was answered by a familiar voice at the airstrip control tower.

'What damage you got?' the male voice asked calmly.

'Cockpit windscreen gone – I only have partial vision – seems I took a bird-strike,' Lukas replied, keeping his own voice calm. 'I might have some trouble landing in the dark.'

'I think I see you to the south-east at about 6000,' the controller came back. 'That means you are on course to land. I am alerting the right people now to make sure you get in safely.'

'Roger,' Lukas answered and wiped with the back of his ungloved hand at the blood flowing into his good eye from the severe cut somewhere on his head. The wind was biting cold but Lukas was hardly aware of it as he desperately sought the landing lights to line up for an approach. There they were! Exactly where they should be. But he also realised that he had lost his binocular vision. He could see the lights beckoning to him but not judge the distance with his usual accuracy.

'Lukas, you need to get your undercarriage down now,' the voice crackled in his ears. 'You are coming in low and fast.'

Lukas glanced at his altimeter but could not read it. It was a blur. He knew he must rely on the little sight he had to make the landing. 'Get her up and circle round for another attempt,' the controller called out over the airwaves.

Lukas could hear a note of panic in the man's voice. Something was terribly wrong. Lukas reached for the gear lever to let down the undercarriage and felt an overwhelming sense of relief when he felt the shudder and whirr of the wheels coming out of the bays. But now the lights seemed to be rushing at him and at the last moment the young Australian aviator was aware that he had misjudged the distance and in seconds he would be touching the concrete airstrip at a speed far too fast for a safe landing.

The aircraft hit the strip with its spinning wheels. They burst on impact and the plane somersaulted into the air to come down on its back, skidding sideways off the strip and into the paddock adjoining the airfield. Lukas did not feel the plane come to a stop. Nor did he hear the distant wail of a siren approaching.

FIVE

Captain Featherstone was wearing a crisp, white naval uniform when Karl wandered into the room designated as the officers' mess in the hotel. It was adorned with traditional silverware and one or two old trophies taken in foreign campaigns from the days of Queen Victoria's rule. The young British officer stood with a gin and tonic in one hand speaking to a major from the English army on the headquarter staff supplying the forward units in Syria. Karl felt a little uneasy being in the mess, which was now filling with high-ranking officers sporting the ribands of the last war on their chests. They were mostly English but there were also a couple of Free French officers.

'Come and join me, old chap,' Featherstone called when the major moved away. Karl breathed a sigh of relief at being recognised by at least one of the mess members. 'What will your poison be?' he asked when Karl was at hand.

'G and T will be fine,' Karl said, and the Englishman signalled to a waiter hovering at the edge of the officers by pointing to his own drink. The waiter understood and went to fetch two drinks.

'Got your kit squared away?' Featherstone asked politely.

'Not much to square away,' Karl replied. 'But the quarters are excellent compared with what I left behind in Syria.'

'If you were wondering,' the English officer said, 'I heard your chaps did well in their attack on the froggy fort and not too many casualties to your platoon. I will obtain a report for you tomorrow, if you like.'

'Thank you, sir, it would be very much appreciated. I guess I feel a bit guilty about leaving them when I did,' Karl replied.

'If it is any consolation, you had no choice,' Featherstone said sympathetically. 'We need you here for a little while.'

The waiter returned and both men took the drinks from the silver platter the waiter held in one hand. Featherstone drew out a packet of cigarettes and offered Karl one. 'No thanks,' Karl replied.

The Englishman lit his own and inhaled the smoke. 'That's right, you don't partake. Bad habit,' he said with a sigh. 'But one has to have some vices.'

Karl glanced around at the rapidly filling mess. The noise level had risen a little but the atmosphere was comfortable. It was hard to imagine that only mere miles north his men were probably once again digging in.

'I normally do not talk shop in the mess,' Featherstone said, leaning towards Karl. 'But matters have taken a sudden turn and I am going to brief you on why you are here. Sadly, I am not at liberty to tell you what the sudden turn has been – Secrets Act and all that. You are probably aware that this campaign has appeared somewhat confused in its strategic objectives.'

'Strategy is not something mere lieutenants worry about much,' Karl grinned. 'Just the tactics of staying alive on the battlefield whilst doing our best to deny the enemy his life.'

Featherstone smiled at the Australian's pragmatic approach to his rank and role in the war. 'Well, to put it in a nutshell, it's a damned mess and the bottom line is that we are really here to help the bloody French on the insistence of that jumped-up chap de Gaulle, who insists that Lebanon and Syria must be secured. From our point of view the nation- alists in Iraq are more of a problem. They could invite the Germans in if they seize power and the oil must remain in our hands at all costs. But I am digressing,' Featherstone said, realising that he could easily launch into a geo-political dissertation on Middle Eastern strategy of no consequence to the Australian's mis- sion. 'We have a problem here in Jerusalem with a Nazi spy ring and we need you to do a bit of undercover work to identify the ringleaders. I have suggested that a German-speaking officer might be passed off as an escapee from one of our POW camps.

As it is, an officer did escape but was killed by the Jewish militia working with us and you just happen to have an uncanny likeness to the man that was killed, who, by the way, was also born in Munich. Needless to say I am not really asking you to volunteer for what could be a dangerous job but really ordering you as a soldier of the King to do your duty.'

'I kind of gathered that,' Karl replied. 'I will do my best so long as I am guaranteed a return to my unit when the job is over.'

'You will have that, old boy, and the gratitude of His Majesty to boot – well, at least British intelligence, anyway,' the Englishman said with a wry grin and offered his hand. 'As we chappies say in the navy, welcome aboard.'

With a sense of irony, Karl realised that before he even finished his drink, he was now officially a spy – whether he liked it or not.

Fully briefed on his mission and suitably supplied with the relevant documents and accoutrements of a German bomber pilot on the run from the British, Karl sat at a table outside a coffee shop in the old part of Jerusalem. The only thing British intelligence had been able to glean from their reports was that this particular coffee shop had something to do with a German intelligence network. They knew that the shop belonged to a shady Corsican by the name of Pierre Cher. It was also known that Cher, a swarthy, solidly built man in his forties, had travelled from North Africa at the outbreak of the war and settled in Jerusalem. He appeared to be married to a woman not known to the British and had a daughter around seventeen years old. Although a French citizen, the coffee shop owner was suspected of being pro-Nazi on the Vichy side. Featherstone had decided not to intern him and his family in the hope that the Corsican might lead them to others involved in espionage and sabotage. After all, Featherstone had snorted, Corsica had also produced Napoleon Bonaparte and his damage to European stability in the nineteenth century was well-known to the English.

Karl wore a shabby, ill-fitting suit stained with dirt. He was unshaven and bleary-eyed – to all intents and purposes a shady character himself. The sun was hot and in the distance Karl could hear the call to pray from one of the many minarets in the old city. He gazed around at the predominantly Arab people passing him in the narrow street surrounded by walls of stone, and wondered how many other races of people had walked such streets throughout history and become conquerors: Assyrians, Romans, Byzantines, Arabs – and even Australian soldiers from the Great War.

'Coffee, monsieur?' a woman's voice at his elbow asked, interrupting Karl's musings on history, a subject he loved very much. Karl glanced up at the young woman and was struck by the stunning blue eyes that stared back at him from behind the veil. He guessed her to be in her late teens.

'No speak French,' Karl replied.

'Do you speak English?' the girl asked.

'*Nein, bitte*, a little only,' he replied and the eyes frowned.

'You are German?' she asked bluntly in heavily accented German, glancing around to see if they were being overheard by the other patrons who sat sipping the thick, dark coffee and playing backgammon on battered boards.

'Yes, I am German and need help,' Karl answered.

The girl understood his plea for help and hovered uncertainly as if mulling over a problem. Then, without a word, she turned and walked away to disappear inside the dingy coffee shop. Karl felt the sweat running down between his shoulder blades and wondered whether he had convinced the girl – or was she going to speak to someone who might do him harm? Alone, unarmed and without immediate support he had good reason to feel the prickles of fear. Spying was a dangerous game at any time – let alone wartime – and he was a complete amateur at this form of warfare.

After a few minutes a man appeared at the door and beckoned him inside with a subtle nod of his head. Karl could see that the man was of Latin appearance and had an air of menace about him that made Karl even more nervous. He had come to the coffee shop unarmed as per his instructions from Featherstone who had also instructed him that they would not be able to provide a cover force in this area of Jerusalem. Too many Arab eyes to inform whoever was working against the British in the twisting and narrow alleys of the old city, he had explained cheerfully.

Karl walked warily into the dimly lit, smoke-filled room. It was occupied by Arab customers who gave him hardly a glance.

'You are German?' the man asked in badly accented German.

'I am,' Karl replied, and glancing around the room with its old stone arches he was surprised to see that it was much bigger than he first appreciated in the dim light.

'Why do you tell me this?' the Corsican asked with a hint of hostility. 'If you are what you say I should inform the British immediately.'

'I identified myself because the girl spoke French – I can only hope that you are a Frenchman loyal to Petain and the Führer. If not, I will pay for my mistake.'

'Who are you?' the Corsican asked without dropping his air of hostility.

'I am pilot officer Karl Harmstorf. I was shot down with my crew three months ago while serving with the Italians over Lebanon. I was taken prisoner by the British but escaped a fortnight ago and was able to make it to Jerusalem because here I thought I might have more chance of getting back to Germany.'

'Why would you think that, Herr Harmstorf – if that really is your name?' the Corsican asked with his arms folded across his broad chest.

Karl shrugged. He would play the man who had lost all hope. 'I have come to the end of my tether, Mr . . .'

'Normally I do not give you my name,' the

Corsican answered. 'But you would probably find out anyway as this is my coffee shop. My name is Pierre.'

'Monsieur Pierre, I came to this part of the city because the odds are you are a patriot to France and therefore might help me escape the British.'

'Or hand you over to them,' Pierre said, but with just a little less hostility. 'In the meantime, you put me in danger with the damned British by being here. My daughter will take you to another place until I make up my mind about you, Herr Harmstorf.'

Karl felt a sudden sense of relief. His acting had paid off – at least he hoped so. But then he felt a foreboding sense that the young woman might also be taking him to his death. What if the Corsican had decided that he was not what he claimed to be? He could end up with a bullet in his head on the out-skirts of the city. How could he make contact with Featherstone?

'You appear a bit apprehensive about my propo-sition, Herr Harmstorf,' Pierre said.

Karl sensed the menace behind the question. 'I have not slept or eaten in a long time,' he quickly replied, rubbing his face. 'That is all.'

Pierre signalled to the girl hovering in the back-ground. She moved forward and the Corsican spoke quietly to her in French. Karl had no doubt that he was the subject of the briefing and wished that he could speak French.

'You come with me,' the girl said to Karl in English. 'Come.'

Karl nodded and followed her to a back entrance

to the coffee shop. Whatever happened in the next few hours would decide his fate. Either he eventually returned to his battalion to fight a war where the enemy was clearly defined, or he possibly ended up in an unmarked grave, never to be seen again, buried in a land far from his beloved Papua and family.

Karl was surprised by the transformation of Marie from a traditionally dressed Arab girl to a modern young Frenchwoman. She had done so to drive Karl to a destination outside the city and now looked a different person. When she noticed his curious, questioning look she said in English, 'It is easier to explain why I am driving. Arab women do not drive in this country – if you can understand what I am saying.'

Karl did not answer but merely smiled, nodding his head as if not understanding but attempting to be polite.

They walked a short distance through the alleys to a sun-warmed house on a broad avenue where Marie spoke French to a man who answered the door. Gesturing for Karl to follow she directed him to the back of the house where an old, battered sedan of dubious mechanical quality was garaged. Karl sat in the cramped passenger seat and Marie took the driver's seat. The car sputtered to life and the young woman deftly manoeuvred it out onto the street.

On the journey no words were spoken and Karl had an opportunity to appraise the girl. She had a slightly olive skin that was flawless and a thick mane of dark hair with just the faintest of streaks of gold. Her eyes were a stunning blue and he could clearly see that she was not altogether European in her parentage. There was something very exotic about this extraordinary beauty that intrigued him.

Their journey took them via a route designed to avoid army sentry points and Karl guessed that Marie had done this journey before. After an hour of driving outside the city they arrived at a squalid Arab village of mud buildings and numerous goats with a view of the Mediterranean Sea. When they rattled in on the pot-holed dirt road the Arab men glared with suspicion and hostility at the car and its occupants and Karl felt uneasy.

'This is where we stop,' Marie said, more to herself than her passenger. 'You can get out Herr Harmstorf.'

Karl stepped warily into the dusty street and instinctively scanned the surrounding locale for possible avenues to escape should things go wrong.

'Follow me,' Marie commanded with a slight frown. 'We go inside.'

Karl followed her into a mud-and-thatch house off the street. It was dim inside and it took long seconds for Karl's eyes to adjust from the hot glare of the day outside. When they did he noticed a rickety wooden table at the centre of the room. But more importantly he also noted a blond-haired man dressed in European clothes sitting behind the table, and closely watching him across a Luger pistol lying on the table. Karl stood in the doorway while the man took a packet of Turkish cigarettes from the top pocket of his sweat-stained white shirt. Karl guessed the man to be in his late thirties and he looked very dangerous. There was a disconcerting hardness behind his cold eyes and no sign of welcome in his face, which only softened slightly at the sight of Marie. Her beauty could do that to any man, Karl thought observing the slight change in the man's demeanour.

'Sit down, Herr Harmstorf,' the man behind the table said in German, pushing a chair with his foot towards Karl. 'A cigarette?'

'Thank you,' Karl replied, taking both the seat and the offered cigarette from the pack that now lay on the table beside the Luger. Karl was fully aware of the significance of the gun on the table and was tempted to snatch it. But it could have been unloaded, a test, he considered. For now he would let things ride as he suspected that the man behind the table was of extreme interest to Captain Featherstone. Possibly the very agent the naval officer was after, he thought. The man was obviously German, judging by his speech and appearance.

When Karl was seated the German held out a match to light Karl's cigarette. 'As an officer in the air force you would naturally be familiar with this gun,' the man said, leaning back in his chair. Karl noticed uneasily that Marie was no longer in the room.

'I am,' Karl replied, taking in a draught of smoke.

'Then you would have no problem showing me how to strip and assemble the weapon?' the man asked, watching Karl's reaction carefully.

The Luger was not a simple machine pistol but

an intricate device in comparison with later models of German pistols such as the Walther. Karl stared at the Luger for a short time. It was not a weapon familiar to many of his army. He knew that if he fumbled the stripping and assembling process he would give himself away in this first test. He reached for the gun and expertly broke the weapon down into its main parts, placing each part on the table in sequence for reassembly. The man behind the table seemed impressed as Karl glanced up at him for approval to reassemble the pistol. In the stripping Karl had noted that the magazine held no rounds. The German nodded and Karl quickly reassembled the pistol.

'That is not a skill easily acquired by a British agent,' the man said, sucking on his cigarette and clouding the still air of the dark room with the acrid smoke. 'You said that you were shot down working with the Italians?'

Karl was surprised to hear this information. He had not volunteered it to the German and guessed that he had some kind of communications system that went back to the Corsican. At least two radios, Karl thought, as he had seen no sign of telephone wires on his car trip into the Arab village. He was beginning to feel more at ease and thanked God that his father had taught him the intricacies of the Luger from one that he had purchased from a prospector down and out on his luck in Papua. Paul Mann had bought the pistol for nostalgic reasons as much as for protection on a dangerous frontier of cannibals and head-hunters, and Karl had spent many hours stripping and reassembling the 9mm weapon in the lounge room of his father's house in Papua. It had been a close thing as the German on the other side of the table might have asked him to strip and assemble one of the newer pistols issued to German officers. Had that been so, Karl would have in most probability been a dead man by now. 'I was, but I escaped from the British and have been on the run for over a week now,' Karl answered.

'Needless to say you don't have any papers to prove who you are,' the German said. 'But you do have European clothing – if you could call the rather shabby condition of your clothes that.'

'I robbed a Jewish house,' Karl replied, hoping that the story Featherstone had fabricated for him would stand up to scrutiny should anything he said need to be verified. Although the Jewish house was not robbed, its occupants would corroborate any inquiries to that effect should the occasion arise. They were on Featherstone's payroll – as were many others hired to support the story of a German pilot shot down – and on the run.

'You will only know me as Fritz,' the German said, without attempting to offer his hand. 'You will be taken back to Jerusalem to a safe house until given future orders.'

'You will help me get home?' Karl asked, feigning excitement.

'I will,' Fritz answered, taking the pistol from the table and slipping a full magazine of bullets into the pistol grip receiver. 'Or kill you, if you do not check out as who you say you are. For all I know you might be one of those damned Jewish agents the British

Special Operations Executive uses in Palestine. So for now you will be watched and I strongly suggest that you do not make any attempt to escape or contact anyone other than myself.' As if on cue a young Arab man entered the room behind Karl. 'Abdul here will be your escort, Herr Harmstorf. He and Marie will take you back to Jerusalem.'

Karl turned carefully to see the Arab standing behind him. He was armed with a Luger tucked behind his belt, and a wicked-looking, curved dagger in a sheath at his waist.

'You can go now,' Fritz said, without rising from the table. 'We will meet again.'

Karl rose and stubbed out his cigarette on the edge of the table. The Arab was careful to remain behind Karl as he walked out of the house and into the squalid street where Marie was waiting beside the car, conversing in fluent Arabic with three Arab children. She was laughing lightly and Karl was struck by the contradiction: the young woman appeared so beautifully angelic at one moment, yet she was obviously working with a Nazi organisation known for its brutality. She glanced up at him and he thought that he saw just the slightest hint of interest that he had left the house alive. Karl cursed himself for feeling attracted to Marie – for she was also the enemy.

SIX

The warm waters of the Pacific lapped along the shoreline of Townsville's harbour. Victoria Kelly did not feel the heat as much as her taller and older companion on the walk as they strolled arm in arm, taking in the late afternoon sea breezes of the tropical capital of north Queensland.

'Uncle Bernie, you should slow down,' she chided gently. 'You are walking too fast.'

Bernard Duvall checked his military pace to accommodate his niece. 'I'm sorry, Cherry Blossom,' he apologised gruffly. 'I've been in Washington too long to change to civilian ways.'

His pet name for his much loved niece went back to when she was a student of Japanese language and culture in California prior to her travelling to Papua, meeting Jack Kelly and subsequently marrying him. Victoria's father had served with distinction with the

United States Army and she had lived in both China and Japan when Colonel Owen Duvall had been posted as a military attaché to those countries.

'So, are you going to tell me why you are here, and why the covert military operation for me to steam down to Townsville to meet you? I smell secrecy in the whole matter, Uncle Bernie.'

The distinguished man with the thick, short-cut, greying hair slowed to a stop to gaze out to the calm waters of the harbour. 'I miss you very much, Cherry Blossom. I kind of hoped that you might come and live with your old uncle in Washington when my brother passed away.'

'I would have except I met the man I was destined to be with,' Victoria replied, also gazing out to sea. 'I am extremely happy sailing with Jack. No two days are ever the same when we are together.'

Bernard Duvall turned to his niece with a pained expression. 'It would be safer if you returned to the States,' he said. 'There will be a war in this part of the world and I don't think it will go well for the Aussies.'

Victoria frowned. Her personal knowledge of the Japanese had long convinced her that what her uncle said was true. She had often thought it was only a matter of time. Sadly, many Europeans could not understand the fierce Oriental belief in saving face, and had trodden on Japanese honour without any respect for their national pride. She well knew of the samurai tradition and had watched it being awakened in the people of the island nation to the north. Like a kamikaze wind they would one day explode out of their home islands to sweep south. 'Then that is all the more reason why I should be by Jack's side when the time comes,' she said with a sad note in her reply.

'I guess you know that my visit here is more than personal,' her uncle said. 'We have been quietly liaising with some members in the Aussie government and defence about putting in place a plan for when the inevitable happens. You can understand that I cannot tell you much.'

'I know,' Victoria said with a sigh. 'I was not the daughter of a military man for nothing. I understand that you work for the Office of Naval Intelligence and that says it all. You forget that a few years back I worked with Joe Oblachinski to film around Papua for the Department of Defense back home and I still keep detailed notes and photographs of places of military interest for Uncle Sam.'

'Does your husband know what you are doing?' the American naval man asked.

'If Jack does, he never lets on,' she said, and added, 'He is an extraordinary man – and husband.'

'From your repeated declarations that he is superman it sounds like I will never be able to convince you that it would be safer to return to the States with your Uncle Bernie,' the naval officer said with a gentle touch to Victoria's face. 'So I am going to ask you on behalf of your Uncle Sam to do some things for us in the name of national security.'

'I half-expected that when I came down to see you,' Victoria said. 'I feel that I can help my country by staying in this part of the world if . . . when, the

85

Emperor unleashes his bushido warriors on the Pacific.'

The American was hesitant to brief his niece and turned again to gaze out at the blue waters beyond the harbour before speaking. 'I cannot tell you how we know but it has come to our attention that the Japs are stockpiling supplies around the islands for their submarine fleet. We know that the Brit navy is also aware and will be mounting an operation to hunt down and destroy those dumps before the Japs declare war on us. I know that you are currently perfectly placed with the operations of the *Independence* to help us locate a Jap agent who is responsible for covert activities right under the Aussies' noses in your part of the world.'

'Why don't you give this information to the Australian authorities and let them hunt down the man?' Victoria asked with a frown of disapproval.

What Commander Duvall could not tell his niece was that United States counter-intelligence had broken the Japanese diplomatic code, which they named Purple, and that since 1939 the US Navy was partially able to read the new Japanese navy code they had designated JN 25. In the intercepts they had stumbled across references to a well-placed agent actively working in Papua, code-named Krait, and his controller, Leading Seaman Fuji Komine. As it was, the USN code breakers were one step ahead of the Japanese agent by virtue of the fact that they had partially deciphered a routine message between Japanese commands that Komine was to be reassigned to the island of Bougainville. As far as they knew, not even the Japanese agent was aware of his new posting. But this information was called intelligence and was on a *need to know* basis. Despite the close cooperation between the United States government and the Australians, it was still deemed by some in the secretive world of counter-intelligence that it would not be wise to reveal too much to a government that just might fall in the opening shots of a war. After all, the Australian government had its finest troops on the other side of the world fighting for the British in North Africa and the Middle East, and the country would be virtually defenceless against a sudden and overwhelming attack from the north.

Bernard bowed his head. 'We are not in a position to leave it to the Australians,' he answered quietly. 'But I can trust you, as a patriotic American, to carry out the task of locating a Japanese by the name of Fuji Komine.'

'I know that name!' Victoria exclaimed. 'It has to be a coincidence, but I know that name.'

Bernard Duvall was startled by his niece's statement. 'How could you know this man?' he asked.

'When I first met Jack there was a tragic incident involving an attempted murder on some friends of Jack's near Moresby. Jack was actually wounded in the incident and later learned that a young Japanese man born in Papua was involved in almost having him and his friends killed. His name was Fuji Komine. His parents still live just outside of Port Moresby and his father is a well-respected boat builder. Young Fuji used to sail with his father all around the islands. In fact, Jack tells me that Fuji was educated in Port Moresby along with his son.'

'It fits if what you say is true. This Komine would be the perfect agent for the area of operations around southern Papua and the islands of the Torres Strait. Have you seen him lately?' Bernard asked, hopeful that he might receive a positive answer.

But his niece shook her head. 'If anyone could track down Fuji it would be Jack,' she said. 'He is a born hunter.'

'I would prefer that we keep your husband, er, Jack, out of this.'

'I trust my husband with my life,' Victoria snapped, annoyed at her uncle's bureaucratic response. It seemed that a bit of Washington had worn off on the man she had always respected for his diverse opinions in the face of plodding government thinking.

'I am sorry, Victoria,' her uncle said apologetically. 'I did not mean to infer that Jack could not be trusted. I suppose I have to go off the record, as they say in the world of newspapermen, and leave how much you confide to your Aussie to your intelligent judgment. But you did not hear that from me.'

Victoria grasped her uncle's elbow. 'You know that my loyalty to Uncle Sam is beyond question and I also trust Jack to be discreet in this matter. I sense that he knows Australia will need the US in the future if it is to survive in a war against Japan – although most of his pompous friends at the club still believe that the Brits will save them. The Brits are hardly in any position to save themselves right now and after all, we and the Aussies share the edges of the Pacific.'

Bernard nodded and turned to walk with his niece back to the hotel where he had organised comfortable accommodation for her. Tonight they would share a meal and he would complete his briefing. Along with his knowledge that the Japanese were in the process of planning a war against the Western powers in the Pacific was his unshakeable trust in his remarkable niece's loyalty and abilities.

A clatter of something metallic and the strong, pungent, lingering smell of chloroform impacted on Lukas Kelly's senses in his world devoid of light. Something had happened and he struggled frantically to remember.

'Easy Lukas,' he heard a soothing male voice say, and desperately tried to recall whose voice it was. His hand came up and he touched a swathe of bandages around his head. More voices now but muted by distance.

Luke's throat felt dry and nausea welled up. As he struggled to sit up to vomit he felt a gentle but strong hand assist him into a sitting position.

'Nurse,' the voice called, but it was too late, and Lukas felt the spasms force up bile to splash on the bed.

'I have him, Mr Oblachinski,' a female voice said and Lukas felt the moistness of a cloth wiping his face.

'Joe?' Lukas queried to ascertain if his mind was functioning.

89

'It's me,' Joe answered and Lukas smelled the strong aroma of cigars when Joe Oblachinski leaned forward. 'Take it easy, young fella, you have just come out of the operating theatre.'

'What happened? I just remember flying Errol somewhere.'

'It seems that you had a bird-strike on your plane and you went down a bit hard on the strip. You are in a private hospital. When Jack Warner's people heard what happened they had you sent by ambulance directly here.'

'Where's here?' Lukas asked weakly.

'A place in LA,' Joe answered and took Lukas' hand. 'A really good place where Jack has ensured you will get the best of treatment.'

'How bad am I?' Lukas asked as he slowly but surely fought for control of his senses. It was still dark and already the young Australian realised that the bandages around his head had obstructed his vision. His head throbbed and so too did his whole body. He cried out involuntarily when a wave of intense pain wracked his head and was not even aware of the needle inserted by the nurse. The morphine took effect and Lukas did not care about the world anymore as the analgesic effect swept over him.

Joe continued to hold Lukas' hand until merciful sleep came. Lukas could not see the tears that rolled down the film director's face.

Joe Oblachinski came every day and sat with Lukas. They talked and the big man in his late fifties, with a paunch that displayed his success in Hollywood, puffed on his cigars when the window was open. The rich aroma was soothing to Lukas who had always associated it with the man who had taken him under his wing. It was because of Joe that Lukas had been able to travel to the United States originally to realise his dream to fly. Under the American's roof with his wonderful wife, Marjory, Lukas had been accepted almost as an adopted son to the childless couple. Marjory Oblachinski reminded Lukas very much of Karin Mann who had virtually raised him as a young boy. Both women had a natural maternal instinct that required someone in their lives to fill a space. Joe had organised Lukas Kelly's flying lessons with the best instructors and when he had won his wings ensured he had employment with the Warner Brothers company as a stunt pilot and flying charters.

Now, doctors would drop in from time to time to examine him, pushing and prodding his body in places where it still hurt. Nurses would routinely visit to carry out maintenance in a manner that reminded Lukas of how he looked after his own aircraft. He knew he was popular with the staff as he refused to complain, or even at times, admit to his pain. Lukas came to recognise each person by their scent and footsteps in his world of darkness. His questions to the doctors about when the bandages would come off his eyes were met with the usual, 'Fairly soon.'

And fairly soon eventually came. Two specialist doctors stood around his bed whilst a nurse carefully removed the swathe of gauze and cotton. 'Try to open your eyes slowly,' a voice said. Lukas recognised it as that of an eye specialist. 'You may experience a little bit of disorientation.'

Lukas opened his eyes and immediately closed them as the light flowing through the bedroom window seemed to be coming directly from the core of the sun. He winced and in a split second before closing his eyes saw the restrained smile of a bespectacled, balding man, only inches from his face.

'It looks good,' the balding doctor said to his colleague. 'The reaction to the light has obviously stimulated his optic nerves. Try to open your right eye only this time Mr Kelly,' the same voice commanded Lukas.

Again the intensity of the light flooded his head and Lukas instinctively closed his eye against the blur.

'Now, the same for your left eye.'

Lukas slowly opened his left eye and suddenly experienced a wave of fear – nothing – just total darkness. 'I can't see anything, doc,' he said in despair.

'You are fortunate to have any sight at all in your right eye,' the doctor said matter-of-factly. 'We had to remove fragments from both eyes after the accident and I am extremely pleased with what Doctor Lowenstein has done to save your right eye. So you will be able to continue seeing fully with your right eye and live a productive life.'

'I'm a flyer,' Lukas said softly with his eyes closed. 'I need both eyes.'

'There are other jobs for a smart young man,' the eye doctor attempted to reassure him. 'At least it seems that if the healing continues as it has, you will be able to see. I will need to make further examinations and tests to ascertain that you do have a functioning right eye.'

Over the next week the tests continued and it was ascertained that Lukas had regained the use of his right eye. Sitting up in bed with a black eye patch and his hair growing thick and curly around his ears, Lukas looked to all intents and purposes like a pirate from one of his friend Errol's movies. Marjory Oblachinski came every day with Joe and from time to time old flyer friends dropped in to wish him the best, talk over aviation news and what was happening in the industry. Other than those visitors he did not see anyone else. The visitor he most wanted to see was Veronica but she did not come. There was not even a phone call to inquire about his health.

Lukas did not ask Joe about her as he knew the Hollywood man disapproved of the beautiful would-be actress. But it was he who brought up the subject finally as Lukas limped along, aided by a walking stick, down a corridor of the white-walled private hospital. 'Veronica has a supporting role in a film being shot at the moment,' Joe said self-consciously. 'Probably why she has been unable to visit or contact you.'

'The doctors tell me that I had six broken ribs, a fractured left ankle, head injuries, and we know about the loss of my left eye. You can add to that the fact that they have missed the broken heart bit,' Lukas reflected. 'No, Joe, I guess I have to face the fact that it is all over. I kind of knew she was too ambitious to really fall in love with a mere pilot. It is better that she does not make any contact.'

Joe patted Lukas on the back. 'Good attitude,' he muttered. 'A son his father can be proud of. Always saw you as a copy of your father,' he continued.

And eventually the day came when Lukas was released from the hospital to return to Joe's big house outside LA. Neither Joe nor Marjory could understand why the young man who had become such an important part of their lives should want to persist in leaving America to return to Australia to enlist.

'You know a man with one eye missing will be rejected for the military in your country,' Joe had tried to tell Lukas, as he packed a small suitcase with his few most valued belongings. 'You may as well stay here where I can find you other work in the industry,' he pleaded.

'There is a bloke over in England flying fighters for the RAF called Douglas Bader and he has two tin legs. If he can do what he is doing for the RAF I am sure Australia can do no less for me with all the hours I have put into flying. Australia is going to need all the experienced pilots it can get if the Japanese decide to have a go at us.'

Joe stood by the door of Luke's room. 'You know that Marjory is very fond of you,' he said gruffly. 'Kind of fond of you myself.'

Lukas glanced up from his packing. 'Joe, I owe you everything that I have achieved here but I have to do this thing, more than ever now. It is hard to explain why.'

'I think I understand but I want you to know that this will always be your home no matter how things pan out back in Australia.'

Lukas nodded and resumed his packing. Pride, a need to win – both factors in why it was so important for him to return to Australia and enlist. Besides, he had not seen his father in years and he also missed the blue waters of the tropics and the green jungles of Papua. It was time to return home.

The farewell at the wharf was a sad time for the three people who stood at the bottom of the gangway. Marjory wept as she hugged Lukas and when it came time to say goodbye to Joe the two men hugged. As Lukas boarded and waved from the deck of the merchant ship destined for the port of Sydney, he was forced to turn away to fight back the tears that flowed from his right eye.

SEVEN

As scheduled by Japanese intelligence the radio transmitter/receiver had arrived in the cargo from Hong Kong. Fuji instructed Sen in its functioning and set the prearranged frequency to broadcast the first message in code to a Japanese fishing boat overtly trawling in the Papuan Gulf. The message was deciphered and relayed to an island off another island occupied by the Japanese since the Great War and where a naval intelligence officer quietly celebrated by pouring a sake for himself. The information-gathering network was in place and functioning, spreading its tentacles into the mainland of the United States of America and to all the isolated islands of the Pacific occupied by the Western powers.

'This is what the Christians would call your bible,' Fuji said, fingering the code book. 'I know that you take your Ford truck into Port Moresby twice a week,' he continued. 'It is then that you will take careful note of what is happening. You will report any shipping movements, troop and aircraft deployments to the Port Moresby region, and as well as doing that you will also transmit meteorological information as to the weather in the Port Moresby district. I will explain later the basics of meteorological data collection and measurement.'

Sen did not answer. The two men were huddling over the small but efficient radio packed into a battered suitcase in the room used as Sen's office, and the aerial wire leading to the roof was disguised as an aerial for a commercial short wave set to pick up Radio Australia.

Fuji had lived under Sen's roof for two weeks and rarely went outside. But when he did he came and went without disclosing where he had been or what he had been doing. His mission to ensure that a communications base was set up strategically close to the important harbour was at an end and he could look forward to being taken off the island by either a fishing boat or submarine and eventually finding his way back to the great Imperial fleet. Sen had explained Fuji's presence to his native staff. He said that Fuji was a relative from the Chinese mainland and obtained their sworn oath that they would not speak of him to any European. Although Sen's native staff did not understand the need for secrecy they dutifully obeyed their employer who doubled their wages. Whatever the need for secrecy was it did not concern mere natives, they told each other.

'You must be by the set at, or before, twenty-three

hundred hours each night,' Fuji said in closing. 'That is when any messages for Krait will be transmitted to you.'

Sen nodded. The arrival of the radio had well and truly cemented his role as a spy for the Japanese and at times he had tossed and turned in his bed, agonising over whether he should betray the son of the boat builder. But he feared the power of the Japanese to reveal that Sen had been helped in the making of his fortune during the Great War by spying for the Germans. That information would not be appreciated by the Australian administration in Papua and could lead him to the gallows for treason, Sen had brooded as he stared at the ceiling of the room. Better to go along with the Japanese, he decided. At least in any coming war he – and his family in Singapore – would be safe if the Japanese invaded Papua and New Guinea.

Sen was pleased to see Fuji's back when the briefing session was over, but the Chinese entrepreneur did wonder where he went – and what Fuji did when he left the bungalow.

Fuji followed the same trail for a couple of hours until he broke through the scrub that ran down to the edge of the beach. Very cautiously he scanned the surrounding area for signs of other people, and when he was satisfied that he was alone, concealed himself amongst the foliage of the low-growing bushes. Now he would wait and see if they would come as he had noted before on prior trips to the beach.

He did not have to wait long until the distant sound of laughter and voices drifted to him on a tropical breeze. He felt himself tense whilst the waiting continued. At last the four girls appeared at the end of the white sandy strip near the headland. Barebreasted and innocent in their place in this Garden of Eden, they were not aware that they were under observation by the Japanese sailor. Each were a study of beauty, befitting their appearance which was more Polynesian than the darker-skinned Melanesian characteristics of most natives along the Papuan coast. They laughed and played girlish games like young women of any culture. But it was one in particular who Fuji noticed most. She was the shortest of the four but the most beautiful in his opinion; petite with long dark hair washing over her shoulders and deep brown eyes that seemed to have a permanent smile. Fuji felt his heart beat in his chest as he strained to identify the girl and was pleased to see that she had come as she usually did in the afternoon. Satisfied he was still safe, he sat back and watched the young, brown-skinned Motu women strolling along in the shallows between surf and sand. He had guessed that they were all in their late teens and all wore the more traditional grass skirts of their culture.

Fuji was fluent in the Motu language as it was commonly used along the Gulf coast by the people who lived in villages built on stilts out to sea. They were a fishing people who traded in the islands and their seagoing skills were second to none amongst the peoples of Papua and New Guinea. Fuji had accidentally stumbled on the four a week earlier when he had walked to the beach for exercise. He had concealed himself then and overheard the girls speaking. He had also learned that the girl who had attracted his interest was named Keela and that she was being courted by a local boy from the village just up the coast. This beach was the girl's secret place away from the gossip and prying eyes of relatives – a place to discuss intimate things with her closest female friends.

Whenever Fuji had returned to his hiding spot overlooking the beach the girls had also come, and the more Fuji had watched them the more he was sure that he was falling in love with Keela. But what could he do? He was a warrior of the Emperor and as such must dismiss all thoughts of such happiness if he were to be strong and able in his mission. Recently there had been many times when he fought with self-doubt. He had not thought of how his return to Papua would flood him with warm memories of his youth when he had been free in an earthly paradise. His exposure to Japan had been dis-illusioning. It was a place of snow and ice in the winters and crowded cities of paper and wood and had not been what he had dreamed of for years.

Now he was back and questioning his place in the world. The one overriding thought that helped ease the pain of being away from his Papua was that the place would again be his home once Japan swept the barbaric Europeans from the island.

Now the girls were close enough for Fuji to once again listen to their chatter. He could clearly see Keela now as she tossed back her hair and laughed, revealing her tiny white teeth as she waded knee deep into the sea. She was not a betel nut user, Fuji noted and smiled. That was unusual in her people, and only endeared her to him more.

Suddenly his smile froze. Keela and her companions stood blissfully unaware of what Fuji could see from his vantage point – a giant, saltwater crocodile was slowly manoeuvring in the sea to launch its deadly attack on one of the girls.

'Get out of the water!' Fuji screamed at the top of his voice in fluent Motu, rising from his hiding place to wave his hands frantically above his head. Four sets of startled eyes fixed on him. The surprise turned to confusion and fear at the appearance of the wildly gesticulating man above the shoreline. 'A crocodile,' Fuji continued in Motu. 'Get out now!'

Keela did not hesitate. The Motu word for crocodile was primeval fear in itself. She almost leapt through the surf to rush up the beach as the other three girls turned on their heels and fled into the scrub leaving Keela to her fate. With one eye on the water, Fuji rushed forward to intercept the girl. He could no longer see the croc and guessed that it had swung away to seek another unwary victim. He grabbed her by the arms and looked into her terror stricken eyes.

'I saw it,' she gasped. 'It would have snatched me.'

'You are safe now,' Fuji said calmly and let go of Keela's arms as a show of his peaceful intentions. 'You can follow your sisters back to the village.'

Keela stepped back to examine her rescuer. 'You are not Motu although you speak our language well. You remind me of Isokihi Komine, the Boat Builder.'

'He is my father,' Fuji answered openly. He was surprised that this young native girl should know of his father but then realised that his father was well known to all along the Papuan coast and beyond for his boat-building skills.

'I would not be speaking to the son of the boat builder if he had not saved me,' Keela said, and began to tremble from the delayed shock of the near-death experience. Fuji took her by the hand and sat her down on the warm sands. 'Thank you,' she said, looking up into his eyes with a searching expression. 'How is it that you were here now?'

'I have watched you for many days,' Fuji replied honestly. It seemed the best course open to him with this innocent girl. 'I thought that you were the most beautiful of all the sisters who came with you to this beach.'

Keela's eyes flared. 'You have been watching us,' she accused. 'You should not have done that.'

Fuji bowed his head. 'I am sorry for upsetting you but your beauty was greater than my dishonourable behaviour in watching you.'

The angry expression in Keela's eyes faded and the smile returned at the almost boyish shyness of the slim, handsome young man standing before her. 'Will you be at the beach tomorrow?' Keela asked with a mischievous twinkle in her eyes.

'I will be here,' Fuji answered.

'Good,' Keela said, turning on her heel and walking in the direction of her village beyond the headland. 'Then it is possible we may meet again.'

Fuji watched her walking away from him with a deliberate sway of her hips. He stood transfixed until she was out of sight, still coming to grips with what had occurred in the last few but critical minutes. His mind in turmoil, Fuji walked slowly back to the scrub at the edge of the beach. The crocodile had intervened in ways that he was frightened of. It had brought the girl into his life.

For a week Keela came to the beach alone. She had convinced her companions that they should not come with her and each day Fuji met with the young Motu girl to sit in the shade of the tall trees off the beach and talk. He came to learn that she and a native boy were to wed but it was to be a traditional marriage arranged by the two families. Keela was coy about her betrothed and Fuji was unaware that she was playing the age-old game of women, by keeping him keen with jealousy. She would boast of the boy's prowess as a seagoing fisherman and how he had sailed each year to the islands where the sun rose.

Fuji had listened and fallen for her wiles but felt clumsy in the ways of romance. He held the view that the woman must be subservient to the man – a perception reinforced by his short time in Japan. But this beautiful young girl with the copper burnished skin and laughing eyes was a free spirit, at one with the sand and sea. Despite all that he believed about a relationship between a man and a woman, Fuji had to admit to himself that he would have possibly deserted his cause for the Emperor to possess her.

'If you are the son of the boat builder, why is it that you do not live under your father's roof?' Keela asked one day as they sat side by side in the shade, gazing out at the placid waters of the Gulf.

Fuji picked up a shard of sea shell and tossed it idly at the beach. 'I cannot answer your question,' he replied and fell silent.

'Do you work for the white men?'

Keela's questions were making Fuji feel uncomfortable. 'No, I work to rid this country of the Europeans,' he said. 'But I cannot tell you any more.'

Keela stood and consciously stretched her arms above her head. Fuji could see the firm swell of her breasts and felt the desire return. He sensed that she was deliberately provoking him and reached up to drag her down beside him. Keela did not resist and Fuji rolled her on her back. 'I want you, Keela,' he said, covering her body with his. 'I think you are the most beautiful woman I have ever seen.'

Keela smiled up at his face and subtly spread her legs apart. Without a further word between them Fuji followed her cue and struggled to pull down his pants. Under a Papuan sun Fuji finally realised a desire that was almost as strong as his loyalty to the Emperor.

EIGHT

When Victoria returned to Port Moresby Jack noticed a subtle change in his wife and guessed that it had a lot to do with her journey south to meet with her uncle. She seemed just a little reserved and even absent-minded at times.

'I am sorry to hear about Lukas,' she had said, sitting with a mug of coffee at the stern of their schooner on her first night home in Port Moresby. 'But Joe's telegram says he is in fine health and will recover. He has his father's resilience.'

Jack stared at the lights of Port Moresby. The schooner was anchored offshore and the sea breeze had a wonderful cooling effect after a hot day under a tropical sun loading stores at the wharf. The crew went ashore and would return when they sailed again to carry valuable goods to outlying islands in the nearer waters of the Coral Sea. 'A bloody bird,'

Jack mused. 'He has flown so many hours only to be blinded and grounded by a bird.'

'He can still go back to flying with one eye,' Victoria offered hopefully. 'I am sure that there are aviators who only have one eye.'

Jack glanced at his wife and under the light thrown by the lantern swinging on the stern could see the genuine concern written in her expression. She was extremely fond of his son and considered him one of her closest friends. 'He was returning to join the RAAF,' Jack said. 'I doubt that the air force will take a one-eyed flyer.'

Victoria knew Jack was right and did not comment. She had long ago learned that both the Kelly men in her life were proud, driven by a strong masculine ideal of being protectors and providers. War to Lukas was the protective side of his nature, and as such, the unfortunate crash had deprived him of his pride to be able to fight for his country in the armed forces altogether. How would the son of Jack Kelly cope with not being able to enlist even as a foot soldier in the army?

'Speaking of the armed services,' Jack said, 'how did things go with your uncle?'

The question was bound to be asked and Victoria was prepared for the answer. 'Do you think we will go to war with Japan?' she asked, turning to Jack.

'Funny question, but I think it is inevitable sooner or later. The Japs are in a corner and I don't think they will stay there.'

'Uncle Bernie thinks that too,' Victoria said slowly, deliberating on how she would enlist her husband's help in her mission. 'He thinks that the Japanese are already active in this part of the world spying on us.'

'They have been doing that for years,' Jack laughed softly. 'Their goodwill naval visits around the Pacific have been intelligence-gathering exercises, so that is not news.'

'Uncle Bernie is a bit more specific. He has a name – a name we both know well.'

Jack raised his eyebrows and took in a breath. He knew whatever his wife was about to say was most probably backed by corroborated Yankee intelligence.

'Who?' he asked.

'Do you remember a young Japanese man who was born here called Fuji Komine? I believe he went to school with Karl and Lukas in Port Moresby when they were in the primary grades.'

'The boat builder's son,' Jack said quietly. 'The little bastard who was with O'Leary when they came to Paul's plantation all those years ago. Yeah, I remember him but last I heard he headed for Japan after the attack.'

'We . . . I think he is back,' Victoria said. 'And is setting up a spy network somewhere around Port Moresby. I feel that we should find him and report the matter to the police.'

'I am not going to ask you how you know all this,' Jack said with a grin. 'But you realise that even if we find Fuji that we have laws, even in Papua, that say we have to have evidence of his spying to lock him up.'

'Surely you Aussies must have some form of counter-intelligence organisation?' Victoria asked.

'Not that I know of,' Jack shrugged. 'Only have those things when we are at war. Other than that, only the coppers.'

Victoria was amazed at Jack's statement. At least the United States had the Federal Bureau of Investigation under Mr Hoover, to monitor any persons or organisations that might pose a threat to national security. Uncle Bernie was right about the Aussies being woefully unprepared. 'Will you help me find Fuji Komine?' Victoria asked. 'I need your help.'

Jack shook his head. 'I think that you have been reading too many of those Agatha Christie novels,' he said, chuckling. 'But I will give it a go – just for you – and Uncle Bernie.'

Impulsively Victoria placed her mug on the deck and hugged her husband. 'Thank you,' she said squeezing him. 'It means a lot to both our countries.'

Jack buried his head in his wife's long hair and smelled its clean, salty scent. He loved her more than his own life, and despite his misgivings about hunting down a name from the past, he would take some steps to help her crusade to save Australia and America from the Yellow Peril. It was growing more possible each day to visualise Japan unleashing its growing military power in the Pacific, as they already occupied French Indochina and most of China. He knew they would not stop there. They badly needed the rubber of Malaya and the oil of the Dutch East Indies and that meant his beloved Papua and New Guinea would have to be in the firing line. As for finding the Japanese boat builder's son – that was another matter. Jack had no qualms about quietly killing the man when he remembered the terrible night Fuji had assisted O'Leary in attacking the Mann plantation. Jack had killed many times before in the trenches of the Western Front and he was not a man to take half measures. Finding and then killing Fuji was simply finishing a job.

Jack had an idea of where to start. He figured that if Fuji was in the district on subversive activities for Japan he would not risk staying around his father's house outside Moresby. And it would be very hard for a Japanese man to remain in hiding in any of the villages, which would not welcome him because of his race – Asian people not being popular with Melanesians. No, Fuji must either be camped out in the bush or holed up with someone sympathetic to the Japanese. The first thought that came to Jack's mind was that Fuji might be given refuge by German missionaries in Papua. But most had declared their basic neutrality in the war against their fatherland and as missionaries they had explained that their loyalty was primarily to God and not the Führer. If anyone could answer his questions it had to be his old friend Kwong Yu Sen – what he did not know about the comings and goings in the district was not worth recording. Yes, he would visit Sen and ask him what he might know about Fuji's return.

'You realise that we have a cargo to deliver,' Jack said, disengaging himself from the hug. 'So I am going to visit someone I know and if he cannot help then we sail in two days.'

'I understand,' Victoria agreed. 'But I have faith in

whatever you do. If you are not successful then I will stop searching.'

'Like hell you will,' Jack growled affectionately. 'I know you Miss Duvall. Once I exhaust my contacts you will no doubt go back to Uncle Bernie and see if he has any more leads. Then you will chase them – with or without me.'

'I would not, Jack Kelly,' she said, with a laugh feigning indignation. 'I would return to being a dutiful wife to my one hundred per cent Aussie cave man.'

Jack reached out to touch his wife on the cheek. 'That's what I love about you,' he said and Victoria took a playful swipe at him. But Jack was too fast, catching her hand, drawing her close and kissing her passionately. He was glad that they were the only two aboard the schooner on this balmy tropical night. Hopefully Lukas would soon return to Papua and Jack could hand over the running of the schooner to his son. Victoria was not the only one with secrets. Jack had one of his own but was just a little afraid to tell his wife what he had done in her absence. He knew he would have to wait for the right time. His promise to Victoria that he would not enlist had been broken and already the papers were signed. The New Guinea Volunteer Rifles had accepted him after he had passed his medical examinations and he had sworn his oath of allegiance for the term of his military service. But when was the right time to tell a woman anything that was bound to upset her? Jack brooded briefly as he led his wife by the hand below decks.

• • •

The following day Jack left Victoria to supervise the final loading of stores and borrowed a horse from a prospector friend. Saddled up, he rode for a couple of hours to Sen's bungalow outside Port Moresby. It was a place he knew well and almost a second home to him in the old days following the Great War. Here he had brought his old comrade-in-arms George Spencer, who had met the beautiful Eurasian beauty Iris, sister-in-law to Sen. Riding east along the rarely used rutted track, Jack remembered the past: how he had gone with George in search of gold in the Morobe province only to have the expedition cost his wartime friend his life from a Kukukuku arrow; how Iris had been taken captive by the infamous Tim O'Leary and disappeared; and how Jack had found out after the death of his father in England that George was in fact Lord Spencer.

Jack sighed when he remembered how he and Iris had been left a fortune in George's will. The only catch was that both had to sign for the release. Dear old George had never foreseen that this might be impossible, as it was when events unfolded as they did. As far as Jack was concerned Iris was forever lost – maybe even dead by now. Easy come easy go. The thought came idly to mind as Jack reined in at Sen's house. He was not aware that even as he dismounted and tethered his horse to a tall tree at the edge of the small lawn, he was being watched by eyes that contained both fear and hate.

• • •

Fuji recognised Jack Kelly immediately even though it had been years since he had last seen him in the company of his son, Lukas. Fuji gripped the handle of the short but finely honed knife he always carried strapped and hidden behind his shirt. It was an assassin's weapon, one Fuji had been trained to use with deadly skill by his masters in Japan.

He crouched by a window and watched Jack walk unconcernedly towards the house, then heard Sen's voice welcome Jack. Fuji knew that what occurred in the next vital moments depended on the Chinese trader.

'Jack, it is good to see you after all this time,' Sen said with a smile, offering his hand. Jack, with a broad smile, shook the extended hand.

'Been a while, old cobber,' he said, standing on the front verandah bordered by the greenery of tropical plants. 'How long? Six, seven years?'

'Longer,' Sen replied without attempting to allow his old friend past the front door. 'I did not have the opportunity to say goodbye when I took my family to Singapore.'

'Yeah, that was a while ago,' Jack admitted. 'But you haven't changed at all, you old Chinese bastard. How is the family?'

Sen winced a little at his friend's statement but knew the derogatory term was used with affection when it came from the mouth of his old friend. 'My son and daughters are growing strong and my wife is well, although I could have used my wife's considerable skills in re-establishing the running of our place here, when I had to return,' he said, without elaborating on the matter of his return to his home in Papua. He offered Jack one of the comfortable cane chairs facing the luxurious, well-kept garden. 'I will arrange to have tea brought to us on the verandah.'

In minutes a young *haus meri* appeared with a silver salver on which perched a teapot and two delicate china cups. Jack knew from past experience that they would soon be sipping the almost clear green tea, Sen's favourite beverage.

When they were settled Sen poured the tea for them both. 'I have heard that all is going well in your life,' he said. 'But I have not heard about your son, Lukas.'

'The young fella will be home soon,' Jack said, taking a sip of the fragrant tea. 'He had a bit of an accident flying in the States but it seems he will be all right.'

'I am sorry to hear of that,' Sen replied. 'I remember him as a fine young man when he was in Moresby.'

'Speaking of young men from the past,' Jack said casually, 'you wouldn't have happened to hear about Fuji Komine in these parts recently, would you?' For a second Jack thought he saw a perceptible change in Sen's normally relaxed manner. It was as if he had stiffened at the mention of the Japanese man's name.

'I last heard that he had disappeared north after the terrible happenings at Paul Mann's plantation all those years ago,' he replied without looking at Jack.

'Other than that I cannot help you. Why do you ask?'

'Nothing of much importance in particular,' Jack lied. 'Just thought I heard on the grapevine that he was back in these parts.'

'Sorry that I cannot help,' Sen continued lying. 'But I tend to keep to myself out here, as you know.'

'No matter,' Jack shrugged. 'It just gave me an excuse to catch up with an old friend if nothing else.'

Fuji frowned at the *haus meri* as she was confronted by him in the house. She knew that she was to see nothing – and know the same – about the Japanese man's residence with her master. Besides, she was afraid of him and sensed that he was a very dangerous man. Fuji let her pass and stealthily made his way to the wall adjoining the verandah from where he could monitor the conversation between Jack Kelly and Sen. The knife was in his hand and he was poised like a spring to use it should things go wrong. He knew by doing so that his stay in Papua would be short lived. If Jack Kelly went missing, Fuji knew that every police officer in the Moresby district would be mobilised to find the famous son of Papua. Killing was a last resort, but not one to be dismissed under the circumstances.

He listened closely and was pleased to hear Sen playing his part. The conversation went on for some time as the two men caught up on years of separation – there was nothing else mentioned about him after the initial questions – and soon the Australian bid his farewells to return to his tethered horse for the ride back to Port Moresby.

Sen came inside and Fuji could see that his hands were shaking. 'It seems that the authorities know of you being here,' Sen said. 'How could that be?'

Fuji was at a loss to explain why Jack Kelly should say that he had been seen in the district. His only conclusion was that a member of the staff had gossiped. 'I don't know,' he said, sliding the knife back into the sheath inside the waistband of his trousers. 'Maybe I should leave here before the police come, instead of Kelly,' he added. Whatever the leak to his security he knew it was time to move on. 'Tonight I will make the broadcast,' Fuji said thoughtfully. 'You will no longer need to fear my presence under your roof.'

At his last statement Fuji noticed the relief flood the normally impassive Chinese man's face. He scowled. The Chinese were a cowardly race, deserving of complete decimation. At least his brothers in the Imperial forces in China were doing their best to see that would happen.

Jack rode away from the house in the Papuan bush. He should have made it a point to visit Sen earlier, he thought with a twinge of guilt. But time had gone so fast and his work with the *Independence* had taken up much of that time. Outside his own race Sen did not have many friends and Jack was one of the few exceptions.

NINE

Although Karl Mann was back in Jerusalem he may
as well have been cut off behind enemy lines,
unarmed and without a compass and map to guide
him home. He sat in a tiny, almost airless room above
a house, which, from the voices below he guessed,
belonged to Arabs. Marie and Abdul had blindfolded
him and forced him down in the seat of the battered
sedan as they had approached the city's outskirts. It
was clear to Karl that they still did not trust him and
no doubt the agent he had come to know as Fritz was
making checks on his story.

He had been held a virtual prisoner for two days
now with just water, a few dates and unleavened bread
for sustenance. A bucket jammed in one corner of the
windowless room was his only furniture other than a
flea-infested straw mattress. There were no visitors, only
the sound of men's voices speaking in Arabic below.

Karl wondered what he should do next. His mission briefing by Featherstone was to report on the identity and location of a German agent Karl now strongly suspected as being the German he had met outside Jerusalem. After that, he had completed what was expected of him for the shadowy Captain Featherstone. But in the briefings that filled his time before setting out for the café in the old section of the city, Featherstone had been a bit vague about how Karl was to extricate himself from the type of situation he now found himself in. When Karl had asked the question as to what he was to do when he achieved the aim of his mission, the naval officer had simply brushed off the answer with 'We will worry about that, old chap, when the time comes.' With a soldier's inherent duty to orders from a superior, Karl had at the time uneasily accepted the captain's explanation. Now he was not so sure that he should have. How was he expected to be successful in his task if he had no way to contact Featherstone? Featherstone and his mob had probably written him off when he did not report back within twenty-four hours, Karl thought morosely, scratching at the itchy stubble of his face. After all, this was war and one more life lost in the course of military events would simply mean he would be listed as missing in action. Or was there more to this mission that Featherstone had not told him? It was dawning on Karl that paranoia was not the exclusive domain of neurotic people. Something did not feel right about the whole affair.

The wooden door of the room creaked open and Karl snapped from his meandering thoughts, feeling a surge of hope when Marie appeared in the doorway. She was once again wearing the traditional dress of Moslem women but he instantly recognised the startling blue eyes behind the veil.

'You come,' she commanded, beckoning with her hand.

Once the door was fully open Karl saw Abdul standing behind her. He rose stiffly to his feet and followed Marie. He noticed that this time Abdul was not behind him when he walked down the stairs behind her.

In the lower room Karl saw Fritz standing by the main entrance.

'I must apologise for the uncomfortable time you have spent here, Flight Lieutenant Harmstorf,' Fritz said without much sound of apology in his tone. 'However we had to verify that you are who you said you were.'

Karl breathed an inward sigh of relief. At least his cover story had stood up to scrutiny and for that he knew he could thank the meticulous work of Captain Featherstone and his organisation, whoever they really were. 'Does that mean you can get me home?' Karl asked.

'We will. Berlin has authorised the means to get you out of here and back for a debriefing. It appears that they think you are an important man.'

Karl felt a twinge of uneasiness. Featherstone had obviously not briefed him on everything that he needed to know about the dead man he was impersonating. Fritz seemed to know a lot more about him than Karl did. 'What arrangements have been made to get me out?' Karl asked, riding on the back of his perceived importance to the Third Reich.

'One of our U boats will rendezvous with a fishing boat tonight off the coast. You will be taken aboard.'

Karl's heart skipped a beat. That the Germans would risk such an important asset so close to the presence of the Royal Navy truly indicated that whoever Flight Lieutenant Harmstorf was in life, it was worth risking a U boat and its valuable crew to save him. The thought chilled Karl. If he was that important no doubt he would be closely guarded to ensure that he did not fall into the hands of the British – something he badly wanted to happen. The future was looking bleak again. He may as well have been back in the jungles of Papua – blind, alone and in Kukukuku country. At least his chances under those circumstances were better than if he fell into the hands of the dreaded Gestapo. At least the lethal little warriors of the jungle killed a man outright for his head and body to eat. They did not indulge in pulling fingernails out and other unspeakable tortures in order to extract information from a man who would be deemed both a traitor and spy. 'That is good,' Karl replied as cheerfully as he could. 'Soon I will be home drinking schnapps and toasting your brave efforts deep in enemy territory.'

'If the damned British navy do not spoil our plans,' Fritz said less optimistically, and Karl prayed that Fritz's pessimism might be well founded. 'In the meantime you will remain here with Abdul, Marie and her mother, Fatima. Fatima will cook you a good meal to give you some strength for your journey. I will return just after dark to take you to the fishing boat that we use. Do you have any questions, Flight Lieutenant Harmstorf?'

'Does Marie's mother make strudel?' Karl asked in an attempt to sound lighthearted.

Fritz broke into what could almost be called a smile. 'I doubt it,' he said, making his way to the door. 'She is really a half-caste Chinese who I have been told once lived amongst the cannibals of Papua.'

Fritz did not see the sudden flush that came to Karl's face. Papua! A name he had never expected to hear so far from home. The casual remark gave him hope. If the woman had once lived in Papua perhaps there was a slight chance she might be sympathetic to him if he called on her help as a last resort.

Karl was allowed to remain downstairs away from the stifling room above the tenement. He guessed that he was somewhere in the Arab section of Jerusalem. If so, he also knew that German sympathisers dominated the back streets and alleys amongst the local Arab population. He knew that if he attempted an escape in broad daylight Abdul would kill him. His only hope was to play along and try to lull his menacing Arab bodyguard into a false sense of security. While he was pondering the options to escape, a woman entered the house wearing the same style of dress as Marie. Karl could see from her eyes that she was part Asian. They were beautiful, partially slanted dark eyes, that somehow reminded Karl of a cat watching him. From the manner of greeting between Marie and the new arrival, Karl guessed that the older woman was Fatima, mother of Marie and wife of the Corsican. They spoke in Arabic and Karl knew that he was the topic of their conversation. Fatima was carrying a cloth parcel and stone jar which she placed on the table. She unwrapped the parcel to reveal a freshly baked loaf of bread, block of cheese and a jar of black olives. Karl was famished and the delicious aroma of the bread wafted in the room.

'You wish to eat, Herr Harmstorf?' Fatima asked in good German but with an accent.

'Yes, thank you,' he replied gratefully. 'I could not help but notice your German has a strong English undertone,' he added and watched the woman's eyes closely for a reaction. 'Where did you learn to speak German?'

Fatima's expression changed at his question and her eyes switched to her daughter standing to one side. 'It is not important where I learned to speak German,' she replied softly, and Karl sensed that her evasion had something to do with her daughter.

'I am sorry,' Karl said as Fatima broke off a chunk of bread and passed it to him. 'I was merely attempting to make some conversation. I have had little opportunity to speak with anyone for the past couple of days.'

Fatima passed bread to Marie and Abdul who then helped themselves to the cheese and olives. Karl declined the cheese which had a rancid smell. The stone jar contained water and Fatima poured its contents into a tin mug she found on the single shelf in the room. Karl accepted the water, washing down the bread. It was now or never, Karl decided, and asked his question.

'I was told that you lived for some time in Papua?'

This time Fatima looked startled. Her eyes swung to him. 'How did you know this?' she asked in a whisper.

'Fritz mentioned it to me,' Karl answered with as much innocence as he could muster. 'I once visited that country and was curious that an Arab woman should have lived there.' Fatima glanced nervously at Abdul. 'Does Abdul speak German?' Karl asked softly, leaning slightly towards Fatima. Their conversation did not appear to interest either Marie or the Arab.

'No,' Fatima answered, but still appeared nervous. 'When were you in Papua?' she countered.

'Oh, in 1938,' Karl replied. 'I was visiting a distant relative over there who had a plantation just outside of Port Moresby. A family called Mann. Did you know them?'

Fatima shook her head. 'I do not know that name but I also once lived just outside of Port Moresby with my sister and brother-in-law, Kwong Yu Sen.'

Now it was Fatima's turn to be surprised by the reaction of the German pilot who had visibly paled. What had she said that should cause such a reaction?

Hardly believing what he had discovered, Karl asked in an almost strangled tone, 'You would not also be known by the name of Iris?'

He did not see the look of shock on Fatima's face as she suddenly pulled the veil further up her face and turned away. Her reaction was noticed by Marie who said something Karl did not understand, which caused Fatima to reply in a short sentence that seemed to reassure her daughter. Fatima turned to Karl with a desperate plea in her eyes. 'How could you know my real name?' she asked.

Karl knew that this was the turning point. Whatever he said next could either save him or condemn him on the spot.

'I am not what I appear to be,' Karl said softly. 'My real name is Karl Mann and it was my father who went in search of you many years ago up the Fly River. He was sent by your brother-in-law, Sen, to rescue you but unfortunately failed. My father was once the best friend of Jack Kelly and I have heard the story of how you were taken captive by O'Leary and spirited out of Papua. I have also heard the stories of how you loved George Spencer . . .' Karl hesitated. He could see the tears welling in Fatima's eyes and felt her hand on his arm.

'Is George well?' Fatima choked.

'I am sorry,' Karl answered gently. 'He did not return from the expedition that he and Jack Kelly went on into the Morobe province. He was killed by natives and mercifully never learned of your abduction by O'Leary.'

Fatima held her hands up to her face and wept openly as the pain of the years swept over her. Marie could see her mother's distress and glared at Karl as she moved to place her arms around her mother in comfort. Karl felt uncomfortable that it had been he who had delivered the news of George Spencer's death and brought anguish to a woman he had only heard about in the stories of Jack and his father which had become part of their family lore. Karl experienced a strange calm. He would use this diversion, calculating how he might overpower Abdul who was well armed with pistol and dagger.

'You German pig,' Marie spat in English. 'What have you said to upset my mother?' As Abdul hovered uncertainly at the edge of the room, Karl continued to pretend that he did not understand her and shrugged with an imploring expression on his face. 'I am sorry,' he said in German.

'What has this man said, Mother?' Marie asked, holding the weeping woman close.

Karl was not sure of the loyalties of the Corsican's daughter but it seemed so far that Iris had not betrayed him. 'I am well,' Fatima replied in English. 'Herr Harmstorf was just telling me how he has lost his wife and children in this terrible war.'

Karl felt his hopes surge. Not only had Fatima lied, and in doing so indicated that she was prepared to protect their secret, but Marie appeared to believe her mother's story and cast Karl a sympathetic look of condolence.

Fatima wiped her eyes with the edge of her veil, and without looking at Karl, sat down on a stone ledge against a wall and stared at the floor. Abdul frowned and snarled something in Arabic at Fatima who ignored him. Karl knew all was not going well and he had yet to enlist Fatima's help in getting a message to Featherstone at headquarters. Just because they had established a bridge between them did not necessarily mean Fatima would help him. The day was moving towards night and when that time came Karl would be shuttled to the U boat and by then it would be too late to help either himself or the mission, which was becoming more confusing the deeper in he got. Karl was beginning to strongly believe that from the outset he had been tagged as easily expendable. Was this simply a mission to uncover a spy ring operating in Palestine? Or was the target something else? He guessed that he would find out within the next twelve hours – if he lived that long.

TEN

Fuji should have known better. Had he not been trained to never use the same track twice? He was almost at the beach to meet with Keela when a young native man stepped out to block his way. Fuji stopped in his tracks and eyed the stranger who he recognised as a Motu. Fuji guessed the boy was around Keela's age and his bare chest rippled with muscle from years of rowing the outriggers in the tropical waters. A deadly machete, honed razor sharp, swung casually in the young man's right hand and the hostility in his stance spoke of death.

'You will die, Jap man,' the young Motu warrior roared, charging with the broad blade swinging above his head.

Instantly Fuji snatched for the knife in his waist-band and assumed a combat half-crouch with the knife extended to meet the attack. All he could think was that his assailant must be the boy Keela told him was her betrothed and somehow he had learned of her liaisons at the beach and had chosen to ambush him on the track.

In the blink of an eye the two men were face to face. Fuji could see the killing rage in his opponent's eyes who was a head taller than himself and had the body of a man in his physical prime. The native boy swung the machete down in an arc but Fuji was fast and brought his free arm up to block the downward swing. Their arms met and without hesitation Fuji thrust the knife at a sideways angle, using all his strength to slide the finely honed blade between his attacker's upper ribs. The blow was perfect and the blade found its mark in the beating heart of the native boy. With a long scream he slumped to the ground, his eyes rolling in pain and the machete fell from his hand. Clutching his hands around the handle of the knife, he feebly attempted to drag it from his chest.

For a brief moment Fuji remained very still, standing above the boy. This was the first man he had ever killed and despite all his training he still felt weak with shock at how easy it had been to rob a man of his life. He continued to watch his attacker until, with his eyes half closed in despair, the native boy stopped breathing. Only then did Fuji remove and wipe the blade clean on tussock-like grass beside the track and replace it in its sheath. Fuji glanced around the surrounding scrub but it appeared the native boy had been alone; no other warriors had appeared to give assistance to their comrade.

Fuji realised that the boy had probably boasted to friends and relatives that he would settle a matter of honour in the traditional way. When he did not return, the news of his failure was bound to spread and possibly even reach the ears of the district police, who would attempt to locate him. Even if the killing had been in self-defence the matter was moot. To be discovered in Papua would disrupt his mission as even now he was preparing to be picked up by the submarine lurking in the Gulf of Papua. His mission had been extended to the town of Rabaul on the island of New Britain. He had important work to do there and this incident had the potential to seriously disrupt the pick-up due to occur within forty-eight hours.

The sun was high overhead and Fuji knew that he was late for his meeting with Keela. Without another thought for the body sprawled on the track he turned to continue his walk to the beach.

Keela was waiting and her eyes widened in alarm at the sight of the blood soaking the front of Fuji's white shirt. She rushed to him and flung herself onto the slim young man. 'Have you been injured?' she gasped.

'It is not my blood,' Fuji replied dispassionately. 'I think it is the blood of your betrothed.'

Keela pushed herself away and covered her face. 'I came to warn you that he was boasting in the village that he would kill you,' she said. 'But you have killed him.'

'It was either him or me,' Fuji frowned. 'He did not give me any choice but to defend myself.'

Fuji felt suddenly weary. How would Keela view the matter of honour settled between men? Fuji had a grudging respect for the man he had killed as he had shown that loss of face was worth risking his life for. That the Motu man had failed to keep face still meant he was honoured as a fallen warrior by Fuji, who fervently believed in the tradition of the samurai, and at least the native boy's soul would not be lost.

'I am glad that you came to me,' Keela said calmly. 'He was a strong man but you were stronger. That is a good thing for the children of such a man.'

Fuji reached out to touch Keela gently on the face. Still shaken from the fight to the death with her betrothed he realised just what the young man's death had really meant. Fuji had put his life on the line for the woman he loved more than life itself. 'Keela, I want you to be my woman.'

'I already am,' Keela answered, eyes downcast shyly. 'I think I am with your child.'

The news startled the normally impassive young Japanese man. He was to be a father! His emotions reeled. Keela was not of Japanese blood and therefore considered by his own people to be less than human. But she now bore his blood within her body. He was a warrior of the Emperor dedicated to the God King. He had been trained to dismiss all personal ambitions and desires. Nevertheless, standing at the edge of a beach in the land where he had been born, with the woman he loved, the mother of his unborn child, standing at his side, Japan and its strictures seemed so far away for now. The reality of his life was right here and now amidst the gentle sounds of the Papuan bush and surf.

'You are not pleased?' Keela asked in a frightened voice.

'I am pleased,' Fuji said. But he was confused by the situation and needed time to sort out his feelings and priorities. 'It is unexpected.'

Keela wondered at his remark. Surely it had to be expected when she was in the prime of her womanhood and had given herself to him each time they had met. Now it was only a matter of what he would do to support her and the child she carried. She had missed her monthly bleeding and the wise old women in her village considered her pregnant. Fuji had been the only man she had lain with. 'What will we do?' she asked. 'I do not know what we should do.'

Fuji considered the situation. It seemed an impossible dilemma. He could not go to Keela's village for not only were the native boy's relatives honour bound to exact revenge, but he was an educated Japanese man who was not fated to live like a savage, fishing from the sea, whilst his woman tended the vegetable garden and children she would bear him. Nor could he take her with him. He was a sailor in the service of the Imperial Japanese Navy. Looking into her trusting eyes he felt a terrible surge of guilt. 'We will find a way to be together,' he said gently, a lump in his throat. 'You will be my woman forever. I will not return here tomorrow lest the dead man's relatives lay in ambush for me. I will get a message to you, one way or the other, at your village, of where we are to meet again.'

Keela nodded in agreement. She did not question the Japanese man. She knew he was different. He was a man who knew so much and had proven his prowess as a warrior. He would be a fitting husband and father to the many children she would bear for him. 'I think you should return now and say that you have not seen me,' he added.

Keela understood and clung to him one last time before turning to walk back down the beach. Fuji watched her walk away and fought back the tears. It was not right that a man of the bushido way expressed personal emotion. This was the second time since he had returned to Papua; the first was when he had lost his father and now he knew he had probably lost the only woman he had ever loved. The lie that he would meet with her again haunted him more than he thought it would. He could console himself with the knowledge that when the Emperor ordered the attack on the Europeans in the Pacific he would return to Papua as a conqueror. Maybe then he would be able to be reunited with Keela and hold his son in his arms.

Having arrived on schedule, the I–47 glided just beneath the surface at periscope depth. Lieutenant Kenshu Chuma slowly rotated the scope to scan the seas and the darkened headland. It was a moonless night and the horizon merged with the inky blackness of the sea. 'Half speed,' he called and the submarine's rate of knots was reduced. Kenshu continued peering through the scope at the headland and grunted with satisfaction when he saw the tiny but distinct flash of light in the preordained sequence of dots and dashes. Komine was at the appointed place as per the instructions that had been radioed to Krait. 'Prepare to surface,' Kenshu commanded, checking the seas once again to ensure that there was no one to witness their ascent to the surface. They were within the territorial waters of Papua without authority from the Australians and this constituted a serious breach of international law. The I–47 had been designated to carry out covert operations for its masters in naval intelligence and such a breach by a naval ship was almost akin to an act of war.

Fuji strained to seek out any disturbance of the ocean's surface following his last periodic signal from the hand torch. Then, from the corner of his eye, he thought he noticed a phosphorescent glow in the distance about 500 yards from the shore. His keen eyesight, well adjusted to night vision, was proved correct when something big and black began to emerge against the horizon. With a deep sigh of relief Fuji rose from his place of concealment in the jungle to pad down the beach to the edge of the surf. Here, he would await an answering flash of light from the coning tower of the submarine. It came when he signalled again from the water's edge. Even now, Fuji thought, standing patiently, the captain would be ordering the launching of a dinghy to fetch him to safety.

Cruising on her powerful diesel engine, Jack Kelly was at the helm of the *Independence* as she slipped through the calm night in the Gulf of Papua. He was not alone on the deck. Momis, one of three deck-hands Jack had employed from the Solomon Islands, was high up the forward mast. Like the majority of his people from the Melanesian islands, Momis' skin was jet black, an almost dark blue hue to it. Naked, apart from a pair of cotton shorts, he was a man in the prime of his life. The Solomon Islander had the task of being lookout for the schooner, which was sailing almost blind on this dark night.

Jack had been forced to leave at sunset so that he would be down the coast at a Catholic missionary outpost by the early morning to deliver desperately needed medical supplies. Victoria had not been fazed by the rushed departure. She was a self-taught master navigator and had plotted their course. As there was little wind to fill the schooner's sails the navigation had been easier when Jack switched over to the auxil-iary power of the diesel engine. Although their course would be true and straight, they were still hugging the coast to conserve fuel. No skipper liked being so close to the shore. Too many things could go wrong, like a fishing boat collision or sudden shift of wind to drive them ashore on the rocky reefs, but Jack was relying on his skill – and a lot of luck – to reach the mission-ary station in the shortest possible time.

Jack had informed his wife of his failure to glean from Sen and other contacts around Port Moresby any information on the elusive young Japanese man. Victoria had been disappointed but suggested they could try again when they returned, as she was certain the Japanese agent was operating in the Port Moresby district. Jack guessed that her certainty was fed by reports from her uncle who was still in Townsville.

'Masta Jack!' Momis suddenly called down from his perch up the mast. 'Big fella thing ahead.'

'What is it?' Jack called back to his lookout.

'Don't know,' Momis replied thoughtfully. 'Me think maybe whale.'

Jack spun on the helm to veer from the course, avoiding what Momis had seen on the surface. He trusted the Solomon Islander's eyesight; the man had the vision of a cat. But the concept of a submarine was not something a Solomon Islander could entertain.

'Not whale,' Momis called with a rising note of fear in his voice. 'Too big for whale. Maybe monster.'

Jack frowned and shifted the accelerator lever to reduce speed. What the hell did the man mean by 'monster'? For now all he could see was the inky blackness ahead.

'Boat approaching from the east, Captain,' the I–47 lookout on the coning tower called quietly to Kenshu.

The submarine commander turned from gazing

out to the shore for sight of the dinghy returning with the agent he had been assigned to recover. 'Where?' he asked, and the lookout pointed into the night off their portside.

'I think over there,' the lookout replied.

Kenshu could see the navigation lanterns of what he calculated to be either a big yacht or even a schooner bearing down on them. Suddenly it seemed to alter course to take it past the sub's stern. That could mean only one thing: that the captain of the other craft had spotted them and was taking evasive action to avoid a collision. Kenshu calculated that the other craft was around 300 yards away and approaching fast. The Japanese captain swore, cursing the unknown boat that had appeared out of the night to compromise his mission. He swung back to see the dinghy come alongside the hull of the submarine with an extra body aboard. At least they had got Komine off the shore. Now what to do about the boat that had obviously spotted them? His question was answered when the radio operator sent a message up to the tower to say that the unknown boat was a Papuan registered schooner, now attempting to make contact with the harbour master in Port Moresby to report the sighting of a submarine. He was even attempting to send coordinates to fix their position.

Kenshu was a man selected by the Japanese navy for his intelligent and decisive manner of command. 'Has he established radio contact yet?' he called down to the radio operator.

'Not yet, sir,' the executive officer relayed back to his

captain from the signal man. This decided Kenshu on his course of action. He was pleased to see that his landing party had scrambled up onto the deck with their passenger and were already stowing the sub's dinghy.

'Prepare to dive and go to action stations,' he called down the tower.

On his command the crew of the Japanese submarine came to life. This time it was not an exercise.

Victoria was at the helm while Jack desperately attempted to establish radio contact with Port Moresby. He had called her up to take over when he finally saw the vague shape of the submarine ahead. Jack had read of sightings of subs around the Australian coast and knew it was important to relay what he had seen to the authorities.

Victoria could also see the submarine now. Its outline became clear against a star-studded night sky. It was an eerie sight and caused the American to feel a rising fear.

'It's an I class Japanese sub,' she called down to Jack at the radio. 'I have seen them in Japan.'

Jack did not question his wife. If that is what she identified the submarine as, then that was what it was. 'Moresby, Moresby, this is the Independence out of Moresby. Over.'

Nothing but the crackle of static came back to Jack over his radio.

'She's diving, Jack!' Victoria called excitedly from the cockpit of the schooner. 'I think we are going to lose her.'

'Damn!' Jack swore. He would have liked the sub to hang around long enough for someone other than the crew of the schooner to corroborate their sighting.

'She's gone,' Victoria called down in a disappointed voice, the excitement of the sighting now fading with the swirling phosphorus that marked where the submarine had been. 'Have you got coms with Moresby yet?'

'Bloody idiots must be on the grog or have their fingers up their bums,' Jack growled angrily. By all his calculations they should still be within radio range of Port Moresby.

'No matter,' Victoria interrupted. 'We can make the report from the mission station radio tomorrow morning.'

'Bit late,' Jack commented with disappointment in his voice. 'She will be well and truly gone. I wonder what she was doing on the surface so close to the coast.'

'Momis has told me that he thought he saw a dinghy pull in beside the sub just before she submerged. They must have gone ashore for some reason,' Victoria speculated. 'A bit disappointing now that the excitement is over for the night. You may as well join me on deck. I will get Momis to fetch us a brew.'

Jack placed the transmitter mike on the chart table and took off the receiver headset, still muttering about the incompetence of the land-based sailors in Port Moresby. He placed his hands on the wooden rails either side of the hatch to the deck and could see Victoria smiling down at him as he started up the steps to join her. It was a funny thought to come to at such a time, he realised, but how much he loved this woman who seemed to shine when things got dangerous.

Victoria was still smiling when the submerged submarine rammed the starboard side of the schooner with her raised bow cable cutter almost lifting the big sailing boat clear out of the water. Timbers splintered, the Solomon Islander crew screamed in panic and Victoria's smiling face disappeared from Jack's view as he was hurled back into the cabin.

'Vicky!' he screamed. 'Vicky!'

Jack was hardly aware of the blood running down his face from a cut across his head. All he could think about was the safety of his wife as he scrambled to his feet and forced his way back up onto the deck. The navigation lantern had spilled kerosene across the aft deck which had been ignited by the burning wick, and the fire was spreading rapidly. As the *Independence* settled back in the sea, water from a hole rammed in her side poured into one of the cargo holds.

'Vicky,' Jack called desperately, but did not receive a reply.

Momis loomed out of the dark, silhouetted by the rising flames. 'Missus Jack overboard,' he gasped in pain and Jack could see that the deck hand's arm was hanging at an unnatural angle.

Jack ran to the side, oblivious of the desperate situation his schooner was in. He ran up and down calling out his wife's name – but still nothing. If she was in the sea he prayed that she might at least be afloat, treading water. But the fact she had not answered his calls caused Jack to feel a terrible, paralysing dread.

Kenshu peered through the periscope at the burning schooner clearly lit up against the night sky. 'She is sinking,' he said to his second in command. 'It will look like an accident.'

'Do you think that we should finish it off?' the 2IC asked.

'No need,' Kenshu replied. 'Our mission is to remain undetected and we have Komine aboard. It is better that we proceed on course for New Britain with as much haste as possible and clear these waters.'

The second in command nodded and the I–47 slipped silently away on her electric engines. She would surface later that night to monitor any radio traffic in the area that might indicate that their position in Papuan waters had been compromised.

Jack knew the only hope of finding his wife lay in first containing the near impossible situation aboard his seemingly doomed schooner. He had to forget Victoria for the moment. Already the *Independence* was keeling over to the starboard where the water rushed in. He rapidly gathered the crew of three together and issued orders for two of them to go below and cram anything they could in the hole where the sub had rammed them. He had been stunned to see that the damage wasn't as bad as he'd feared, as the tough timbers had absorbed much of the impact, and that the hole could be plugged with mattresses, boxes of cargo and pieces of lumber. Above deck Momis doused the fire, which had only succeeded in singeing the planking of the deck.

It was as if the boat had the constitution of its owner, Jack mused. After half an hour he was satisfied that the *Independence* would not sink – although she was low in the water and tilting at an angle to the starboard. When he was satisfied that the situation was under control he turned to the medical condition of his crew. Momis had broken his arm but the other two men had little more than minor cuts and bruises. Jack's own gash was in need of a doctor but he simply gritted his teeth and got one of his men to sew the skin together with a needle and thread. Jack had attempted to use the radio once more to transmit a mayday call but it was out of action. The schooner's dinghy was gone too, having been dislodged on impact. Jack prayed that Victoria had found it in the dark and had been able to scramble into it. He called Victoria's name throughout the night until his throat was sore and hoarse. He knew that he would have to wait until first light before any effective search could be made but when the sun rose over the still calm seas Jack noticed that they had drifted towards a little beach not far from the headland. There was no sign of his wife anywhere and in the back of his mind he tried to tell himself Victoria was okay; that she had found the dinghy and both had drifted away in the night, and since they were so close to the coast, that she would be able to row ashore – or even see the schooner and row to them.

'Look, Masta Jack,' Momis shouted, his arm in a makeshift sling that Jack had improvised for the broken arm. 'A native boat.'

Jack turned his eyes to the headland where he could see a Motu-style outrigger paddling towards them. It was crewed by four strong native men, and when they came alongside Jack asked them to return to shore and contact Port Moresby. Jack further explained that there would be a big reward for their help, and the men rowed away enthusiastically to fetch help. Within minutes of the outrigger leaving, Jack and his crew saw a small flotilla of other native outriggers rowing towards them.

Word had spread to the nearest village that a big boat was in trouble just offshore. With any luck there would be salvage for the villagers if the crew had left the stricken ship. They were disappointed when they arrived but cheerful nonetheless at some of the small items Jack parcelled out from the cargo. Their company was welcome and at least now the crew had a means of getting off the schooner should it decide to give up the ghost and sink.

Later that afternoon a ketch sailed into sight. Aboard was a police inspector from Port Moresby. He had received the news and had come to help tow the badly damaged schooner back to harbour. Jack asked if Victoria had been picked up but the inspector shook his head.

'Sorry, old chap,' he said sympathetically. 'We will

have a couple of crates up as quickly as possible to carry out a search. Aircraft can cover a lot more area than ships alone.'

Jack knew the policeman was right but was frustrated by the lack of immediate action to go in search of his wife.

'Masta Jack.' Momis nudged nervously at Jack's elbow as he stood on the deck of his schooner with the police inspector. 'I think the native boys have found your missus.'

'Where?' Jack asked, grabbing Momis by his broken arm in his excitement, and causing him to wince in pain.

'Over there, Masta Jack,' Momis grimaced until Jack let go.

Both Jack and the inspector turned to see a small outrigger being paddled towards them from the sea. It was manned by two rowers and between them Jack could see a body lying face up in the bottom. Jack instantly recognised his wife's face, now pale and wax-like. He knew immediately that she was dead.

ELEVEN

'God willing' was an expression Iris had become familiar with. She knew it was fate that had brought her past into the present. Her conversion to Islam had helped her cope with her hard and lonely life in the land of a people who believed that their path in life was in the hands of a higher being. God had sent this young man across the sea from Papua for a reason. What reason? Fatima's life in that far-away place was as dead as the man she had loved as a young woman. She stood outside the stone building where Karl was kept and in the shade of the narrow street attempted to make sense of his God-sent role in her life.

So much had happened since the terrible day she had left the shores of Papua in an Arab slave dhow. She had been forced to live as Pierre's virtual slave in French-controlled North Africa. She at least had met a tall, handsome Legionnaire from Germany in the Corsican's bar. He had brought some happiness to her hard life. Wolfgang had been a gentle, intelligent young man who had shown kindness to Fatima when she had still been known as Iris, and in time love had bloomed and led to the birth of Marie. But then Wolfgang had been killed in a back alley brawl. Two men she had come to love in her life had died by violent means. But it was God's Will.

When Pierre had found out that Marie was not his daughter, Iris had thought he would kill them both. But he had grudgingly accepted Marie as his own child – albeit with occasional outbursts of rejection. Fatima had never told her daughter who her true father was as it was easier to live with Pierre that way. It was also the only way she could protect her daughter from the violent, brutal temper of the man.

Fatima did not know Paul Mann but she knew Jack Kelly. He had been George's best friend and a man who Fatima knew her fiancé had trusted with his life. If this young Australian of German birth was close to Jack Kelly then he must be a good man, Fatima rationalised. However, he was also the enemy and his assuming the identity of a German aviator seeking an escape route out of Palestine was obviously a ruse to betray her and her daughter – along with the others – to the British. That could only mean certain death for them all by a military firing squad. Surely the goodness of Allah would not allow His devoted follower to be slain by the infidels? Somehow she did not believe that was why Karl Mann had come into her life. It was time to go inside and discreetly continue their conversation. They would again speak in German. That way neither her daughter nor Abdul would understand. Nevertheless they would still have to be careful.

'From the stories Uncle Jack told us it seems that George Spencer was really a British aristocrat, Lord Spencer,' Karl said quietly, attempting to make his tone sound conversational. 'It also seems that if you were back in Australia and able to prove your identity, you and Jack would share the fortune George left to you both. Under the conditions of his will it required both your signatures to make the claim. I don't know why that was so but Uncle Jack seems to think his friend George wanted to ensure Jack would look after your interests if anything happened to him.'

Fatima listened as Karl told her as much as he could about her family in Papua. The more she listened the more real the scent of the frangipani became in her mind.

'Why do you work for the Nazis?' Karl asked.

'I do not,' Fatima replied. 'My husband is loyal to Petain and his government in Vichy.'

'There are also many Frenchmen fighting for freedom from the Nazi occupation of France,' Karl pointed out. 'You do not have to remain loyal to an unjust cause.'

Searching the eyes behind the veil, Karl could see the pain in the woman's soul. He also felt a tiny hope that by reminding her of Papua he might have swayed her loyalties.

'I am sorry Herr Mann but my daughter is the most precious thing I have in my life,' Fatima finally said. 'I will not risk her life under any circumstances.'

'What if I could get you and your daughter out of Palestine and back to Australia?' Karl countered. He did not know how this was possible under the current circumstances but he had nothing else to offer. 'You would inherit a fortune that I know you could use to help not only yourself but also Marie. She is a beautiful young woman and has her whole life ahead of her. Do you honestly think she is better off here?' He could see that Iris was considering his proposal and guessed that somehow she feared her common law husband enough to dismiss the tempting offer. 'All I would need you to do is go to the King David Hotel and ask to see a Captain Featherstone. Tell him where I am and what Fritz has planned for me and I promise that both you and your daughter will receive protection and an eventual passage to Australia.'

'Your offer is tempting,' Iris conceded. 'I have wondered if Allah has sent you here to fetch us back to Papua and my family. But I must also consider the wrath of my husband and that I am now a follower of the ways of Mohammed. This place is close to the roots of my life now.'

Karl was becoming desperate. Abdul still stood nearby, guarding him until Fritz came to smuggle him to the rendezvous he had with the U boat. It had not passed by the Australian officer that the knowledge of a U boat's location was worth much in military terms. The dreaded steel sharks of the sea had wreaked a terrible toll on supplies crossing the Atlantic, and there was a strong possibility that they may even bring the besieged British Isles to surrender as the rise in shipping tonnage sunk outstripped the ability of the Americans to replace the losses. So far Britain was losing the war in the cold waters of the Atlantic Ocean, and being able to get a message to Featherstone about the German sub was vital. It was no less significant than him taking a strategic hill or French fort in Syria. Indeed Karl had come to accept that leading Featherstone to the U boat was becoming more important than his own life. He was after all a soldier and expected to take such risks. At least this target was worth it.

'I could possibly help you slip away from here,' Iris said. 'I could find an excuse to have Abdul leave his post for a short time.'

Karl again experienced a surge of hope at her suggestion. At least she was not going to betray his real identity. 'I wish I could do that but I am an officer of His Majesty and must do my duty. I need you to go to the hotel and seek out Captain Featherstone. Tell him all you know about where I am and the fact that I am going to be picked up tonight by a submarine. It is all I can do.'

Iris did not answer. However she had considered a very dangerous plan to excuse herself from the presence of Abdul. She turned and walked to Abdul and said something to him in Arabic. He answered angrily and glared at Karl. In a couple of strides, Abdul crossed the room to slam Lukas in the side of the head with the butt of his pistol. Karl saw swirling

147

red stars but stood his ground. Without a further glance at Karl, Iris left the room. Wavering on his feet, Karl felt sick with despair. Whatever she had said was not what he had hoped for. The bread and olives he had consumed seemed to be rebelling and he fought off the nausea. It seemed that all hope was gone and now it was time to keep a clear head to seek a means of escape. But Abdul was watching him with more than casual indifference, his hand close to his pistol.

Fritz arrived just after sunset and Karl watched his reaction to a short discussion he had with Abdul in Arabic.

'I see that Abdul and Fatima have looked after you,' Fritz said with a thin smile. 'I am sure that you will have a lot to tell the Gestapo in Berlin, Herr Mann.'

So she had betrayed him after all, Karl thought sadly, staring at the Luger in Fritz's hand which was pointed at his belly. It was all over. Fritz continued. 'Fatima also mentioned that you asked her to contact a Captain Featherstone. I have heard of him. He works for the British Special Operations Executive and thus I can only conclude that so do you. Your knowledge of their activities makes your capture worth the risk of a submarine pick-up. So the operation to get you out of Palestine is not wasted after all.'

Karl had not even heard of the SOE. So at least under torture he could not betray much to the

Gestapo, he thought bitterly. He cursed Featherstone to hell for allowing him to be trapped in this world of dark intrigue. He had enlisted in the Australian Army to fight a war on the battlefields, leading men with what he hoped would be skill and courage, not to be part of this devious war of espionage. Spying was just a case of relying on luck to stay alive and now Karl knew death would probably come to him in some lonely and unglorified way.

As Abdul secured Karl's hands in front of him with a rope all Karl could think about was being deceived by the woman who his father had once attempted to save. It was the ultimate betrayal.

Karl was bundled into the dark, now deserted alley. The curfew had forced the populace indoors and as Karl stood flanked by Abdul and Fritz he wondered how they would transport him to the seashore. His question was answered when he heard the distant sound of a car engine. He recognised it from days earlier when he had first been taken out of the city. The car came to a stop and in the dim light Karl could make out Pierre behind the wheel.

Without a word Karl was bundled into the back seat. Abdul got in beside him and jabbed the barrel of the pistol painfully under Karl's ribs. All Karl could hope for now was that they would be stopped by a British patrol. The noise of a car on Jerusalem's roads was bound to attract attention. Maybe the German agent's plan was not so well thought out after all, Karl thought. Even so, he suspected he was still a dead man if they were stopped. It did not take much strength to pull a trigger. At least he would have the satisfaction of knowing that in all probability his executioner would in turn be killed by a patrol of armed British soldiers. He sensed from the tension in the car that what he was thinking was also in the thoughts of his captors.

With a crunch of a transmission badly in need of adjustment the car lurched into motion. Karl strained to listen in on the conversation between Pierre and Fritz in the front seat, but as they were speaking in French he could not keep up with what was being said. French had never been a favourite subject when he was at school and nor was Latin for that matter. What he could deduce was that both men were very tense and even concerned. That was to be expected, Karl thought, since they were placing themselves in great danger to transport him.

After an hour or so outside the city they came to the beach. Karl knew that they had arrived as he could smell the salt air and hear the gentle hiss of the Mediterranean Sea against the shore.

Abdul gestured with the pistol, indicating that he was to get out. Karl obeyed and stretched his legs once he was standing outside the car in the dark. He considered whether it was worth making a break for freedom but knew that he would not get far with his hands bound.

'Walk,' Fritz commanded.

Karl stumbled in the dark and was hauled to his feet by Fritz. 'I would just as soon shoot you now,' he hissed in Karl's ear. 'You are in my opinion a traitor to the Fatherland where it seems you were born. It is only what you know about the SOE that keeps you alive for now.'

Regaining his balance Karl wondered if he could get the German agent to shoot him now so he could avoid the Gestapo. He was already imagining some dank, dark cell in Berlin, dripping with his blood as he screamed out what little he knew. But he doubted that Fritz would grant him a quick death.

· He was marched through the dunes to the beach where a small open fishing boat with a single mast rocked in the gently lapping surf. The moonless night was illuminated faintly by a single lantern at the stern of the boat, which was manned by two men dressed as Arabs. In the boat lay a mess of fishing nets. Karl was forced aboard and felt a heavy hand on his back force him down to his knees. Fritz said something and Karl suddenly felt the weight of the nets tossed over him, their weight forcing him face down and helpless into the bottom of the boat where he could smell the strong stench of tar and fish.

He heard the small concealed motor splutter into life and the boat was pushed out from the shore. As far as Karl could ascertain, Pierre and Abdul had remained ashore. Only Fritz and the two silent crew members were accompanying him to the meeting with the U boat.

For what seemed like about ten minutes, Karl could feel the vibration of the engine pounding against his cheek through the planking of the fishing boat. Suddenly the engine stopped and the boat rocked in silence on the swell of the sea. A hand hauled him to his knees and out from under the nets. Karl gazed over the side of the boat and felt his will to live falter. The sinister shape of a submarine was silhouetted against a brilliant night sky of stars. The U boat was about a hundred yards off the fishing boat's portside and drifting towards them. Half a dozen men were scurrying on the deck of the U boat, preparing to grapple with the fishing boat and draw her alongside. For a moment Karl thought he saw a flash on the horizon followed by a strange whisper in the air. It was a sound he was very familiar with and he instinctively crouched on his knees lower in the boat.

The shell exploded in a shower of water, drenching the occupants of the fishing boat. The U boat was being fired on and suddenly the night was lit as a powerful, piercing searchlight fixed the U boat. The crew scrambled back to the conning tower as the sub prepared for a crash dive to avoid the finger of light and shower of shells that now poured down on her. Karl did not hesitate and with all his strength he barrelled into Fritz who had swung on him with a pistol. With his impressive size and weight, Karl easily cleared a path to the edge of the fishing boat where he dived into the safety of the inky dark waters.

In the water Karl struck out as best as he could, wanting to quickly make some distance between himself and his captors. He could hear the sound of the fishing boat's engine as it came to life and lumbered off into the cover of night. The searchlight did not follow the fishing vessel but instead kept the U boat in its grasp.

Karl stopped swimming and began to tread water. He did not know how long he could do this with his hands tied but was determined not to die a lonely death so far from his beloved Eden. Somehow he kept himself afloat while the shells continued to bracket the U boat as she desperately blew her tanks to take in water for a crash dive to safety. Another searing flash in the night and a heavy explosion indicated that the unseen ship firing on the sub had scored a direct hit. Fragments of metal spattered down around him as he fought to keep afloat. Karl did not cheer the hit. To do so would have meant taking in sea water. Was drowning a more pleasant way to die than from a bullet? He didn't really want to find out.

TWELVE

The well-meaning Methodist minister droned on about God's Grace, intoning prayers for the dead. Sweat trickled down his stiff white collar as he held the prayer book in his hands. Jack Kelly stared at the simple burial casket being lowered into the grave. Rock solid and seemingly without feeling he stood under the blazing sun.

Around him in the dusty cemetery outside Port Moresby a small group of men stood, hats in hand. They had known Jack from the days when they were young prospectors on the Papua and New Guinea frontiers, both before and after the Great War. They had come to pay their respects to a lady who they all had seen bring happiness and serenity to their old friend.

Amongst the mourners stood Paul Mann with his wife Karin and their daughter, Angelika. Tears poured down Karin's face and she dabbed at them with a tiny lace handkerchief. She held Paul's hand as he remained stony faced opposite his estranged friend, Jack Kelly.

'Dust to dust, ashes to ashes . . .' the young minister said, and the tough old prospectors replaced their broad-brimmed hats as the coffin was lowered into the ground.

Jack bent down to take up a handful of Papuan earth. Paul saw a fleeting expression of gratitude in his old friend's eyes. He alone understood Jack's seemingly unfeeling demeanour. They had been men who had survived the carnage of the Western Front and had sadly come to a point where the public expression of emotion was not something that came easily anymore. To those who had not been there this stolid stance in the face of personal grief was alien.

The minister moved to Jack's side and mumbled the usual condolences. Jack nodded. Old friends came one by one to awkwardly offer their sympathy. How did one express sorrow for such a loss?

Finally the graveyard was empty except for Jack and the Mann family. It was Karin who stepped forward to gently embrace Jack. 'Oh, Jack, I am so sorry,' she said. 'We all loved Victoria.'

Jack bowed his head and the tears flowed uncontrollably. The tears became sobs. Not even the conditioning of a past war could now contain his grief and in Karin's embrace the pain of loss overwhelmed him. 'God, I miss her,' Jack sobbed. 'The bastards murdered her.'

'Come home with us, Jack,' Paul said. 'You need time to be with your family.'

Jack stepped back and wiped his eyes. In the simple offer he found a tiny fragment of peace. 'Thank you, cobber,' he replied. 'I will accept your offer. We have much to catch up on.'

At the Manns' copra plantation west of Port Moresby, Jack sat on the verandah of the comfortable timber-and-iron bungalow surrounded by lush tropical gardens. The explosion of flowers around the house brightened the outlook to the beach and happy laughter drifted from the stately rows of coconut palms where the native labourers tended the plantation.

It had been a week since the funeral and in that time the tender care of Karin and Angelika had helped heal a fraction of Jack's emotional wounds. The company and conversation of Paul had eased his grief a little more, and such was the easy manner in which he was treated it was as if the men had never been apart for the past two years. If nothing else, Victoria's death had brought the Mann family back into his life.

'You have a visitor,' Paul said, striding across the front yard towards the verandah. The tall, middle-aged man with Paul wore a dark suit not usual for the tropics and sweat glistened on his face. Jack could feel the authoritative presence of the stranger as he approached.

'Mr Jack Kelly?' the man asked, extending his hand. 'I am Victoria's uncle, Bernard Duvall.'

Jack took the hand and felt the firm grip. 'I have heard a lot about you,' he said. 'Victoria told me that you were in Townsville.'

'I came as soon as possible when I was informed of Victoria's death,' Bernard said. 'Sadly, I was unable to be at her funeral.'

Jack could see the pain in the American's face when he mentioned the funeral. It made him aware that the loss of his wife was also the loss of a beloved niece. 'Would you like to pull up a chair and join me?' Jack offered gently. 'I am sure that the sun is beyond the yardarm somewhere in the world.'

The expression of gratitude in Bernard's face was a reward in itself as he sat down in one of the battered cane chairs under the shade of the tin roof.

'I will go and see Karin,' Paul said. 'And we are able to provide you with a bed for the night, Mr Duvall, if you would prefer to spend a little time here?'

Bernard glanced up at Paul. 'I would like that, Mr Mann,' he responded. 'It is mighty hospitable of you.'

'I thought that you and Jack might need a little time together. It would be good for you both.'

Paul disappeared inside to speak to Karin and tell her that they had another guest. He took a bottle of schnapps onto the verandah and discreetly made excuses to go back to the packing sheds.

'I have heard how your schooner was rammed by a Jap sub,' Bernard said as Jack poured them both a shot of the fiery liquor. 'Naturally the Japanese government denies any such event occurred. They suggest that the collision was probably caused by a whale.'

'What do you think?' Jack asked bitterly.

'That you were rammed by a Jap sub because you were in the wrong place at the wrong time,' Bernard replied, gazing across the yard through the rows of coconut trees to the beach below. 'I think that you know not to ask me how I know,' he continued. 'But it was the I–47 commanded by Lieutenant Kenshu Chuma – on a mission to pick up an agent, Fuji Komine. I believe you know Komine.'

Jack paled. Fuji! It was as if the attack on the Mann plantation years earlier had come to life again and the intervening years had been merely an intermission before Fuji finished something personal against him and Paul. Jack did not doubt the American naval man's knowledge. He suspected that he had access to secrets so sensitive that even to confide what he already had was breaching all that he stood for. Jack was grateful. 'I tried to find him when Victoria came back from seeing you,' he said. 'I only wish I had tried harder. Maybe Victoria might be alive today if I had found the bastard. Then the Jap sub would not have been in the wrong place at the wrong time.'

'It's not your fault,' Bernard offered. 'You and I have both seen war and know how fickle the gods of fate can be. Komine was sent here to set up a network. We believe that he has done that but all we know is that the agent in the Port Moresby district is code named Krait. We were kind of hoping that you might be able to help us find out who Krait is.'

'Why me?' Jack asked. 'I'm no bloody spy.'

'Because it would have meant something to

Victoria. She always was a patriot. I suppose you could say to uncover Krait would honour her memory.'

Jack stared at the wild bloom of colour in the garden and remembered how the heavily scented, waxy frangipani flowers had been his wife's favourites. Other than having Victoria alive and by his side, the thing he desired most in his life now was to wreak revenge on the men responsible for her death. Maybe it was an impossible hope as the Japanese were not at war with his country, but in finding Krait there was a good chance of tracing the link back to Fuji. 'If I can I will try to find out who Krait is,' Jack replied. 'And I do not promise to take him alive.'

Bernard shifted uneasily but tacitly agreed with Jack's sentiments. 'Just don't get yourself into trouble in doing so,' Bernard warned. 'The conversation we had never occurred.'

Bernard Duvall stayed at the plantation for the night and proved to be a pleasant guest. After the evening meal the three men removed themselves to the verandah to drink more of Paul's fiery schnapps and reminisce about the Great War, in which all three men had served for their respective countries.

As they sat chatting Jack mused on the task he had accepted. He did not care that he was probably indirectly already working for the United States. Right now their priorities were also his. The *Independence* had been beached and was now undergoing repairs and Lukas, according to his last letter, was due home soon. So at least his son could take control of the business. Jack wondered if he would ever be able to step aboard his ship again when it held so many memories. If only he had lost the schooner and not his wife; inanimate objects could be repaired as they did not have souls, his mother had once told him. However the *Independence* was different; over the years it seemed to have been invested with Victoria's soul.

Thousands of miles away Lieutenant Karl Mann sat in a comfortable leather armchair in a hotel room of the King David Hotel. Opposite him, Captain Featherstone sat puffing on a cigarette, its smoke swirling lazily around his head under the slowly rotating ceiling fan.

'Fatima is an extraordinary woman,' Featherstone said. 'It took great initiative to play her hand the way she did.'

Karl frowned. The SOE man had explained how she had seemingly betrayed Karl to gain the confidence of the network around her. By doing so she was beyond suspicion in the eyes of the German agent in the vital hours she needed to be out of sight of Karl's captors. This enabled her to slip away to make contact with the SOE man at the King David Hotel.

At first Featherstone had been stunned by her revelations about the planned U boat rendezvous and even more amazed when Fatima revealed a little about her own background. But he had acted immediately and, making contact with the Royal Navy, he was able to go through headquarters channels and have a British destroyer stationed to ambush the U boat. The destroyer had one vital piece of equipment that the German submarine did not have – radar – and with this they were able to locate the surfaced U boat in the dark. Although no wreckage of the U boat was found, the skipper and crew of the British warship were claiming a kill. The explosion before the sub was able to submerge indicated a direct hit on her hull.

When the warship had steamed over to the last sighting of the surfaced sub they had picked up Karl in the water. At first the sailors thought they had captured one of the sub's crew. A string of oaths in a broad accent soon convinced them otherwise. They had picked up something just as odious – a colonial!

When the destroyer docked, Karl was able to have his identity confirmed and he was taken under military police guard to British headquarters to be debriefed on the operation.

'Did you pick up Fritz and his people?' Karl asked.

'Sadly, the man has slipped through our fingers but we have faith in our Jewish allies eventually locating him for us. They have eyes and ears all over Palestine and no love for the Germans or any of their Arab allies. Thanks to you we have an idea of where to start looking, and also thanks to you we may have bagged a U boat. I have put you in for a gong to recognise the risks you took for King and country,' Featherstone added casually. 'But I am afraid you will not be able to tell anyone how you earned it – a bit like our chaps who won their VCs back in 1919 when they led attacks on the Red fleet in their home ports. They got the medals but could not tell anyone why they had them. Personally, I think that you have a nose for our rather secretive operations.'

'With all due respect for what you do, sir, I am looking forward to returning to my battalion.'

'Understandable, old chap,' Featherstone said. 'Not everyone's cup of tea dodging around in back alleys saving the world without seeing the sun. The offer remains should you ever decide to jump boat and join us.'

'If that is all,' Karl said, standing. 'I have been informed that I will be joining a truck convoy heading north with supplies.'

'If there is anything we can do for you, old chap,' Featherstone said, thrusting out his hand before Karl could put on his hat and salute. 'Don't hesitate.'

'Just a couple of things, sir,' Karl replied. 'First, I think I have earned the right to know the real aim of the mission which almost cost me my life.'

'Ah, yes,' Featherstone frowned. 'I think an explanation is deserved. As I briefed you before the mission, we had need to locate the German agent and confirm our suspicions concerning the role of the Corsican.'

'But there was more,' Karl quietly prompted. 'Wasn't there?'

'There was,' Featherstone replied, and Karl noticed that it was the first time that he had ever seen the British intelligence man look uncomfortable. 'We knew that the man whose identity you assumed was of some great importance to Berlin.

We guessed that they would go to any means to get him back – maybe send a seaplane or E boat for the rendezvous – but the deployment of a U boat was a surprise and only confirmed the dead man's value. You see, when he was captured he was in possession of some papers whose veracity we had to test. It's all part of our game to confirm such matters by any devious means possible. Fritz and his network were of importance to us but not as much as confirming the identity of the man you pretended to be. Now we know, and the bagging of the U boat was a bonus beyond our greatest hopes.'

'I don't suppose you are going to tell me any more about the man I was supposed to be,' Karl said with a note of bitterness in his voice.

'Sorry, old chap,' Featherstone answered apologetically. 'A need-to-know matter. But what is your second request?'

'Make sure that the promise to get Iris . . . Fatima and her daughter Marie back to Australia is kept,' Karl said. 'I think the lady deserves that much for her role in your mission.'

Featherstone broke into a broad smile. 'I can promise you that much, Mr Mann. I have already made arrangements to ship her and her daughter back to the antipodes within the week. My department is arranging to send word to her brother-in-law in Papua of her arrival. In the meantime, they will remain as guests of His Majesty here. Can't have them wandering around the town – under the circumstances.'

For reasons of security Karl appreciated that Featherstone really meant that Iris and Marie were actually under a form of 'house arrest'. At least they would be safe and well treated. 'Thank you, sir,' Karl said gratefully. 'The fact that Iris is still alive has ramifications for a very good friend of mine in Papua. All going to plan and allowing for the vagaries of the law, both he and Iris are fated to be very rich people when they next meet. It has been almost a quarter of a century since they last saw each other.'

'Ah, that smacks of intrigue, not unlike the world at the front you are leaving for,' Featherstone said with a chuckle. 'Or maybe a love story in the truest traditions of romance.'

Karl was not about to disillusion the English officer and was at least grateful to be able to get Marie out of Palestine. There was something about the young and beautiful woman that had touched him. At least in Australia he might get the chance to see her again. If he survived the war, that is, he thought, closing the door behind him.

'I hate you, Mother,' Marie screamed. 'How could you do it?'

Iris stood by the hotel window, gazing down at a section of British soldiers changing the guard at the King David Hotel.

'I did what I did for you,' Iris replied, calmly turning to her daughter standing in the centre of the room and raging at the world.

'You betrayed my father to the damned British. God knows if he is still alive.'

'Knowing Pierre as I do, I doubt that the British

will have captured him. I suspect he is up in the hills with his German friends at this very moment planning his return to Casablanca.'

The two women stood facing each other across the hotel room provided by Captain Featherstone. Iris remained dressed in the chador whilst Marie wore a European skirt and blouse. It was a true contrast of generation and culture as Marie had never adopted her mother's religion but was at her father's insistence loosely a Catholic. The Corsican held only contempt for the people who he had mixed with for most of his life and regarded the Moslems as people who had invaded Corsica in the past and attempted to force their culture on his own.

'I will escape from here and join my father at the first possible opportunity,' Marie warned, lowering her voice. 'We will leave Palestine together.'

Iris had expected this resistance from her daughter. She had virtually been taken to the hotel under armed guard when Featherstone sent a patrol of military police to fetch them. 'Please sit down, Marie,' Iris requested gently. 'There are things you should know before you make any foolish decisions to escape to Pierre.'

Marie remained standing, glowering at her mother, her arms folded defiantly across her breasts. 'Why should I believe anything you are about to tell me? Traitor!' she spat.

'Traitor?' Iris questioned with irony in her voice. 'Traitor to what?'

Marie walked to the window to gaze down on the street below. 'You have sided with the British against our government in Vichy,' she replied with her back to her mother. 'That is an act of treason.'

'I am not French,' Iris answered. 'The only country I can feel any real affiliation to is Papua which is under Australian administration. So I am not siding with the British.'

'The Australians are puppets of the British,' Marie snorted. 'What difference does it make?'

'You don't know the Australians like I do,' Iris said. 'They are good people.'

Marie swung away from the window to stare at Iris. 'You have betrayed my father. That is a treason in itself.'

'He is not your father,' Iris replied quietly. 'Your real father was killed on orders I suspect strongly came from Pierre. Your real father was a gentle, wonderful German soldier in the French Foreign Legion. Have you never suspected that Pierre was not your father?'

Marie paled, her hands fell to her side. Iris could see that what she had told her daughter about her parentage had struck a chord. It was as if the girl had been struck dumb.

Yes, Iris thought, you have always suspected something was wrong. The times Pierre scorned you when you were young, the lack of real feeling in their father–daughter relationship. You must have suspected all was not well. 'I swear on my love for you and in the eyes of Allah that what I tell you is true,' Iris said aloud. 'Pierre helped another evil man kidnap me many years ago from my family. I was raped and he forced me into slavery. The piece of paper saying that we are man and wife is a forgery and when he learned of my pregnancy he attempted to kill me.'

'I cannot believe that,' Marie finally said. 'My father would not do that.'

Iris stood and suddenly dropped her chador around her ankles. With horror Marie stared at her naked mother. She had never seen her unclothed before as her mother's modesty had forbade revealing herself to anyone other than her husband. But what was even more horrifying were the terrible scars covering her mother's body. 'This is what your father did to me in a rage when he learned I was carrying you. I would have died and so would you except for an old kindly Moslem woman who took me in and cared for me until you were born. Pierre came for me and only when I threatened to kill him if he ever attempted to hurt you did he accept that you were part of my life, if not his.'

'He was the only father I knew,' Marie uttered. 'He must have wanted me.'

Iris picked up the chador and dressed. From a hidden pocket she produced a small leather satchel and removed a scrap of well-worn paper. 'This is your certificate of birth,' she said passing it to her daughter. 'Read it.'

Marie took the paper and read the entry. Iris could see from the expression on Marie's face that the French birth certificate confirmed all that she had said.

'It does not list Pierre as my father,' Marie whispered.

'He insisted that his name not be linked with

your birth. He could have done so but rejected you from the day you were born.'

Marie slumped into a chair and stared with unseeing eyes at the floor. She was hardly aware of her mother's arms around her as the tears rolled freely down her face. The betrayal had not been by her mother, Marie realised between silent tears. It all made sense now, but that did not stem the flood of pain. The only family she really had was her mother.

Captain Featherstone was true to his word and within twenty-four hours Iris and Marie were transported out of Palestine and heading for Australia. For Marie a whole new world was waiting on the other side of the world. For Iris, she was finally going home to her family in Port Moresby.

THIRTEEN

The great expanse of sail flapped with the rising gusts of wind and the *Independence* leapt forward with the stiff breeze. Momis and the two other Solomon Islander crew members were back on deck with broad grins spread across their dark faces.

Lukas Kelly spun the great, teak-spoked wheel to steer into the best breeze he could find and, responding to his touch, the schooner heeled over at an acute angle, and sliced faster through the white caps. Flying fish glided from wave to wave as if attempting to outrun the schooner, racing with the sou-westerlies of the Gulf of Papua.

Momis and the crew cheered as they gripped masts for balance on the sloping deck and Jack Kelly smiled. It had been almost half a year since the death of his wife and it had only been the return of his son from the United States that had brought Jack back onto the deck of his schooner. Lukas, with his black leather eye patch jauntily in place over his left eye, had helped by taking charge of the business.

'Since the services won't take a one-eyed former flyer I figured you might have a berth for a pirate,' Lukas had said. 'I brought my own eye patch and will get a parrot as soon as it is possible.'

With that, father and son had returned to the sea. As the months passed Jack's resumption of his friendship with the Manns and the return of his son snapped him from the lethargy of not having anything to live for. Not a day passed when something aboard the schooner didn't remind Jack of Victoria but he was able to console himself that her soul almost possessed the schooner itself.

On some nights when his father was at the helm under a starry sky Lukas had heard Jack talking aloud as if speaking to Victoria. Lukas accepted that his father was not going mad, merely missing the woman who had only brought love and happiness to his tormented life, and he would creep away, allowing his father the privacy that a man and spirit might share.

Jack made his way to the helm with a half mug of steaming tea for his son.

'Thanks, Dad,' Lukas said taking the mug from his father. 'With this wind we will make port in a day.'

'Then unload and return to Moresby,' Jack added. 'And be home for Christmas with your Uncle Paul and Aunt Karin.'

Home, Lukas thought. Papua was truly home. Home was a Christmas at the Mann plantation, sharing the warmth of their unconditional love. Karl

Mann had been like a brother, sharing his life when they had been school friends together. And now Lukas envied Karl for the fact that he was fighting overseas for his country whilst he, Lukas, was safely sailing the tropical waters of the South Pacific.

Letters from Karl had arrived from the Middle East, describing the world he was seeing as an infantry officer plodding through the craggy, arid lands of the Bible. How Lukas would have given his good eye to be with Karl, sharing the adventure and danger. Surely there was some way he might be able to get into the action? He was physically fit and the only disability he had was the loss of his binocular vision. He could see extremely well from his good eye so why would the army at least not take him? At every chance he had, he read the latest reports in the newspapers of the Australian armed forces' successes in North Africa and the Middle East. They had only plagued him with guilt at what he considered was shirking danger when he should have been fighting. It was just part of the Kelly blood to be a fighter.

Jack, on the other hand, had secretly been pleased that his son was unable to enlist. For Jack knew the horrors of war, which young men at first believed was a grand adventure. To have his son home beside him meant more than any fortune he was likely to gain with Iris returning to Australia en route to Papua. Tom Sullivan, his old friend and family lawyer, had written to Jack informing him of all that had transpired. The inheritance left to Iris and him was now being released from England under the terms of Lord George Spencer's will. Tom Sullivan had gone on to say that it would all take some time as the war in Europe had caused chaos in London where the records were kept. Nevertheless, in the end he and Iris should inherit a small fortune. Needless to say, Jack would have preferred to have George back rather than his fortune, and he was sure Iris felt the same way. Jack had known great money when he owned a gold mine and was very aware of just how fleeting fame and fortune could be. After that, Victoria and the schooner had become his life and in that alone he had been content.

When the current cargo was delivered Jack planned to return to Moresby and take time off with a trip down to Cairns for a week's pre-Christmas leave with Lukas. It would be a chance to catch up with old friends and do some Christmas shopping.

Jack returned to the cabin with a rare smile on his face and, glancing across at the calendar hanging on the wall, idly realised that he had not brought it up to date in the last couple of days. Leaning over the chart table, Jack ripped away the pages, each with its own numeral.

He stood back and thought what a wonderful day this was, with a lucky number. The numeral was a big black eight and the month above the numeral read December. On the eastern side of the International Date Line it would have read Sunday, 7 December, 1941.

The sails were unfurled and Lukas motored the schooner skilfully towards the sturdy wooden pier built by the native converts of the Church of England mission. Their arrival always caused excitement for they were bringing the wondrous produce of Western civilisation to be distributed to the mission staff.

Jack stood by his son at the wheel, puffing contentedly on his briar pipe. 'The boys look a bit agitated,' he mused, watching with an experienced eye. He could see the Anglican priest, the Reverend Bill Smith, dressed in working clothes, waving to them at the end of the pier.

Carefully, Lukas steered the *Independence* to the wharf whilst Momis and his fellow Solomon Islanders leapt from the boat to trail the ropes securing the schooner.

'Have you heard?' The reverend called excitedly above the din of the idling engine.

'Heard what?' Jack replied as the engine cut out.

'The Japs have just sunk the Yank fleet in the Hawaiian Islands. We heard the news on the station wireless. It looks like we will be at war with Japan.'

'God almighty,' Jack swore. 'That means they will come after us for sure.'

'We have unconfirmed reports that they have launched attacks all over Asia . . . Hong Kong, Malaya, Singapore and the Philippines,' the reverend said, helping Jack ashore.

'Kind of lucky we have some supplies for you then,' Jack said. 'It might be a bit hard in the future if the Japs are coming south.'

'I am sure the government will have a plan to evacuate us if that is so,' the Anglican priest said.

'Well, at least to get all European women and children back to Australia.'

Jack did not comment. Privately he did not have much faith in the government having any contingency plan for such an event. War in the Pacific had come too suddenly, despite a lot of warning signs out of Asia. Maybe now it was too late.

The cargo was unloaded under Momis' supervision whilst Jack and Lukas walked up to the thatch buildings that constituted the mission station to take tea with the Reverend and his wife, Gwen. Jack could feel the fear in the airy room, although Gwen appeared calm as she busied herself with delivery of the tray for their morning tea of fresh baked scones and strawberry jam. The Anglican priest and his wife also had a fourteen-year-old daughter and were grateful for the fact that she was currently at a boarding school in Brisbane. Jack reassured Gwen that he would personally bring the *Independence* back to fetch them if the Japanese appeared to threaten their part of the world. His promise was gratefully received and after the morning tea, Momis came to inform Jack that their work was done.

Gwen handed Jack a small canvas bag of mail to be posted from Port Moresby and their farewells were made at the wharf. Then the schooner steered away to swing about and take a course back to Moresby.

At sea Jack broke open the supply of arms he carried aboard: two bolt action rifles and his old Webley Scott service revolver. Not that he figured they would be much good against a Jap naval vessel but at least they were reassuring to have at hand.

A watch was posted throughout the voyage but the trip was uneventful. The welcome sight of Port Moresby came into view within five days at sea and when Jack and Lukas went ashore the first thing they sought was news of the war. All they had heard since the attack on Pearl Harbor confirmed Jack's worst fears: the Imperial Japanese Navy had sunk the mighty British battleships *Prince of Wales* and *Repulse* off the east coast of Malaya. The dreadnoughts had been assigned to the Pacific by Britain as a supposedly tangible warning to the Japanese.

Within hours of contact with the Japanese both capital warships lay at the bottom of the ocean after being attacked by flights of torpedo and bomber aircraft. When Jack heard the news he immediately thought about Bernard Duvall. At least the Yanks had seen this coming, he thought. Now Australia would have to reach across the Pacific to its neighbour and seek help. If Singapore fell then it would herald the end of Britain's role in defending Australia in Asia. Jack was also acutely aware that they would be fighting for their very survival and that Papua and New Guinea would be the front line to the defence of Australia. Christmas and leave in Cairns were far from Jack's thoughts. What was uppermost in his mind was his role in the fight to come. There was no way anyone could keep him out of his second world war. Acceptance of his enlistment in the New Guinea Volunteer Rifles had been approved and he was now Sergeant Jack Kelly.

• • •

Sweat streamed down Fuji's face as he chipped away at the vegetable garden with a hoe. Once Sen had helped set up his contact with one of his less than reputable Chinese business acquaintances, it had been relatively easy blending into the Chinese quarter of the New Britain township bordered by the range of volcanoes. For a substantial wad of Australian bank notes the Chinese businessman had asked no questions of his paying resident. Fuji spoke no Chinese so both men communicated in English. Fuji posed as a Chinese labourer and found himself working in the garden to avert any suspicion from neighbours. He despised his Chinese employer and the squalid corrugated iron lean-to he had been allocated at the bottom of the vegetable garden for his quarters. It had no sides and the heavy rains ran through to soak his few personal possessions. The Japanese sailor vowed to settle with the Chinese shopkeeper when his comrades eventually arrived. Fuji understood the strategic importance of Rabaul Harbour, considered one of the best in the world. It would be needed as a staging post for any invasion of the Australian mainland. Its protected waters were capable of holding a fleet and were deep enough for submarines to come and go on their deadly patrols. The surrounding high ground could be reinforced with troops to protect the harbour from any attempt to counter-attack.

Oh how Fuji had dreamed of being aboard one of the great aircraft carriers or battleships of the Imperial navy when the arrogant Americans had been defeated at Pearl Harbor so easily. Instead, he had been instructed to remain around the township of Rabaul to watch and report on any moves the Australians might make to fortify the strategic port. They had even left a radio with him when he had been put ashore weeks earlier. The radio was well hidden in the jungle and he had no trouble slipping away from the Chinese trader to make his scheduled reports. He had been successful in sending his latest report on the deployment of the poorly equipped infantry battalion sent from Australia and of the coastal guns guarding the harbour's entrance, as well as general reports on a list of key government targets in the town and surrounding area.

Sooner or later his comrades would come to Rabaul and seize the town. Maybe by then the Australians would have surrendered their country, Fuji thought, bending over to tug at a particularly stubborn clump of weed. He hoped this would not deny him the opportunity to prove his worth in battle and he even experienced a pang of guilt at the fact that in Rabaul he was not really in danger's way.

Fuji did not mind the hard physical work which kept him fit, but as he chipped away at the rows of yams he continued to curse his Shinto ancestors. The war had begun and he had been left in a backwater.

Rabaul continued to bake lazily under a tropical sun as if there was no war but Fuji knew that would all soon change. The world would come to understand that nothing could stop the Japanese southern advance down the Asian mainland and across the Pacific waters.

Part Two

THE KELLYS' WAR

January 1942

FOURTEEN

Z day arrived before Christmas Day in Papua.

Z day was the code name assigned to the evacuation of all European women and children from the Papua and New Guinea territories commencing the eighteenth day of December 1941. It did not include those female missionaries and nurses who chose to stay nor non-European women and children.

Paul Mann saw Karin and Angelika off on the steamship *Neptuna* bound for Cairns and Townsville. He owned a small property in Townsville so his family had somewhere to stay upon arrival in Australia. The sudden but not unexpected war in the Pacific had changed their lives dramatically. Jack stood beside Paul Mann, wearing the uniform of the New Guinea Volunteer Rifles. On his sleeve Jack wore the rank of sergeant. In the Great War he had risen to the commissioned rank of captain but Jack did not mind reverting back to a rank he had once held in the trenches of the Western Front, as the NGVR had had a slot for a senior NCO and Jack had taken it without hesitation. At least he was back in uniform and doing his bit with a unit raised locally to defend Papua and New Guinea. The officers and men making up the NGVR were drawn from all sections of the Island's colonial society: government clerks, prospectors, merchants, plantation owners and managers, scientists and many more. Had many of the same men attempted to enlist in the armed forces of Australia they would probably have been rejected on the grounds of age, and so many of the officers and men had seen action twenty years earlier in the Great War. A unit of the NGVR was in Rabaul alongside a battalion sent up from Australia and Jack was to fly out of Moresby on the morrow to join his unit in Lae. He guessed it might be a long time before he, his son and his friend Paul Mann would be together in one place at the one time.

'They are not evacuating Sen or Iris at the moment,' Jack said bitterly, standing beside his friend and watching the ship pull out into the channel to steam away from Port Moresby. 'But I suppose that the government in its wisdom believes it has to keep the Chinese out of Australia.'

Paul stayed on the wharf until the ship was a small dot on the horizon. Although Jack remained with his best friend he was impatient to head for the hotel as the influx of troops from Australia made it harder to get a beer at the bar.

'I have read that the Japanese have bombed Rabaul,' Paul said, turning to walk down the wharf for the town. 'It won't be long before Moresby comes under attack.'

'Just a matter of time,' Jack agreed. 'Lukas is sailing for Rabaul tomorrow. The navy has given him some hush-hush charter to take some bloke there on government business.'

'We . . . Lukas must be careful, my friend,' Paul cautioned. 'The seas are a dangerous place at the moment. And so are the skies. The Japanese have formidable aircraft.'

'You know,' Jack said, 'I have never asked you your views on the Japs coming into the war on the side of your German countrymen.'

'I could not fight my countrymen as my son does,' Paul answered. 'But the Japanese are a different matter. I do not know why Hitler should have even considered signing a pact with them.'

'Like he signed a pact with Stalin in Russia and look where that went,' Jack sneered. 'Paper treaties don't mean much to your Herr Hitler.'

'He is not *my* Hitler,' Paul snapped. 'The man will destroy Germany for the sake of his personal ambitions, especially now that the Americans have come into the war.'

Jack dropped the subject. Prior to the war Paul had expressed some admiration for the man who had returned self-esteem to his people. Even the conquest of France was viewed by Paul as a natural way of subduing Germany's historical enemy on the continent, although he had disagreed with the unjustified

183

occupation of such neutral countries as Holland, Belgium and Norway. 'Well, let's just have a drink. You may as well stay aboard the *Independence* tonight with Lukas and myself,' Jack said, slapping Paul on the back as they walked into town. 'Hopefully you will get to join Karin and Angelika soon enough in Townsville.'

'That may be some time,' Paul replied. 'I am going to stay here and try to help keep the Japanese out of Papua.'

Jack was taken by surprise by his friend's statement. 'How do you, a German, expect to be able to help?'

'I have ways,' Paul replied mysteriously. 'Ways that I cannot tell even you, my friend, because I have sworn to remain silent.'

Jack glanced sideways at Paul and saw the grim expression set on his face. Whatever Paul was involved in had the smell of official secrecy and Jack did not question him any further.

Kwong Yu Sen was now transmitting information on the scheduled basis and feared that somehow he might be discovered. The presence of his sister-in-law Iris only added to his guilt of betraying the people who had come to trust him. There were times he had considered fleeing Papua rather than work for the Japanese, but now even that option was gone as the Imperial forces of the Emperor overran Asia and most of the North Pacific. No, he was trapped in Papua and with things going so well for the Japanese in the Pacific it was only a matter of time before they occupied Port Moresby. What was there to stop them? At least he had the consolation that he and his family in Singapore would be looked upon favourably by the Japanese when they came, unlike any Europeans captured by them.

When Iris had arrived alone in Port Moresby she was greeted by Sen, who was surprised to see that his sister-in-law was alone.

'It is good to see you, Iris,' Sen had said formally. 'Your return is a joyous moment for all the family.'

Iris had stood with just one small suitcase by her feet on the wharf busy with the business of war: cargo ships unloading war material and troops straight from Australia sent to reinforce the Port Moresby garrison. Captain Featherstone had arranged to ship Iris and Marie to Australia but it had been Tom Sullivan who had arranged the last leg of her journey to Papua. Both mother and daughter had been his guests in Sydney – part of the service to the estate of the late Lord Spencer, Tom had explained shrugging off their gratitude when Iris tried to thank him for his generosity and hospitality. For the voyage out Marie had been surly to her mother but when she arrived in Sydney she was captivated by its sunshine and the easy-going ways of its citizens. Tom Sullivan arranged for the young woman to meet some French friends who, with open arms, took the exotic, beautiful young woman into their fold.

When Marie had approached her mother over leaving Sydney with her for the journey to Papua she had been unusually contrite explaining that she wanted to stay. Papua sounded too primitive for her liking. Iris listened to her daughter's pleas sympathetically. In the back of her mind was the fear that her beloved Papua might come under intense Japanese attack, placing Marie in extreme danger. She agreed to Marie's request to stay and Tom Sullivan, charmed by the young French beauty's wiles, was kind enough to find Marie employment in one of his many booming businesses.

Despite Tom Sullivan's insistence that Iris remain in Sydney with her daughter, Iris had a need to visit her home in Papua at least for a short while. There were the ghosts of her past that required exorcism and so she bid Marie a tearful farewell, promising to return.

On the car trip back to Sen's bungalow outside Port Moresby, Iris had soaked in the sounds, sights and smells of the country. With her eyes closed she could almost imagine that she was a young girl again, riding her horse to the nearest village to chat with the native women and on the way home stopping to pick flowers. When she opened her eyes she was aware that only the countryside had not changed much in the years she had been gone. Everything else was gone; her sister-in-law and children were now living in Singapore under threat of occupation whilst her brother-in-law appeared to have aged prematurely under the burden of being separated from his family. There was a terrible shadow over the land, she thought as she gazed at the countryside through the window of Sen's small Ford sedan. She had instinctively sensed something less than warm in Sen's welcome to her at the wharf. It could be just the stress of knowing that his family were in Singapore living under threat by the Japanese, she had told herself, that made him so distant. Whatever it was, Iris thought, travelling on the dirt track to Sen's place, it was of no real consequence. All she had come home for was to see the place where she had met the man she had truly loved all her life, for the last time. She just wanted to stand on the verandah overlooking the lush tropical garden and remember the tall, almost awkward Englishman. The journey to Papua was not unlike a pilgrimage to Mecca. For Iris, it was a spiritual journey before returning to the material world of an inheritance.

Morning came with scudding clouds and a stiff breeze. Jack lay in his bunk aboard the schooner and wished that he had not drunk so much the day before with Paul who snored in a bunk on the opposite side of the cabin.

With some effort Jack heaved himself out of his bunk and padded to the sink to wash away the dryness brought on by the over-consumption of alcohol at the Moresby pub. He vaguely remembered that Paul had kept up with him and their old friends from his prospecting days. It was unusual to see the normally reserved man drink so much and Jack could only put it down to the fact that he was attempting to drown the thoughts of being separated from his wife and daughter.

'Are you two alive?' Lukas called cheerfully down from the deck. He had not been afforded the opportunity of getting drunk with his father. Someone had to remain aboard and supervise last minute details before they could set sail this day.

'Just,' Jack moaned, rinsing his face with the cold water. 'But I am not sure about your Uncle Paul.'

At the mention of his name, Paul Mann rolled over to blink at the first rays of the rising sun filtering weakly down through the porthole between breaks in the clouds. 'I am alive,' he groaned, and let his legs hit the floor. He sat at the edge of the bunk. 'But I wish I wasn't.'

Jack raised a feeble grin. 'Never seen you get so drunk before,' he said, throwing his friend a wet cloth to bathe his face. 'Wait 'til I tell Karin how you played up last night in the bar.'

'I didn't – did I?' Paul questioned in a shocked voice before realising that Jack was kidding.

'Well, old friend,' Jack said, 'time for you and I to go ashore. Our passenger should be here pretty soon.'

'I am your passenger,' Paul said quietly lest he split his head with undue sound.

'You are kidding?' Jack asked. 'You can't be the man Lukas is taking to Rabaul.'

Paul enjoyed the effect his announcement had made on Jack. 'I am.'

'But why the bloody hell didn't you tell me this yesterday?' Jack asked. All he had known was that whoever the passenger was, he had the highest government clearance.

'I was sworn to secrecy by your military people

not to tell anyone,' Paul replied, rubbing at his eyes to remove the imagined grit. 'Not even you and Lukas. I am not supposed to tell you anything, as you can understand.'

Jack stared at his friend with new respect. Whatever the mission was it must be dangerous. Paul Mann, former highly decorated officer in the Kaiser's army, was undertaking a mission in Rabaul for the government of his former enemies on the battlefields of France and Belgium. 'Cobber, whatever you are up to has got to be bloody interesting,' Jack said in awe. 'So what the bloody hell are you up to?'

Paul heaved himself to his feet and felt the gentle rock of the boat's decking below his feet. 'I wish I could tell you,' Paul said. 'But I swore an oath to secrecy. I know you will understand, old friend.'

Jack nodded. He understood but did not agree. Whatever Paul had been asked to do had the smell of danger about it and Jack feared for his friend's life.

Shaved, washed and back in uniform, Jack hefted his kitbag on his shoulder and climbed up to the wharf. Momis and the Solomon Islander crew had returned from a visit to a village outside Moresby where it was rumoured alcohol and women could be found. They were a sorry sight as it seemed they had also found a fight. Momis had a swollen lip and the other two had half-closed eyes. Jack did not ask. At least they had got back to man the schooner.

Now it was Jack's turn to watch a boat depart. In the last twenty-four hours it seemed all the people he cared about were sailing from his life. He waited until the schooner was well out into the channel before turning to go to the airfield where he had a plane to catch.

FIFTEEN

Built in the shadow of active volcanoes, the township of Rabaul had known tragedy in its short history. An eruption had occurred in the late 1930s, nearly destroying the town. Just prior to Lukas and Paul sailing for the island a series of violent earthquakes had shaken the town and surrounding country.

Paul would have liked to have explained to Lukas the secret mission he was carrying out on behalf of Australian naval intelligence. Paul Mann had agonised over his role in this second war of his life. He had a son risking his life for his former enemies and yet Paul felt the whispers of 'coward' in his own life. Once he had been a soldier, and now knew it was again time to cast his lot to protect his adopted homeland and family from this new and ruthless enemy which was poised to invade Papua. In the end

Paul's conscience had led him to the offices of naval intelligence and hence to this journey to New Britain. The Royal Australian Navy had long recognised the strategic importance of Rabaul Harbour and Paul now had a small but important part to play in the overall scheme to secure specific objectives in the event of war. But war had come suddenly to the Pacific, so now the mission had to be carried out under the most dangerous of conditions.

Paul sat at the chart table finishing his morning mug of coffee and poring over a chart of the harbour only a few sailing hours away. The schooner wallowed and slapped through a rising sea and outside the cabin the sky was awash with low scudding rain clouds threatening a downpour. The weather was a reflection of Paul's brooding thoughts about his mission and his agonising over disclosing it to Lukas, who he regarded more as an adopted son. If he could not trust Lukas Kelly then he could trust no one, he considered. Maybe he could . . . Paul's thoughts were suddenly interrupted by Lukas's cry on deck.

'Uncle Paul! Get up here, quick!'

Paul scrambled from the table scattered with charts and up the ladder into the early morning sunlight. Off their starboard bow through the scudding rain squalls was Praed Point, and Paul could see what had caused Luke's urgent call. Many aircraft circled and dived at a coastal battery guarding the entrance to Rabaul Harbour. The distant sounds of explosions and machine gun fire drifted to the schooner.

'Japanese aircraft,' Paul said. 'The poor bastards manning the coastal guns are taking a hammering.'

He glanced at Lukas behind the wheel who stood gaping and realised that this was the first time Lukas had witnessed the scenes of war.

The aircraft peeled away and with growing fear Paul noticed that they were directly under the flight path of the Japanese dive bombers as they droned lazily away from the smoking ruins onshore. His fear was justified when one of the aircraft peeled away from its formation and came down at them to level off just above the waves. It was coming straight on.

'Swing the wheel!' Paul screamed. 'Get her over.' In an instant Paul had appraised the situation and realised that they were being lined up for a strafing run. The fountains of water already spouting ahead and clawing their way towards the schooner verified this. Unopposed, the Japanese pilot had been able to line them in his sights for an easy run of machine gunning them from bow to stern.

Lukas obeyed and the big schooner heeled over to present a three-quarter target to the pilot's guns. The bullets slammed into the hull and deck which exploded with slivers of timber. Paul could feel the shudder of the bullet impact under his feet and instinctively threw himself down whilst Lukas half-crouched behind the wheel, continuing to turn the schooner about. The deckhands had sought cover behind the hatch openings.

All could hear the terrifying roar of the engine directly overhead and feel the draft of its propeller. When he glanced up Lukas was aware of the great red roundel on the wings. The Japanese aircraft was climbing into the blue sky and the thought of the rifles below came to Lukas. Not that they would prove very useful against a modern fighter plane but at least he was not going to lose his ship without some kind of a fight.

'It looks like it's leaving,' Lukas gasped. 'Must be out of ammo.'

Paul could also see the plane continuing to climb in the direction of the disappearing formation and agreed with his observation. The formation would have expended all they had on their primary target onshore. It just happened that this one pilot had a little bit left over and chose to use it up on a target of opportunity.

'Anyone hurt?' Lukas called and was relieved to hear that all reported that no injuries were sustained. Paul turned to Lukas who was swinging the sailing ship back on course.

'You did well,' Paul said, placing his hand on Lukas' shoulder. 'You kept your head.'

Lukas was visibly shaken. He had paled under his tan and Paul could see the receding fear in his eyes. 'I thought we were dead,' he rasped, his mouth suddenly dry. 'I could see the flame from his guns and even saw the bastard's face when he flew over. I swear he was smiling.'

'We were lucky,' Paul reassured. 'That is all part of war.'

'Were you scared?' Lukas asked.

'Scared out of my wits,' Paul replied.

'At least you were able to react. If we hadn't heeled over he would have caught us from stem to stern. Your decision was not one of a frightened man.'

'It was fear that caused me to make a split second decision, never forget that,' Paul said gently. 'Believe me Lukas, I was scared . . . Now it's time to check for damage and for you to steer us safely into the harbour. We have a job to do and I fear that what we just witnessed is only the tip of the Japanese sword.'

Lukas steered the schooner under motor past Matupi Island and into Simpson Harbour. As they approached the townships, even from the deck they could see an eerie absence of the bustle of an important town. Recent volcanic eruptions from the surrounding mountains had clothed much of the town in grey dust and the visits by the Japanese bombers caused smoke to rise from twisted wharfs and burning buildings. The once peaceful, pretty town of old German colonial buildings looked wounded and worn.

Paul slipped an old .38 revolver that Jack had given him many years earlier into his belt and gathered together a small blanket-wrapped swag of a few personal items. He dropped it on the deck and stood with Lukas. 'No one to welcome us ashore,' he said. 'Place looks deserted.'

'Maybe they are all indoors or in shelters somewhere,' Lukas agreed, gliding the *Independence* into a berth at a deserted wharf showing signs of damage.

'I don't like it,' Lukas said, surveying the area while Momis and his boys leapt ashore to secure the schooner. All Lukas could see were the rib-skinny native dogs roaming the streets alongside their better kept four-footed European cousins. The place was like a ghost town.

Lukas glanced at the rifle leaning against the railing, hoping that he would not have to use it. 'I don't think you should continue with your mission, Uncle Paul.'

Paul Mann hefted his swag over his shoulder but hesitated. 'I have to honour my oath to those who have put their trust in me,' he said uncertainly.

'I think the bloody Japs must be already ashore somewhere and the town has been deserted. It looks like the residents have gone bush up into the hills.'

'Then I will find out when I go ashore,' Paul replied. 'There is no reason for you to stay around. Better you get away now.'

'You have rocks in your head, Uncle Paul, if you think we are going to sail away without you.'

'You were paid to get me here,' Paul argued. 'Now your job is done. Besides, officially Germany is an ally of the Japanese so even if they take me I can always fall back on that.'

'I have a bad feeling that they will not bother to take the time to check you out – just shoot you on sight,' Lukas countered.

Paul knew Lukas was worried for his safety but he had once been a soldier and understood the meaning of following orders. 'If it seems that the Japanese are already here I promise I will return with you. If they are not then I must continue with my mission.'

'Fair enough,' Lukas agreed. 'I will hold you to your word but the first sight of any Japs and we get out of here quick smart. You want me to come with you, Uncle Paul?' Lukas asked.

'Best you stay here with the boat,' Paul replied. 'It might be an idea to have Momis and the boys stand by on the wharf ready to slip the ropes if we have to leave in a hurry.'

Not all the town was deserted. In the Chinese quarter, people still went about their business. After all, as Asians, they did not count to the European administration when it came to evacuation plans and all that they could do was wait in fear for the Japanese to come. They attempted to convince themselves that with good fortune they might just be left alone.

Meanwhile, Fuji Komine was elated. His brothers were a mere few hours away from occupying the strategic port nestling between the volcanoes, but he had work to do before then. There was bomb damage assessment and the location of any military forces to be located and reported to the fleet off the coast. Now he could move freely, as he would still be considered a Chinese national by any European administrators he may stumble upon in the town. He was not armed except for the knife but felt he did not need to be under the current circumstances.

The first place he had decided he must investigate was the wharf district. It was important to send a comprehensive report to his superiors on the state of the docking facilities. With an air of confidence Fuji set out for the wharf jutting into Simpson Harbour.

• • •

Paul moved cautiously into the town of low-set colonial buildings.

'Who are you, cobber?' a voice challenged him from a building.

'Paul Mann out of Moresby,' Paul replied, sensing that he may be in the centre of someone's rifle sights.

A middle-aged man stepped from a shop. He was unarmed but gripped a wooden crate of supplies. 'Herb Boyd,' the man said. 'I was just closing down my shop. You got transport?'

'Just arrived by boat,' Paul answered. 'What's going on around here?'

The man placed the crate on the road and wiped his brow. The crate contained vials of quinine, tea, bags of sugar and other essentials needed to live for a short time in the bush. 'We have reports that the Japs are just offshore with a bloody great invasion force. It's too big for our boys to take on so anyone left is heading up into the hills and inland. I would strongly recommend that you don't hang around here very long.'

'Do you have transport?' Paul asked.

Frowning, the Australian shopkeeper glanced at Paul. 'You a Kraut?' he asked bluntly. 'Thought all you blokes had been interned from here in '40.'

'I was born in Germany,' Paul replied. 'But I am a loyal Papuan.'

'That's okay with me,' Herbert Boyd said, thrusting out his hand to Paul. 'You can come with me, old chap. Just give me a hand with this stuff and then we will be off. I have a car parked around the corner.'

'Thanks, cobber,' Paul said. 'I just have to report

back to the skipper of the boat that brought me here that I will be all right. I can tell him to leave immediately.'

'No worries,' Herbert grinned, taking up his crate of supplies. 'Just hope your mate gets his boat out of the harbour before the whole bloody Jap navy arrives. I will wait for you around the corner but don't be too long. We have to get up the hills before dark.'

'I will be quick, my friend,' Paul reassured him.

Fuji stared not so much at the schooner as at the young man with the eye patch who stood on its deck. Years had passed but not faded Fuji's memory of an incident that had brought great loss of face to his father. On the beach off the Mann plantation Fuji had sworn to kill one of the men responsible for his father's humiliation. It was Lukas Kelly, Fuji thought, as the memory of the day renewed the hatred in him. This day was his. The naval forces of his country were poised to deliver his countrymen to Rabaul and here – only a matter of a few yards away – was a chance to settle old scores. Fuji was elated.

However, the rifle he could see leaning against the boat's rail and within reach of Lukas Kelly dampened his joy. He was only armed with a knife. What he needed to do was get close enough to Kelly to use it. Fuji could also see the three Solomon Islanders with the schooner and correctly guessed that the men were crew. They were another problem to overcome, but such was his desire for revenge that he knew he would come up with something. So preoccupied was he in keeping the schooner and its crew under observation that he did not notice the figure approaching from the town.

Paul Mann frowned. The Asian man watching the *Independence* was doing so in a very covert way. He was crouching out of sight as if not wanting to be seen by Lukas and the boys. Maybe he was a Chinese desperate to get off the island by hijacking the *Independence*, Paul thought, drawing the revolver from its holster. 'Hey, you. *Rausim!*' he roared, waving the pistol to emphasise his meaning.

Startled, the man spun around and for a brief moment their eyes met.

'Fuji!' Paul exclaimed in a whisper. He could never forget the young man who had brought death to the Mann plantation years earlier and whose name had been linked to Victoria's. It was obvious that Fuji also recognised him as his eyes widened in alarm. The sudden, totally unexpected meeting froze Paul to inactivity but not so Fuji. He came out of his half-crouch behind a pile of heavy ropes to sprint away, ducking and weaving in the expectation of a volley of shots from Paul's revolver. Fuji flung himself off the wharf in a shallow dive to splash into the waters below.

Paul caught his breath and flung his arm out to fire the pistol in the direction Fuji had taken, but the bullets ripped through empty space.

Lukas had heard Paul's shout and then heard the

shots. Without hesitating he snatched up the rifle and ran to the schooner's railing. He could see a figure running, then diving from the wharf into the water. Lukas' attention was on searching out his Uncle Paul and he was relieved to see him standing on the wharf with his pistol drawn.

'It was Fuji Komine,' Paul called. 'The bastard is somewhere in the water.'

Lukas returned his attention to the spot he had seen Fuji disappear beneath the waters but nothing remained except a ripple. Scudding clouds and rain squalls were covering the bay but the sound overhead was ominously distinct. Lukas looked up but could not see the aircraft which, he had to conclude, could only be Japanese. Paul was at the edge of the wharf, scanning the waters for any reappearance of the Japanese man.

'Got to get you out of here, Uncle Paul,' Lukas called, manning the helm in readiness to cast off. 'If we don't and the Japs see us we will be sitting ducks.'

Paul slipped his revolver into his waistband and ran to the *Independence,* which was already being pushed away from the wharf. He stopped at the edge of the pier and flung revolver and holster to Lukas as a low-flying Japanese floatplane skimmed in over the waves of the harbour. Fortunately for the departing schooner the pilot was making a run over the town and not the wharf area. No doubt a recon mission, Paul thought, staring after the rapidly disappearing seaplane now climbing back into the low clouds of the rain squall. Nature had been kind to them, he considered, as the squall provided an effective cover for Lukas and his boat.

'Uncle Paul?' Lukas yelled, picking up the pistol and holster from the deck. 'Get aboard!'

'No need,' Paul said, cupping his hands to be heard over the sound of the schooner's engine. 'I have my mission – the Japanese are not here yet.'

Lukas held up the revolver with a questioning frown on his face.

'Better you have it,' Paul shouted and Lukas shrugged.

'I will see you back at the Moresby pub, then?' Lukas shouted as his schooner disappeared into the squall. 'That's a promise.'

The last he saw of the man was a lone figure standing fearlessly on the edge of the bombed wharf. It was not right to leave him, Lukas told himself bitterly. What could he do? He had left the second most important man in his life to an almost certain death. Lukas felt the pain rising in his chest. It was no wonder the tears flowed down his cheeks. His Uncle Paul was so much like his own father. They were men born of a different age when the word hero had real meaning. One war was not enough for tough old warriors like Paul Mann and Jack Kelly. Never before had Lukas felt so alone but he tried to console himself with the words his father had spoken about the *Independence* one night just after he had returned from America. 'She is kind of special,' his father had said, sitting under a starry sky. 'She now has the soul of Victoria to guide her in rough seas and bad times, and she won't let you down.' Lukas hoped so, for somewhere in the squall was an entire Japanese invasion fleet and he definitely did not want to bump into it.

Paul Mann did not fear Fuji Komine. He suspected that the Japanese man was not about to come looking for him if he thought he was armed. Paul turned and walked back into the town where he found Herb Boyd patiently waiting for him in his car. It was time to get out of Rabaul and up into the hills. Then after he'd completed his mission he hoped to satisfy Luke's promise of eventually joining him for a beer at the Moresby pub.

SIXTEEN

Lieutenant Karl Mann stood at the rail of the once luxurious trans–Atlantic liner now converted to a crowded troopship and stared at the disappearing coastline. The sun was blood red over the sea named for that very colour. Early February in the northern hemisphere was the end of winter and by steaming south they were returning to a hemisphere where summer was now ending.

Karl had returned to his unit to see combat in Syria and southern Lebanon and in one hard-fought, bloody action his company commander had somewhat reluctantly mentioned Karl in dispatches. The personal animosity between superior and subordinate had seemed to be heightened when Karl returned to duty with the battalion as a platoon commander and was unable to divulge where he had been or what he had done during the time he was seconded to the SOE. When the paperwork recognising Karl's contribution to the sinking of a U boat arrived at the company HQ Major Jules fumed. Whatever his platoon commander had done had won him the highly prized decoration of a Military Cross. Jules felt an intense jealousy for the German-born officer's receipt of such an award and the thought of the beautiful riband of white and purple stripes adorning Lieutenant Mann's chest was more than he wanted to consider. Major Jules was pleased that he had not been given the job of informing Karl of the award as the task had been done by the battalion's commanding officer who liked and respected his young lieutenant.

At least Jules had been able to not recommend his platoon commander for promotion, citing his time away, albeit only short, from infantry operations as a contributing factor. Karl had shrugged off the lack of promotion when he had been informed that he would remain a platoon commander. Major Jules would have liked to recommend him for a logistics posting but the award of the MC decoration curtailed that plan. A medal bestowed for courage did not help the army fight the enemy if the recipient was stuck behind a quartermaster's desk.

Now, the campaign in the Holy Land was over and they were sailing home. The news of Japanese victories in the Pacific left none in doubt that the next enemy they would face on the battlefield would be the Japanese. Karl's men had expressed their concerns for the fate of family and friends in Australia if the Japanese advance could not be checked – and it was a fear Karl shared. The Americans were fighting a desperate battle in the Philippines whilst the British, Indian and Australian troops were besieged at Singapore. Should the fortress of Singapore fall, then nothing could stop the Japanese advancing to the frontiers of New Guinea and then Papua, and onwards to Australia. Such was the situation reported to Karl's troopship currently en route to Australia via India.

Karl watched the great red globe sink into the waters. His thoughts drifted to Marie and he wondered where she might be at this moment. A letter from his mother dated 9 December said that Iris had returned to Papua and that she, Angelika and his father were to be evacuated to Australia. Karl was relieved to hear that his family would be relatively safe. With any luck his unit would be posted to northern Australia as a jumping-off point to the Pacific war, and if that was so he might once again see his family. It had been a couple of years since he last had seen his mother's tears and his father's grim countenance when he marched off to war. Oh, how he missed his sister Angelika and the happy days at the plantation.

Paul thanked the Australian shopkeeper for the lift and waved to him as he drove away to seek safety with others fleeing into the mountains to avoid the Japanese.

With the help of Herbert Boyd, Paul had now completed his first objective, making contact with the Catholic mission inland from Rabaul. The priest was a German who administered a station along with some Irish nuns. He was the same age as Paul and they shared much in common without knowing it. Both had served as infantry men in the trenches of the Western Front and both hailed from Munich.

'My name is Paul Mann,' Paul said, shaking the tall, distinguished priest's hand. 'I have a copra plantation near Moresby.'

'I am Father Kurt Stempel and I must say that you have come a long way,' the priest said, his white cassock flapping in a gentle breeze. 'What brings you to my mission station in these troubled times?'

'I will speak bluntly,' Paul said. 'I have come to ascertain where your loyalties lie now the Japanese have come into the war on Germany's side.'

Father Stempel glanced around his mission station. Native children dressed in European clothes and holding books were filing from a thatch-covered wooden building shepherded by an old nun wearing the full-length garb and head dress of her order. 'My loyalty is to my congregation,' the priest answered in German. 'I am a priest and the Australian authorities have kindly respected my religious neutrality in this war. Before we continue with this discussion, which I can see is of great importance to you, can I offer you a cool drink in my office?'

'That would be nice, Father,' Paul answered gratefully. The sun was hot even after the heavy rains. 'I will accept your hospitality.'

Paul followed the priest to a long dormitory-style building with a small room at one end. He admired the neat, clean grounds of the mission station as much as the healthy appearance of the people who worked with the priest and Irish order of nuns.

The office itself was spartan but befitting a man of God. A portrait of the Pope and a crucifix adorned the wall behind the table which served as a desk, and two chairs and a sideboard made up the rest of the furniture in the office. From the sideboard Father Stempel produced a carafe of water with lime wedges floating in it.

'I regret I cannot offer you something stronger,' Father Stempel said. 'My supply of Irish whisky has been curtailed by the war. Do sit down and enjoy the water.'

'Thank you,' Paul replied. 'I do not want to take up your time as I have the Lutheran mission station to visit as yet.'

'I presume that you will ask Pastor Bernard Benchler the same question that you have asked me?' the priest questioned.

'That's right,' Paul replied, sipping the water from a glass. 'I have been given the task of ascertaining from all Germans still resident in New Britain their attitude to the Japanese occupiers.'

'You mean, would we put ourselves in a position to actively assist the Australians should they seek our assistance in the future?' Father Stempel asked, leaning forward across the table. 'That is a very dangerous question to answer.'

'Maybe I should have asked you in the confessional,' Paul said with a wry smile. 'I believe it is in your teachings that a priest cannot divulge what has been said to his confessor in the sanctity of the confessional box.'

'On spiritual matters, no,' Father Stempel replied. 'But you are talking matters that belong to Caesar – not God.'

'So if an Australian came to your mission seeking aid and sustenance in these times, you would turn your back on him?'

'No,' the priest replied stiffly. 'Nor would I turn away a Japanese person who also came to me under the same circumstances. And, if you are wondering, I am not a Nazi but merely a priest whose concerns are with the spiritual concerns of my people.'

'What of the nuns?' Paul asked. 'What will the Japanese do with them when they eventually come?'

'The sisters are of an Irish order and Ireland is a neutral country in this war. They will respect international law on such matters.'

Paul gazed out the window to where the nuns were playing soccer with some young boys on a dusty stretch of ground in front of the building. A couple of the nuns were very young, laughing as they picked up the hems of their flowing white habits and chased after the ball with a youthful exuberance still unbroken by the rigid mores of their conservative vocation. He hoped the priest was right about the Japanese respect for neutrality but Hitler had not respected neutrality when he invaded the Low Countries and Norway. 'I suppose you have answered my question, Father Stempel,' Paul said, swallowing the contents of the glass. 'I should endeavour to make contact with the Lutheran mission station as soon as possible and was wondering if I could impose on your hospitality and ask if you have some form of motorised transport at the mission station.'

'I have a car,' the priest replied. 'You are welcome to use it to visit my friend Pastor Benchler. But I will need it back as soon as possible.'

'Thank you, Father,' Paul said, rising from his seat and extending his hand. 'I promise it will be returned within a couple of days.'

The priest also rose. 'Be very careful, my son,' Father Stempel said. 'I have heard from the natives that the Japanese are already fanning out in search of any Australians who have not been able to get off the island. Your questions may be construed as you actually working for Allied interests when in fact you should be loyal to your country and cause.'

'I will remember that,' Paul said, facing the priest. 'I hope to be well away from this island before the Japanese catch on to what I am doing here.'

'Then go in peace and God be with you,' Father Stempel said gently, raising his hand in the traditional gesture of the blessing. 'I will fetch Sister Ursula who will show you where we have hidden the car in the jungle,' Father Stempel added with a grin. 'I thought that might be a wise idea in case the Japanese decide to confiscate it from the mission.'

'Then you are not about to render unto Caesar,' Paul grinned, baiting the priest.

'Not my car,' Father Stempel replied. 'I have a worldly attachment to it.'

• • •

Paul was assisted by a cheerful, ruddy-faced nun of middle age to get the car out of its hiding place just near a copra plantation that the missionaries managed. She did not ask any questions, knowing that Father Stempel would brief her on the stranger when he was gone.

The car spluttered into life and Paul waved to the horde of native children who chased the car out of the mission station until he picked up enough speed to leave them in a swirl of dust. As he drove Paul found himself praying that his mission would be over before the Japanese made their way up into the mountains. He knew time was short but it was imperative to contact the Lutheran pastor before Paul made his way to a prearranged rendezvous with the coast watcher assigned to liaise with him. Like Paul, the coast watcher was now working deep in enemy territory as the invading Japanese swept the island with their patrols, searching for any possible pockets of armed resistance. His role was to observe Japanese troop and naval movements in his territory. All Paul had was a location and time to meet with the unnamed observer. As with everything else he had been told in his briefing by the naval officer in Port Moresby, for security reasons the information was in his head, not on paper.

Paul was acutely aware of the extremely lonely and dangerous task he had accepted. He only hoped that his family would not learn of what he was doing until he at least returned safely to them. For some strange reason, as he drove along the narrow, rutted dirt road hugging the side of the jungle-clad mountain, he thought about his son. Mostly he regretted that he had not demonstrated his overwhelming love for Karl when they last had seen each other.

'Stupid,' Paul said, banging the dashboard with his fist. 'So stupid to be so stubborn.'

He would have been amused to learn of the parallels his life was taking with that of his son. But for now he only experienced the pain of separation. He had survived one war but he felt he would not survive this one. He only hoped that what he was doing now would help to one day bring back the old world he and his family had known in Papua before the war.

Fuji had been taken at bayonet point to a former government office by a marine detachment of the Japanese navy. He now stood to attention before an officer of the dreaded *Kemptai* detachment sent ashore with the first wave of troops capturing the tropical township of Rabaul. The screams of women and the sound of shattering glass were audible even downtown from the Chinese quarter and the noise chilled Fuji. They were the sounds of an army raping and murdering defenceless civilians, and although he had heard stories of such events from navy men who had served in China, he had not expected his countrymen to behave in such a manner. The military police sergeant, a squat, pockmarked former policeman from a rural area outside Tokyo, glared coldly at Fuji. 'Your story of being an agent for naval intelligence has been verified,' the sergeant said. 'And because of your ability to speak English I have permission to have you transferred temporally to my detachment until you are reassigned back to the navy. We have work here for you, interrogating any Europeans we round up.'

Fuji felt his hopes of a transfer back to the decks of a warship sink. He wanted to be able once again to proudly wear the white uniform of the navy rather than this continuing service living a life divorced from the glory of combat. The unexpected, almost fatal contact with Paul Mann and Lukas Kelly the day before had unnerved him. It had been a bad omen and now being separated from the navy rankled him. 'I understand, Sergeant,' he replied. 'I will do my duty.'

In the hills beyond Rabaul, Paul Mann made his contact with the Lutheran pastor. The man had been less than sympathetic to his question and Paul had left the mission station to return the Catholic priest's car. As he approached the Catholic mission to return the car before seeking out the coast watcher somewhere south of Rabaul, the bad feeling he had experienced whilst driving away was turning into outright crippling fear.

SEVENTEEN

Paul finally relaxed when the buildings of the Catholic mission came into sight through the stand of tall palms. But as he slowed the car and drove into the wide clearing where the boys had kicked a football with the nuns earlier, he immediately felt a feeling of dread return. The whole station seemed deserted. He brought the car to a stop and from the corner of his eye saw that the mission station was not entirely deserted after all. Five Japanese soldiers stepped from behind the school rooms, bayonets fixed and their rifles pointed in his direction. He glanced over his shoulder and could see another six soldiers step out of the grove of palm trees behind him, cutting off any possible escape.

Paul stepped carefully from the car with his hands in the air. 'I am German,' he called in that language, but received no response from the five

Japanese soldiers now advancing on him. He stood by the car as one of the soldiers wearing the rank of an officer and carrying a pistol shouted orders to the men in the palm grove. They too advanced on Paul.

'Hands up! Speedo!' the officer screamed in English when he was mere paces away. To emphasise his point he swung the butt of his pistol, striking Paul across the face. Paul staggered but refused to fall and steadied himself to face the Japanese officer who was a good head shorter than him.

'Australia no good,' he shouted, spraying spittle in Paul's face. A fanatical fire burned in his dark eyes. 'Japan number one.'

'I am a German citizen,' Paul said, switching to English, but it was apparent that the Japanese officer's vocabulary was limited to just a few words and phrases and he did not understand.

When Paul spoke it only infuriated the officer and he launched another vicious assault on him with his pistol butt. The blows opened a gash under Paul's eye, and he felt blood welling from the wound. Paul felt both fury and helplessness in the same heartbeat and knew that if he retaliated he was a dead man. As far as he could ascertain, someone had betrayed him. Or the Japanese had mistaken him for an Australian. Paul struggled to remain on his feet.

Finally the Japanese officer ceased hitting him and stepped back. Blood had spattered over the front of his green uniform and he said something to his men as he walked away. For a terrible moment Paul thought that the officer had ordered his execution, as two of the soldiers had raised their bayonets in a manner that seemed to indicate they were about to stab him to death. Remembering the agonising deaths that bayonet wounds had caused soldiers in the Great War, Paul decided that he would rather be shot. However, the soldiers only prodded him with the sharp points, pushing him in the direction of a truck that rumbled into the yard. When Paul turned his head he recognised it as one of the European types used around New Britain before the war. But what was chilling was its cargo. Paul could see five obviously maltreated Europeans in the back, guarded by Japanese soldiers. One of the badly beaten men was Herbert Boyd.

With his hands in the air Paul was marched to the truck with the shouts of 'Speedo' and the jabs from the bayonets to hurry him along.

Paul scrambled over the tailgate of his own accord as none of the European civilians, cowering under the guns of their guards, dared to assist him. Paul caught Herb's eye and saw a look of fear and defiance. Paul was kicked to the floor of the truck's tray and found himself jammed up against the shopkeeper.

With a lurch, the truck moved away from the mission station and onto the dirt road.

'Where do you think they are taking us?' Paul whispered from the side of his mouth.

'Rabaul, I think,' Herb replied quietly.

'No talk!' one of the guards screamed and Herb was smashed in the side of his head with a rifle butt. He slipped sideways with a groan and lay in a pool of blood, which slowly seeped from the back of his head. Paul made a move to help him but felt the crack of a rifle butt on the back of his own head. A red haze of stars momentarily blocked his vision and the groan he heard was his own. Then mercifully came oblivion as he slid into a world of darkness.

When he finally came to he vaguely recognised the buildings slipping past as those of Rabaul. Herb was sitting up, his hair caked with blood. He glanced at Paul and despite the chance he would be struck again, asked softly, 'You all right?'

Paul nodded carefully, his head throbbing from the beating. The truck came to a stop outside a building that Paul guessed was once a government office. Japanese soldiers in green uniforms and with bayonets fixed to their rifles swarmed everywhere.

The prisoners were bundled from the truck and stood in a huddle surrounded by their captors.

'Could kill for a fag,' Herb muttered to Paul. 'But the little yellow bastards took everything I had when they caught me.'

'No talk!' a guard yelled and raised his rifle to slam Herb again. He suddenly desisted in the action, coming to attention as whatever had saved the Australian from a further assault came from the building. Paul turned his head to see an immaculately dressed Japanese officer wearing a sword appear on the steps, flanked by a squat, frog-faced NCO and a Japanese man dressed in a European white shirt and trousers.

'God in heaven!' Paul swore under his breath. It was Fuji Komine – a face he could not forget.

The Japanese officer said something that Paul took as an order and turned his back to return to the building with his subordinate whilst Fuji alone remained on the steps to address the prisoners.

'You are unworthy prisoners of the Emperor of Japan,' Fuji said in a commanding tone. 'As such you have forfeited any rights for good treatment unless it is in the interests of the Imperial forces of the Emperor. You will be questioned before being taken to a holding camp where your fate will be decided. If you cooperate you will be well treated.'

With his short welcoming speech at an end Fuji turned and disappeared into the building. It appeared that although Paul had recognised Fuji, Fuji did not appear to have recognised him. How long could that last? Paul wondered with rising despair. Fuji would not forget the past and hence his fate was sealed. It was bad enough being taken prisoner but as a German citizen he might have been able to bluff his way out of the imprisonment and escape. However, if Fuji recognised him he would be aware of his close contact with the Australians, which would be construed as siding with them. Whatever cover story he could come up with as a German would be taken apart by Fuji in an interrogation.

For hours the six men were forced to stand under the blazing tropical sun in front of the government office, whilst thirst and weariness plagued them. Their guards did not allow them to sit down or have any water as they waited and Paul suspected that they were being softened up for questioning. The promise of water might work better than a beating when it came to getting whatever answers the Japanese wanted. Paul prayed that he would not be asked about the coast watcher. He was not sure how long he'd be able to endure torture. He had no doubt their captors were more than capable of extracting information by the crudest and most brutal methods.

The sun was setting when the frog-like Japanese NCO reappeared on the verandah of the government office and issued orders to the guards, who made it known with kicks and jabs from their bayonets, that the prisoners were to get back in the truck that had brought them to Rabaul. Exhausted and thirsty, the prisoners scrambled aboard the tray and were joined by their guards.

'What the hell do you think the bastards are going to do with us?' Herb whispered in Paul's ear when he leaned against him.

'Take us to a gaol of some kind,' Paul whispered back.

Then Paul's blood ran cold. Fuji had appeared on the verandah and was walking over to the truck. He scarcely spared the prisoners a glance as he stepped up into the cabin of the truck. The truck lurched into motion and took a road out of Rabaul. The prisoners remained silent but the expressions on their faces reflected growing concern. They had not been interrogated but simply driven away from the island's capital and Paul had a bad feeling when he glanced at the guards in the back with them. There was something distant in their expressions that was very ominous, as if they knew something but did not want to share their secret.

After an hour's drive the truck stopped at a deserted coconut plantation. The usual shouts, jabs and kicks harried the prisoners off the truck and one of the guards produced some thick fishing line and began binding each man's hands behind his back.

The sun was on the horizon and the sky was taking on the soft glow of approaching night. Paul stood assessing his situation as the knot was tied behind his back, the line biting painfully into his wrists.

'Paul Mann?' a voice asked from his elbow, and Paul turned to look directly into Fuji's surprised face. 'It is you,' Fuji continued. 'I did not realise that we had captured you. If I had known, I would have insisted on your interrogation.'

'Then you also know that I am a German and I believe that as a citizen of that country I should not be a prisoner,' Paul answered quietly.

'You forfeited your nationality when you shot at me,' Fuji scowled. 'I doubt that your loyalties are to Germany. I see you as a traitor and deserving of a traitor's death.'

'So you plan to kill us?' Paul asked, wondering at the calm he was beginning to feel. Faced with the inevitable, his only regret was that he would never see his family again and this sadness dulled any fear. He did not want to die but his fate was out of his hands now.

Fuji looked away. Now that the moment had come to settle an old score he no longer had the same burning desire to see this man he had known from his childhood executed. Fuji now only saw a weary and helpless man. Time had taken the edge off his need to seek revenge for the slight to his father's honour. 'I will ensure your death is quick,' he said quietly lest the other prisoners overhear him. 'Would you prefer to be shot or bayoneted?'

'Shot,' Paul replied. 'A clean shot.'

Fuji nodded and walked away as the guards stepped in to force their prisoners into the rows of coconut trees. Herb was behind Paul as they were marched single file into the gathering darkness. 'The bastards are going to kill us,' he said. 'Aren't they?'

'I am afraid so, my friend,' Paul answered sadly. 'There is nothing we can do.'

'I can do something,' Herb muttered savagely. 'I'm not going to lay down and let them kill me.' With that the Australian suddenly made a break from the file of prisoners and attempted to sprint into the rows of neatly cultivated trees some hundred yards away.

The guards shouted and raised their rifles. Paul reacted quickly. He wasn't going to just let the Japanese lead him meekly to his death either. 'Run!' he shouted to his fellow prisoners and launched into an awkward sprint.

He could hear angry shouting and rifle shots behind him and although he knew he had little to no chance of escaping he would at least try. The bullet that hit him just above the shoulder and near his neck stung, flinging him around in a pirouette. Before he could regain his balance Paul felt a searing pain in his back and knew that he had been bayoneted from behind. He cried out in pain while the Japanese soldier forced him to the ground. Paul tried to roll over to face his executioner but felt the long knife being withdrawn before being plunged into his back again, this time grazing his ribs where it was deflected by the bone.

Paul was vaguely aware of more shots and the sound of men dying as he lay on his stomach feigning death. There were footsteps around him and a terrible silence broken only by men moaning in agony. Then the horrible sound of bayonets being stabbed into flesh finally cut short the moans. With all the willpower he could muster, Paul held his breath. He was face down and could just see the tip of a boot near his face. The only sounds now were Japanese voices chattering and laughing. Blood welled in a thick pool around his head and he could feel it warm and wet against his cheek. A searing pain wrenched at his body as once more a bayonet was thrust into his back. The coup de grace was to ensure no life still existed in his body. The overwhelming instinct was to scream and beg for mercy but Paul continued to feign death, lying still as the sound of footsteps and voices receded. Finally he heard the sound of a truck driving away but he continued to lay face down for another hour in case there was a detail left behind to ensure that no one had survived the massacre.

When the sun was below the horizon and the crickets ruled the night with their chirping calls, Paul forced himself to his knees, then to his feet. He stumbled to what he could see was a body already growing cold to the touch. He knelt to feel the man's skin. 'Is there anyone alive?' he called softly but received no answer.

His wounds were serious and Paul knew that he

would die unless he received help. Alone in the dark that did not seem possible and he despaired that he had only postponed the inevitable. Whatever he did, he must get away from this place.

A click broke the silence. Just the faintest noise and Paul recognised the sound of a safety catch being slipped on a rifle. The Japs must have sent back a patrol, he thought. Now he truly was dead.

Sen had been hospitable but distant in his dealings with Iris when she had arrived from Australia and all seemed to be going well until one night Iris stumbled on a secret that disturbed her. It had been a hot and still night when Iris found herself tossing and turning. Thirsty, she had left her room to go to the kitchen when she thought she heard voices coming from Sen's office at the back of the house. Curiosity became stronger than her need for water and Iris crept to the closed door of the office. It was unlocked and very cautiously she swung it ajar to peek inside. Sen was crouched over something that looked like a small suitcase. He had earphones on and was talking softly in Chinese. She had seen similar equipment used by the German agent in Palestine and knew immediately what it was. Sen paused and finally appeared to end his conversation by reassembling his radio and sliding it into a panelled slot in the wall which was carefully concealed. Whatever her brother-in-law was doing had to be subversive. A spy! He must be transmitting to the Japanese – why else would he need to hide the radio?

Cautiously Iris closed the door and retreated. As thirsty as she was, it was better to go straight back to her room so as not to give the slightest hint to her brother-in-law that she had been up when he had been transmitting.

Iris found her way back to her room and lay down under the mosquito net. Her mind was racing. What was she to do? Would it be better to forget what she saw in the late hours of the night? Or should she bring up the subject with Jack Kelly when she next saw him?

EIGHTEEN

Jack felt every one of the fifty years he had been alive on earth. The trek from the goldfields township of Wau down to the coast in the Gulf of Papua entailed days of traversing a dank forest in extreme humidity, to say nothing of the mud and sheer climbs of 2000 metres, and the nights of uncomfortable sleep when the temperature dropped to just above freezing. Jack persevered in good company, as a couple of his fellow NGVR soldiers were also about his age and knew plenty of the same curses and oaths. Accompanying Jack's section was a large party of native carriers for the supplies they were to eventually pick up from the coast.

His unit of volunteer residents of Papua and New Guinea were now under the command of the newly formed ANGAU. The Australian New Guinea Administration Unit had been put together in mid

February to coordinate the efforts on Australia's front line in the Pacific war. No matter what the government was doing in Canberra it made little difference to Jack and his comrades. Each day in the tropical jungles was just another day of exhaustion, isolation and sweat and the men were dogged by malaria, dysentery, pneumonia and a thousand other diseases hardly known to medical science. If Jack ever thought of his country as Eden, the parts he seemed to find himself in now had been a bit neglected by God. It was a garden of weeds, snakes, leeches, painful heat rash and death.

The last part of the journey from Bulldog, the base camp in the hills, was by canoe down the Lakekamu River. Some of the NGVR soldiers were held over at the base camp whilst Jack continued with his carrier section to reach the coastal camp of Terapo. Three days later, he and his party finally burst out of the jungle to view the welcome blue-green waters of the Gulf.

Sitting in the canoe, Jack removed his broad-brimmed hat and gazed out at the sandbar that blocked large ships from coming inshore to offload cargo. A procession of surf boats and canoes ferried the supplies to the shore. Focusing on a schooner at anchor in the mouth of the river, a broad smile creased Jack's weary face. 'Bloody hell,' he swore. 'The *Independence*.'

It had been over two months since he had said goodbye to his son and best friend at the Port Moresby wharf and so much had happened since then. Jack gave orders to his crew to continue paddling towards the big boat.

• • •

'Dad! You old bastard,' Lukas shouted down from the deck of the schooner, overjoyed at their unexpected meeting. 'What the hell are you doing in this neck of the woods?'

'What's it bloody look like,' his father grinned as the canoe bumped at the side of the schooner. 'Help your old man aboard.'

Jack turned and gave orders for the native canoeists to paddle ashore and get some rest before they commenced their work of ferrying stores ashore. With Momis' help, Lukas heaved his father aboard. 'Good to see you, Dad,' Lukas said, hugging Jack to him.

'I'd kill for a cold beer if you have one,' his father said, disengaging himself from the heartfelt embrace.

Jack followed his son below, where Lukas opened a crate of beer. They were not cold but Jack had not tasted the malty dark ale since his last night in Lae and as hot as it was it still tasted good.

'Well, what have you been up to?' Lukas asked when they were both settled either side of the chart table.

'Bloody running all over the country up around my old mining claim,' Jack replied. 'Me and the boys are supposed to stop the Japs if they land anywhere in the Morobe district – at least that is what the bloody government back in Australia has commanded. Pretty obvious that they don't really have a clue how small and under-equipped we are, or that this is some of the roughest country anywhere on earth. We kind of get the feeling that the government boys think we are some sort of guerrilla force, which

I guess we are. Anyway, changing the subject, how did things go taking your Uncle Paul to Rabaul and back? Is he with Karin?'

Lukas took a deep breath. 'Obviously you didn't hear the news,' he said slowly. 'Uncle Paul would not come back with me. We arrived the day the Japs went ashore and I had to run for Moresby.'

A silence fell between them for a short while as Jack gathered his thoughts. Word had come back that the Japanese were in control of the island and killing any European they could get their hands on. The 2/22 Battalion sent from Australia just prior to invasion and the NGVR detachment already in place had fought as courageously as they could against massively overwhelming odds but had been forced to retreat from the shores of Rabaul into the mountainous, jungle-covered inland. The 2/22 Battalion had virtually ceased to exist on the rolls of the Australian army and its last inane orders from Canberra had been to hold out to the last man – regardless of the fact that no reinforcements or any supplies were to be sent to assist them. It was an act of suicide. Reports said that there were survivors scattered in the jungles and mountains but the Australian government had made no effort to rescue them, such was their overriding panic at the current state of the Japanese southward advance. The unstoppable enemy was expected to land in Port Moresby and then the Australian mainland at any moment. Already Japanese bombers had hit Darwin and other coastal towns of northern Australia.

Jack knew all this and felt empty. It all seemed so

bloody hopeless. The Japanese just continued to roll south and men like Paul were thrown away on missions that were probably just about as hopeless as everything else going on around him. It was a sheer waste.

'I suppose you haven't heard anything?' Jack finally asked, breaking the silence. 'No word on whether Paul got out.'

Lukas shook his head.

'I've heard a rumour that Keith McCarthy is calling for volunteers from our ranks to put together a flotilla to go to New Britain and rescue survivors,' Jack said. 'I think I will be volunteering.'

'That's got to be madness,' Lukas said. 'The waters between us and the eastern islands are crawling with Jap ships and planes. It's suicide.'

'Maybe,' Jack conceded. 'But I think we have to do it. There are cobbers from the NGVR over there still and we can't let them down. Besides, I am kind of hoping I might be able to get word on Paul.'

Lukas stared at a space in the corner of the cabin. 'Looks like I will become part of your navy,' he said with a sigh. 'Figure the *Independence* will be needed. Kind of ironic when you consider that neither the navy, army nor air force will take me because I only have one eye,' he continued with a wry smile. 'But it's okay to volunteer the *Independence* for what bloody well looks like a suicide mission.'

'For anyone else except a Kelly,' Jack said, leaning forward and gripping his son's hands. 'I can't promise that either of us will get out of this war alive but I can promise you that so long as you keep your head down you might have a chance . . . I wish I could say something more reassuring, son, but this is war and all we can do is live from day to day with something called hope.'

Jack felt awkward, wishing that he could have lied and found the words of a philosopher to make the man he loved above all else feel secure. Unfortunately, he had seen first hand over twenty years earlier just how random war was, and who lived and who died was very much down to chance. His secret prayer was that if God existed he would take his life and spare his son.

'I know, Dad,' Lukas replied gently. 'It would take a lot more than the Jap navy to stop me and the *Independence* getting through.'

'Well, I have to go and get the supplies off the old girl,' Jack said, gazing around the cabin with a warm feeling of being home, surrounded by so many wonderful memories of Victoria within the walls of the schooner's hull. 'I have a feeling we will meet up again when McCarthy puts his navy together. I expect the *Independence* to be the flagship of the Kelly navy.'

Lukas rose to see his father topside. They exchanged handshakes and Momis rowed Jack ashore in the schooner's dinghy. The supplies would be offloaded and taken back up to Wau, and from past experience Jack knew that there would not be enough of whatever they were unloading to equip the small force that was expected to face the might of a Japanese invasion in the Morobe province.

The unloading went ahead without mishap and

before the sun sank over the Gulf, Lukas had up anchored, waved his father goodbye and sailed on a course back to Port Moresby. The war in the Pacific was only three months old, Lukas thought as he stood at the helm guiding his ship through the night, and already it seemed that he had lost someone he loved. Lukas doubted that Paul could possibly be alive. War was something for young men like himself, Lukas thought. Not old men.

Leading Seaman Fuji Komine stood at attention in the office that once belonged to an Australian administrator in Rabaul. A smashed portrait of the English King lay on the floor and behind the desk sat Lieutenant Kenshu Chuma, captain of the I–47.

'You have done well,' he said, perusing Fuji's report. 'And I know how hard it has been to live amongst the barbarians in the course of your sacred duty to the Emperor. I have been impressed by your record of service prior to your detachment to our intelligence services. That, and the fact you speak English and know these waters, is why I have a position for you on my boat. I need a good man with your skills for the special patrols I have been assigned, but I will not force you to accept my offer.'

Fuji had come to like this young officer in the course of the I–47 transporting him around Papuan waters. He had graduated from the naval engineering academy at Maizuru and it was well known that only the best of the young officers in the Imperial navy were given command of Japan's submarines. In the cramped and claustrophobic confines of a sub only men of the highest calibre could survive the deadly underwater war. Fuji had always considered returning to one of the great capital ships to continue his service but was now being offered the honour of joining Japan's elite.

'I have no submarine training,' Fuji replied. 'But if you can make it possible for me to join your crew I would be truly honoured, sir.'

'I am aware that you have no training, Leading Seaman Komine, but with your proven record of initiative and courage I am sure you will soon learn the ropes. Your duties will still have much in common with what you have done for our intelligence. I have special tasks to carry out to help defeat the enemy and you are the man I want.'

For the first time since joining the navy Fuji felt appreciated and a feeling of elation swelled in his chest. 'Thank you, sir, I would be honoured to be part of the I–47 in whatever sacred tasks you have been assigned.'

Kenshu, dressed in the only set of neatly ironed dress whites he had aboard his submarine, stood and stiffly shook Fuji's hand. 'Welcome aboard, Leading Seaman Fuji. You will report to the I–47 immediately with whatever you may have with you. You will be allocated your post aboard and looked after by my senior NCO. Do you have any questions?'

'No, sir.'

'Good. You are dismissed.'

Fuji stepped back and snapped a crisp salute before turning on his heel and marching out of the office onto the busy Rabaul street now crowded with Japanese uniforms. How strange life was, he thought as he hurried back to the Chinese quarter to pick up the few possessions he had carried with him on his travels. Fate had brought him to Rabaul to meet once again with a man from his past and kill him, and now he was to become a part of a submarine crew patrolling Papuan waters where his father's boats had plied their trade for the Europeans of the island. The thought of his father – and his mother – suddenly saddened the Japanese sailor. No doubt the Australians would have interned them at best. At worst . . . he did not want to consider that his enemies might act in the same manner that of his own countrymen. At least he could hope that the inherent weakness of the Australians, with their concept of humanity, meant his parents were still alive. Oh, but the day would come when he returned to Port Moresby as a conqueror and could parade before his parents as a hero. What would his father say then? For a moment he wondered about Keela carrying his child. It was a dark and confusing thought, for no respectable Japanese man could ever claim the child as his own. The Motu girl was of an inferior race, below even the Europeans according to the customs of Japan. But Keela had given him moments of such peace and pleasure that Fuji found he could not agree with the dictates of his Japanese heritage.

He reached the lean-to in the Chinese merchant's garden where he had resided while waiting for his comrades to come. He could smell the stench of death and avoided the bloated body of the man who had sneered at him although he took his money. Killing the Chinese merchant had been another promise he had fulfilled. Recovering the small linen bag that held little else than a set of chopsticks, a bowl and a spare set of clothing he headed back to town. At least now he was back in uniform and ready to fight the enemy from the sea. He could fight a war that would bring victory to the Emperor and spread the concept of the Greater East Asia Co-Prosperity Sphere to the enslaved peoples of Asia and the Pacific. If nothing else, Fuji was an optimist as well as a survivor.

NINETEEN

Karl Mann had never been to the South Australian capital of Adelaide before and he was impressed by its broad streets and beautiful architecture. He and his battalion had crossed the Indian Ocean without incident and caught the nostalgic scent of the eucalyptus trees off the coast of Western Australia – at least many of his troops claimed so.

Karl knew that Jack Kelly's birthplace was in South Australia. Being born to an Irish father and German mother was not unusual; many German immigrants had settled in the state when it was still a colony and their beneficial impact on Australian society was most felt in this corner of the continent than anywhere else. Even town names spoke of their presence. Jack had once told him how many of the second generation German immigrants, being so desperate to support Australia, had changed their names from Schmidt to Smith, or Neumann to Newman so that they could enlist in the first AIF to sail overseas and fight on the Western Front. Many of the little war memorials that sprung up after the Great War in towns all over South Australia were inscribed with the anglicised names of men with German blood who had died for the cause of their new country.

The heat of the southern summer was different from that of Papua. Standing on a street in the state's capital Karl could feel it sucking the moisture from him, whereas in Papua it settled on the skin and ran in rivulets. 'Looking forward to getting back to Sydney,' Lieutenant Colin Pitt said beside him. 'Not much in Adelaide except churches and cemeteries.'

The two officers had become close friends on the voyage. Both were platoon commanders who had served in Syria, although Colin Pitt had joined them near the end of the campaign to replace a platoon commander wounded in action. Pitt had worked for a time in Port Moresby as an engineer with the Department of Public Works and this gave the two men a common bond. Pitt was a stocky, heavily muscled man of medium height with a barrel chest. Despite his comparative lack of active service he was well liked and respected by the thirty men he led. The MC riband Karl now wore on his uniform impressed Colin, as did the mystery as to how Karl had earned it. But he liked Karl even more because he was modest about his official recognition from the Crown for services to his country.

'Me,' Karl said, 'I am looking forward to getting up north.'

Colin acknowledged the salute given by a couple of soldiers rambling along the street and gawking at the pretty girls who had left their shops and offices to go to the parks to enjoy a lunch break.

'The Japs have taken Rabaul, Singapore and just about finished the Yanks off in the Philippines,' Colin said. 'You think we will be in time to stop them in New Guinea?'

'I don't know,' Karl replied. 'I only wish we could get up there a bit faster.'

Colin Pitt understood his comrade's wish. Unlike the men of his platoon who hailed from the Australian mainland, Karl was a Papuan at heart and the Japanese advance south was directly threatening his homeland. He knew his mother and sister were in Townsville but neither he nor his family had received word of his father. His mother had written that Paul had stayed back in Moresby after they had been evacuated. He was supposed to return to the plantation and carry on with production but from what she could gather, Karl's father had last been seen sailing with Lukas Kelly from Port Moresby to a destination that was classified by the government. Karin had made frantic inquires of the authorities in Townsville, but had come up against a stony wall of silence.

The letter had been brought aboard Karl's ship off Western Australia and since then he had been able to make a telephone call to his mother, whose joy on the phone turned naturally to tears of relief to have her only son home and alive. A chance to visit his mother and sister was another reason Karl was impatient to travel north with his unit. He had learned at a briefing by the company commander to his officers that they would travel east from Adelaide to Melbourne and then on to Sydney by rail. From Sydney, so ran the rumours, they would be sent to Queensland to carry out training before being shipped to New Guinea to counter the Japanese advance.

At the moment the only Australian units facing the best of the Japanese land forces were a few militia units of poorly equipped and under-trained young soldiers barely old enough to shave. The situation was grim and Australia was fighting for its very life. The Australian Labor Prime Minister, John Curtin, had defied the imperious British leader, Winston Churchill, and had ordered the bulk of his best fighting units home to face the new threat. Curtin had also broken with tradition by looking across the Pacific to America for assistance as the two nations shared the edges of the great expense of water.

Karl was worried about his father and felt helpless that he was at the far end of Australia, unable to make his own inquires as to his whereabouts. For now there was little he could do until the battalion was sent north and then hopefully on to the jungles of Papua and New Guinea where he would be at home.

• • •

Any message at the battalion orderly room for Karl to see the commanding officer immediately was bound to cause a feeling of apprehension. The CO was a distant man and for him to order a mere junior officer to report to him was unusual. Karl made a quick mental inventory of duties he may have neglected in the course of journeying from Syria to Adelaide. The orderly room clerk cast the young officer a sympathetic look. 'Might not be too bad, sir,' he said, typing up another request for boots for the quartermaster. 'I can tell the adj that you are here.'

'Thanks, Corp,' Karl said in a hollow voice.

The corporal slipped away and knocked on the adjutant's door. A quick, muffled conversation was followed by the adjutant, a captain, appearing in the orderly room.

'Lieutenant Mann,' the young captain said, 'the CO is ready to see you now.'

Karl hoped his uniform was up to inspection standard when he followed the adjutant into the CO's spacious office. He came to a halt and snapped a smart, regulation salute.

The CO was a full colonel and a man who had seen action in Palestine with the Light Horse in the last war. He was tall and patrician in appearance with a shiny bald spot on his head, and on his chest he wore the military ribands which demonstrated his distinguished military career.

'Lieutenant Mann, sir,' the adjutant said, and without asking the CO's permission, took a chair at a corner of the room. Karl guessed that the working relationship between the two men was such that a liberty could be taken without disrespect to the senior officer of the battalion.

'Stand easy, Mr Mann,' the CO said kindly, placing his fountain pen on the shiny desk and looking up from the papers on his desk. 'I have summoned you because of an unusual signal that came through to BHQ yesterday from Ceylon. It seems when you were detached from us in the Middle East you made some interesting friends,' he added with just a touch of mirth. 'And those same friends of yours – from God knows what cloak and dagger department – have requested that I ask you to volunteer for some secret unit in Victoria.'

Karl stood stunned at his CO's words and glanced at the adjutant who sat in the chair with his legs crossed.

'I suppose if it is secret then I cannot ask what I am volunteering for, sir?'

'I suppose you are right, Mr Mann,' the CO replied with a wry smile at the corner of his lips. 'But I can tell you that by volunteering you will probably beat the battalion to New Guinea.'

The thought of getting to Papua as soon as he could appealed to Karl. It could mean seeing his family sooner rather than later. All life was a gamble and war the worst one of all. Karl was a soldier used to quick decisions.

'Whatever it is, sir, I will volunteer.'

The CO glanced at his adjutant, who then nodded back at Karl. 'You are sure of your decision?' he asked. 'I personally would not like to lose an officer I consider one of my best and brightest but would only do so in the interests of the service.'

'Yes, sir,' Karl replied, without the conviction he knew he should have displayed before a senior officer. 'I am sure the army has something in mind for me. It certainly did in Syria.'

Without another word the CO signed a paper before him and held it out to the adjutant, who left his chair to step up to the desk smartly. The adjutant held out his hand to shake Karl's. 'I concur with the boss,' he said. 'Our loss is the army's good fortune – wherever you go.'

Karl took the hand in a hard grip.

The CO stood up and also extended his hand. 'Tonight we shall have your farewell in the mess. It seems you are to take a train to Melbourne tomorrow night and report to military district HQ for further orders. Good luck, Mr Mann, and I pray that we meet again.'

'Thank you, sir,' Karl said. 'I am going to miss the battalion. It has become my home.'

The CO knew the words were sincere. The battalion meant mates.

'Well, you will have a lot to do before you leave us, clearances and all that, so I won't hold you up any longer except to say that you may not be in good shape when you do get on the train. Oh, did I mention that you will be reporting to your new posting as a captain? The orders came through this morning and your promotion is effective as from twenty-four hundred hours tonight. I would like to be the first to say it is a well-earned and overdue recognition of your services to your country. Congratulations, Captain Mann,' the CO added with a broad grin. 'So you will be shouting the mess the first round tonight.'

Karl was stunned by the news of his promotion and knew his farewell in the officers' mess would be a night he would rather forget in the morning but remember with fond thoughts in the future. He saluted the CO and marched out of the office with the adjutant behind him.

'I would like to add my congratulations on your promotion,' the normally aloof adjutant said, uncharacteristically slapping Karl on the back and handing him two extra star pips to make three on each shoulder epaulette. 'I don't know what you have volunteered for, Karl, but whatever it is, be bloody careful.'

'Wish I knew a bit more,' Karl conceded. 'But all will be revealed when I reach Melbourne, I suppose.'

Lieutenant Colonel Keith McCarthy and Lieutenant Commander Eric Feldt were two remarkable men in the right place at the right time. McCarthy was a soldier whilst Feldt a navy man assigned as the director of the coast watchers – a courageous band of men who worked behind enemy lines, reporting on Japanese movements and strength. Along with their loyal native comrades the coast watchers were always in constant danger from betrayal or discovery and many lost their lives to a brutal enemy.

So it was that McCarthy made the suggestion to

Feldt that they organise a few coastal boats and slip over to New Britain to rescue any survivors from the NGVR and the 2/22 Battalion. The fact that New Britain and its surrounding waters were dominated by the Japanese navy and air units did not even come into the equation when volunteers from the NGVR were called up for the rescue operation. Without hesitation they came forward: tough former gold prospectors and others who had worked the frontier of New Guinea and Papua, men who had lived with danger all their lives and saw the proposed operation as little more than going into the dreaded Kukukuku country in the early days between wars. Jack Kelly was one of the men who stepped forward.

'I have a schooner currently being skippered by my son,' Jack said standing, leaning with his hand on a wooden table in a tin shed which had once been a mining office high in the mountains of Wau but was now an NGVR HQ room. Outside the air was crisp and clear. Mist lay in the valleys below and the birds of the forest provided a sweet song around the isolated fortress west of the Japanese.

'I am offering the services of the *Independence*, Mick. I have a mate over there and I promised his missus a long time ago I would never let him down. So the boat is going even if you do not give approval.'

Major Mick Campbell sat back in his chair to avoid the chin thrust forward. 'You know this is an NGVR op, Jack. We don't take on civvies.'

'Then I will enlist my son as an NGVR rifleman,' Jack said smugly, leaning back from the table.

'Didn't your son lose an eye in some aeroplane accident?' Major Campbell asked with a frown.

'Cobber,' Jack said with a pained expression, 'if the NGVR were going by the standards of the bloody army in Australia none of us would have passed the medicals. Besides, he is young and fit and one eye has not stopped him doing his work running supplies up to us in the Gulf.'

Mick Campbell sighed in resignation. 'Okay, Jack, but don't put down that he only has one eye on his enlistment papers.'

'Not a problem,' Jack answered. 'He has a glass eye – the best the Yanks could turn out – and no one will know the difference.'

'Okay,' the major agreed. 'The *Independence* is in. Just leave the details with the orderly room and I will give you a cooee when we are ready to use her.'

'Thanks, Mick,' Jack said, snapping a smart salute at the rim of his slouch hat. 'Young Lukas will make a bloody good soldier and you won't regret his enlistment.'

'Like his old man,' Major Mick Campbell replied with a wry grin. 'So take some time off and go down to Moresby and tell young Lukas that he is now part of our navy. We have a flight out tomorrow and I need someone to deliver dispatches to HQ.'

'Thanks, Mick.'

Jack left the tin shed and stopped to consider the situation. He had known that he'd be able to get his way with the major who had once worked in his company managing his gold dredging operations in the Morobe district. The great gap in rank between sergeant and major was not even a consideration between men who had trusted and respected each other long before the army separated them with its hierarchical structure.

Iris found the hidden radio and the code books that confirmed that Sen was indeed working for the Japanese. She sat back on her heels and stared at the battered suitcase containing the apparatus. Since the time she had seen Sen using the radio she had wondered what she should do. For now she would think about its implications for her life, Iris thought as she carefully replaced the suitcase in its hiding place beneath a panel in the wall. What Iris did not know was that any tampering with the suitcase left a trace. A few hours after she replaced it Sen discovered that the tiny thread of very fine fishing line was broken. His secret was no longer his alone. Someone had removed the set and then replaced it.

A chill of fear possessed the Chinese spy. Had it been one of the native staff? Sen sat back in a chair, staring at the incriminating evidence. Whoever had removed the radio had to have seen him conceal it at some stage, he concluded. And if that had happened then they must have suspected that he was transmitting to the Japanese.

Iris! The thought seemed to come naturally to Sen. She was a resourceful woman to have survived so long, but if she knew of his covert activity then why had she not done something at this stage? A colder chill came to Sen: because she had not had recent opportunity to contact the Australian authorities in Port Moresby, he told himself.

He walked to a window in his office and gazed at the garden below where butterflies flitted amongst the flowering shrubs. Sen cursed the day so many years earlier when he had taken what the Christians called the thirty pieces of silver from the Kaiser's intelligence services.

The wounds throbbed and Paul Mann feared infection. Weeks of keeping on the move with Rifleman Sandy Robinson down the Gazelle Peninsula to the southern end of the island of New Britain had taken a toll on both men.

Sandy Robinson was in his early twenties and had been a clerk with the government administration before enlisting in the NGVR. Cut off from his platoon in the retreat back into the island, the Australian soldier had stumbled on the site of the massacre and rescued Paul. It was the optimism of the soldier's youth that kept Paul struggling through the sweating days and chilling nights. Sandy was always alert to the enemy now prowling the island in search of survivors, whereas Paul could have just sat down and given in to his wounds which had begun to heal although not as quickly as he wanted. Sandy had cared as well as he could for Paul by bathing the wounds and covering them with makeshift bandages torn from a spare shirt he had in his meagre kit. He had washed the bandages whenever possible and used them again but with the lack of food, sleep and medicine Paul knew he was at constant risk of infection in the humid jungle.

Now in the highlands Paul sat with his back against a rainforest giant and stared bleakly at the ocean in the far distance. Unshaven, dirty, gaunt and in rags, his hopes to continue evading the Japanese patrols diminished with each passing day even though the young soldier had been able to scrounge enough food for them from friendly villagers en route.

The cautious approaches to the villagers had been carried out by Sandy as betrayal to the enemy was a real fear. Their luck held though and along with the food generously given, the villagers were also sometimes able to give Sandy snippets of information as to the whereabouts of other possible groups of survivors. Sadly, each piece of information proved incorrect.

So the two men trudged south, using nothing more than their survival instinct to distance themselves from Rabaul and the surrounding districts, where a build-up of Japanese forces was creating a major Pacific base of operations.

The crack of a twig or sudden silence in the rainforest would cause a rush of fear. Sandy with his .303 rifle was ready to go down fighting rather than be captured and executed. Luck continued to be with them and Sandy calculated that they were halfway down the island on the western side.

'How you feeling?' Sandy asked, squatting beside Paul and leaning on his rifle.

'I can keep going,' Paul replied with a weak smile. 'Maybe one more day,' he said.

'Got to come across one of those coast watch fellows sooner or later,' Sandy said, scratching at his neck where his beard grew. 'When that happens he can arrange to get us off this bloody island and home.'

Paul had been reassured every day by the young man that they would find a coast watcher, but how this would happen Sandy was unsure. The days had blurred into weeks and time had lost meaning as they just kept trudging on their course south, always attempting to catch glimpses of the shimmering sea to spot a ship flying a friendly flag. But the only ships spotted had been those flying the Japanese ensign. It was as if the Australian navy had ceased to exist, although the occasional American aircraft spotted high in the sky reassured them they weren't completely alone.

Sandy was just about to rise when Paul seized his arm. 'Don't move,' he hissed, staring over Sandy's shoulder. 'We have visitors.'

Sandy let his hand slip to the pistol grip of the rifle, his finger on the trigger. 'Japs?' he asked quietly.

'Not Japs,' Paul replied. 'Natives. Four of them, but they are armed. They look like native police boys.'

They were well away from any known villages and the appearance of the faces in the bush was ominous. Weak and exhausted from the arduous trek, the men would be easy targets for tribesmen who had lived for years beyond the frontier. The threat that they may pose was equally as dangerous as that from the Japanese. Sandy turned slowly to face the four men standing only ten paces away. The first thing he noticed was that they all carried Australian-issue rifles and wore tattered remnants of the native constabulary uniform.

'You that Paul Mann fellow?' one of the natives asked in pidgin. 'Coast watch fellow sent us to bring you to him,' the speaker continued. 'Local natives told us you were in this place.'

Paul was curious as to how the native constable knew his name. His unasked question would be answered soon enough when the former native police led the two exhausted men to meet the mysterious coast watcher.

Lukas Kelly was stunned to find himself sworn into the NGVR. His dream to carry arms in the defence of his country had come true. Now he stood proudly with his father in the Moresby hotel amidst many others wearing the army uniform of the NGVR.

'But what about the medical?' he asked his father as they stood at the bar.

'Kind of got the papers fixed for that,' Jack answered, swigging beer from a tumbler. 'Seems when you did your medical you had no trouble seeing from your left eye. All you have to do is remember to wear the glass one.'

Lukas accepted that his father had the power to falsify papers. So now he was Rifleman Lukas Kelly. Up until now his military experience had been with the army cadets as a school boy. His father had explained that the main reason for Luke's enlistment onto the regimental roll book was to give him legitimacy in the forthcoming operation to rescue survivors of the 2/22 Battalion and the NGVR from New Britain. At least his enlistment also made him a lawful combatant if he was unfortunate enough to fall into Japanese hands, although whether this would make any difference to his treatment as a prisoner of war was hard to say.

'So when and where do I report for duty?' Lukas asked, pouring another glass of beer from the bottle on the counter.

'You will get that information in due time. For now all you have to do is stay with the *Independence* until I contact you. Just remember that your old man is a sergeant whilst you are a lowly rifleman,' Jack added with a grin. 'McCarthy has been ferrying Yank missionaries and downed pilots between Finschhafen and Lae for the last couple of weeks but Jap activities are closing down the escape routes. What you must keep under your hat is that the assembly point will be Luther Haven at Umboi Island in a few days time. From there we intend to cross to New Britain and pick up those we can.'

Lukas sucked in his breath. The crossing was almost suicidal. 'Do you think we will find Uncle Paul?' he asked.

Jack stared at the bottle on the counter and the raucous din of voices around him muffled his reply. 'I bloody well hope so.'

Both men fell into a silence. On the morrow Jack was to return to the highlands to rejoin his unit. He had been able to wrangle extra leave in Port

Moresby to liaise with his son to procure the services of the *Independence*. It was also an opportunity to spend some time with him and the schooner away from the edge of the battle area as it crept closer to Wau. For now they would drink together and strengthen that special bond of father and son. Tomorrow was an unknown in their lives and Jack was very aware that by enlisting his son he was putting his life on the line.

TWENTY

It took two days and nights travelling on foot with the native policemen for Paul Mann and Sandy Robinson to reach the coast watcher's camp, where they were welcomed by a middle-aged man wearing civilian clothes and a battered old hat. A bolt action .303 rifle was slung over his shoulder.

'Irvin Rockman,' he said, thrusting out his hand to Paul. 'I heard you blokes were in the area. Not much gets past my boys.'

Paul accepted the gesture from the coast watcher, a man with searching grey eyes, a broken nose and an unshaven tanned face. Although he was thin he appeared fit. 'It is good to meet you,' Paul replied as Irvin turned to Sandy.

'You with the NGVR?' he asked. 'Heard some of your mob were wandering around the scrub.'

'Rifleman Sandy Robinson,' the NGVR rifleman

said, shaking hands with Irvin. 'I was cut off just after the Japs landed around Rabaul and haven't seen any of my mates since.'

Paul glanced around the campsite that overlooked the ocean below. It was well concealed in the hillside of thick rainforest and he could see blackened cooking pots and a lean-to shelter made from saplings. It had a temporary look about it. Under the lean-to Paul could see a heavy AWA radio transmitter/receiver. The native police moved quietly and cautiously around the camp, alert to any subtle changes in the sounds emanating from the jungle surrounding them. Each native man was armed with a Lee Enfield .303 rifle which was – as Paul noted with a soldier's eye – kept in immaculate condition. The former native policemen appeared confident and formidable which inspired a sense of security in Paul after the dangerous weeks of trekking south with Sandy.

'Ought to get a brew on for you blokes,' Irvin said with a broad smile. 'Doubt that you would have had much opportunity to have a cuppa in the last few weeks.'

Paul and Sandy nodded.

'See you have a few cuts and scratches,' Irvin continued, eyeing Paul's old wounds which were still oozing under the dirty bandages. 'I'll get one of the boys to rustle up some clean bandages and antiseptic but we won't be able to hang around for much longer. My intelligence sources tell me that the Japs are onto me and sending a patrol this way soon. So we will have to go walkabout again.'

In no time Paul and Sandy had a steaming mug of sweetened black tea in their hands and Paul's wounds had been cleaned and redressed. He sat with his back to a tree and luxuriated in the effect of the hot tea on his stomach. Irvin was going about a well-practised routine of breaking camp and dismantling the valuable radio for transport to another location. His men knew their roles and there was little fuss in the preparations to move. Sandy had volunteered his services while Paul rested recovering a little of his strength for the strenuous trek ahead. A combination of age and his debilitating wounds had slowed him down and he prayed that he would not cause the coast watcher any delay in reaching his next position.

When Paul was finished with the tea Irvin strode across the small clearing to him. 'You up to a bit of a walk?' he asked in a concerned voice.

'I can keep up,' Paul replied. 'If I cannot I will stay behind.'

Irvin handed Paul an old revolver. 'Keep this with you,' he said. 'I've only got twelve rounds for it but it's better than nothing.'

Paul accepted the pistol. 'Thank you, my friend,' he said. 'I promise that if I choose to remain behind at any stage I will use all twelve rounds to good effect.'

'I heard that you were an officer in the last war with the Kaiser's army,' Irvin said. 'So was I. Where did you serve?'

'Western Front,' Paul answered. 'I met Jack Kelly there.'

'I know Jack,' Irvin said. 'Good bloke.'

'What is going to happen to Sandy and me?' Paul asked.

'I don't exactly know,' Irvin answered, scratching under his beard at his neck. 'There is a move to evacuate those who have evaded the Japs from some points to be secured, but none that I know of in my area. Either you have to turn around and go north to meet up with the others escaping or you remain with me until something can be worked out.'

'So it is not looking good for us to get off the island,' Paul replied gloomily.

'Looks that way, old chap,' Irvin corroborated. 'Not much I can do except report that you are alive and then it's a matter of waiting until the people in Moresby make a decision to get you off one way or the other.'

Irvin signalled for his party to move out. One of the native coast watchers led the way with his rifle in his hands. The report from the nearest village had spoken of a Japanese patrol of at least platoon strength, around thirty men armed with rifles, automatic weapons and a small mortar. Irvin Rockman knew that his smaller and less well-armed section was no match for a confrontation with the Japanese. Their only hope of survival was to melt into the jungle until the Japanese tired of the chase. And that he did, with Paul and Sandy in tow and the Japanese patrol a mere two hours behind them.

• • •

Sweat poured down Paul's face and stung his eyes. He was on his hands and knees, inching his way up a steep slope, using tree roots as handgrips. Ahead of him was a native coast watcher working hand over hand to negotiate the slope. How much more could he take, Paul wondered over and over again. They had been travelling for almost seven hours with little let-up in country that seemed to be nothing but jungle and deep ravines and sharp ridges. Then finally he was at the top of the gully and lying on his stomach, sweat soaking his shirt and trousers, and Sandy standing above him. Irvin was already ahead with his men who had hauled the wooden crates used to transport the cumbersome radio set up the steep, scrubby slope to the bush-covered ridge above.

'I'll give you a hand,' Sandy said in a weary voice, stretching out his hand to Paul. 'Irvin says we don't have very far to go before we pitch camp for the night. I –'

Sandy's voice was cut short by the stuttering of a Nambu light machine gun and he suddenly pitched forward with a startled expression on his face.

Paul's old military instincts screamed *ambush*! The Japanese had somehow got in front of them. The chatter of the rapid firing was joined by the blast of rifles and the screams of men joining the battle on either side of them.

Sandy fell on Paul, who dragged him back down the slope to avoid the hail of bullets ploughing up the ground at the lip of the slope. Below the slope Paul and Sandy were safe from the line of fire.

'Jesus, it hurts,' Sandy groaned, fighting the almost

unbearable pain of his numerous bullet wounds. He lay on his back and Paul could see where the Nambu had stitched a close pattern of wounds through Sandy's hips and stomach. It seemed that he had taken the full volley when the gun opened up, and had Paul been standing then he too would have been hit. Grass and leaves rained down on both men as they lay below the ridge.

'Oh, God it hurts!' Sandy screamed, no longer able to contain the terrible pain. 'For God's sake Paul, do something!'

Paul realised that he had his pistol in his hand. As the sound of the close-quarter fighting continued on the ridge, he could hear Irvin calling orders to his men. They were probably about twenty yards away in the thicket of saplings clinging to the ridge. At least he was still alive but the situation was confusing. How many Japanese were they up against? Was this the end for them all? The machine gun continued to fire on them in bursts.

Paul glanced down at Sandy's pain-wrecked face staring up at him. He had seen similar wounds many times before and knew that under the current conditions his friend would die an agonising death. He had to turn off all emotion and not think about Sandy as his friend anymore but merely as a human in extreme pain pleading for the means to avoid the inevitable prolonged suffering.

Paul pulled the trigger of the revolver and the bullet entered Sandy's head, causing a fine mist of red to shower Paul's hand. 'I am sorry, friend,' Paul muttered as Sandy stared up at the sky with sightless eyes.

He placed his hand on Sandy's face as a gesture of respect for the man who had once saved his life. There was nothing else he could do and he expected that he would probably be soon joining his doomed comrade in death.

The silence came as suddenly as the late afternoon, and with pistol pushed forward Paul scanned the lip of the slope for movement.

'Hey! You blokes all right?' Paul heard Irvin's voice call.

'Over here,' Paul replied.

A few moments later he saw Irvin's worried face appear at the top of the slope.

'Sandy?' Irvin asked, and Paul shook his head.

'We have to keep moving,' Irvin said. 'My boys got the Jap MG crew but two others escaped. Looks like we stumbled onto a forward scouting party so the rest won't be far behind after the ruckus we made.'

Paul stripped Sandy of his identification tags, rifle and spare ammunition. There was no time to bury him. The jungle would be his grave.

'What happened?' Paul asked when he was on top of the ridge.

'The little yellow bastards sprang an ambush on us,' Irvin replied bitterly. 'But they bit off more than they could chew with my boys. Buka, over there . . .' Irvin said, indicating a black face baring betel-stained teeth and holding up two Japanese soldiers' heads, 'was able to outflank the Jap gun crew and finish them off with his machete. He gets to keep the Jap machine gun as a prize for his prowess. It seems we must have walked through their ambush site and they only woke up to us when they saw Sandy, the poor bastard.'

Paul almost pitied the dead Japanese soldiers. He wondered how they had felt, looking up at the big native warrior wielding his razor-sharp machete above his head before he decapitated them.

'We have to get this show on the road,' Irvin said.

Paul hefted Sandy's rifle into his hands. He hoped that he would get a chance to use it on the Japanese and avenge his friend's death – and assuage his guilt. There was nothing else he could have done under the circumstances, he continued to reassure himself. But he had lost a friend who had saved his life and now the Japanese would pay.

Momis had a fever and lay groaning in his bunk below decks. Lukas took his temperature with the thin thermometer and ascertained it was well above 97 degrees. He could only guess that his leading seaman was down with a bout of malaria.

Lukas consulted his charts and plotted the position of the schooner just north of the port of Morobe in the Huon Gulf. The weather was fair and the sailing good. He picked up the dividers and calculated that he could be in the township within hours before sunset. At least he might find medical aid for his leading hand. Lukas bawled up orders not to spare the sail.

• • •

Late that afternoon, Lukas waited patiently on the verandah of the hospital staring out at a grove of palm trees rustling gently in the breeze. A nursing sister appeared in her clean white dress and starched nursing bonnet.

'I am Sister Megan Cain,' she said when Lukas turned away from his view of the countryside. 'Your man should come through but I will be keeping him in overnight to see how he is in the morning.'

Lukas was attracted by the bright blue eyes and warm smile of the young nursing sister. She had a pretty if not beautiful face, spattered with freckles. Her lips were full and under the nursing hat Lukas could see that her hair was a lustrous chestnut colour. Her hips were broad and her bottom well rounded without being what he would consider fat. She exuded a sensuality he sensed immediately and guessed her age to be a couple of years younger than his. 'Thank you for your help, Sister,' Lukas mumbled.

'So it is your boat in the harbour,' Megan commented, keeping eye contact. 'I love yachts.'

'The *Independence* is a bit more than a yacht,' Lukas bridled. 'She is a blue water trading ship.'

'I did not mean to cast aspersions on your boat, Mr Kelly,' Megan hastened. 'I just meant that she appears to be a fine seagoing craft.'

'No aspersions taken about my really big yacht,' Lukas replied with a slow smile. 'Maybe we could drop rank and exchange first names and you could come down to join me in a late afternoon drink on deck.'

His brazen approach had unsettled the nursing sister. There was just the slightest flush under her light tan and freckles.

'What is your first name, Mr Kelly?'

'Lukas,' he replied, offering his hand. 'Or some people call me Luke – whatever you prefer.'

Megan took the firm but gentle grip. 'I think Lukas sounds very dignified,' she said. 'And I will accept your rather forward offer to have a drink with you when I go off my shift.'

Lukas was surprised at her acceptance and immediately wondered why he had made the offer so impulsively. Whatever it was, it kept a smile on his face as he walked back to the jetty and his really big yacht.

Megan drove down to the wharf in the hospital's car and came aboard just as the sun was sinking below the jungle-covered hills behind the tiny township of Morobe. She was wearing a light skirt that flowed around her legs, and her hair flowed over her shoulders. The red lipstick she wore accentuated the sensuality of her lips and Lukas could see what had attracted him to her in the first place.

'Gin and tonic?' he asked as he helped her step aboard. He had changed into the best pair of slacks and short-sleeved shirt he owned and hoped that his clothes did not smell too strongly of mothballs.

'G and T will be fine,' Megan answered when she was aboard, scanning the schooner with an appreciative eye. 'Where is the rest of your crew?'

'I, uh, gave them some shore leave to go and buy some betel nut,' Lukas answered, hoping that he did not sound guilty of plotting for them be alone. Despite her sensuality Megan Cain did not have the air of a woman who would abide any clumsy sexual overtures. 'They will be returning later this evening. I had my cook leave us with a curry and rice for supper – if that is okay with you.'

'Curry and rice sounds fine with me,' Megan said, turning her attention back to Lukas who was standing just a little bit awkwardly by the mast. 'So where do we park ourselves?'

Lukas indicated the area at the aft of the boat where they could watch the sunset. Megan made herself comfortable while Lukas brought up the bottle of Gilbey's and a bottle of tonic water which he poured into a couple of glass tumblers.

'To the return of peace and good company with equally good food and conversation,' Megan toasted, raising her glass to Lukas who responded by raising his own and saying, 'Cheers.'

'So, tell me all about yourself,' Megan said, sipping the slightly bitter drink. 'And don't leave out how you have come to look like some dashing Caribbean pirate with that eye patch. You strike me as a man with a past full of adventure.'

Lukas was hardly aware of time passing. They talked into the night with the ease of two people who had known each other for years. Lukas told his story only when Megan delicately drew it out of him. In turn, Lukas learned that Megan was the daughter of a wealthy Queensland squatter from the

Cloncurry district. She had pursued a nursing career, as was traditional for many of the daughters of wealthy landed gentry in the Outback. Eventually she would return to the district, where she would be expected to marry the eligible son of another property owner.

'I don't have anyone in mind back home,' she said. 'I am going up to Finschhafen next week to the Lutheran mission station. Will you be sailing up that way in the foreseeable future?' she asked.

Lukas suddenly smelled his unattended curry burning on the stove in the galley. Without hearing her pointed question he muttered a curse and dashed for the galley where the curried meat had turned into charcoal. Lukas moaned at his incompetence and took the heavy pan from the stove to dump the contents in a bin. 'Sorry about dinner,' he called up from below. 'How about a corned meat sandwich?' he offered lamely. 'I make the best corned beef sandwiches in the Pacific.'

On cue, Lukas appeared above deck carrying two huge corned beef and chutney sandwiches on a cracked plate. Megan accepted his apology for a meal with good humour and Lukas forgot the question she had asked. They had just finished the sandwiches and a strong mug of tea when Lukas's crewmen returned, mumbling their greetings shyly to Megan. Lukas wished that for just once in their lives they had disobeyed him and returned late. Their punctuality meant escorting Megan back to the hospital. Perhaps he would not see her again for a long time – if ever.

'Well,' Megan said with a sigh. 'It has been a truly

wonderful evening, Lukas. I wish I was sailing with you to all those exotic ports you must visit.'

Lukas laughed. 'The only exotic ports the *Independence* will be sailing to are full of troops waiting for supplies – not much else. I doubt that you would want to be going with me to those places.'

Megan placed her hand on his arm. 'I think sailing with you would have been reward enough,' she said quietly. 'But for now I must return to go on duty on the late shift. I hope I get to see you in the morning when you come for your boy.'

'I will walk you to the car,' Lukas said, acutely aware of her touch. 'And I will see you in the morning.'

He walked Megan to the car and took her hand formally. It was a moment he did not want to end and his hand lingered in hers. 'Until tomorrow,' he said, reluctantly releasing her hand and opening the door of the sedan.

'Goodnight, Lukas Kelly,' Megan said, putting the car into motion and driving away into the night.

Lukas stood on the wharf, watching her disappear. Shaking his head in bewilderment at the hours they had just spent together, he walked back to his schooner. Megan had a serene beauty that could smite a man's heart, he thought when he reached the rail of the *Independence* and hauled himself aboard.

When Lukas came to collect Momis he was disappointed. Momis was weak but well enough to return to the schooner. However, Megan had been called out in the night to attend to a native woman in a nearby village. Lukas would have liked to have stayed in port but there was a war on and it was time for him to set sail back into dangerous waters.

TWENTY-ONE

Lukas was assigned his first task of ferrying Lutheran missionaries from Finschhafen to the port of Lae. Along with the missionaries, the small fleet of coastal boats mobilised from Papuan waters also picked up downed pilots and civilians who had made their way to nominated pick-up points.

Lukas was acutely aware that it was becoming increasingly dangerous working in the tropical seas off Papua and New Guinea as the Japanese navy manoeuvred to cut off the sea lanes. With his father's help Lukas had been able to spirit an old .303 Lewis machine gun aboard to beef up protection for his schooner. It came with a case of extra rounds of drum-like magazines of ammunition and Momis had taken over the role of the schooner's machine gunner with relish. Jack had instructed the Solomon Islander in its maintenance and use and Momis proved to be a keen student. Out at sea he had been allowed one precious magazine of ammunition to practise his marksmanship on tins tossed overboard into the wake of the *Independence* and after half a magazine Momis had proved to be a natural shot, with the tins disappearing under a hail of controlled bursts from the gun. A slap on the back from Lukas brought forth a proud smile of healthy teeth stained by betel nut. The machine gun was fixed to the bow railings where it could be swivelled to confront an aerial threat or cover shore landings, and Momis was never very far from his new love.

Off Finschhafen, Lukas anchored the boat to meet with a small dinghy motoring out from the crowded wharf, which was occupied by other coastal boats also taking aboard refugees. He stood at the portside to assist the passengers being brought to him. Beside the helmsman, a uniformed NGVR man, there were only three other people – two young women and a middle-aged man.

When the dinghy drew closer Lukas could see that one of the young women was a striking, fair-skinned beauty whose long, lustrous dark hair was piled up under a broad-brimmed straw hat. The other he recognised as Sister Megan Cain, and immediately broke into a broad smile of unconcealed delight, waving to her.

'You young Lukas?' the helmsman of the dinghy called up to the deck of the *Independence* when it drew alongside.

'That's me,' Lukas replied as the engine in the dinghy was turned off and the small boat drifted alongside the schooner.

'Cameron Fleay,' the NGVR soldier called back cheerily. 'I heard from your old man that you were stupid enough to sign up with us. How's the eye?' Lukas flinched – out of habit he was wearing his black leather eye patch. 'Got to be the worst-kept secret in Papua and New Guinea,' Cameron continued with a broad grin. 'Don't worry, half the blokes I know in the unit should be in an old people's home. Give us a hand aboard.'

Lukas hurried to throw down a short rope ladder and the first of the dinghy's passengers scrambled aboard with grace and agility. Carrying a small, battered cardboard suitcase, the pretty young woman with the lustrous dark hair turned to assist Megan and then the older man on deck. As she climbed aboard, the wind whipped the hat from her head, causing her hair to flow over her shoulders.

Very independent, Lukas thought when she politely declined his assistance with a smile. Finally, Cameron came aboard after securing the dinghy to the schooner.

'Should introduce your passengers,' he said, grasping Lukas's hand in an iron grip. 'This is Pastor Schmidt from South Aussie. He has a Lutheran mission station up country.'

Lukas took the man's hand. 'Just call me Lukas,' he said cheerily. 'I don't go much for last names aboard the *Independence*.'

'Sister Cain is from Brisbane and was working at the local hospital.'

'So I finally get to sail to all those exotic ports you visit,' Megan said smiling, taking Lukas' hand in hers without shaking hands. 'And I hope you have improved your cooking skills since we last met.'

'Good to see you again,' Lukas replied. 'I was kind of hoping that it would not be the last time after treating you to one of my burnt offerings.'

'Gather you two have already met,' Cameron said with a grin. 'And this is Miss Ilsa Stahl, she is a Yank correspondent for some paper back in her country, but needs a lift back to Port Moresby.'

Lukas turned to the dark-haired girl and was met by a frank appraisal. 'Nice to make your acquaintance,' he said.

'Well, I have to get back to the wharf,' Cameron said. 'Next time I see your old man I will tell him I saw you in the company of a couple of beaut-looking sheilas.'

Lukas found himself blushing under his deep tan. When the NGVR soldier was over the side and the engine of his dinghy kicked over, Lukas gave orders to Momis to sail. It did not pay to be too long in waters where boats congregated. The armed Japanese recon flights were constant and the target tempting to Rabaul-based aircraft.

'If you come with me,' Lukas said to his three passengers, 'I will show you where you will be quartered for the voyage to Lae.'

It was strange, Lukas thought, showing the three to the closed-off bunks, that two of his passengers had German names. Lukas had heard that the Australian government had replaced interned German missionaries with Australians of German descent in the

Lutheran Church, and when the pastor thanked Lukas he did so with a broad Australian accent.

Megan also thanked him. 'I have to admit that I missed your company and conversation after you sailed away,' she said with a bright smile that highlighted the sparkle of her eyes. 'And I have had the good fortune to meet your father since you and I met in Morobe. He was in charge of a party to oversee our evacuation. You are very much like him.'

'Kind of hope not,' Lukas grinned. 'I heard that he was a real rascal in his early days around Papua and New Guinea. Well, I should let you settle in and when you are up to it I will have one of my boys brew up a cuppa.'

Lukas next checked on Ilsa, who had been given his cabin. Having given up his quarters he would sleep on deck or beside the chart table. He knocked lightly on the door and entered on her invitation. She was unpacking her small suitcase and turned to meet his eyes. 'I just thought I would tell you that when you are settled in I am putting on a billy of tea and some sandwiches.'

'Thank you, Lukas,' she answered. 'You are very kind.'

Lukas detected a trace of German behind her American accent and on an impulse he asked in German, 'Which part of Germany are you from?'

Startled, Ilsa answered in her native tongue. 'I was born in Munich but I am an American citizen. How is it that you – an Australian – speak German so well?'

Lukas switched back to English. 'I had a good

teacher,' he said with a sad smile and did not elaborate. A day did not pass that Lukas did not think of his Aunt Karin and her family. 'When you are ready you are welcome to join me in the main cabin for tea.'

Lukas went above deck to supervise the changing of sails and oversee their course south. The ocean was at its best and the winds were in their favour. Momis had the helm but kept his eye on the Lewis gun mounted at the bow. Lukas sensed that his employee, who was more like a friend, was hoping that a Japanese aircraft might turn up so he could get a shot at it. But Lukas prayed that their trip would be uneventful. He knew they had little chance against a fully armed fighter plane or a bomber determined to sink them. Their only hope was to sail undetected in these dangerous waters.

Satisfied with the sailing, Lukas went again below decks, where his three passengers had gathered for sandwiches and tea. He was already scheming how he would get Megan alone so they could pick up where they had left off in Morobe. There was just something about the woman that made him feel good whenever his thoughts turned to her. It could not be love, he convinced himself. But it was nice to be around her.

'I cannot adequately express my thanks for you taking us aboard,' the pastor said when Lukas entered the cabin. 'I thought Miss Stahl, Sister Cain and I would be abandoned at my mission station. We were the last to leave.'

'It is my pleasure to have you aboard,' Lukas said,

pouring himself a mug of black tea and stirring in a teaspoon of powdered milk. 'But I cannot promise smooth sailing. If we come under aerial attack I want you to remain below where you are better protected. In the unlikely event that we might sustain enough damage to sink us, you will find life jackets at the end of your bunks. When you get the chance, it is a good idea to practise putting them on.'

A short, tense silence followed Lukas's briefing as the grim reality of war at sea sunk in. They did not look at him and it was Megan who broke the silence. 'Well, if it ever comes to that the sea looks very inviting. I always liked swimming.'

Lukas smiled. She has guts, he thought admiringly.

Lukas chatted with the pastor and learned that he had been brought up from Australia to replace his German counterpart. Megan entered into the conversation to talk a little of her work and only Ilsa remained silent about her life, except to say that she was a journalist for a Christian magazine in America and had volunteered to do a story on the Lutheran missionaries in faraway, exotic New Guinea. At the time she had steamed from the United States, America was at peace with Germany and the core of her story was to be about how the Australian government, allied with Britain, had treated the German men of God during their war against Germany. America had a substantial German immigrant population and it was a sensitive subject for her readers.

Night came without incident and after dinner Lukas took his post at the helm for a six-hour shift. Momis found a place beside his beloved Lewis gun to curl up and sleep. The winds blew stronger and the schooner picked up speed. It was a beautiful, moonless night and the Australian was able to relax just a little. He was sailing without lights and knew that detection by any subs, ships or aircraft belonging to Imperial Japan would be very difficult. He thought that all his passengers had retired for the night and was therefore surprised to be joined by Ilsa, who had kindly brought him a mug of strong tea.

'I hope you don't mind,' she said standing beside him. 'But I found your supply of coffee and made myself one.'

'Should have thought about that myself,' Lukas said. 'I am not used to catering to Yanks although I did spend many years in your country.'

'I hope you mean the States,' Ilsa replied.

'California, to be precise. I had a job flying the movie stars around and doing a bit of stunt flying for movie directors. I mostly worked for Jack Warner, a really nice bloke.'

'You are full of surprises,' Ilsa said. 'My father used to love the movies. He especially liked the Errol Flynn and John Barrymore films.'

'I knew Errol pretty well,' Lukas said. 'As a matter of fact he was my last passenger before my plane took a bird-strike and went down just outside of Los Angeles. That is how I lost my eye – and the woman I thought I loved.'

'She was killed in the crash,' Ilsa gasped.

'No, her love for me was killed in the crash,' Lukas replied with just the slightest hint of a smile for things that had cured themselves with time and distance. Now he had a war to occupy his thoughts and remembered how his father had once said there were no guarantees of survival for anyone. Not that Lukas felt he would be killed in this war. That was something that only happened to someone else.

'Oh,' Ilsa said in a small voice, reflecting her slight embarrassment for presuming the worst. 'Was she a person in the movies?'

'Probably by now she is,' Lukas said, swinging the great ribbed wheel to counter a wave attempting to force the schooner off course. 'I don't get much opportunity to catch up on the flicks unless I happen to be in Port Moresby.'

'Are you sailing for Port Moresby after Lae?' Ilsa asked, suddenly interested in his mention of the frontier town. 'Because if you are, I would very much like to sail there.'

'I am not exactly sure,' Lukas frowned. 'I guess so, if the boys don't need me for another ferry run.'

'Could I please stay aboard and sail with you to Port Moresby? I have urgent business there.'

Lukas glanced sideways at the beautiful young woman leaning towards him with the tilt of the deck. 'I suppose that would be all right,' he replied. 'Maybe you could give our cooking a woman's touch. A few meals just like your mum used to make.'

'My mother did not like to cook,' Ilsa replied quietly with a scowl on her face.

Lukas sensed from her answer that he should not make light of her mother – whoever she was – and so dropped the subject of Ilsa's possible role in the ship's galley. 'For a Yank, you know how to brew a good mug of tea,' he said, and the tension seemed to evaporate. Although curious, he did not feel that he should ask why she wanted to go to Port Moresby. Maybe that was the nature of journalists, he thought. They just wandered around the countryside looking for stories.

'Thank you for agreeing to let me stay aboard after Lae,' Ilsa said, finishing the last of her coffee. 'Maybe I could learn to cook,' she said as she left.

Lukas realised that she was attempting to apologise for her reaction. He was pleased that she had asked him if she could sail on to Port Moresby. She was an interesting, somewhat enigmatic woman but she held no sexual attraction for him.

Ilsa had only been gone for a few minutes when Megan appeared on deck wrapped in a big woolly jumper he recognised as one of his own. 'You seem to have a cavalcade of admirers tonight,' she said, settling down beside Lukas at the helm.

'I don't know about admirers,' Lukas grinned. 'At least Ilsa brought me a mug of tea.'

'I would have brought you a cold beer,' Megan retorted. 'But it's too bloody cold up here for that.'

'It can get a bit nippy at night out here,' Lukas replied. 'Considering that we are sailing in tropical waters. Anyway, what brings you on deck?'

'I was feeling a bit confined below decks,' Megan said. 'And I thought that you might like some company on your watch.'

'With you, yes,' Lukas answered. 'Maybe you would like to try your hand at the helm of my really big yacht,' he grinned.

'Touché,' Megan answered. 'I do know the difference between a schooner and a yacht despite the fact that I am but a mere country bumpkin from Cloncurry.'

'Well, the bridge is yours,' Lukas said, standing aside to allow Megan to take the great spoked wheel in her hands.

She was surprised how much it attempted to twist and turn in her hands – and how much she was forced to fight the running sea below the keel. Lukas stood back and attempted to light his pipe in the stiff breeze. He gave up when the wind whipped out every match, and placed the pipe back in his pocket.

'Do you know,' Megan said, 'I can understand why you love sailing so much.'

'And why is that?' Lukas asked, stepping closer.

'There is just something about the beauty of being under those magnificent stars with nothing to disturb the serenity of the moment. It is very intoxicating.'

'It is not always this peaceful,' Lukas said. 'We are just lucky tonight that we have a good wind at our backs and clear skies. Sometimes the situation is reversed and even I wonder at why I choose to skipper the *Independence*. At times she can be as fickle as a woman.'

'I protest,' Megan said with a tone of mock indignation. 'Not all women are fickle, Mr Kelly. Some . . .'

Her statement was cut short as a big, unseen wave forced the schooner to slew in a trough, wrenching the steering wheel from her hands. Lukas immediately stepped behind Megan and grasped the spinning helm to steady the course. As he came up against the young woman he could clearly smell the heady scent of her hair blown free by the wind. His body was pressed against her back and his arms enveloped her waist as he gripped the helm. Megan did not protest and he felt her press back against him. Then her hands came down to grip his arms and she wrestled free from his embrace of her body. He had not expected her reaction to be so strong and was bitterly disappointed.

'Keep your eye on the road,' she said, twisting to face him. 'We would not want to have an accident at sea,' she added in a teasing tone.

Lukas released his embrace so she could step aside and wrap her arms around her body against the cold. He was confused by her seeming defence of her virtue when he thought that she had signalled her physical need for him. 'I am sorry,' he said. 'I hope that you did not interpret what just happened as anything but an accident.'

'I don't know what you mean,' Megan replied sweetly. 'I consider you a gentleman who would not take advantage of a lady. I think that it is time to bid you a good night and go below,' she continued, stomping off towards the hatchway with her arms still wrapped around her.

Completely bewildered, Lukas watched her walk away and disappear below the edge of the hatch. He was mystified as to her sudden change of mood and sighed. *I was right. Bloody fickle*, he thought to himself.

• • •

When Megan found her cabin she lay down on the bunk, still hugging herself. 'Megan,' she muttered to herself. 'You are a stupid woman.' She had experienced an almost overwhelming need to give in to her strong feelings for Lukas but held back. She tried to convince herself that her reservation was simply about her need not to get involved with a man living a very precarious life.

'Bloody war,' she swore softly. Possibly next time she would give into her feelings for the captain of the *Independence*. She had been attracted to Lukas the very moment she had laid eyes on him standing on the verandah of her hospital at Morobe. Even on the night they had shared his corned beef sandwiches, Megan had fallen under the spell of this funny, unassuming man.

'Maybe next time,' Megan whispered softly, before falling into a deep sleep.

Lukas was dozing on the deck when the sun rose over a tranquil sea and Momis was at the helm as the passengers stirred from sleep below. Lukas could almost believe that the war did not exist, so peaceful were his waking dreams. The clatter of pots and pans below reminded him it was breakfast time. He had a good supply of fresh eggs aboard and thought about a plate of scrambled eggs.

A distant buzzing noise intruded on his waking thoughts.

'Jap man plane!' he heard Momis call from the cockpit.

Lukas came fully awake and rolled onto his feet to frantically scan the skies. Then, as his searching gaze swung past the rising ball of the sun, he saw it. It was just a tiny dot against the sun but the noise of its single engine was growing louder as it came in towards them.

Momis had already deserted the wheel, which spun slowly as the schooner keeled on its side to fight the stiff morning breeze. 'I got the gun, Masta Lukas,' he yelled as he sprinted excitedly past Lukas, who turned on his heel to take control of the helm. Everything was happening so fast. Gripping the wheel, Lukas attempted to steer the schooner into a zigzag course on the open seas. He had been in this situation before and knew that only pure luck could save them. Even in his moment of fear he felt a partial envy for the pilot of the Japanese aircraft. As it grew closer, he identified it as being a Japanese Model 11, twin seat fighter floatplane. Probably on a recon mission, Lukas hoped. Maybe it would just buzz them and fly on.

He saw the twin flashes from the plane's nose before he heard the staccato sound of its nasal twin 7.7mm machine guns. Spouts of water whipped up by the bullets clawed their way towards the schooner at a terrifying speed.

'God almighty!' Lukas swore. 'Not again.'

The aircraft did not attempt to take any evasive action as it flew head on towards the *Independence*. Momis had the Lewis operating and carefully squeezed off a series of bursts to range his machine gun. His aim proved true, and the approaching aircraft suddenly swerved away as the bullets ripped through the fragile skin of the plane, even scoring a hit on the windscreen, shattering a small hole just above the pilot's head.

'Me tink I got Jap man!' Momis whooped triumphantly.

But Lukas knew better. The plane climbed, wheeled high in the sky and made another dive at his ship. Now Lukas had a clear view of the two small bombs the plane carried under her wings – and of the machine gunner sitting in his open cockpit behind the pilot.

Momis swung the Lewis around to meet the new approach. Smoke curled from the barrel and was whipped away on the breeze as the schooner was heeled over in the continuing attempt to zigzag.

'Let him have it, Momis,' Lukas yelled down the deck. 'Give the bastard your best.'

Momis lined up the diving aircraft. It was a shallow dive and the Solomon Islander remembered what Masta Jack had said about firing in front of a flying aircraft. He had told him over and over about that and now Momis would see if Masta Jack had been right. He squeezed the trigger but this time kept his finger hard back. The machine gun belted into his shoulder but Momis did not feel it as his blood was running hot with excitement. It had come down to a duel between himself and the Jap man in the sky. The .303 bullets hosed into the air, seeking the diving seaplane. As Momis continued to empty the round magazine at the oncoming plane, he was aware from the corner of his vision that two objects were hurtling towards them. Then the seaplane seemed to swerve to one side and peel away from the two objects in the sky. Momis ignored them and followed the aircraft around until the gun suddenly went silent as the magazine emptied. The Solomon Islander stood amongst the pile of brass rounds rattling around his bare feet. As he bent to grab a magazine of fresh rounds he heard Lukas scream, 'Get down!'

Momis stood up to see why Masta Lukas had yelled at him to get down. At that moment the bombs impacted and exploded.

TWENTY-TWO

Iris sat in the garden of Sen's bungalow at dawn, a battered copy of the Koran in her lap, contemplating what she should do concerning her knowledge of her brother-in-law's espionage activities. Delicate butterflies flitted amongst the shrubs and from the house she could hear the sounds of life. There was the houseboy's raised voice, chiding the cook for spilling sauce on the floors just after he had cleaned them, and the clatter of pans as the cook returned to the kitchen.

Iris had thought that by now she would have been on her way back to Sydney to join her daughter but the immigration authorities in Australia had not as yet authorised her return. A matter had come up concerning her racial origins and under the strict criteria of the White Australia policy a bureaucrat had protested her coming back into the country. The first Iris had learned of the delay was when she received an official letter stating that for the moment her case was under review on racial grounds. Iris had been confused as she and Marie had travelled to Australia from the Middle East without any problem. She did not know it then but Captain Featherstone had cut through red tape to authorise her trip to Australia. His influence ended once Iris reached the shores of the Great Southland and now she was in the hands of petty bureaucrats who were exercising their power over her life. Iris was growing desperate to leave the Port Moresby district – and particularly her brother-in-law's house. Although he was part of her family through marriage he was also working for the hated Japanese and this Iris viewed as real treason on account of what the Japanese were doing to her people in China. Her own activities in Palestine had been carried out under coercion but she could not see any tangible threats to Sen. For all she knew, he was probably betraying the people who had trusted him for years in Papua, for nothing more than money. To report him to the Australian authorities would not in fact be a betrayal but an indication of her loyalty to the Australian cause in their war against Japan.

From past experience Iris knew that the Australians were a very fair-minded people. However, she also knew that approaching the Australian authorities in Port Moresby was a risky business. They could react by imprisoning her in the process of taking Sen into custody. Iris needed someone to undertake the betrayal instead, someone who was trusted to both herself and the Australians. The names came almost immediately to mind – either Lukas Kelly or his father would be perfect. Both knew her and were also well known and respected in Papua.

Almost immediately Iris felt the gloom return. The Kelly men were God knows where in Papua or the Pacific. Whichever one was to return first would do. In the meantime it was a matter of keeping on very careful guard against Sen, who had been particularly distant towards her since she had gone to his office and discovered the radio.

The bombs hit the water and detonated just off the starboard side of the schooner, spraying a deluge of water over the men on the deck and knocking Momis from his feet. The Japanese floatplane climbed over the mast and from where he lay Lukas thought he could see a thin streak of grey smoke trailing from the engine cowling.

'You okay?' he called to Momis, who struggled to his feet with water cascading down his bare chest.

'Me oright, masta,' Morris replied shakily, turning to peer at the low-flying plane flying away from them. 'Me tink me shoot 'im down,' he shouted jubilantly. 'Jap man plane, he no oright.'

Lukas could hear a distinctive coughing noise in the once steady throb of the departing aircraft's engine. One of Momis's bullets must have found a mark, he thought, and felt like whooping a victory cry of delight. Had the *Independence* claimed its first kill for the war?

'I think you are right,' he called back to the beaming Islander. 'I don't think the little bastard is going to make it home.'

The aircraft was heading for the horizon trailing a thin plume of oily smoke and Lukas could see that it was in definite trouble. But to claim a kill they would need evidence to show the authorities in Port Moresby. Boy! What a story he could tell his father. Rifleman Lukas Kelly of the NGVR had shot down a Jap plane. As captain of his schooner the kill would be accredited to him, with due recognition going to Momis as the gunner.

The aircraft was close to the horizon and Lukas made a quick bearing on its course. It was like a wounded bird seeking the safety of quiet waters. With any luck they might even find where it had gone down and take the pilot and his gunner prisoners – if they were still alive.

The pastor, Ilsa and Megan came on deck as soon as they heard the two men shouting their elation above them. The attack had been so sudden and unexpected that they had only time to scramble for life jackets and get them on. Blown from their feet by the bombs exploding in the water nearby, by the time they had regained their balance the fight was over. They were visibly shaken but had the courage to come above deck. Megan checked if anyone required her medical expertise. She could not see blood or other signs of injury to either Momis or Lukas. Both grinned savagely at her questioning expression. 'We got the bastard,' Lukas exploded happily. 'And now it's time to go and claim our kill before the sharks do.'

Megan had her doubts about his enthusiasm to hunt the downed aircraft. What if the fight had attracted less than welcome attention from Japanese ships or other aircraft in the area? Lukas Kelly looked every bit the old style pirate with his savage expression and she had no doubt it was some kind of male bravado to be prepared to risk all in pursuit of a trophy.

Megan was right to have her doubts. The pilot had been able to transmit a mayday call before ditching his aircraft in the sea. The call was picked up by a surfaced Japanese submarine assigned for rescuing pilots shot down over water. She was the I—47 commanded by Captain Kenshu and aboard his boat was Leading Seaman Fuji Komine.

The Japanese captain quickly plotted his course to the downed aircraft and gave the order to dive. Daylight was upon them and other craft would be prowling about. It would be a furious dash underwater to the last known location reported by the Japanese pilot as he ditched his plane in calm seas. The submarine's captain knew without a doubt that the distress signal would have been picked up by Allied stations listening in New Guinea as well as by patrolling enemy warships. The plane had come down very close to his own location in the Solomon Sea so he calculated that he had the best chance to rescue the pilot.

Submarine and schooner both raced for the same location oblivious to the other's proximity.

• • •

Sweat trickled down Fuji's face as he wiped up the last of his meal of dried fish and rice from the bowl with his fingers. He could hear the conning tower hatch slammed shut and the submarine's crew scrambling to man their stations. 'What's happening?' he asked a sailor scurrying past towards the torpedo room.

'We are going to pick up one of our pilots,' the sailor replied over his shoulder.

Fuji wiped his fingers on his loin cloth. He would take up his station in the engine room, where he assisted the officer to maintain the sub's diesel and electric engines during actions. The heat of the tropics in the confined quarters was beginning to dissipate as the sub descended into the cooler levels of the ocean. Fuji had adapted to being a submariner with ease. He was able to operate in waters he had come to know in his youth and at last felt he had a place in the Japanese navy. He was now part of a lethal fighting machine, prowling in search of the enemy. It was like living in the belly of a shark – a predator of the unwary.

Fuji's primary role was not in the engine room but up on deck, where he would be when the time came to be slipped ashore on various intelligence gathering missions. So far he had not been deployed on land as the I–47 had been assigned a roving charter to locate and destroy enemy shipping, and rescue downed pilots.

Fuji had heard from others in the crew that the young, ambitious captain of the I–47 was not pleased with the current tactics employed by his superiors in the Imperial navy. He had closely studied their German ally's tactics of forming wolf packs of U boats to intercept convoys or armed armadas of capital ships. It was with force of numbers that the Germans had been successful in sinking a massive amount of British tonnage. In his quietly spoken opinion, the captain believed this single use of Imperial subs was a tragic waste of a war-winning tool. But he did his duty despite his personal opinions and now could at least see some wisdom in his superiors' deployment of his own sub. A comrade was in trouble and they were best equipped to rescue him.

Just after the attack by the Japanese seaplane the wind had suddenly dropped and Lukas had been forced to use the schooner's engine to power them through the relatively placid seas. This made him a little uneasy as his speed had been reduced. He knew that he was dallying in dangerous waters when he should have been making all haste away from the location of the Japanese floatplane. However, his desire to find the downed aircraft and possibly take its pilot prisoner overrode all caution.

Just before midday Momis spotted the stricken aircraft floating upside down in the sea. 'I see him!' he yelled like an old-time whaling man spotting his prey.

Even Megan felt her misgivings disappear when she was able to see the wreckage. She too had become caught up in Lukas's infectious enthusiasm to pursue his war at sea although she secretly feared for his safety. 'I see it,' she called in her excitement, grabbing Lukas by the arm as he swung the helm to track towards the downed aircraft. Under her fingers she could feel the steel-hard muscle of his arm.

'Jap man, he on top of plane,' Momis continued, peering towards their target. 'Me tink he oright.'

'Looks like I will be conveying four passengers to Lae,' Lukas said, cutting back on the engine to bring the schooner into a glide towards the plane. 'Albeit one just a little unwilling.'

He was aware that the pilot would most probably be armed but was satisfied that the revolver on his hip and the Lewis mounted on the bow would be sufficient to convince the Japanese pilot he was a prisoner of war. Lukas was only a stone's throw from the floating plane wreckage when Momis shouted the warning. Any excitement that Megan may have felt disappeared in a flash as the calm waters were disturbed by the black bow of a surfacing submarine on the other side of the downed plane.

'God almighty!' Lukas swore, as the rest of the surfacing sub came into sight and so too did the rising sun ensign on the conning tower. 'I think we have big trouble.'

Now Megan gripped Lukas' arm in her own terror. She had heard the stories of how Europeans were treated by the Japanese. All she could do was pray for a quick and merciful death.

Captain Kenshu had picked up the profile of the *Independence* in his periscope a quarter of a mile away. Somehow it had looked familiar and when the I-47 moved closer he could see the schooner's name proudly displayed on the bow. Either he was staring at a ghost ship or his efforts to sink the schooner before the war had failed. Kenshu was not superstitious but thanked his illustrious ancestors anyway for giving him a second chance to finish what he should have done many months earlier. He called for Fuji to join him on the sub's bridge. There was no rush to immediately sink the schooner which had unwittingly sailed into a trap. He would send over a boarding crew to see if anything of military value could be found and then have his deck gun sink it, thus saving valuable torpedoes for bigger targets.

'Boarding crew prepare to go over,' he commanded his executive officer. 'We have a schooner to board. Leading Seaman Fuji, you will go with the boarding crew to act as interpreter in any interrogations.'

Lukas was momentarily frozen into indecision at the sight of the Japanese submarine now fully surfaced and with armed crew spilling from the open hatches. He cursed himself for his stupidity and wished now that he had attempted to establish radio contact with a coast watcher to merely report the suspected location of a downed Jap seaplane. But his pride had got the best of him and he had ploughed, boots and all, into an unexpected trap. His three passengers stood on the deck, white-faced and silent, watching the Japanese sailors manning the 5.5 inch deck gun whilst others hauled up two rubber dinghies from below and launched them expertly into the sea beside the surfaced sub.

Momis refused to leave his precious gun but had the sense not to appear threatening with it. It was no match against the far superior firepower of the enemy. Lukas' other two crew members stood sullenly apart, staring accusingly at their captain who had got them into this terrible predicament. The Japanese dinghy crews rowed with strong strokes through the water, one heading for the downed pilot and the other towards them.

'What do we do?' Megan asked in a whisper, although the Japanese boarding party was still a good 200 yards away.

'We don't have much choice,' Lukas replied weakly, his stomach churning with bitterness. How could he have been so foolish as to have endangered his passengers for the sake of his own pride? 'We wait and see if the little bastards will at least let us go in our dinghy before they sink the *Independence*. I suspect that is the best we can expect.'

'You are not very reassuring,' Megan retorted. 'I thought you might have had a better idea.'

'I'm sorry,' Lukas replied. 'I can only ask your forgiveness for my stupidity. I acted like a bloody drongo.'

The dinghy, manned by four armed sub crewmen, was almost alongside them when one of them carefully stood up, balancing himself against the gentle swell of the sea. 'Let the captain of the *Independence* show himself,' he commanded.

Lukas was struck by his perfect English and walked to the railing to show himself. 'I am the master of the schooner, *Inde*–' His reply was cut short when he stared down into the eyes of Fuji Komine. 'Fuji?' he uttered loud enough to be heard, noticing that his appearance at the rail had also visibly shaken his former primary school mate.

'Lukas,' Fuji almost stammered. 'We are coming aboard,' he continued as harshly as he could. 'If you have any arms they are to be disclosed now and all passengers and crew are to assemble forward.'

Lukas turned to his passengers and crew, who moved forward as they had been instructed.

'All hands on heads,' Fuji continued as he took hold of the railing and scrambled aboard to wave a pistol at Lukas and the rest of the group, now standing uncertainly with their hands in the air whilst the schooner rocked gently beneath their feet. The rest of the boarding party followed.

'I would appeal to your honour to spare the crew and passengers,' Lukas said when Fuji stood before him. 'If for nothing else but old times sake.'

'You are the enemy and have allowed yourself dishonour in being so easily captured,' Fuji sneered. 'You cannot expect to be treated with honour.'

'A bloody civilian schooner against your sub,' Lukas spat. 'You call that a duel of *honour*? If nothing else I was able to shoot down one of your glorious navy planes,' he continued, indicating the wreckage of the floatplane in the water.

'It was you who shot down our plane?' Fuji asked with just a hint of respect in his voice. 'With what?'

'With my Lewis gun mounted on the bow. Your pilot was trying to sink me.'

Fuji turned to his companions guarding the prisoners and spoke to them in Japanese. As they muttered in response their expressions seemed to indicate a little more respect for the master of the schooner and his crew. 'I told them of your feat,' Fuji said, turning back to Lukas. 'Your capture carries with it a little less dishonour.'

'If you are an honourable man, Fuji, you will allow my crew and passengers the use of the schooner's dinghy and appropriate rations so they can be picked up by one of our own. I know that you are not about to let me go alive but at least for the sake of our links with Papua, let them go.'

'It is not up to me,' Fuji hissed quietly. 'I agree that we should let your crew and passengers go, and you are right about me killing you. I have no doubt you have forgotten that day on the beach at the Mann plantation when your friend Karl Mann struck my father, forcing him to lose face before his son. Such matters must be paid for in blood.'

'That was when we were kids,' Lukas exclaimed. 'You mean to say that you are still carrying that minor incident as a chip on your shoulder even now? What sort of drongo are you?'

Fuji's face reddened and with the speed of a striking snake he struck out with the butt of the pistol and hit Lukas in the face. Lukas felt the butt strike his nose and although blood instantly spattered over both men the Australian did not instinctively attempt to put his hand to his face. To do so would show the

Japanese sailor he had hurt him. Lukas had only one weapon to hurt the man before him – his pride and defiance.

Then it all happened so fast. The first Lukas knew of the approaching aircraft was an urgent hooting sound coming from the surfaced submarine, followed by shouting from the conning tower. Fuji and his boarding party must have recognised the signal, as looks of alarm crossed their faces followed by expressions of uncertainty. As Fuji was in command of the boarding party he knew that he had only precious minutes, if not seconds, left to return to the submarine before it was forced to crash dive for safety. He glanced around desperately to ascertain the situation and spotted the low-flying twin-engined, snub-nosed Beaufighter bomber approaching from the east.

Lukas was in no doubt of what he must do if they were to survive. He lunged for Fuji and both men went down on the deck. Momis roared and charged the three remaining Japanese guards, who fired in panic, caught between their need to flee the oncoming aircraft bent on killing them, and their duty to execute the prisoners. One of the Japanese guards made his choice and opened fire on the prisoners. Two in the party died almost instantly as bullets ripped into their close packed ranks. The remaining boarding party did not wait to finish off those still standing. They were already leaping into the dinghy leaving the schooner behind.

Fuji lashed out at Lukas, striking the bigger man in the face once more. With a grunt of pain Lukas relaxed his grip. Suddenly he was aware that Momis' thick brown arms were being thrust between him and Fuji. Lukas rolled away as Momis hauled up the smaller man and tossed him over the side. With a splash, Fuji hit the water and sank from sight.

Without hesitating, Lukas scrambled to his feet, blood trailing from his nose. He threw himself towards the Lewis gun. The low-flying RAAF aircraft roared overhead, her nose-mounted machine guns blasting a stitch of bullets into the hull of the Japanese sub.

Lukas swivelled the Lewis gun towards the submarine's deck, where the gun crew had been waiting for their comrades to clear the decks of the schooner before firing. The bullets from the Lewis gun splashed across the water, seeking out the submarine's gun crew. They fired wildly in retaliation and Lukas heard the shell pass dangerously close overhead to explode in a column of water a few hundred yards away.

The sound of the Lewis gun firing on a continuous burst was drowned out by the roaring sound of the aircraft overhead firing its own machine guns. The noise was deafening but Lukas knew the sub teetered between destruction and survival – and a submarine caught on the surface by an armed aircraft was like a turtle on its back.

The I–47 did not wait for the return of its boarding party but commenced its dive to the deepest depth it could allow, until only white water marked where it had been moments before. The Beaufighter climbed to make another run and Lukas tore off the empty magazine when the Lewis gun stopped firing to slam on another. As he did so he turned to see the bodies of his comrades crumpled in pools of blood, staring skyward with sightless eyes. With a sob of fury Lukas turned to find the dinghy with the three Japanese sailors. It was a hundred yards out and he carefully set the sights on the machine gun. With controlled bursts of fire he poured the .303 bullets into the bunched sailors in the dinghy. His aim was true and the water surrounding the small craft soon turned crimson. If any were left alive then the blood would bring the sharks to finish them off. His rage spent, it was time to turn to the welfare of his crew and passengers – those that were left alive.

The Beaufighter made a rolling turn to swoop over the *Independence* and with a waggle of its wings made another turn to fly to its airfield somewhere in New Guinea or Papua, leaving Lukas as the victor in the schooner's second clash with the I–47.

Fuji was not dead. As the RAAF Beaufighter strafed his submarine, he swam to the upturned wreckage of the floatplane and clung to its bullet-riddled wing, while the I–47 submerged. He was about to wave to the dinghy containing his comrades when he saw them lashed by machine gun fire from the *Independence*. Immediately he slid off the wing and took shelter, treading water behind the downed aircraft, out of line of sight to the schooner. He saw the *Independence* motor away and waited, clinging to the wing. A pack of sharks suddenly appeared, swimming lazily around the submarine's dinghy. To his horror Fuji watched them glide in to savage the bodies of his former shipmates. With the *Independence* out of sight Fuji was able to climb onto the wing of the floatplane, having thankfully escaped the sharks which eventually had finished their feeding frenzy and disappeared.

Night came and so did a terrible thirst, driving Fuji to the point of madness. Clinging to the wreckage, he was hardly aware of the dark shape surfacing. The captain of the bullet-riddled I–47 had waited until it was safe to resurface to repair external damage brought about by the strafing. A lookout noticed Fuji and a dinghy was sent to fetch him aboard.

For the captain of the I–47, his two contacts with the Papuan registered schooner had proved a defeat. That a mere wooden schooner could escape being sunk by him on two occasions caused the young captain to brood on the spiritual aspects of destiny. Should he ever again encounter the schooner, he would use one of his precious torpedoes against it, ensuring its total destruction.

Kenshu mourned the loss of shipmates. At least he had been able to save Leading Seaman Fuji, he reflected as Fuji was hauled aboard. He would get his submarine back to Rabaul for urgent repairs – and when the repairs were completed he would return to Papuan waters.

TWENTY-THREE

Returning from a base camp in the mountains west of Lae, Jack Kelly, with his rifle on one shoulder and kitbag over the other, hardly recognised the town of Port Moresby as he stood amidst the wasteland of bombed-out houses and government buildings. The extensive damage had been the result of Japanese air raids nearly every second day against the troops sent up from Australia to protect the vital port facilities. Jack was pleased to see that the town's pubs still operated, providing some relief from the stress of war. But to Jack, Port Moresby was now a dreary place filled with the unfamiliar, frightened faces of young soldiers far from home.

'Jack Kelly – you old bastard. How are you goin'?' a voice yelled across the street which was littered with sheets of corrugated iron and shards of metal shrapnel from the bombs.

Jack turned to see a familiar face. 'Sergeant Groves . . . thought you would have more sense than to hang around here. I thought you would have gone bush with the kanakas.'

The police sergeant strode across the street and enthusiastically shook hands with the man he had once had the task of dumping, completely inebriated, at the door of his friend Paul Mann. A severe tongue-lashing from Karin Mann was far worse a punishment than being locked up for the night on a charge of being drunk and disorderly, Sergeant Ian Groves considered.

'I see that you signed up again,' the police sergeant said, observing the three stripes on Jack's arm. 'Hope I don't have to arrest you for being akwilly.'

'I'm not absent without leave,' Jack grinned. 'So you can go and harass a few unfortunate lads who are.'

'So what are you doing back in Moresby?' the police sergeant continued.

'I got some leave and was hoping to meet up with my young fellow when he gets back with the *Independence*. You haven't heard anything about the schooner's whereabouts by any chance?' he asked.

Ian shook his head. 'All I have heard was that the *Independence* was on the ferry run between Finschhafen and Lae a few weeks back – that's about it.'

'Thanks, cobber,' Jack said. 'Guess I will head out to Sen's place for a day or two.'

'Kwong Yu Sen?'

'Do you know any other Chinaman by that name?' Jack replied. 'Why do you ask?'

'Maybe nothing, Jack,' the police sergeant answered, removing his hat and scratching his balding head. 'I know Sen is a cobber of yours from way back. It is just something I overheard on the military grapevine. Our signals boys have intercepted radio transmissions coming from out his way. But since they haven't been able to triangulate they cannot specifically say they are coming out of Sen's place – just from his direction. Whoever is sending the signals is transmitting in a Japanese code of some kind. The sig boys are always vague about that sort of thing though.'

'If they are working off a bearing, the signals could be coming from a Jap surface ship or sub in line with Sen's place off the coast,' Jack offered.

'The signals people are pretty sure that the transmitter is in a static loc.'

'Got to be a mistake,' Jack replied. 'I have known Sen for years and he is not capable of working for the Japs. After all, the Chinese hate the Japs as much as we do. It just doesn't make sense that he would betray his friends. Maybe someone does have a transmitter out near his place. Anyway, I promise you I will have a bit of a look around.'

'Thanks, Jack,' the sergeant said, replacing his cap. 'Hope you hear from that boy of yours soon. I know young Lukas and fortunately for him he is no chip off the old block.'

Jack grinned, shook the sergeant's hand and turned to walk through the bombed streets towards the track out to Sen's place.

A good three-hour slog brought him to the gate

of Sen's bungalow in the Papuan bush and he was immediately greeted by the old gardener.

'*Yalia, yu stap gut or nogat?*' Jack asked.

Yalia replied with a wide smile. '*Mi orait, Masta Jack.*'

'*Masta Sen, i stap we?*' Jack asked, and Yalia waved his arm in the direction of the house.

'*Tenk yu tru,*' Jack said, pushing the gate open to walk along a neatly kept gravel path flanked by brilliant bougainvillea flowers. He was pleasantly surprised to see Iris sitting on the verandah, a book in her lap, and Jack marvelled at the serene beauty of the woman who had suffered so much in the last two decades. 'Iris, how are you?' he asked as she rose to greet him.

'Jack, it is wonderful to see you so well considering what you have been doing lately,' Iris said with a genuine smile of pleasure. The man reminded her of better times when she was in love with his English expedition partner, Lord George Spencer. Impulsively, Iris took his hands and gazed searchingly at his face. 'You have been unwell,' she continued with a frown. 'I see it in your eyes.'

'Just a touch of malaria back up in the hills. My CO gave me a bit of leave in Moresby to help me to fully get back on my feet. So I thought I might head out your way to see if Sen might have a place for me to put my head down for a couple of days.'

'I know he will be more than pleased,' Iris replied, leading Jack to a cane chair. 'I will have the *haus meri* fetch us a pot of tea and scones.'

Jack slumped gratefully into a well-worn,

comfortable cane chair and placed his rifle against the wall. 'How is Marie?'

'From her last letter she is well and happy working for Mr Tom Sullivan in Sydney,' Iris replied after issuing orders to the *haus meri*. 'Mr Sullivan has put her in charge of selling his French perfumes to cosmetic departments. It seems that her accent helps the sales along and she is doing well financially. She even has her own flat and –'

Iris cut herself short when Sen appeared on the verandah wearing a white tropical suit and matching hat. Jack rose to greet his friend.

'The housegirl said you were here,' Sen said, and although his tone was friendly enough Jack subtly noticed that his old friend did not extend his hand. 'Are you just visiting or looking for a bed?'

'Good to see you, old cobber,' Jack said, feeling a little uncomfortable at the way Sen had asked the question. 'I was hoping that I might be able to stay a couple of days if that was okay with you. Moresby is not much of a place to take leave at the moment with all the bombing that has gone on.'

Sen seemed to be considering the request and Jack sensed that he would be some kind of imposition to his old friend. 'Look, if it is not convenient I can return to Moresby.'

'No, no, Jack, you are always welcome in my house,' Sen said, waving off Jack's protest. 'I can put you up in the shed behind the store room – if that suits you?'

'Anywhere with a roof and a soft bed will do,' Jack replied. 'It beats where I have been putting my head down for the last few weeks.'

'Then the matter is settled,' Sen said, finally extending his hand. 'I see tea and scones are about to be served and I hope that you don't mind if I join you.'

Jack pulled over another cane chair and the three sat together amidst the beauty of the tropical garden, a serene oasis in a world of turmoil. The hours passed pleasantly with much talk of how Iris should invest her inheritance from her former fiancé.

As the afternoon drew on, one of the native servants was called for. He guided Jack to his sleeping quarters in the store room. It was a neat, clean corrugated tin shed with a camp stretcher, mosquito net and kerosene lantern, and a packing crate which acted as a low table. The room was empty but well ventilated with its high roof and latched windows.

Jack dropped his kitbag and rifle beside the camp stretcher and thanked the houseboy. He was weary, the bouts of malaria had sapped his strength, and he lay down on the makeshift bed. Sleep came easily and soon Jack was dead to the world. When the houseboy returned to take Jack to dinner in the main house, he could see that the Australian soldier was still in a deep sleep and quietly left him undisturbed.

Some time later Jack felt his shoulder being shaken. 'Jack, wake up.'

He slowly opened his eyes and was surprised to see that he was in a world of total darkness.

'Must have slept a bit longer than I thought,' he mumbled with the sleep still upon him. 'Iris! What time is it?' he said, pushing himself onto his elbows and blinking away the sleep.

'I think it is about midnight,' Iris replied uncertainly. 'I need to talk to you about a very urgent matter.'

Jack fumbled for the kerosene lantern. With the expertise of a soldier, knowing where all vital pieces of kit were left in the dark, he found a box of matches and struck a light for the lantern. In the flaring of the match he could see Iris's worried face. He lit the lantern and placed it on the wooden crate, realising that he was still fully dressed. Instinctively Jack sought out his rifle by the bed. It was still there, he thought with relief. He had been fortunate that he was not deep in enemy territory, where to be approached so easily could mean death.

'What is so urgent,' Jack asked, rubbing his eyes with the back of his knuckles, 'that it brings you here at this hour?'

'I have waited until Sen went to bed before coming to see you,' Iris said.

Jack could sense her fear. 'Why all the secrecy?'

'I have come to you because I could not think of anyone else I could trust with what I know,' Iris said. 'Can I trust you, Jack?'

'I can't see why not,' he replied, but with just a hint of wariness. 'What's up?'

'I think my brother-in-law is reporting to the Japanese. I know he has a radio transmitter.'

The revelation brought Jack fully awake. 'Are you a hundred per cent sure? Can you prove what you are saying?'

'I have seen him making a transmission and have since learned that a Japanese man by the name of Fuji was staying with him just before I arrived in Moresby. The natives who work for Sen talk, and the houseboy confirmed the rumour.'

'Why haven't you reported your suspicions to the police in Port Moresby?' Jack asked.

'I am virtually a non-person to the authorities here on account of being Eurasian and was afraid that if I did report Sen, your government might just imprison me for simply being in the same house with a spy. I was waiting until either you or Lukas came to visit.'

In the dim light of the small room Jack frowned. 'I believe all that you are saying,' he said. 'And what you are saying leaves me with no other choice than to confront my old friend. First, I will need you to show me where the radio is hidden.'

Fear flitted across Iris's face. 'I am afraid to go to his office. He may discover us.'

Jack reached for his rifle. 'Not much he can do when I have this,' he said grimly, turning her expression of fear to reassurance. 'So let us go and speak to Sen.'

'There is something else,' Iris said as she followed Jack, who held the lantern in one hand and trailed his rifle in the other. 'I have heard from the girls here that this Japanese man who visited my brother-in-law has a woman in a village down on the coast. They say the woman is pregnant to him.'

'Do you know her name?'

'She is a Motu girl called Keela,' Iris told him. 'She lives in the village not far from here.'

Jack did not reply as they reached the front verandah of the darkened house. He stopped, placed the lantern on the ground and pulled back the bolt of his rifle to feed a round into the chamber. 'You carry the lantern,' he whispered.

Together, they entered the house and went to Sen's office. Iris told Jack where the radio was hidden; he placed his rifle on the floor and dropped down on his knees to slide the panel aside. When he flipped the catches on the battered suitcase, he found himself staring at the radio. He had hoped that Iris was wrong but the evidence before his eyes was damning enough.

'It was only a matter of time,' Sen said sadly from the doorway behind them.

Jack turned cautiously with the aim of reaching the rifle at his fingertips. But when he glanced up he could see that Sen was not armed.

'I don't understand,' Jack said in a voice laced with sadness and disbelief. 'I have known you for years and would have trusted you with my life. How could you work for the Japs considering what they have done to your relatives in China?'

'I had no choice, Jack,' Sen sighed. 'Somehow, I am glad that it was you who found out and not some stranger.'

Jack stood and faced the smaller man. 'You are working for the very people who want to kill us all . . . why?'

'It was what you call blackmail,' Sen said. 'But I will tell you all about it over a glass of scotch. You won't need your rifle,' he added when he saw Jack swing it up to cover him. 'I have long resigned myself to this day and do not want to see any harm befall my family. That is all I ask.'

Jack nodded and eased the rifle down. He could see in his old friend's eyes that he had accepted his fate. The three of them went to the living room, where Sen had a well-stocked liquor cabinet. He produced a bottle of good scotch and three tumblers. Iris remained silent, awed by the events that had transpired so quickly. She had expected resistance from her brother-in-law if he thought he might be cornered – not complete capitulation.

'Before the last war I was approached by the German authorities in New Guinea to work for them,' Sen began. 'I think it was 1912 or '13,' he said. 'They asked me to move into Papua and spy on you Australians.'

'Why you?' Jack asked.

'Because I already had a well-established native recruiting business, which made it easier for me to be accepted by Europeans needing labour for the gold mines and plantations. I was able to send reports on just about everything.'

'You used me in your spying?' Jack asked, dumb-founded by the extent of his friend's espionage history.

'No, Jack, you were a genuine friend who I always liked and respected. I have never used you.'

But this was a lie as Sen had used Jack and Paul Mann to dispose of the infamous and brutal recruiter of native labour, Tim O'Leary. He had been well aware that the formidable expertise of the two men would rid him of a man who had the ability to betray him to the Australians for his spying role in the Great War. 'My role should have ended with the war but when the Germans signed their pact with the Japanese I was transferred to Japanese intelligence because of my value to their operations in this part of the world. Fuji Komine returned in disguise to threaten me with exposure to the Australian authorities if I did not comply with him. My first loyalty is to my family. I had to do what I was told. I did not want to help the Japanese, and being Chinese I despise them as my ancestors have loathed the Monkey Men for centuries. That is all I can say except that I would do anything to prove to you how much I regret going along with Fuji.'

Jack stood and walked back to the library, returning with his rifle. 'There is something you can do to prove how much you regret your decision to work for the bloody Japs,' he said, flicking the safety catch off the rifle and unexpectedly passing it to his old friend. Startled, Sen took the rifle. 'Point it at me, Sen,' Jack said. 'Believe me, all you have to do is pull the trigger and I will no longer be a witness to your spying activities. But if you put the rifle down I will shift heaven and earth to help you and your family get out of this mess. I have friends who can help.'

Slowly, Sen rose to his feet, pointing the rifle at Jack.

Petrified, Iris remained seated, mouth agape in horror. Jack Kelly was crazy, she thought. Sen would kill him and then kill her.

The rifle was levelled at Jack's chest, and the men

stared into each other's eyes. Seconds felt like minutes to them both, until finally Sen passed the rifle back to Jack, butt first. 'I doubt that you would have done that with a loaded rifle, Jack,' Sen said with the slightest hint of humour.

Jack took the rifle, grasped the bolt back spinning a live round into the air. Its brass case gleamed gold in the light of the lantern as it spun and clanked onto the floor. Sen's eyes grew wide with shock. 'I needed to know if I could trust you,' Jack said, placing the rifle beside him.

'What if I had pulled the trigger?' Sen gasped.

'We have known each other for too many years,' Jack replied, picking up his tumbler of scotch and swigging the lot down. 'And if you had, I would have been dead wrong in my estimation of you.'

Sen shook his head. Jack Kelly was the only man on earth he would ever trust. Such was the power of his old friend. Now his family's fate was in the hands of the Australian.

TWENTY-FOUR

With clearance granted by the harbour master, Lukas sailed the *Independence* into Port Moresby. In a cargo hold the shroud-wrapped body of Pastor Schmidt lay alongside that of a blanket-wrapped Solomon Islander. Megan had insisted that both men should be buried ashore rather than disposed of at sea as Lukas had wanted – and she had got her way, Lukas having calculated that they were close enough to Port Moresby to allow such a request.

Entering the port, those remaining gathered on deck to view the array of shipping that filled the harbour. Ilsa Stahl was disappointed with her first sight of the township of Port Moresby. Standing at the bow of the *Independence* she saw that what had once been a quaint town of corrugated iron-roofed buildings nestling in the hills was now a town devastated by the Japanese air raids. Wisps of smoke rose here and there from the bombed buildings and the port was crowded with cargo ships unloading vital war supplies for the Australian garrison ashore. The surrounding hills were scorched bare and the red earth was revealed like blood on the landscape. Her first impression was not of a town but of a half-costructed open-air factory.

'It was not always like this,' Megan said quietly beside her. 'I remember Moresby as a lively, colourful town filled with characters of the sort to be found nowhere else on earth.'

'It must have been wonderful before the war came here,' Ilsa said. 'I wish I had seen it then.'

'Lukas told me that he had radioed ahead for you to meet one of your journalist colleagues when we get ashore,' Megan commented. 'If he is not there, you are more then welcome to doss down with me in Moresby until you find him.'

'Thank you, Megan, but I am sure Mr Fay will be waiting for me. If I have any trouble I will take you up on your kind offer.'

They fell into silence as the dock neared, with the schooner manoeuvring to a small place between two huge American cargo ships. The noise of industry was clearly heard across the water, with men swearing as they unloaded the pallets of supplies in the tropical heat. Ilsa winced as she was not used to such profane language in her genteel world of New York's religious circles. Megan seemed immune to the colourful language and Ilsa guessed that as a nurse amongst male patients she had heard it all before.

'You don't blame Lukas for what happened off Lae,

do you?' Megan asked suddenly as if it had been bottled up in her. 'He was only doing his job as a soldier.'

Ilsa turned to gaze at her travelling companion. 'I do not blame Lukas,' she replied. 'It is war and such things happen. I am sad because I can see how much the pastor's death has affected him. If you think that I resent him, you are wrong. It is just that I knew the pastor well and he was like a father to me. So I feel his loss strongly.'

Megan turned away to watch the wharf glide closer. Momis was running along the deck with the mooring ropes and Lukas had an expression of complete concentration as he delicately swung the helm this way and that to ensure he did not collide with the two cargo ships. Behind the intense look on his face Megan could see the anguish and wished she could convince the master of the schooner that neither she nor Ilsa blamed him for their very close call with death. How different it all had been only months earlier when everything seemed so stable in this part of the world, she thought. Then it had been a time for dances, tennis parties, picnics and trips to the beach. All that had finished when the men had left to enlist.

They docked and Lukas assisted the two women ashore. 'Thank you, Lukas,' Ilsa said, and impulsively reached up to kiss him lightly on the cheek.

Startled, he stiffened but accepted the gesture as one of sympathy for the anguish he carried. 'I hope we bump into each other sometime in the future,' he said. 'I am sorry for the loss of the pastor. He was an exceptional man for what he did.'

'I am sure God has measured his sacrifice and found him not wanting,' Ilsa responded. 'I hope we meet again one day.'

Lukas watched her walking down the wharf, dodging the chaos and ignoring the wolf whistles from the bare-chested, sweating men who paused to watch her walk by. She was a rarity in a world now dominated by men, since the majority of European women and children had long been evacuated from Port Moresby. Only the native labourers did not express their admiration for the beautiful young woman who suddenly appeared amongst them. To do so would bring the wrath of their European companions down upon them.

'Well, Lukas,' Megan said, lining up to bid farewell to the *Independence*'s captain. 'I will be seeing you – but hopefully not in my hospital.' He pushed forward his hand.

'If it is good enough for Ilsa to give you a kiss goodbye then it is good enough for me also,' she said with a mischievous smile, and reached up and pulled his face down to hers. Again, Lukas stiffened, but tasting the sweet softness of her mouth, relented. Then just as he was melting she pulled away from him.

Cheers and wolf whistles followed from the dockhands below. 'Good on yer, cobber,' he heard, and 'Who's a lucky bugger then?'

'Well, Rifleman Lukas Kelly, if you are up at the hospital you just might see me again,' Megan added, fully aware of the impact her unexpected kiss had on him.

'Momis,' Lukas called to his leading seaman, 'help the missus get her bag up to the hospital.'

Momis responded immediately and scooped up the suitcase.

'Thank you,' Megan said and turned to walk away with a definite swing of her hips. Lukas watched her until she disappeared in the clutter of the wharf. He was still stunned as to what exactly her pleasant gesture meant. She lived after all in a world full of eligible men – and must have known it. He was not an officer and not even really in the fight against the Japanese. So what could she see in him?

Eugene Fay was waiting for Ilsa when she came and stepped ashore in Moresby. 'Miss Stahl, over here,' he called, dodging a canvas-backed military truck.

Ilsa could see a middle-aged man wearing American military fatigues and sweating profusely enough to make the green uniform look almost black in patches. He wore glasses and had the world-weary, disillusioned look all war correspondents bore. Most risked their lives to write reports which their editors then deemed too horrific to print for readers complacent with the official line of government propaganda.

'Mr Fay, it is good to meet you,' Ilsa said, taking his hand in a brief handshake.

He took her suitcase and indicated a Dodge sedan. 'Call me Gene,' he said with a bright smile. 'I have transport and you will be staying with me out near the Seven Mile airfield until you are reassigned to God knows where in this asshole at the end of the earth. So welcome to hell. At least it is not as bad as where you left. No doubt you have heard that the Japs have taken Lae, and the Philippines seem to have been lost. Things are not looking too good in this part of the world.'

'I had not heard,' Ilsa said, opening the car door while Eugene Fay took his place behind the wheel.

'Still trying to get used to this goddamned right hand drive,' he mumbled as he fumbled with the ignition. 'Bloody Aussies do everything like the Limeys,' he continued as the car coughed into life.

'I notice that you have picked up one of the Australians' favourite adjectives,' Ilsa said with a wry smile.

'Yeah, which one?' Eugene asked as he put the car in gear.

'Bloody . . . you must have a lot of contact with our Australian allies.'

Eugene Fay glanced at Ilsa from the corner of his eye. 'Pretty observant for a woman,' he said. 'Sounds like you might have the makings of a war correspondent yet.'

'Has my accreditation come through?' Ilsa asked, referring to the eagerly sought official acceptance by her government to allow her to work in the field with their troops and those of the Allies.

'I gotta tell you that I was kinda surprised that Uncle Sam passed you,' Eugene said, honking the horn at a slow-moving army jeep in front of them. 'You being a German-born person and all. All I can say is that you must have some pull with the government back home.'

Ilsa did not reply. Between her late stepfather's valuable work for the American government against Hitler and the power of the Lutheran church with her local senator, she had been granted the credentials.

Eugene chatted on about what he knew of the war to date. The war in the Pacific was only a few months old and the Japanese had conquered the whole of Asia and most of the Pacific. They stood poised to take Port Moresby before consolidating and striking at the Australian mainland. Already, devastating bombing raids had been launched against northern coastal towns on the Australian mainland. Darwin, Broome and other towns had taken a battering from the weight of bombs dropped on them and the Japanese had also destroyed valuable shipping and aircraft. So far the loss of life to the raids had been a well-kept secret from the population of the southern cities to avoid feelings of panic.

'Do you think that Port Moresby is under an immediate threat of invasion?' Ilsa asked.

Eugene scratched his head as they passed a deserted native village on stilts jutting into the sea. 'I have a bad feeling that we are next in this part of the world. I have talked to a lot of Aussie officers and men and they feel it is only a matter of days before the Japs come.'

'How would they come?' Ilsa asked, already filing the information away as material for writing her own stories from the Papuan front.

'My guess is it will be by sea. Since Pearl Harbor we really haven't had a chance to lick our wounds. It only makes sense that the Japs will continue their momentum with their navy leading the way. This war out here is shaping up to be a naval war in a big lake called the Pacific Ocean.'

'Do you think the Australians can hold the Japanese at Port Moresby?'

Eugene frowned. 'These guys were good back in the last war but what they have sent up here are boys who were too young to join their expeditionary force and be sent to the Middle East and North Africa. Maybe if they had their boys back from the Middle East they might make a stand but not with what they have now. No, without Uncle Sam backing them and a properly trained force they don't stand a chance. It's only a matter of time before you and I find ourselves being pulled out.'

Ilsa fell into silence. She had originally travelled to Papua and New Guinea to seek out her real father, and to do so she had accepted an assignment with her newspaper. Then the onset of war in this part of the world had disrupted her plans. Now Papua was facing an imminent invasion from a brutal enemy and as a war correspondent Ilsa would be in the front line. At least she could make a name for herself reporting on the war first hand. There was no fear in her decision to stay, more an elation at being able to be a part of history. Was this strange desire to face danger something she had inherited from the man who had sired her? She had loved her stepfather as if he had been her biological one but a desire to find her roots was also strong. When she located her Uncle Paul and Aunt Karin they would be able to tell her where this Jack Kelly was.

Sen was now a double agent – a rare prize to the Australian counter-intelligence people. His full cooperation brought a promise of security for his family, as Jack had promised. With his code name of Krait he was still trusted by his Japanese handlers and could now be used to transmit misinformation.

Sen's bungalow was discreetly turned into an agency of Australian counter-intelligence with a full-time staff of carefully screened personnel liaising with the armed services of the Australian government. His native staff were warned, on pain of death, to ignore any unusual comings and goings or activity around the house, and they did not have to be told twice. A further increase in their wages helped seal their silence and they also took a certain amount of pride in being considered part of the war effort against the Japanese men.

Sen transmitted what the counter-intelligence people required of him and Jack was not permitted to speak to his old friend again. Not that he had much choice as the wheels of the military ground into action and isolated Sen from all outside contact. Jack was allowed to stay on in the store room and took walks down to the beach. He would strip off and take long swims in the tropical waters, then rest on the beach under the shade of the overhang of coconut trees.

Four days after the night of Sen's revelations of his espionage activities for the Japanese, Jack received word that the *Independence* had docked in Port Moresby harbour after a perilous journey from Lae. He spruced himself up and hitched a ride into town with an Australian corporal from the Signals Corp. Let off at the wharf he walked down the pier to the familiar sight of his schooner. Lukas was on the deck with Momis, inspecting new ropes that had been delivered that morning. He glanced up to see his father walking towards him only feet away.

'Dad!' he called from the deck and Jack leapt aboard with the nimbleness of a young man. The two man fell into a crushing bear hug – tears welling in both men's eyes. 'I thought the Japs might have got you by now,' Lukas said, holding his father at arm's length to gaze into his face. 'They almost got us.'

Jack could see a change in his son. There was a sadness he could not conceal beneath his wide smile of welcome. Something had happened since their last meeting.

'What happened?' Jack asked, and Lukas seemed to crumple.

'I lost a couple of good people out of Lae,' Lukas replied. 'Lost them because of my own stupidity.'

'How about we go below and you tell me all about it,' Jack said. 'I'll put on the billy and you can tell me over a cuppa.'

Lukas nodded, brushing away the tears with the back of his hand. He felt stupid, like a kid again, for breaking down so easily at the mere sight of his father – that rock in his existence who seemed completely impervious to the worst life could throw at a man. But he was also overjoyed to meet once again with the only person in his life who could really understand what it felt like to lose people that you had been responsible for.

Jack filled the two chipped mugs with hot black tea and sat at the chart table while Lukas poured out the events of the last two weeks: the shooting down of the Japanese floatplane, the dash to it and how they had been intercepted by the Japanese submarine. It was when he continued with the actions that had transpired after Fuji came aboard that Lukas began to hesitate.

'I was entrusted to ferry my passengers to Lae,' he said. 'And I lost the pastor and one of the boys. Ilsa said that the pastor threw himself in front of her and Megan – Sister Cain – to protect them from the Japs when they opened fire. If it had not been for him, Ilsa and Megan may have been killed. It should never have happened. I . . .' Lukas fell into silence, staring with blank eyes at the chart on the table.

'It may not be any consolation but you are a soldier in the NGVR and you did exactly what I would have done under the circumstances,' Jack said, leaning forward to place his hand on his son's head. 'Your primary job is to fight – not flee – in the face of the enemy. I know that is a tough thing to ask of my only child but we are at war, and if the Japs keep going south we won't be around to even reflect on such terrible decisions. You made the right decision and the pastor also bravely made the right decision. This war is all about protecting our women and children – not about simply fighting for your government. You said that you might have killed Fuji Komine,' Jack said, diverting his son's attention from his self-recrimination. 'From what I have learned lately, Fuji was assigned to a Jap sub, the I–47 on special duties. That was the same sub that rammed the *Independence* when Vicky was killed,' he said. 'I only hope that the RAAF sank it.'

'From what I saw it looks pretty certain that they have put her down,' Lukas reflected.

'If that is so then I can sleep just a little easier,' Jack sighed. 'It is kind of ironic that you were present to see the death of the submarine that took Victoria's life and kill the man who was indirectly involved in the death of Dademo all those years back. Maybe there is an Old Testament God who believes in an eye for an eye after all, because I know I do.

'So what happened to the two sheilas you were ferrying?' his father asked with a playful shove of his son's shoulder. 'You fall in love with both of them?'

'Dad!' Lukas protested. 'A man does not mix business with pleasure – you know that.'

'So which one?' Jack persisted. 'You said that you eventually brought them both to Moresby.'

'Sister Cain has been assigned to the medical services here,' Lukas answered. 'Miss Stahl, the Yank, was a bit of a mystery woman. She said that when she got to Moresby she was going to look up some relatives but I told her any German residents had been interned back in Australia.'

'I thought you said she was a Yank.'

'She was born in Munich and emigrated to

America with her father about ten years ago. Because we had quite a few Germans around this part of the world before the war, I asked her who she was looking for, but she said it did not matter as she had an address. She was a bit mysterious about the whole matter.'

'Looking for German relatives at this time can be a touchy matter,' Jack said. 'She was probably a bit sensitive about divulging who they were for that reason alone.'

'Maybe you are right,' Lukas frowned. 'Anyway, she was met by a Yank when we arrived. It seems that they are looking after her.'

'So it was Miss Stahl who caught your fancy,' Jack teased. 'And not Sister Cain who I had the pleasure of meeting briefly up around Morohe way.'

'I didn't say that,' Lukas retorted. 'As a soldier sailor I haven't been to all the ports yet.'

Jack laughed at his son's joke. Long ago he had made reference to a sailor having a girl in every port. Lukas was still young and had plenty of time to find a long-term relationship in the future. Future? What bloody future? His son should seize any scrap of romance that came along in his life. And besides, Jack had immediately liked Megan when he had met her. The war was only in its infancy and Lukas might not be around to see it mature. Jack had learned that lesson from his own terrible experiences in the trenches of the last war.

Jack and Lukas spent half the day chatting, renewing their deep bond with one another. The other half of the day was spent in the hotel bar getting blind drunk until an air raid came. They spilled out onto the street to seek a slit trench, which they tumbled into, roaring with drunken laughter in the midst of the earth-shattering explosions around them. It was the only weapon they had to hide their fear of losing each other. When the bombing was over they stumbled back to the wharf to see that their schooner had escaped undamaged. The three were still together despite all the Japanese threw at them.

The following day Jack rediscovered the painful world at the end of a drinking binge. He lay in his bunk listening to the water lapping at the hull of the boat and the irritating, clanking sound of men at work on the wharf. Through the haze of his hangover something started to niggle at Jack's memory. Not a matter of great importance it was just that the name Stahl rang a bell somewhere. Where had he heard that name before? He groaned and closed his eyes. Stahl, it had something to do with Paul Mann, he remembered, and then promptly forgot to remember anything else lest it tax his brain and cause a worse headache.

It had only been forty-eight hours since Megan had taken up her duties at the hospital and already she had held the hands of two dying young soldiers. Both had been victims of the terrifying bombing raids and their horrific injuries were beyond repair by medical science. In peacetime she was used to witnessing the death of the elderly but in time of war it was the young.

Weary and emotionally drained, Megan found herself in the garden of the hospital. She sat on a bench staring listlessly at a native gardener, the final words of the second young soldier echoing in her head. He had cried for his mother before fading into the grips of death. Why was it that young men did this? She had heard the plea so many times in the last few months.

'A penny for your thoughts,' a voice said softly.

'Wha . . .?' Megan snapped from her gloomy thoughts to see Lukas standing awkwardly in the garden, a sprig of bougainvillea in his hand. She had not noticed him enter the hospital garden.

'You looked so tired and sad,' Lukas said, passing the flowers to Megan. 'I thought these might make your day better.'

Megan smiled sadly at the gesture, noticing that in wrenching the small branch from the shrub Lukas had pricked his hand on the thorns. 'Let me look at your hand,' she said, placing the flowers on the seat beside her and reaching for Lukas's hand in her professional way. The cut was not severe but she continued to hold his hand.

Lukas sat down beside Megan, his hand in hers. 'Looks like you are having a bad day,' he said sympathetically. 'Maybe I have the remedy.'

'And what is that?' Megan asked.

'Well, if you can get a little time off – at least be away overnight – I can take you from here to a place of tranquillity, safe from the bombs.'

'Australia?' Megan asked with a wry smile.

'Ah, no, not Australia, but my aunt and uncle's

plantation not too far from here,' Lukas said. 'I promised my Aunt Karin that I would check in on their place whenever I got the opportunity. I have a couple of days off before I sail again and thought that you might also like to get away. It is recommended medicine for what seems to be ailing you.'

'I would like that, Doctor Kelly,' she said with a smile. 'I will ask for a day off. The matron here is very nice and I am sure that she will be sympathetic if I promise to do a double shift down the road.'

'Well, if it is possible we can leave this afternoon,' Lukas said brightly.

'I think that is a possibility,' Megan responded. 'I have just come off my shift, so I will go see the matron straightaway.'

'Good,' Lukas said, reluctantly releasing his hand from Megan's. 'I will drop back this arvo to pick you up.'

Megan glanced up at him. 'Lukas, thank you for the flowers. They mean a lot to me.'

'Ah, it was nothing,' he said awkwardly.

'I wouldn't say that,' Megan replied. 'You had to spill some of your blood to get them.'

Lukas grinned, waved his hand and walked away with a spring in his step.

That afternoon he returned in an old T-model Ford truck. He had borrowed it from a friend who worked at the harbour, with the promise that he would get his crew to catch a good feed of fish. Megan was waiting in front of the hospital, a small suitcase by her feet. She was wearing a colourful cotton frock and broad-brimmed straw hat. The sight of her made Lukas think of the healthy country girls of Australia's Outback. He smiled. She was from Australia's Outback. Leaning over, he opened the passenger side door. 'Hop in,' he said. 'We should get to the Mann plantation in a couple of hours.'

Megan threw her suitcase on the back tray of the truck and stepped inside. That he had not stopped the truck, got out and opened her door, did not concern Megan. He was, after all, an Aussie male. But one she was attracted to and the anticipation of getting away from war-ravaged Port Moresby with him was something she knew would be an adventure in itself.

TWENTY-FIVE

A native boy, wearing the traditional lap-lap of
his people and carrying a machete, greeted
Lukas upon his and Megan's arrival at the old Mann
plantation.

'Who are you?' he asked suspiciously in pidgin.

'Masta Lukas Kelly,' Lukas answered with a broad
grin, recognising the grown up son of Dademo.
'Don't you know me, Rabbie?'

The young man stared at Lukas for a brief
moment and broke into a broad smile of his own. 'It
is you, Masta Lukas,' he said. 'Me think maybe you
are dead. Me think you been killed across the sea.'

'Not dead – just feel that way sometimes. I have
come back to look at Masta Paul's place for him.'

'I have looked after the masta's house and trees,'
Rabbie said, puffing out his chest. 'I don't let those
bush kanakas go near the house.'

Lukas could see that Rabbie was staring at Megan. 'This is my woman, Missus Megan,' he said by way of introduction.

'Good to meet you Missus,' Rabbie said in halting English. 'Good you be here, Missus. Name belong me, Rabbie.'

'Good to meet you, Rabbie,' Megan said, offering her hand in friendship, which Rabbie accepted self-consciously.

Lukas informed Rabbie that he would like to have a look around and the young man led the two up to the house with its tin roof and wide verandahs. He opened the gauze door which squeaked back on its rusty hinges and Lukas and Megan stepped inside the former residence of the Mann family. Although everything had a layer of dust, Lukas was surprised to see that the house and its contents were intact despite the absence of its owners. Rabbie had been telling the truth when he said he had been looking after his former masta's interests.

'Place all correct, Masta Lukas,' Rabbie said in pidgin, and Lukas paid him a compliment on the good job he had done looking after the place.

'Me and the missus will be all right now,' Lukas said. 'We will be leaving in the morning. I have some money for fish if you have any?' he asked.

'Me have big fish caught today,' Rabbie answered. 'For you, the fish is a gift.'

'Thank you, Rabbie. I will tell the masta that when he returns he is to give you a raise in your wages for the good job you are doing.'

Rabbie beamed. 'I will get the fish for you,' he said, turning to walk out the door.

'What did you say to Rabbie when you introduced me to him?' Megan asked suspiciously, taking hold of his arm. 'I do not speak pidgin but I thought there was something about me being your woman.'

Lukas looked sheepish. 'I kind of said that you were my missus,' he replied. 'It was just a simpler way of explaining your presence here.'

'Am I?' Megan asked.

'Are you what?' Lukas replied, feigning ignorance.

'Your woman?'

'That's a question that only you know the answer to,' Lukas answered with a warm smile. 'As for me, I already know how I feel about you.'

'I think it is time that we went for a swim in that delightful bay I noticed as we drove into the plantation,' Megan said, evading the line that the conversation was taking. 'I hope that you brought your swimming trunks because I packed my cossie. So where is my bedroom?'

'I guess you get my Uncle Paul and Aunt Karin's room,' Lukas said. 'I will show you.'

Lukas led Megan to a large well-ventilated room with a mosquito net hanging from the ceiling over a big double bed. Megan immediately stripped the bed of its musty sheets and rummaged in a tall wardrobe to find a clean set. Lukas left her changing the sheets while he went in search of a few items they would need for the overnight stay.

In a matter of minutes Megan appeared beside him in the living room wearing her one-piece swimsuit and bathing cap. Lukas gave a wolf whistle. He had already changed into a pair of swim shorts. 'Last one down to the beach has to cook dinner,' he said, allowing Megan to get her foot out the door first.

Neck to neck they raced down to the beach with Megan splashing into the placid warm tropical waters first. 'You have to cook!' Megan yelled as she fell back to luxuriate in the cleansing water.

'I was kind of hoping that,' Lukas muttered, throwing himself at her. Laughing, she moved quickly away and he splashed face down, missing her altogether. For an hour they larked about like two children on holidays, then swam to a sandbar not far away where they could stand with water to their waists, gazing back at the little beach fringed with coconut trees swaying gently in the late afternoon breeze. It was then that Lukas took Megan in his arms and kissed her. This time she did not resist, returning his passion with her own. They remained in the embrace until Megan suddenly broke away.

'Race you to the beach,' she said breathlessly. 'The loser has to find the kindling for our cooking fire.'

It was Lukas who, as the sun began to set, scrounged around under the grove of coconut trees for the driftwood to make a fire on the beach.

Lukas disappeared for a moment back to the house and returned with a cane basket, an old army blanket and a big coral fish that Rabbie had left in the kitchen for them. Megan had removed her bathing cap and her hair flowed to her shoulders.

She had already lit the fire and Lukas, preparing the meal in the traditional way of the coastal people of Papua, placed the fish wrapped in plantain leaves into the colder coals of the fire, along with some yams. From the picnic basket he produced a bottle of red wine. 'No one seems to drink this froggy stuff,' he scowled. 'I would rather have a beer but couldn't get my hands on any. I just hope that you like plonk.'

Megan stretched like a cat beside the fire. 'It just so happens that I was brought up on wine,' she said. 'My father served in France in the last war and acquired a taste for it. We always had wine with our meals. They were mostly sauternes and hocks.'

'Well, I don't think wine drinking will ever catch on in Australia,' Lukas growled, prying out the cork with some difficulty using a length of fencing wire. The cork finally came out and he poured equal measures into tin mugs. Megan sniffed, then sampled the wine. 'Not a bad choice for one who professes not to like wine,' she said.

Lukas took a sip. 'It could grow on you if you couldn't get a beer,' he grudgingly conceded. 'Well, here's a toast to this moment lasting forever,' he said, raising his mug.

'And to the hope that we are not forced to once again partake of corned beef sandwiches,' Megan responded, raising her mug and sighing.

'Not this time,' Lukas said, kneeling before the fire to poke more wood into the flames. 'This time you will see just how well a Kelly man can cook.'

'A surprising feature for a man as rugged as

Lukas Kelly,' Megan said teasingly. 'I thought you might be a man who feels a woman's place is barefoot, pregnant and in the kitchen.'

'I might have, once,' Lukas replied. 'But this war is changing everything. It's not right that women like you, being virtually in the front line, should be subjected to war without a lot of respect from us men.'

'Like it or not, we are,' Megan said. 'I doubt that all men are as sensitive as you.'

'Sensitive?' Lukas asked, glancing at her. 'What's sensitive about me?'

'It is just something that I see in you,' Megan said dreamily, rising to join Lukas, who was kneeling by the fire. Without a further word she placed her arms around his shoulders and drew his face to hers. This time, having initiated the embrace, she did not break it. Together they lay back against the old army blanket and Megan rolled over onto Lukas. The kiss continued, Megan's tongue probing his mouth. 'Are you sure?' he gasped as she lay over him. Megan sat up, straddling his hips, and rolled down her swimsuit, revealing her small but firm breasts. For a moment Lukas thought he was dreaming. He reached up to gently touch her rigid nipples with the tips of his fingers. She continued to undress, struggling from the swimsuit and dropping it beside the fire. No words were needed. Lukas quickly stripped off his shorts and they knelt face to face by the fire. Lukas felt his world reeling as they came together in the act of giving body and soul to each other. Megan's nails dug deep into Lukas's back but he scarcely felt their sharpness. He had made love to many other women but for the first time that he could remember, this experience was wonderfully different in a way he could not fully understand. All he knew was that he did not want the moment to end.

Megan suddenly shuddered and fell limply across Lukas' chest. He held her to him, feeling the sweat from her body mingle with his.

Hours later they were forced to eat corned beef sandwiches again as somehow the fish had been forgotten. Naked on the blanket, they lay back, softly whispering words of love to each other while gazing at the seemingly endless stars.

'I never dreamed that you felt that way towards me,' Lukas sighed. 'You always seemed to be avoiding any attempt I made to show you how I felt.'

'I have always been attracted to you,' Megan said. 'From the very moment I saw you standing on the verandah of the hospital. But I tried to tell myself that nothing could come of it.'

'I don't understand,' Lukas said softly.

Megan rolled on her side, pulling gently at the hairs on Lukas's chest. 'I am frightened that I will lose you in this war. I have already seen friends lose the ones they loved and I swore that I would wait until the war was over before committing my feelings to any man.'

'So I caused you to break your oath,' Lukas teased. 'I'm sorry.'

'It must have been the wine,' Megan replied, rolling back beside Lukas to stare at the night sky.

'You hardly had any before you attacked me,'

Lukas grinned, and Megan straddled him again. Before the sun came to rise over Papua, Lukas Kelly knew he was truly in love.

Paul Mann counted thirty-four bombers high overhead and carefully plotted their bearing. From under the canopy of the rainforest he could see them fill the patch of blue above as slow-moving cruciform in the sky. He knew that they were the Japanese bombers now designated with the Betty name by the Americans, because he had trained himself in aircraft spotting from a chart issued to Irvin Rockman in his coast watching duties.

'Time to get back to camp,' he said to Amaiu, who knelt beside him, using his rifle as a prop. The former native policeman, dressed in little else than a pair of shorts and a bandolier of .303 rounds across his chest, stood, stretching his legs. Amaiu was tall and solid for a Tolai man and that, along with his high intelligence, had secured him a position in the colonial police force and made him such an asset to Irvin's small unit.

Amaiu led the way. Silently the two men cautiously moved along the half-hidden trail back to the base camp where the radio transmitter was located. For weeks now Paul had been with Irvin and his party of coast watchers waiting for news of whether there was a way to evacuate him from the island. When Irvin came down with a bad bout of malaria Paul had automatically assumed the tasks of reporting enemy shipping and aircraft movements to

Allied headquarters in Australia using Irvin's code name.

The two men had forged a friendship based on being of similar age and both having had experiences as soldiers in the Great War. They knew that their short bursts of radio transmissions would have been noted by Japanese signallers using radio direction finders. They also realised that they would be high on the enemy's agenda for capture and execution because of their valuable role. Thanks to their work and that of other coast watchers in the Pacific region, the Allies had been able to scramble aircraft to fly out and sink Japanese landing craft filled with troops, thus impairing their military objective of continuing south. It was a holding war, but critical to the overall American strategy of mobilising its vast industry to produce even more munitions. The war that the coast watchers waged was one of the loneliest and most dangerous being fought by any soldiers anywhere at the time. A game of cat and mouse with the numerically larger forces detailed to hunt them.

'Paul, old cobber,' Irvin greeted his unofficial colleague when the two men returned to their camp deep in the rainforest. 'I heard the bastards flying overhead. Did you get any info on them?'

Paul knelt by Irvin, who lay in a hammock strung low between two rainforest giants. 'How are you feeling, my friend?' he asked before delivering his report for transmission.

'Had better days, but I am up to sending any information you might have,' Irvin replied, hoisting himself unsteadily from the hammock. Paul could see how sweat-stained Irvin's shirt was and knew that he had probably weathered another bout of high fever followed by chilling sweat.

'I counted thirty-four Bettys on a bearing of one ninety south at ten forty hours.'

Irvin rose with some effort and shook his head to clear the fog that made him teeter like a drunken man. Paul rose to assist him but was waved off. 'I will be okay after I have something to eat and drink,' Irvin said with a weak smile of reassurance. 'Just a dash of the collywobbles – that's all.'

Paul respected his wish and walked with him to the radio concealed beneath palm fronds. The party of men was barely visible in their hide even in bright daylight. They had become very good at camouflage and only by chance or bad luck would their camp be spotted. Careful steps had been taken to avoid aerial observation and the covert contact Irvin's men had with some trusted villagers miles away provided them with an early warning of approaching Japanese patrols.

Amaiu manned the bicycle-like apparatus to pedal enough power to the radio, and Irvin transmitted the warning to the Allies. Contact was made and the warning was already being passed on to the appropriate command for analysis. The coast watcher had done his job.

'We will have to make another move soon,' Irvin said when he had completed his report. 'It seems things are getting a bit hot around here. Kesanarulu returned while you and Amaiu were down at the observation post with news that the Japs have just moved a company-sized unit into the village. Seems that they are still onto us and Kesanarulu doubts that his contacts in the village will remain very steadfast if the Japs start playing rough in their usual fashion. The good news is that he was able to bring back some fresh pig meat and rice for us.'

Paul took a deep breath and sighed. This would be their fifth move in two weeks, each move was a back-breaking trek carrying the heavy radio equipment on their backs. But the radio was the centre of their universe – their sole reason for being behind enemy lines – and without it they may as well have gone home.

Paul wandered over to where he'd left his meagre kit: a change of clothes, a revolver and few spare rounds plus a Japanese rice bowl he now called his own. His boots had been patched many times and he calculated that they only had about another ten miles wear in them before they would be beyond repair. Supplies were low and most of their food was scrounged from local villagers who were neither sympathetic nor hostile to the coast watching party. As far as they were concerned the war was something between the Europeans and Asians and only became personal when the Japanese came to their villages, raped their women and murdered their boys for the sheer savage pleasure of inflicting pain. Then they were either cowered into submission or moved to take revenge. It was the latter that was most useful to Irvin in his intelligence gathering. The coast watchers had been fortunate so far and the ambush when Sandy Robinson had been killed had been the last clash they had with the enemy. Sandy's death had caused Paul many sleepless nights, reliving the moment he had killed the young soldier in an act of mercy. It seemed as if there was no balance in life to offset what Paul was beginning to view as the murder of an innocent man. He had not spoken of his terrible decision to Irvin, who presumed that Sandy had been killed by Japanese bullets.

'There is something I should tell you,' Irvin said, sitting himself down next to Paul and wrapping his spare kit into a piece of tent canvas. 'I have been in contact with ANGAU. It seems that there is going to be some kind of rescue attempt of the boys still evading the Japs. I haven't told you before because I didn't want you to get your hopes up but now it doesn't matter. We are too far outside their rendezvous points of embarkation. So it seems that you will have to remain with me until the situation changes.'

'I thank you for telling me, Irvin,' Paul said. 'But I do not expect that I have any importance to your government anymore. My mission to ascertain who could be trusted under occupation was a failure. Just a little too late to achieve much.'

'You have not failed here,' Irvin said. 'With me being laid out you have taken over to keep up the flow of information back to HQ. Maybe some of it has resulted in the waylaying of Jap plans. Maybe between us we have sent a few ships to the bottom or caused one or two planes to be blown out of the sky. Who knows? So don't go thinking you have failed over here. You are a cobber of the best kind.'

Paul smiled. He still remembered the first time

he had heard the Australian slang for a friend. Jack Kelly had used it when they had been reunited in Port Moresby just after the Great War when Paul had emigrated with Karin and his son, Karl and his troubled sister, Erika, from Germany, leaving the troubles of the Old World behind them. Paul now treasured its use by men like Jack and Irvin as it meant an unconditional acceptance into an exceptional band of men.

'I miss my family,' Paul said quietly. 'I hope Karin and Angelika will be safe in Townsville.'

'That your wife and daughter?' Irvin asked.

'Yes, I also have a son. Last I heard he was serving somewhere in the Middle East with the army. He is an infantry officer.'

'I have a son in the RAAF who I last heard was flying fighters out of Darwin. It's a terrible irony that we fought the last war so this would not happen to our children,' Irvin said. 'I am sure that your family will be okay.'

'I hope the same for you,' Paul responded.

'Well, time to get back on the track and get out of here before our little yellow friends find us,' Irvin said, rising to supervise the relocation of his campsite. 'Maybe something will happen to get you home to your missus and family,' he added reassuringly.

Watching his friend walk away, Paul let out a deep sigh. *Just words*, he thought sadly. He was rapidly losing hope that he would ever get off the island alive. This war was now too big for anyone in a position of authority to be worried about an individual yearning for his family. For Australians the matter occupying their every thought was surviving the impending invasion and subsequent enslavement by the Japanese Emperor.

It was Sen who quietly told Jack Kelly of Paul Mann's predicament. Jack had wrangled a pass to Sen's residence from an old friend involved in the tight security surrounding the bungalow. An officer with the new administration of ANGAU, he had listened as Jack explained how he needed to visit Iris to discuss their inheritance.

'I suppose since it was you who brought Sen's activities to our attention it's not likely that you would be a threat to security,' he said, leaning back in his chair, chewing the end of a fountain pen. He sat up and reached into a drawer of his desk and withdrew a pad of official government forms. 'This will get you to the OC out there and it will be up to him whether you are allowed to see this Iris sheila,' he said, scribbling his signature on the form. 'I can't promise more than that.'

Jack took the form and hitched a ride with a supply truck out to Sen's residence. He was unsurprised to see the guards posted around the house, as Sen's counter-intelligence role was of vital importance in providing misinformation to his Japanese controller, who still did not appear to realise that their man near Moresby was a double agent.

Jack charmed the young officer from army intelligence into allowing him a brief talk with Sen. Jack was impressed at how the house had been converted to a signals centre with an area soundproofed for Sen to work in. It was a busy place with signallers manning the radio sets, hunched forward with their earphones over their heads, jotting down incoming transmissions and turning knobs to scan for allocated frequencies. Obviously a decision had been made to shift counter-intelligence signals out of Moresby to a place safe from bombing. Sen's place was ideal as it was unobtrusively tucked away into the surrounding forest.

In truth, Jack had really wanted to see his old friend again and Iris had only been his excuse to do so. No matter what Sen had done, he still remained the man who had helped Jack so much in the past, including helping with the purchase of his first ship, the lugger *Erika Sarah*.

Under the scrutiny of an armed guard Jack and Sen were allowed to walk in the garden.

'Paul is trapped on New Britain,' Sen whispered.

Jack pretended not to hear him.

'Do you know where?' Jack asked, equally as quietly.

'I overheard the duty officer discussing his evacuation from the southern part of the island when he was in contact with a coast watcher there. It seems that your government cannot do it so Paul is stuck. They can't reach him, but I know about the rescue mission the NGVR are mounting to get survivors off the island.'

'Is there any way you can tell me where Paul is?' Jack asked with a pained expression.

'I am afraid not,' Sen replied, stopping to gaze

back at his house. 'It was only good luck that I actually overheard the transmission and Paul's name mentioned. It seems that he is doing a valuable job as an assistant to the resident coast watcher.'

'Momis comes from the south of the island,' Jack said. 'Maybe if we could get him over there on the *Independence* he might be able to use his clan links to locate Paul.'

'That is not a good idea,' Sen said. 'You know that the Japanese are consolidating their grip on New Britain. You would be blown out of the water before you even got close.'

Jack fell silent, contemplating the awesome task should he pursue it. 'I just can't leave Paul to die,' he finally said in a despairing tone. 'He is like a brother to me.'

'I suppose if anyone can do it, it will be you, Jack,' Sen said, turning to walk back to the house. The guard had signalled that their time was up, reminding Sen that he was still officially under house arrest for his crime of treason.

'I guess that I should drop in and see Iris,' Jack finished. 'That is why I am supposedly here.'

TWENTY-SIX

When Jack Kelly returned to the wharf at Port Moresby supplies were being loaded aboard the *Independence* by the three newly hired native crewmen. Lukas, stripped to his shorts, was overseeing the operation.

Leaping aboard, Jack greeted his son and motioned for him to follow him below. Lukas gave a short order for Momis to take over the loading.

'I have some news about your Uncle Paul,' Jack said.

'What about Uncle Paul?' Lukas asked, rummaging in a cabinet for a rag to wipe the sweat from his brow.

'He is alive and somewhere in the south of New Britain.'

'Then he will be on the list for evacuation,' Lukas said with relief. 'Thank God.'

'I'm afraid not,' Jack said. 'It seems he is too far south to be picked up. The Japs have tightened the net around the island and last I heard from my sources at HQ the only shipping allocated for the rescue must head south to Townsville or Cairns after the survivors are picked up. It's risky enough and the south of the island has been struck from the list. Paul is stranded, without any hope of getting off.'

Jack did not have to elaborate. Lukas knew that being stranded in Japanese-occupied New Britain was as good as a death sentence. Paul Mann was not a young man and the rigours of evading Japanese search parties would wear him down to the point that he could easily make a mistake costing him his life. 'What can we do?' Lukas asked, suspecting that his father had already formulated a plan.

'You and I sail over to New Britain, put Momis ashore to ask questions of his clansmen around the south of the island, find Paul and sail for Townsville.'

'As simple as that,' Lukas smiled, a touch of irony in his statement. 'How do you get permission in the first place to carry out such a risky mission? You are on active service like I am with the NGVR. We are not in a position to go sailing around without permission.'

'I was not thinking about asking permission,' Jack replied. 'If I did, the CO would stamp the mission as suicidal and stop me from going.'

'I was kind of thinking a bit along the same lines,' Lukas said. 'Our chances of succeeding are a lot less than the chances of being killed.'

'I promised Karin a long time ago that I would never allow anything bad to happen to Paul,' Jack said quietly, gazing out of a porthole at the Moresby harbour filled with shipping. 'That promise still stands. Besides, I know Paul is stupid enough to do the same for me. You are not obliged to sail with me.'

'You actually think that I wouldn't come with you?' Lukas said, shaking his head in bewilderment. 'We have been up against the odds and always won before,' he added. 'Like when we first bought the *Erika Sarah* all those years ago.'

'It may be better if you stayed behind on this one,' Jack said. 'I don't know if I could go on living knowing that it was me who led you to your death.'

'It's war, Dad,' Lukas said, reaching out to grasp his father's shoulder. 'We take our chances together.'

Jack gazed at his son's face and saw the grim determination. It was an expression he knew well. 'I think the old girl could do with a bit of upgrading in the arms department though,' Jack said. 'We sail in twenty-four hours. I will get clearance from the harbour master and see if I can scrounge up a little extra to help us out with the schooner's defence.'

Jack had a real skill for obtaining the unobtainable and returned before nightfall with a smile across his face that spoke of an afternoon filled with drinking and success. He was driven to the schooner's place at the wharf by an American engineers officer in a jeep.

'Lukas,' Jack called from the wharf. 'Get Momis and the boys up here to help me unload.'

Lukas popped his head above deck and saw his crew already scrambling over the side to assist in the unloading of the jeep. Jack stood by puffing on a cigar as the crew picked up the wooden crates and took them aboard. Lukas wondered what was in them.

'Like you to meet my old cobber Captain Madison,' Jack said to his son when he joined them on the wharf. 'This is my first mate Lukas Kelly, and number one son. Captain Madison and I have had a mutually successful afternoon.'

Lukas nodded to the tall American in his immaculate uniform.

'Pleased to meet you,' the American drawled. 'Your old man says that he once owned a gold mine out here.'

'That's right,' Lukas confirmed, but wondered at the statement with growing suspicion.

'You prepared to countersign these papers then?' Captain Madison asked, producing a couple of sheets of crumpled paper that appeared at first glance to be property deeds. Lukas glanced at his father who gave him a wink.

'Are these the deeds to Dad's gold mine?' Lukas asked when the papers were handed to him.

'He says they are,' the American replied. 'Your old man reckons that because the Nips will surely overrun your mine, he is prepared to hand over the deeds to me in exchange for one or two things I was able to put my hands on for him.'

'So why would they be any good to you?' Lukas asked, glancing up at the captain.

'One day, Uncle Sam is going to kick the little yellow bastards all the way back to Japan,' Madison answered. 'And when that day comes I will own a gold mine here in New Guinea.'

'I suppose you will,' Lukas replied with surprise at the American's optimism. 'If my father wishes to trade whatever he has with you then I will countersign the letter granting you possession of the deeds. But I have to ask, how do you know they are genuine?'

'Before the war I was a lawyer back in Tennessee,' Madison answered. 'I know a title deed when I see it.'

Lukas signed the papers Captain Madison put before him and with a handshake the American got back into the jeep and drove away.

'Get the stuff aboard,' Jack ordered, and the crates were lugged onto the deck of the schooner. Lukas and the crew stood about them with an air of curiosity. Jack tossed the remains of his cigar stub over the side and, with a jemmy, opened the first crate to reveal an air-cooled .50 calibre machine gun lying on its side.

'Bloody beauty,' Lukas exclaimed at the sight of the powerful weapon. 'Where did it come from?'

'A downed Yank bomber, I believe,' Jack said, standing back to allow the crew to gaze upon the weapon capable of long range and hard hitting accuracy. 'There is more,' Jack said, levering open the next crate to reveal two .45 Thompson sub machine guns.

Lukas' eye lit up and he retrieved one of the sub machine guns from the crate. His father continued to open the other crates. Mills grenades were stacked in one, a couple of Browning .45 semi-automatic pistols and tins of ammunition for all the weapons in another.

'Tried to get a forty mills Bofors but Captain Madison baulked at that. Just a little too obvious, he thought. But I was able to scrounge a couple of these,' he said, retrieving a strange-looking device. 'They fit on the end of the Lee Enfield and can be loaded with a grenade, then a blank round is used to project them, turning the rifle into something like a mortar.'

'All for the Hindenburg mine,' Lukas laughed. 'It played out years ago. Not worth the paper it was written on.'

'The title was real enough,' Jack said, lighting another cigar and puffing contentedly on it. 'Besides, you never know, with Yankee know-how he just might get it working again – if we win the war. And if he doesn't, it couldn't happen to a nicer bloke than a bloody lawyer. I have no doubt that they are just as bad in the States as here. So let's stow this below and we can show Momis and the boys how to use the stuff once we're out of the harbour. From what you have told me about Momis' prowess with the Lewis I reckon that he has earned the right to be first gunner on the fifty cal.'

Momis grinned at the praise heaped on him by Masta Jack and gazed lovingly at the big machine gun lying at his feet. He could take on the whole Japanese navy and air force with such a gun, he thought.

'I will get clearance to sail at zero one hundred hours tomorrow,' Jack said. 'In the meantime I am going to nip back into town and see if I can scrounge a carton of beer for the trip. Your Uncle Paul will need one when we pick him up. Don't expect me until around midnight. I will probably have a couple with the boys.'

Lukas turned his attention to having the weapons moved below as his father clambered over the side onto the wharf. There was a lot to do before they sailed.

A mere few miles away Ilsa Stahl had finished her first assignment. She had been talking to the soldiers from an American engineers unit working at the Seven Mile airfield, having been granted permission by their commanding officer to obtain their views on the war in the Pacific. The soldiers were taken by her elegant beauty and charming accent, and talked freely of how they missed families, girlfriends and wives back home. Ilsa took down her notes in short-hand while Gene Fay stood to one side, smoking a cigarette and gazing across the airfield shimmering under the heat of the tropical sun. From sandbagged emplacements scattered around the vital air-strip, the long barrels of anti-aircraft guns aimed skyward. Around the adjoining scrub lay the shattered fuse-lages of airplanes caught on the ground by Japanese fighters and bombers. In the distance the low hills baked in the tropical sun. With any luck he might be reassigned to London where the real war was, Gene thought. Albeit it was a place where bombs were a regular disturbance in the night but it was also still somewhere where you could find a bath and a good bottle of scotch. Port Moresby was the end of the world.

'I have enough for an article,' Ilsa said, strolling across the dusty field dressed in baggy trousers and an ill-fitting fatigue shirt.

Gene realised that he was ogling the young woman but so too was the group of men she had just left. She certainly had a fine figure, despite the camouflage uniform she wore.

'I had a talk with an Aussie contact of mine,' Gene said, joining Ilsa as she walked towards their car. 'He's a police sergeant based in Moresby by the name of Groves who does a bit of liaison with the Aussie army. He said he knew your uncle and his family well.'

Ilsa turned towards the journalist. 'Does he know where he is?'

'Sorry,' Gene said, shaking his head. 'It seems that your aunt is down Townsville way and your Uncle Paul was assigned to do something over in Rabaul about the same time the Japs hit. No one Sergeant Groves has spoken to knows his fate since then.'

Ilsa's expression showed her disappointment as the American newspaper man hurried to add, 'I might have some good news for you on the other guy you asked about, Jack Kelly. The Aussie sergeant said he has seen him around Moresby on sick leave from his unit.'

This time Gene could not read the change of expression of Ilsa's face. When they reached the car he flicked his cigarette into the dust.

'Does your police contact know where I might contact him?' she asked quietly.

'Sure,' Gene replied, opening the door to the driver's side of the car. 'You came in on his son's schooner from Finschhafen. It seems that Jack Kelly stays over on the *Independence* with his son while they are both in Moresby.'

Ilsa gripped the open car door to prevent herself from fainting. Lukas Kelly! She had not known Lukas' family name when she had been aboard the schooner. Now she was learning that it had been captained by her half-brother!

'Are you okay?' Gene asked when he noticed the shocked reaction to his news.

'Just a little too much sun,' she said, regaining her composure and slipping into the passenger seat. 'It is nothing more.'

She sat silently on the short trip back to their tent tucked away from the airfield at the foot of the hills. She was now wondering whether she should even attempt to make contact with her biological father.

Jack Kelly returned to the wharf at twelve thirty in the morning. It was dark and guarded by nervous sentries. 'Just heading down to the *Independence*,' he informed a soldier challenging him. The guard recognised Jack and let him pass.

Jack strolled to where the big cargo ships were silhouetted against the moonless night sky and froze when he stared into the empty space where the *Independence* had been docked.

'She sailed about an hour ago,' the sentry said to Jack when he hurried back to him. 'I thought you knew.'

Jack shook his head and cursed. So the little bugger thought he could do it on his own, Jack reflected bitterly. 'Damn you, Lukas!' he roared. 'You stupid bugger, you will get yourself killed.'

TWENTY-SEVEN

Lukas Kelly did not feel guilty for leaving his father ashore. He knew that he had done the right thing and that his father would return to his unit when his leave was up in Port Moresby. Now Lukas could attempt the rescue of Paul without his father's life being endangered in what amounted to a near-suicidal mission. He was now better armed, although no real match for the Japanese navy, but at least he had the firepower to take on any Japanese aircraft that should attempt to sink him — so long as they were alone and not in squadron strength.

The sun was just rising and the sea was choppy as Lukas steered the *Independence* on a course eastward. Momis was at the helm and Lukas pored over his charts of the coastal region east of Port Moresby. Navigating a course was hard enough, let alone having to consider being intercepted by an enemy surface ship.

Ilsa sat in her tent and stared at the canvas wall. Missed him by mere hours, she recriminated herself. The police sergeant had told her that Jack Kelly had been returned to his unit. He had been put aboard a lugger two days after his schooner had sailed from Port Moresby, supposedly to resupply a post down the Papuan coast. The police sergeant could not tell Ilsa exactly where Jack Kelly's unit was. 'Just somewhere up around the Bulolo–Wau area.'

So Ilsa started asking questions about her father's unit. She was establishing contacts – aided by Gene – and heard of the New Guinea Volunteer Rifles. From what she could gather it was a strange collection of men who were truly affiliated with Papua: gold miners, plantation owners, public servants and a few adventurous regular army types. It was as if the unit had sprung up like some sporting club to have a go against the Japanese, and from what she could glean from her contacts they were the men most in contact with the enemy's front lines – tough bush men who had come to consider themselves a match for an enemy most saw as supermen.

She was able to read an order sent to the NGVR from the Australian army headquarters: 'YOUR TASK IS TO PREVENT ENEMY CROSSING MOUNTAINS.' The Australian liaison officer, smitten like most men around her, laughed at the order. 'The poor bastards are outnumbered, suffering from lack of essential medical supplies and weapons, and our government sends them this signal. It's a bloody joke. Not that you got this from me, but I think they are heroes and the people back home should read about what they are doing collecting intelligence right under the Nips' noses. And keeping the gate closed on our flank. They are the only ones currently standing between us and the Japs who have landed all along the east coast.'

Ilsa was intrigued by the little bits and pieces she was collecting on the Australian military unit tasked with holding off the whole Japanese army, from their bases in the goldfields high in the mountains west of the ports of Lae and Salamaua, where the Japanese had landed to seize the vital airfields. She was learning more about the mysterious Jack Kelly from men who had known him at different stages of his life: war hero, gold prospector, prosperous gold mine owner, skipper of coastal sailing ships and finally a soldier again. All spoke highly of a man of honour who was good for his word and a handshake.

Ilsa also learned of the tragedy that came to her father with the loss of his American wife, Victoria. It was rumoured that his schooner was almost sunk after being rammed by a Japanese submarine in a time when the two countries were supposed to be at peace.

Her half-brother was also an interesting young man who, it was said, had killed an infamous criminal when he was still in his teens in defence of her Uncle Paul's family. The more she heard about this side of her biological family, the more she started to understand the impulses of her own life. The man she had long thought was her father had often told her that she was nothing like her mother except in physical appearance. He had said she must have taken naturally after her real father. Ilsa had resented Gerhardt Stahl for saying that she had not taken after him. She still loved and mourned for the man who had risked his life to get her out of Germany. He would always be her real father.

'Knock knock,' Gene said, entering the tent that served as their office. 'Do I see a pose in pensiveness before me?' he asked lightly when Ilsa glanced up at him from behind the tiny fold-down table that served as her work desk.

'I was just thinking how boring reporting from Moresby is,' she replied. 'When do we see some real action?'

'This will do me,' Gene grunted, searching about for a field chair to sit on. 'The goddamned Jap air raids are as close as I want to be to this war.'

'How would I go about getting up to the gold-fields around Wau?' Ilsa asked.

Gene stared at her with a look that questioned her sanity. 'You don't,' he replied, rummaging in his shirt pocket for his crumpled pack of cigarettes. 'It's all Aussie stuff and not much interest to readers back home. We are down here to await the great white armada, should it ever arrive in these waters, and then tell the folks back home how we are winning the war. At least here you can still get a cold beer and a hot shower. No doubt the first may not appeal to you as much as the latter.'

'I would like to write an article on the unit that was responsible for evacuating American missionaries from Finschhafen a few weeks ago. That would be of interest to readers in the US.'

Gene lit a cigarette. 'I didn't know that anyone was opposing the Japs,' he answered.

'From what I have heard, an Aussie unit called the New Guinea Volunteer Rifles has men out in the bush monitoring Japanese movements on the east coast around Lae and Salamaua. The unit is composed of men recruited locally from Papua and New Guinea.'

'They sound a bit like our Minute Men from the War of Independence when we fought against the Limeys,' Gene said. 'A kind of militia made up of civilian soldiers.'

'I suppose they are,' Ilsa conceded. 'That could be the angle for my story.'

'They are Aussies though and I know the folks back home wouldn't even know where Australia is let alone be interested in any story about them. Forget it – besides, you haven't got a snowball's hope in hell of getting up there. It's too rugged and dangerous, and if the Japs don't get you malaria or starvation will.'

'But my fath–' Ilsa checked herself. 'Maybe you are right,' she ended and stared out at the shimmering heat. Soon dusk would come and she had been invited to the American engineers' club for drinks. There she would ask some more questions and possibly find a way up to the front. Ilsa smiled to herself. She was aware of the impact she had on men and knew it gave her the edge in a male-dominated world.

The itch of the sweat under the beard he had let grow upon his return to the NGVR was driving Jack Kelly mad. He knew the slightest move could mean death as the Japanese patrol of ten moved across their front. Lying beside him was Rifleman Andrew Pettit and between them they only had one Webley Scott revolver. The choice had been made to leave rifles behind to allow the two-man observation patrol to creep as close as possible to the airfield now under enemy control. They had lain for three hours, watching the activity around the airfield, counting aircraft types and the number of take-offs and landings. The information would be relayed back to Moresby via radio from a base in the mountains.

The two men considered their hide at the edge of the scrub to be reasonably secure from view but not from any enemy patrol that might get lucky and stumble on them.

Jack could see that the patrol was not at full alert. The men had no doubt been roused from lighter duties at the Lae airfield and sent out on a clearing patrol of the perimeter. They carried their rifles slackly, and had Jack been in command of a better armed fighting patrol he could have easily ambushed and wiped them out.

The Japanese patrol came to a stop a mere ten yards from where Jack and Rifleman Pettit lay under their camouflage of grass and tree branches. Jack could hear them chattering. Rifles lay on the ground at their feet as they sat around wiping sweat from their faces and smoking cigarettes. Jack could see that the senior NCO in command of the patrol had not put out sentries to provide a forward alert system. From what Jack knew of the Japanese strategy it seemed that the enemy was consolidating the Lae area and continuing to stick, in the main, to the roads with motorised patrols. It seemed that the threat of the NGVR in the hills was working. The Japanese did not have enough intelligence about their actual strength and were being cautious. If nothing else, the NGVR had contained the enemy's forces to the coastal region – at least for the moment.

Very slowly – inch by inch – Jack reached under his neck to scratch the itch. He glanced sideways and could see the fear in the young rifleman's wide eyes. Jack flashed a broad grin to reassure him. It appeared to work as Andrew Pettit returned the gesture with a weak, sickly grin of his own. He had the revolver and it was pointed at the nearest Japanese soldier only about five yards away. Should they be detected, Pettit would fire at the nearest soldier and both men would leap up and run like hell. It was their only means of surviving.

Ten minutes passed and the patrol continued to sit around chatting, laughing and smoking cigarettes. Ten minutes felt like ten hours to the men watching their enemy from ground level. The itch returned but this time Jack did not attempt to scratch it.

The Japanese soldier nearest them stood,

stretched and bent down to pick up his rifle, turning to stare directly at Jack and Andrew's position. Both men felt the fear grip them. Life had come down to split seconds of decision. The enemy soldier wore glasses but still appeared myopic. Jack knew he was actually staring directly at them and he watched the soldier's face from under hooded eyes to see if there was any change in his expression.

The NCO in command of the patrol shouted an order and the soldier staring at them turned his head. The rest of the patrol were rising to their feet, picking up weapons. It was obviously time to move and Jack thanked God for the sergeant thinking about getting back to his mess and indulging in a sake drinking session. Maybe he thought the idea of the patrols a bit idiotic, Jack considered as he lay hugging the hot earth, thinking too that no sane man would attempt to creep in this close to his enemy and stake out an observation post in broad daylight. The patrol sauntered away and when they were out of sight Jack let himself take a deep breath.

'Bloody too close for comfort,' Andrew whispered. 'I thought we were goners.'

'You kept your head,' Jack replied. 'I was worried that you might bolt when that Jap was looking in our direction.'

'I was watching to see what you would do,' Andrew replied. 'I figured that you had done something like this in the last war.'

'Not if I could help it,' Jack grinned. 'It's too bloody dangerous.'

When night fell the two men wriggled from their hide to make their way cautiously on foot back to base along the Markham River. Their report was more valuable to the Australian military than their lives. They were, after all, in the opinion of the Australian government, expendable in these dark and desperate days.

TWENTY-EIGHT

The jungle-covered ridgeline finally levelled off and Paul Mann felt the throbbing in his body ease when Irvin signalled a rest. Collapsing against the buttress roots of a rainforest giant, Paul Mann sucked in air for his tortured lungs. The climb had taken from first light to midday and the torrential rain had turned the route into a river of thin mud, which streamed down to grease every inch of ground. They struggled hand over hand, then as if on cue, the rain ceased as soon as they found the level ground, but only to be replaced by a steaming, water-logged air.

Irvin was on his feet but used his rifle as a crutch to support his weight. He lifted his head and smiled weakly at Paul. 'Getting too old for this,' he rasped. 'A man should be back in Rabaul at the club sipping a gin and tonic and discussing the local cricket selection.'

Kesanarulu moved past Paul to take up position on the trek to their new base of operations. The forward scout cast the German planter a sympathetic look and wondered why old white men would want to be in a young man's war. In seconds he had disappeared into the thick green scrub.

'I was . . .' Paul froze mid-sentence when he saw Irvin suddenly raise his hand for silence. Paul slipped his hand to the pistol at his hip and wrapped his hand around its butt.

'You hear anything?' Irvin hissed.

Paul could see the former native policeman tense. He shook his head. He could not hear anything except the silence. No bird calls – just the pounding of his heart in his ears.

Then it came. A burst of machine gun fire from the direction Kesanarulu had just gone in, then a strangled scream and the explosion of rifle fire.

'Japs!' Irvin shouted.

His men looked about desperately for a place of safety and Paul could hear the excited chatter of a single Japanese voice calling out orders. He guessed it was a Japanese commander redeploying his troops because when the shooting stopped he could hear men crashing through the scrub, pushing along the ridge towards them. Paul knew what he must do.

'Give me your rifle!' he screamed at Irvin, who was for a second transfixed by indecision.

Irvin swung on Paul. 'What?'

'Give me your rifle and ammo,' Paul replied, holding out his hand. 'I will hold them at bay while you get the boys back down off the ridge.'

Irvin appeared confused at Paul's request. 'Your bloody rifle and ammo!' Paul screamed again. Irvin quickly gathered his thoughts, shaking off the confusion. It was obvious what his friend had in mind. 'C'mon, get out,' Paul urged. 'We don't have time to argue.'

Paul rose from behind the buttress of the tree and strode over to Irvin. The Japanese had already begun probing the undergrowth in front of them with rifle and machine gun fire, the bullets flicking fragments of vegetation down on them. He snatched the rifle from Irvin. 'Get out of here while I hold them off,' he shouted at the coast watcher. 'I will follow you down later.'

Irvin slipped the bandolier of .303 rounds from over his shoulder and handed it to Paul. 'Make bloody sure you do,' he said, taking Paul's revolver from him in exchange for the Lee Enfield. Without answering, Paul walked back to the flat rising buttress of a tree and placed himself in a firing position behind it as Irvin rallied his men to follow him back down the ridgeline and off the side into the steep, jungle-covered ravine below.

Paul laid the belt of ammunition beside him and flipped open the pockets on the bandolier for ease of reloading. He quickly slipped the sights to minimum range and waited. He did not have to wait long as a bullet smacked the timber beside his cheek, showering him with chips of wood. He could not see the man who had shot at him but nonetheless fired into the dense bush to bring the Japanese advance to a cautious halt while they redeployed to neutralise his position. At least he had bought time for Irvin and his men.

Paul worked the bolt to eject the spent cartridge, reloading and seeking a target. Fortunately he noticed a flash of movement to his right as one of the Japanese attempted to outflank him. The soldier was good, going to ground, Paul thought grimly as he swung his rifle and fired three shots into the area. A strangled yelp of pain gave him satisfaction. A hit.

Sweat poured into Paul's eyes and he wiped it away with the back of his hand. The bush to his front seemed to explode as two squat Japanese soldiers rushed at the tree with bayonet-fixed rifles. Paul fired point blank, hitting one of his attackers in the chest, but he did not have time to work the rifle bolt and reload so he rose to confront the second soldier. He was vaguely aware of the smell of fish on the man's breath as the bayonet slid into his stomach. The pain was like fire and his roar of rage a combination of pain and anger. With all his strength he slammed the brass-plated butt of the Lee Enfield into the Japanese soldier's face, splitting his forehead. His opponent teetered and blood splashed them both as the soldier went down at Paul's feet, dragging the rifle and bayonet from Paul's belly.

Paul Mann screamed but his cry was cut off by the hammering of bullets stitching his body from a Nambu machine gun. He crumpled forward over the two dead men at his feet and lay in a strange state. The pain had gone from his body and he knew that he was dying. 'Karin,' he whispered as the blood flowed from his wounds. 'My love, I . . .' A bullet fired from a few yards away smashed the final words and life from the former German officer. There had not been time for tears as Paul recalled the one person who had loved him without asking anything but his love in return.

The Japanese emerged from the bush warily. Surprised to see the age of the European who had so quickly taken the lives of three of their comrades, they vented their rage by repeatedly stabbing at Paul's body with their bayonets.

Irvin had heard the short but sharp battle on the ridge while picking his way down into the ravine. He guessed Paul was probably dead by now. The shooting had stopped and the Japanese would rally to pursue him and his party. At least they now had a chance of disappearing in the thick undergrowth and evading their hunters. Paul Mann's sacrifice was not in vain.

Irvin's war was one of stealth and cunning. At this he had become very good and by nightfall he had succeeded in losing the Japanese. Within a day he and his men had established a new base in the mountains and transmitted a brief account of the presumed death of the heroic German planter from Papua. Signing off, Irvin reflected on whether those safe in Australia would ever recognise the lonely, unobserved courage of a man who had chosen to put his life on the line with little chance of survival. Holding his head in his hands, Irvin sighed at the futility of it all. Would what any of them did ever be recognised? Not if the Japs won the war, he thought.

• • •

Lukas Kelly was only a day's sailing from the southern end of New Britain when he was relayed the news of Paul Mann's death over the schooner's radio. With a heavy heart, the young Australian now abandoned the mission and turned the *Independence* about, for the return trip to Port Moresby.

Lukas had signalled the Australian authorities of his mission when he had cleared the southern tip of Papua near Milne Bay. It had been in a rough code of his own making, which he knew the receiver would understand if he was a follower of cricket. No doubt any Japanese listening into his frequency would not have long to decode what he had said. But it did not matter. His mere schooner was of little consequence to the might of the Imperial Japanese Navy.

Lukas had been correct in his assumption and the translation was passed on to a Japanese duty officer in Rabual who pigeon-holed the information as low priority. In due time the target list was re-coded and transmitted to Japanese surface ships and submarines working in the waters around the Papuan coast and northern Australia. To all naval commanders who received the signal, the schooner was simply classified as a target of opportunity should they come across it in their patrols.

All, except one. The commander of the I–47 put the schooner at the top of his list. It was a matter of saving face to destroy the *Independence*. Lieutenant Kenshu plotted the last estimated location of the schooner and guessed its destination. This time he would use a torpedo, despite the cost to the Emperor of deploying such an expensive weapon against a light surface craft.

Part Three

FUJI'S WAR

Early 1942

TWENTY-NINE

The sweet song of a butcher bird warbled from the tall eucalyptus trees close to Karin Mann's house outside Townsville. The distinctive Queensland-style bungalow built on stilts had been the first property Paul had purchased when they originally reached Australia after the Great War and it had always been their Australian home away from Papua. Karin was sitting on the front verandah shelling peas when she saw the distinctive red bicycle pedalled by a telegram boy from the Post Office. Squinting against the haze of the hot day she saw that the tiny figure at the end of the track leading to her home was cycling towards her house.

'Angelika,' she called over her shoulder. 'The post office boy is coming.'

Angelika wiped her floury hands on her apron and emerged from the kitchen, where she was preparing dough for bread-making. She joined her mother on the verandah and watched the boy approach. Karin gripped Angelika's wrist as the boy dismounted from the bicycle. He leant it against the fence and walked into the yard. In his hand he held an envelope.

'You Mrs Mann?' he asked from the bottom step.

Karin nodded and the boy could see how pale she appeared. He had seen that same pale expression on other women's faces when he arrived with a telegram.

'I got a telegram for you,' he said and walked up the steps to pass it to Karin. Without another word, he turned and walked back to his bicycle; he had two other telegrams to deliver this day and a long way to go.

'I would rather you open it,' Karin said to her daughter, who could see how her mother's hand trembled as she passed the envelope to her.

Angelika reluctantly accepted the telegram and slit open the envelope. Karin watched the expression on her daughter's face and knew that the message was not good.

'Is it my darling Paul?' she asked in a whisper.

'Yes, Mama,' Angelika answered, tears welling in her eyes as she dropped the telegram on the verandah. 'It is about Papa,' she said with a sob. 'The telegram says that he was reported missing in action somewhere in New Britain. But he wasn't even *in* the war,' Angelika stumbled back inside the house where she could go to her room and sob.

Stunned, Karin retrieved the telegram and read the terse words from a government official telling her that she no longer had a husband. Missing in action was tantamount to being dead. Why had the telegram been sent by someone in the government when, as far as Karin knew, her husband had nothing to do with the Australian military? He was a German by birth, after all, and thus an enemy alien. For some reason she thought of Jack Kelly, then she shook her head. No, Jack had always promised to keep Paul out of danger. It was not possible that he had anything to do with Paul being MIA.

Karin collapsed onto the chair, spilling the shelled peas across the verandah. What was worse than knowing that Paul was most probably dead was not knowing how this had all come about. Her beloved husband was supposed to join them in Townsville, not be missing in New Britain.

'Paul,' she gasped, the reality of her loss slowly dawning on her. 'Oh, Karl, not you next,' she sobbed, knowing that she would not be able to live if another telegram arrived at her little house.

Captain Karl Mann's posting was to No 7 Infantry Training Centre in the beautiful but rugged national park of Wilsons Promontory in southern Victoria. No one in the military district's headquarters in Melbourne seemed to know much about the infantry training centre's activities when he asked around.

As soon as Karl was trucked to his new assignment he was acutely aware this was not a standard infantry school. The security was tight and when they drove in he immediately noticed the establishment had few soldiers. Those he saw appeared in all sorts of strange dress and carried a variety of unusual weapons. The men themselves had a hard, confident look about them, and the training school was not laid out in the orthodox manner. There was definitely a very secretive air about the whole place, accentuated by a series of explosive blasts echoing from the thick scrub not far from where he had been dropped by his driver.

'Captain Mann?' a soldier asked after popping out from a tent with its sides up to catch the cold air. 'The boss will see you straightaway.'

Karl noticed that the soldier did not salute him as protocol dictated but he had enough sense to ignore the infraction of rules.

'Thank you,' Karl replied, hefting his kitbag over his shoulder to follow the soldier to a tent at the edge of the scrubby bush. Karl stood at the entrance until a voice bade him enter. He stepped inside and blinked in disbelief. The face that greeted him was all too familiar but certainly out of place in Australia.

Karl immediately saluted.

'Ah, congratulations on your promotion and gong,' Captain Featherstone said with a broad smile. 'Good to see that you accepted our invitation to join us.'

A little dazed, Karl accepted his handshake. 'I am kind of surprised to see you in our part of the world, sir,' he said. 'I thought that you were returning to London.'

'Have a seat, old chap,' Featherstone said, indicating a fold-out army-issue canvas chair. 'Smoke if you wish. We have a lot to talk about.'

Karl guessed that the British SOE man was not about to go into any discussion on why he was in Australia. And Karl was not about to ask him.

'I must say that it is good to renew an old and respected acquaintance,' Featherstone continued, lighting up a cigarette and taking a seat opposite Karl. 'As you have probably noticed already, this is not actually an infantry training unit. The name is just to divert any unwanted interest from our friends on the other side. It is a commando training unit established to train you Aussies in a new kind of warfare. Well, old to us, but new to you chaps. We call it guerrilla warfare and it takes a very special kind of chap to fight that kind of war. In my opinion, knowledge of guerilla warfare is going to be invaluable in the years after the war. I am not able to convince all my colleagues of this as they cannot see how the Japs have destabilised the Far East with their idea of the Greater East Asiatic Co-Prosperity Sphere. I suspect that when we eventually drive the sons of the Emperor back to Japan they will leave in their wake armies of nationalist guerrillas to resist our return to our former territories of Malaya and the Pacific. Our armies will require men with the expertise you will learn here as a commando.'

'You really think that we will win this war?' Karl asked with an edge of cynicism.

Featherstone looked at Karl as one would a child. 'Of course we will win. We have the industrial might of the USA on side now and our intelligence sources tell us that even Admiral Yamamoto, who carried out the attack on Pearl Harbor, has advised the Emperor that he can only promise that he will win the opening battles but not the war against our American cousins. I personally met Yamamoto whilst he and I were in the States on attaché duties back in the 1930s. Good poker player and an expert on oil supplies. As I remember he was a good chap on the wrong side. You know, the Yanks were so impressed with him that some of their oil companies actually approached him to leave the Imperial navy and go and work for them in the American oil industry. Needless to say he declined, but that says a lot for the dedication of the man to his country. But we are digressing from the topic of your role with us in the future,' the British naval officer continued. 'I think that you are made of the right stuff to have a future in your army after the war.'

Karl was rather surprised at the patronage he sensed that he was being given by the British, given he was the son of their former enemy and a colonial to boot. 'I was not thinking about a career in the army,' Karl replied. 'When this bloody war is over I hope to return to my old job as a patrol officer in Papua and New Guinea.'

'Ah, yes,' Featherstone answered. 'That is why I think you are just the man to deliver a talk to the lads here tonight.' Karl raised his eyebrows. 'Your experience is quite considerable in that part of the world and we are deploying a company or two there. A highly trained small force up against the Japs will help slow them down. As a matter of fact they will be working alongside the NGVR and I believe you have a couple of friends serving with them – a Sergeant Jack Kelly and his son, Rifleman Lukas Kelly.'

Karl was stunned. Lukas serving in the army? Karl knew from his mother's letters that his best friend was not medically fit to do so, and he had a sneaking suspicion that Jack probably had something to do with bending rules. 'If qualifying as a commando gets me back to Papua, then I am in, sir,' Karl said.

'Good man,' Featherstone said. 'As our rather enthusiastic Captain Calvert says, he will teach you to blow up everything from bridges to brigadiers. You will learn how to kill with your hands, live off the land, use every type of weapon available and escape from the enemy if captured. You will become the new kind of warrior for a new kind of war.'

Six weeks later Captain Karl Mann marched out of the No 7 Infantry Training Centre a much fitter man with a new range of deadly skills. His training had been more gruelling physically and psychologically than he had ever imagined. As promised, Karl learned new deadly skills of hunting and killing the enemies of the King. He proved to be one of the top students and gained the respect from all ranks for his demonstrated abilities in commando warfare.

Karl did not see the enigmatic British SOE man after the first week of training. He disappeared as mysteriously as he had arrived in Australia but somehow Karl knew that he would again meet this man who had taken so much interest in his life. At times Karl suspected that his destiny was being guided by faceless men working out of offices in London and Canberra, and whatever they had planned for him was unknown. For now he would be returning home to fight a guerrilla war against a tough and relentless enemy in the jungles of Papua and New Guinea. All he had to concern himself with was just staying alive.

When Karl reported to army HQ in Melbourne he was taken aside and informed of his father's death in the Pacific Islands. He was given no other facts as to why or specifically where, only told his death had occurred on the island of New Britain. But now Karl had a personal reason to wage his war against his new enemy, the Japanese.

At sea Lukas Kelly sometimes found it hard to comprehend that he was in a war zone. And on such a day as this, as Lukas stood at the helm, guiding his schooner south with a gentle nor-easterly in his sails, pushing his ship through gentle seas of frolicking dolphins gliding on the wake of his bow, he found it especially difficult to believe his country was at war.

Only Momis sitting cross-legged at the bow cleaning his beloved .50 cal machine gun reminded him of the conflict that was always ready to intrude into this peaceful world of blue seas and even bluer skies.

The loss of his much loved Uncle Paul weighed most heavily on Lukas during the nights when he was at the helm. On such nights he could reflect on his life and the people he loved. His father, for instance, should have been retired but the war had forced him back into service as a soldier in the NGVR. When Lukas was in a reflective mood the gentle memories of his precious time with Megan at the Mann plantation came to him. Just thinking of her smile and kiss alleviated the stress of skippering the *Independence* in enemy-patrolled waters. She had a way of gently growing on a man, he thought with a warm feeling.

'Radio fella call you, Masta Lukas,' one of the crew called up from the hatchway.

'Take the helm,' Lukas called back and the Solomon Islander clambered on deck to steer the big schooner.

Lukas went below, placed the headphones over his head and clicked the button to respond to his code name. The message transmitted across the waves from a radio operating out of Port Moresby ascertained his latitude and longitude. Lukas had calculated that he was about twelve hours sailing from Port Moresby just off the Papuan coast.

'Stand by, *Independence*,' the voice replied. Lukas sat patiently in front of the radio as a long silence followed.

'Calling *Independence*, over,' the disembodied voice finally broke the silence.

'*Independence*, over,' Lukas said into the mike.

'*Independence*, you are to continue your current course and investigate possible enemy activity at loc able charlie. I repeat, loc able charlie, niner.'

'Roger, loc able charlie, niner,' Lukas confirmed.

The Moresby operator signed off as did Lukas. Transmissions were kept short to avoid interception and fixing by Japanese radio monitors scanning Allied frequencies. Lukas took the headphones off and placed them on the table. He did not have to record the code for the pre-assigned area of operations as he was already familiar with it from past visits. He swore softly. The area of operations was near his father's friend Kwong Yu Sen's house. What did the Chinese man have to do with this?

Lukas went on deck and took the helm to steer a course closer to the coastline. He couldn't help but feel that he was steering his ship into a dangerous intrigue.

THIRTY

Captain Karl Mann knew Sydney well. As a boy he and Lukas had been sent south from Papua to attend boarding school there and when they had returned to Papua they left a lot of friends behind. So when Karl stepped off the train from Melbourne at Central Station it was an opportunity to go in search of one or two old friends before continuing his journey deep into northern Queensland.

Karl had been granted two days' leave in Sydney and knew who he would catch up with first. He rummaged in the pocket of his uniform trousers to retrieve some coins for the telephone. His first call was to the offices of Tom Sullivan. If anyone could provide him with some snatches of news from Papua, it would have to be Tom.

Karl was transferred to Tom's office and was warmly greeted by the solicitor. 'I am having a small party at my office tonight,' Tom said. 'Your call couldn't have come at a better time. The party is to celebrate a big contract one of my best employees has just secured.' They chatted for a short time about what they knew concerning Jack Kelly, Lukas and Iris. 'Do you know what ever happened to Marie?' Karl asked.

'Aha!' Tom said. 'Come tonight and all will be revealed.' Before Karl could ask any more questions Tom Sullivan said he had a client to cope with and made his excuses to cut the conversation short. 'Six o'clock at my office, and don't be late.'

Karl placed the phone in its cradle and stepped out of the booth to the salute of a passing soldier. He would check in to a hotel room arranged for him by the army and then fill in the afternoon by going to see a film in the city. He was looking forward to catching up with the solicitor, whose house he had spent many wonderful days at years earlier when Lukas had been seeing Sarah Sullivan, daughter of the colourful lawyer.

When Karl emerged from the Capitol Theatre in the centre of the city it was just after 5pm. The evening was balmy and Sydney hardly appeared to be a city under threat from Japanese forces. People still went about their business as if the war did not exist, except for a few who carried gas masks in containers. Needless to say there were many more uniforms to be seen in the street, both American and Australian, and when the sun was down the city would go into a state of darkness in compliance with the blackout regulations.

It was only a short tram trip to Tom Sullivan's legal offices and Karl arrived within minutes. In the anteroom he was met by Tom himself, who limped towards Karl with a beaming smile and his hand outstretched. 'Captain Karl Mann, MC,' he said taking Karl's hand. 'How the devil are you, young fella?'

Karl could feel the pressure of the solicitor's handshake and winced, as he had done when as young lads he and Lukas had gone to the Sullivan residence on the occasional weekend leave from boarding school. Tom Sullivan was held in awe for his position in Sydney society. The father of the beautiful but snobbish Sarah had been an intimidating figure in those days before the war. Now Karl and he shared something in common, both men having won the coveted award of the Military Cross. 'I'm fine, Mr Sullivan,' Karl replied, releasing the grip. 'It is good to see you, too. How is Mrs Sullivan, and Sarah?'

'The wife has gone to the country to stay for a while,' Tom answered, ushering Karl to a door. 'She fears that the Japs are going to land any day and come marching down Pitt Street. As for Sarah, well she is married to a young banker who is doing very well for himself.'

From behind the door Karl could hear the murmur of voices and a record player beating out a popular big band song. When Tom opened the door the eyes of those in the room were upon them. 'Everyone, this is a young man who I would like to introduce you to, Captain Karl Mann.'

Karl nodded and his eyes swept the room. There

was a mixture of both men and women of varying ages, all dressed in smart civilian clothes and obviously employees of the legal firm. They smiled back at Karl and when Karl's eyes came to rest on the most beautiful young woman in the room he felt a sudden shock.

'Your answer to that question about Marie,' Tom said, slapping Karl on the back. 'The party is being held because Marie closed a big contract with the largest shopping chain in the state.'

Karl could see that Marie was equally shocked. She stood in the company of two well-dressed young men in flash business suits and stared, mouth partially agape, almost tipping the flute of champagne she held onto the plush, carpeted floor.

'You should go over and make yourself known again,' Tom said with a wink. 'Not that Marie will tell me what happened in Palestine but at least I know enough to suppose that you had some kind of adventure together.'

Karl almost burst into laughter at the mention of an 'adventure together'. How could he tell the solicitor that at one stage the beautiful young lady standing so poised in the board room might have killed him – given the right circumstances. Instead, he mumbled that he might do that, and accepted a glass of champagne thrust into his hand. Before he could take another step he found himself caught up in a conversation with one of Tom's legal partners in the firm, discussing the campaign in Syria. The older man had served in Palestine with the Light Horse in the Great War and the conversation lapsed into a reminiscence of favoured recreational places in Jerusalem.

Karl kept glancing across the room to where Marie stood with the two young men. He had hoped to catch her eye but she appeared to be consciously avoiding him. 'Marie has a fine future with Tom's enterprises,' he heard the older man state. 'A combination of her French accent and exotic beauty is enough to convince Old Nick himself to desert Hades.'

Karl could agree with that. Dressed in a chic, body-hugging skirt and blouse, Marie was the epitome of a modern young businesswoman. Karl had been impressed by her beauty when he had first laid eyes on her in the Jerusalem café but transposed to this environment, she truly shone. He decided however that Marie was more interested in the two young men whose company she shared, and drank his wine faster than he should have. The evening wore on with a rotation of Tom's business acquaintances and colleagues introducing themselves and showing a passing interest in Karl's experiences as a soldier recently returned from the fighting in the Middle East.

Not used to the heady wine, Karl excused himself to leave the room. He had noticed a balcony running off from the anteroom that overlooked the city and decided that it was a good place to take time out from the monotonous questions about the war from the well-meaning but boring people. Unnoticed, he slipped away quietly. It was dark on the balcony and Karl lit a cigarette and leaned on the rails, gazing across the street to a space between the tall buildings where he could see the waters of the Harbour sparkling under a full moon. Karl felt a rare moment of peace. Behind him he could still hear the muffled laughter from the party and the clink of crystal champagne flutes.

'I did not speak to you at my party,' Karl heard the familiar voice say. 'I was embarrassed.'

Karl turned from the balcony rail to see Marie framed by the door. 'Hello, would you like to join me?' he asked.

Hesitantly, Marie stepped forward to stand beside Karl. She gripped the railing and stared towards the Harbour. 'It was a shock to see you tonight,' Marie said softly. 'I thought I was doing a good job of putting Palestine behind me.'

'It was a bit of a shock for me, too,' Karl said.

'You are now a captain, no?' she asked, turning to Karl.

'Yeah, and I hear that you are Tom Sullivan's up and coming executive for his retail enterprises. That's a long way from serving Arabic coffee in your father's café.'

'Pierre was not my real father,' Marie answered quietly. 'My father was a German Legionnaire.'

Karl was surprised at her confession. 'So we share common blood,' he said.

'I will always consider myself French,' Marie countered. 'I was raised as a French woman.'

'Whoever you are, I think that you are an extraordinary woman,' Karl said, turning to puff on his cigarette and watch the smoke curl away.

'Do you have a cigarette for me?' Marie asked.

'I had the impression that you don't smoke,' Karl teased. 'It is not a good habit to get into. Sadly, of late I have found the practice soothing for the nerves.'

'I don't smoke,' Marie replied. 'But I have a need of a cigarette now.'

Karl held the packet out to her and when she had retrieved a cigarette he lit a match. Marie took the hand in which he held the match and drew it to her. The cigarette flared.

'I think that I am nervous too,' Marie said, taking a short puff. 'But I will not continue smoking after tonight.'

'You have no reason to be nervous around me,' Karl said reassuringly. 'I will be leaving soon on the train to Brisbane.'

'You are going back to the war?' Marie asked.

'It looks that way,' Karl said, not making eye contact.

'Thank you for your earlier compliment, Captain Mann,' she said. 'I was afraid to walk up to you this evening because of what had happened when we were in Palestine. I thought that you might hate me for my role in your treatment at the hands of the German agent.'

Karl stepped back from the railing and laughed softly. 'That is all part of the beast we call war,' he said, facing Marie and noticing for the first time how frightened and nervous she appeared. He could not remember seeing her as vulnerable before in Palestine. 'I do not blame you or your mother for what happened. As a matter of fact we would not be having this conversation had it not been for the brave actions of your mother.'

'I think that you are right,' Marie said. 'I feel that fate brought you into my mother's and my life for the better.'

Karl felt a surge of respect and gentle love for the young woman. Her life before Australia had obviously been hard but she had the spirit to fight her way into a new life divorced from her old one. 'I would like to see you again,' he said.

Marie impulsively touched Karl's face with her hand. 'I would like that,' she said. 'I will make a confession to you. When I first met you I thought that you were a very handsome man. And now, in this place far from Palestine, I still see the same handsome man who I sense has a gentle soul.' She leaned forward and kissed Karl on his lips. 'That is to say thank you, Captain Mann.'

'My name is Karl,' he replied. 'Captain belongs to the soldier – and he is not all of me.'

'Karl,' Marie said. 'It is a strong name – I like it. But now I must return to my party or they will come looking for me.'

'I guess you should,' Karl conceded reluctantly.

'Until we meet again, *au revoir*.' Marie said, turning to leave the balcony.

Karl watched her walk away and sighed. Bloody time was against him, he swore under his breath. He turned, lit another cigarette and gazed at the Harbour. Something magical had happened in his life. Whatever it was he knew it would go with him into the jungles and battlefields of Papua.

He was not sure that it was love but he was certain that the attraction between him and Marie was mutual.

When Karl had finished the cigarette he returned to the party to bid Tom farewell. Marie was again standing across the room in the midst of a group of people. He caught her eye and she smiled.

Karl made his way home through the darkened city to his hotel. He fell on his bed, his head reeling from the champagne and memory of what had occurred on the balcony. As brief as the encounter had been, it had filled him with a reason to return and see the beautiful young woman. It was strange, he mused, staring at the ceiling, that war had brought them together. He only hoped that war would not drive them apart.

'I thought that you might like these,' Karl said awkwardly, standing in the anteroom of Tom Sullivan's office.

Marie gazed at the bouquet of flowers Karl held out to her and glanced up to smile at the soldier. '*Merci*, Karl,' she said, taking the arrangement of white, waxy gladioli from him. 'How did you know that I would be here?'

'Tom told me that you were due for a meeting with him this morning and I thought since it was my last day in Sydney that you and I could enjoy the splendid day outside.'

'But I must work,' Marie said.

'No you don't, young lady,' Tom Sullivan's voice

boomed from behind her. 'You take the day off and enjoy yourself.'

Marie turned to the solicitor standing in his office doorway and flashed him a grateful smile.

'Thanks, Tom,' Karl said, and turned to Marie. 'How would you like to go for a ferry ride to Manly and have lunch on the beach?'

'That sounds splendid,' Marie replied, still holding the flowers. 'But am I dressed for lunch?' she asked.

Karl's slow smile lit up his normally serious expression. 'For fish and chips, you are,' he said.

Marie handed the bouquet to Tom and placed her handbag on her shoulder. She took Karl by the arm and led him towards the door. Her tender gesture felt good and Karl was acutely aware of the wonderful scent of the perfume she was wearing.

Later, they stood at the bow of the ferry crossing the Harbour. It was a beautiful sunny day with just a touch of coolness in the autumn air. The little ferry glided past the great man o' war ships from the Australian and Allied fleets. Yet, among the reminders of the war were a few delicate-looking sailing skiffs dancing across the blue waters of the Harbour, crewed by those who had chosen to avoid their offices in the city on such a beautiful day.

Marie stood close to Karl, gripping the ferry's rails. The thump thump of the boat's engine was like a heartbeat and Karl watched her serene expression of joy as the ferry made its way towards the Manly pier, passing by the sandstone headlands dotted with the spindly vegetation of the foreshores.

'Almost there,' he said unnecessarily, the ferry's crew already preparing the ropes and gangplanks for landing.

'It is a beautiful city,' Marie sighed. 'I am glad that I came here.'

'Have you been to Manly before?' Karl asked as the ferry glided into the pier.

'No,' Marie answered, taking Karl by the arm to steady herself as the ferry bumped into the wharf. 'But Mr Sullivan has told me that you and your friend Lukas Kelly used to spend a lot of time here when you were on leave from your school.'

'Tom has told you a lot.' Karl smiled.

'That is because I asked him,' Marie replied mysteriously.

They stepped off the ferry and walked up the wharf. Seagulls scurried in front of them as they stepped out onto the street fronted by a hotel. Together they walked up the street past little shops. Marie would occasionally stop to look into the window of a dress or hat shop. Karl was aware that she had the ability to turn men's heads as they passed and Marie was aware that she received more then one look of envy from the women on the street. They were a fine-looking pair: the tall and well-built young captain wearing the ribband on his broad chest indicating his proven courage in war, and the petite, exotically beautiful young woman.

Karl stopped at a fish and chip shop, ordered two servings and was handed newspaper-wrapped parcels steaming with the aroma of salt and fish. He handed one to Marie and they then walked to the end of the street, where the Pacific Ocean rolled onto the beach of yellow sand.

'We can sit on the beach and feed the seagulls if you don't like the chips,' Karl said.

'I like chips,' Marie answered. 'I have had them before.'

Sitting side-by-side in silence, with their legs tucked up, they ate the chips with their fingers from the top of the packets, torn open to retrieve them. Karl was hungry and ate his meal unself-consciously while Marie picked delicately at her packet. They watched the great breakers crash on the shore. The beach was virtually deserted as the swimming season was over and only those who wished their solitude haunted the sands.

'When do you leave?' Marie asked.

'Tonight,' Karl said, tossing a chip to a gathering of gulls waiting patiently. With squawks and a flurry of white feathers they fell on the chip, chasing the lucky recipient for a share.

'That is too early,' Marie commented, also throwing out a chip to the gulls now gathering for more, with the same noisy result. 'Do you know where you are going?'

'Just somewhere up north,' Karl answered, not wanting to think about what lay ahead in the jungles of Papua and New Guinea.

Marie did not question him any further on the subject. She strongly suspected that Karl was going somewhere dangerous. 'It was nice talking last night,' she said quietly.

Karl turned his attention away from the squabbling seagulls. 'You may think I am what we say in Papua is, *long long luk*. That means to be crazy, but I never forgot your face in all the time after I met you. I don't know why but the memory of you stayed with me when I went back to the front and even when I travelled home. When I saw you last night it felt to me that a dream had come true.'

'I felt the same,' Marie answered. 'It is hard to say why I should feel this way about a man I hardly know. But it is through you I have found myself in a place that I now love. My mother has told me that it was because of what you did that we were able to be here.'

'Then it is only gratitude that you feel,' Karl said, with just the trace of bitterness in his voice.

'Oh, no,' Marie replied, impulsively gripping Karl's arm. 'It is more than that but I am afraid to . . . what do you say . . . commit myself to my feelings. All I know is that I like you very much.'

'That's a start,' Karl grinned. 'It's just too bad that we don't have more time to progress with that.'

'I do not understand,' Marie said with a puzzled expression on her face.

'It doesn't mean anything in particular,' Karl replied, glancing at his watch. He knew that he would have to make his way reluctantly back to the city to catch the train out that evening. 'I suppose we should go.'

They caught a ferry back to Circular Quay and sat side-by-side on the seats outside the passenger cabin talking about their lives. The conversation came easily, with laughter just as easy. When they stepped off the ferry at the end of the trip Karl realised that he was only a few hours from travelling out of Marie's life, possibly forever.

Karl walked Marie back to Tom Sullivan's office just before the staff streamed out to catch trams and trains home.

'Well, it has been a wonderful day,' Marie said, extending her hand to his. 'I wish that you were not going.'

Karl felt her warm touch. It was almost painful to say goodbye and he vehemently cursed the war to hell. How could it be that a stupid war was keeping any chance of love and happiness from the young? 'I would like to thank you, Marie,' he said softly. 'I hope that we can see each other again, one day.'

Marie gazed up into his eyes. 'That would be nice,' she said. 'Please be careful.'

Karl nodded. He could no longer bear standing amid the rush hour crowds walking around them and hurrying to their transport to the suburbs. At that moment he would have given everything he had to be one of those civilians if it meant staying in Sydney. With a sad smile, he turned and walked away, leaving Marie standing alone watching his retreating back.

Soldiers and kitbags, crying women and confused children farewelling loved ones off, stood on the railway platform. Steam from the great locomotive's coal-burning engine hissed and wreathed its way along the raised concrete siding. Sydney was falling under the influence of night as Karl stood beside his kitbag waiting to go aboard the train.

Soldiers passing him saluted self-consciously and he returned the gesture absent-mindedly. Only a couple of hours earlier he had been gazing into Marie's eyes, smelling the sweet perfume of her body and touching her hand. Never before had he felt so alone.

A whistle blew and a uniformed guard called to the predominantly khaki-clad men, with their slouch hats and rifles over their shoulders, to board. Karl bent down to pick up his kitbag and suddenly heard his name called. He stood up and turned to see Marie hurrying down the platform through the milling crowd of boarding soldiers.

'Karl!' she called again and threw herself into his arms.

Karl held her body against his and could feel the pressure of her hips. 'What are you doing here?' he asked.

'I could not let you go without telling you that I think I am falling in love with you,' she said and suddenly pulled his head down to hers. The kiss was long and sweet. 'Come back, *mon cheri*,' she gasped. 'I will miss you.'

'That was the progression I mentioned this afternoon,' he said with a broad smile on his face as he held her to him and took in the scent of her hair. 'Kind of makes the going worthwhile so I have a very good reason to return.'

'All aboard,' echoed down the platform and Karl

was aware that his train was about to pull out. He snatched up his kitbag, grabbed Marie one more time and kissed her on the lips, as her arms wound around his neck. A couple of soldiers hanging out of a window cheered them as Karl dashed for the open door of the already moving train. He leapt aboard and waved to Marie, who was now a diminishing figure amongst the tearful women and children left on the platform. 'I love you,' he called, but his declaration of love was obliterated by the long, loud tooting of the train's whistle. Soon, he could see her no more, except in his heart.

Lieutenant Kenshu called Fuji to the conning tower when the I–47 was on the surface. 'Leading Seaman Komine,' he said, staring into the inky night of scudding rain-squall clouds. 'I have orders to put you ashore to locate and ascertain whether your agent, Krait, is still not compromised.'

'Yes, sir,' Fuji responded.

Kenshu turned his attention to the sailor who had gained a reputation as an outsider amongst a tight-knit crew. Living outside Japan for many years in Papua set him aside as almost a foreigner to the young crew of men who hailed from the home islands of the rising sun. Not that he was held in suspicion by any of them, when it was so apparent that their captain held Komine in high regard for what he had done in the opening days of the war. It was just that Leading Seaman Komine was a taciturn and brooding man who rarely attempted to fit in.

'It is a dangerous mission,' Kenshu said softly. 'I have a feeling that counter-intelligence thinks that the man you recruited may have gone over to the enemy, otherwise they would not dare risk my boat in these waters so close to Port Moresby. I just thought that you should know how important the navy feels this mission is.'

Fuji bowed his head. He had great respect for his captain but had come to detest working in the claustrophobic confines of the smelly submarine's belly. He missed the smell of the earth and forests. He had often pondered how strange it was that he should consider Papua home more than the islands of Japan, where the snows came in winter to freeze his fingers and toes. There was a rumour that a fleet was being assembled to carry out an invasion of Port Moresby, and Fuji, who rarely prayed to his ancestors, did so, begging that the invasion would take place soon so that he could be posted to Port Moresby to follow the progress of Keela's pregnancy. The thought of her bearing his child had more of an impact on him than he thought it would, although it still disturbed him that their child would be born mixed race. As much as he had attempted to put the Emperor's divine mission to conquer the Pacific first, Keela haunted him in those times when he would retreat into gentle memories to escape the realities of life in the submarine. At least there was a chance he might be able to make contact with Keela on this mission.

'You will be armed,' Kenshu continued. 'And you must not be taken alive under any circumstances.'

'Yes, sir,' Fuji replied. The captain's order went

without question. He knew that to be captured and interrogated by the enemy might allow them to locate and destroy the I-47 should he be weak and break under torture. He knew that he was still a mere man and not a god, like the Emperor. 'Do we know when I will be put ashore?' was the only question Fuji asked before going below to resume his duties in the engine room. It was bold of the sailor to ask a question without invitation but Fuji sensed that the young captain was also a compassionate man.

'Soon enough,' was all the captain answered before continuing to scan the dark horizons for any signs of enemy surface ships.

'I feel that the Japanese are growing suspicious of my transmissions,' Sen said, pacing the garden of his home. 'Only, it is what you call a hunch.'

The Australian major standing in the garden with him lit a cigarette and blew smoke into the hazy morning air. Butterflies drifted in and out of the blaze of tropical flowers. Major Colin Shaw was in his fifties and had seen service in the Great War as an officer in Palestine with the Light Horse. In the intervening years he had worked with the New South Wales Police Force where he had risen to be a detective investigating violent crime in Sydney's back streets. He had also belonged to a militia unit and now both jobs combined to put him in the intelligence service and have him posted to Port Moresby. The free meals in greasy cafés during his police service had added weight to the once hard body and stretched his army uniform more than it should have, but it was his keen brain the army needed in its counter-intelligence war against the enemy, not his body.

'You say you have a hunch about being compromised,' Major Shaw said, puffing more smoke into the air and watching it drift on a breeze. 'Then I am prepared to back you. As a copper I often had to trust my feelings about some situations. It's a kind of instinct we hone from working with some real bad bastards. You have anything you can recall that makes you think the little yellow bastards on the other side are onto you?'

'It is in the tone of my radio contact,' Sen said slowly, exploring the reason for his concern. 'Just something in the way he accepts the information I transmit for you.'

Major Shaw pulled a pained face and scratched his forehead. 'If I have to close down this operation I don't know what will happen to you.'

Sen had already considered the options he faced at the hands of the Australian authorities; he would be of no real use to them once the operation to deceive the Japanese was terminated and would be left facing treason charges – unless they quietly killed him and he was simply listed as a missing person.

'It does not matter what becomes of me,' he sighed, gazing into blank space. 'I do not know the fate of my family. My life means little to me now.'

'Hang on,' Colin Shaw interrupted. 'Don't go thinking that we are going to do away with you. We're not some kind of drongos to do that to a man who has helped us. You might do a bit of time for your activities before coming over to us but I doubt that you will end up hanging.'

Sen was surprised at the Australian major's seeming kindness towards him. 'I would like you to know, Major, that my assistance against the Japanese was willing. I am a man of conviction and the threat to expose my past by the Japanese was the greatest punishment that could be inflicted on me – not the threat of death, as you may think. I was ashamed that I was living a life betraying the people of this country who were my true friends. Now, I would welcome death in the knowledge that I was able to redeem just a little face.'

Major Shaw was impressed with the Chinese man's remorse. He prided himself in being able to judge a man's character from years working the streets and here, he sensed, was a man who was truly contrite and even prepared to go further to redeem himself.

'You know, Mr Sen,' Major Shaw said, flicking his cigarette butt into the shrubbery, 'even if we close down your work here I am sure that I could trust you to work for us in some other capacity. You would be a free man but, I will warn you, whatever is ahead will be dangerous and the only reward your redemption. I am sure that we can make any record of your subversive activities disappear. You interested?'

'Major Shaw,' Sen said sadly, 'I have nothing to lose except my shame.'

The Australian officer thrust out his hand in an unexpected gesture. 'Welcome to my world, Mr Sen,' he said. 'Nothing to lose and a war to win. And now, all I have to do is make you disappear in a blaze of glory for the Emperor so that your controllers think that you were killed before you could be compromised. That should convince them that all your transmissions were fair dinkum.'

Sen knew that once his old identity was destroyed he would rise from the ashes newborn. It would be a new – but dangerous – beginning for him.

'You will be sent back to Australia,' Major Shaw said formally to Iris as she sat in the living room now being efficiently rid of any semblance of military counter-intelligence operations. Boxes were being filled around them with papers and pencils, tea cups and radio equipment. 'I will be arranging your transport but you will only be allowed a single suitcase for your personal possessions. Needless to say, you are sworn to absolute secrecy on all that you have seen and heard here. I do not have to elaborate on the penalties for breaking the oath that I am about to have you sign under the Official Secrets Act. I should emphasise that it is well and truly in your interests to comply. Do you understand what I am saying?'

Iris could not believe her ears. How ironic, she thought. After having her readmission into the country questioned by immigration authorities she was finally going to be sent to Sydney where she would be reunited with her daughter.

'I understand what you are saying, Major,' Iris replied. 'I am sure your trust in me will not be misplaced.'

'Good,' Major Shaw replied gruffly. 'I also believe that you are in line to inherit a fairly large amount of money.'

'That is true, Major,' Iris replied with a note of surprise. 'How did you know about the inheritance?'

'Jack Kelly is an old mate of mine,' the major finally smiled. 'He told me to make sure you two were well and truly looked after or he would do something bad to my manhood.'

Iris warmed to the army officer, who she had first perceived to be a gruff and imposing bully. 'Did you know Mr Kelly from the Great War?'

'No, I met him in Sydney years ago when he was a big name in business circles. Jack was well known for his work looking after the interests of war widows and the blokes who had served and were looking for work during the Depression. He is one fair dinkum cobber.'

'I have not been told of the fate of my brother-in-law,' Iris said, changing the subject. 'I would have liked to say farewell to him and thank him for his hospitality.'

'He is being taken care of,' the major replied uncomfortably, clearing his throat. 'You do not have to be alarmed,' he added when he noticed the concerned expression cloud Iris's face. 'He has been taken from here to work elsewhere.'

Iris had to be satisfied with the explanation as it was clear the major was not about to elaborate.

Iris quickly packed the very few personal possessions she had and a truck drove her into Port Moresby, where Major Shaw had prearranged passage on a cargo ship returning to Australia.

She stood sadly on the wharf, clutching her suitcase and staring vacantly at the island in Port Moresby's bay. When she turned to gaze across to the shore she noticed a scraggly frangipani tree with its creamy, delicate flowers in bloom. It made her sad thinking of the loss in her life of this place that could have been her home.

THIRTY-ONE

'You're going back, Jack, whether you like it or not,' Captain Michael Higgins said, standing over Jack Kelly, who was lying on his back under a mosquito net on a camp stretcher. The camouflaged post, halfway from the base camp in the mountains to the west of Lae, nestled amongst the damp, dripping foliage, was a long way from any facility that could cope with Jack's recurring bouts of malaria. His delirious dreams took him into a surreal world inhabited by ghosts and monsters. Even as the commander of the outpost bent over him, Jack shivered uncontrollably in the grips of the deadly illness.

'I can ride this one out, Mick,' Jack replied through gritted teeth, struggling to raise himself to a sitting position. 'Couple of days and I will be back on my feet.'

'Not bloody likely,' Captain Higgins said. 'I am

organising for you to be littered down the track and back to Moresby. I can't afford any man to be laid out so close to the Japs. Jack, you are going, and that's an order.'

Jack slumped back on the sweat-drenched blanket. He knew that the young officer – a regular and graduate of the military college of Duntroon in Canberra – had made the same decision that Jack would have made when he had been a company commander in the Great War. He realised that his stubbornness to remain was merely a manifestation of his fierce pride – and his need to prove to himself that he could still stand and fight for his country despite his age. He was into the fifth decade of his life and still a fit man, but age was slowing him down. His body had cried out in agony with every strained muscle and torn ligament. Jack faced the fact that he no longer wanted to fight in another war, he was just too tired. All he wanted to do was go south, collect his inheritance and build that house on the hill overlooking the Tweed River. He would then be able to sit in a little boat fishing for flathead or bream in the magnificent wilderness of lakes adjoining the Tweed.

Jack Kelly lay on his back, shivering and remembering. The tears flowed – not for himself but for the memory of Victoria, who he missed so much. Not a day passed since her death that he did not think of her and he called her name whenever he was in the grips of the fever. She would not be with him to bask in the serenity of the Tweed Valley's unspoiled rainforests and drift on the tranquil waterways edged by the mangroves.

The blackness came once again and Jack drifted back into his fevered dreams whilst a soldier watched over him in the shadows of the jungle hell west of Lae and the enemy.

Creeping cautiously forward, Fuji gripped the butt of his pistol with a sweaty hand. The drop from the I–47 had gone without incident and Fuji had come ashore alone as he had been ordered to ascertain why Sen had ceased transmitting. Now Fuji crouched in the darkness not a hundred yards from Sen's bunga-low. The dark night hid the house from him and he could barely see his own hand in front of his face. The eerie silence worried him. Not a dog barking, he mused, nor the sound of native labourers chatting around a kerosene lamp, chewing betel nut. It was all silent darkness. Knowing that he would have to wait until first light before making his next move to con-tact Sen, Fuji relaxed. He would snatch a short sleep and allow the touch of dawn to wake him.

When the first rays of the sun appeared Fuji rubbed the sleep from his eyes and was shocked at what he saw. Where the house once stood was noth-ing but a burnt-out shell. The storage sheds and any other substantial buildings had also been burned, leaving blackened sheets of corrugated iron on the ground amid the charred timbers that once sup-ported them. He could not see any sign of the native people who had once worked there and the ghostly silence from the night before continued into the day. No wonder Krait had ceased sending messages, Fuji thought. The Australian military had discovered the existence of the radio and either captured or killed the Chinese man. Something did not feel right about that assumption, however. Fuji knew the Australians well enough to know that they would not simply burn down a man's house just because he was captured or killed. From what Fuji could see, the destruction had been very systematic.

The I–47 was not scheduled to return for another three days so he had enough time to seek out one who might be able to answer his questions. He might risk discovery and probable death but at least he was home and in a world he knew much better than the land of the rising sun.

On his first day of being back on Papuan soil Fuji stripped off his naval uniform and changed into a native lap-lap. He used a dye he carried in a *bilum* to taint his skin colour so he could pass as the offspring of Motu and Chinese parents. His pistol and uniform were buried in a shallow hole not far from the beach where he had first met Keela. He also buried a small canvas bag of essential supplies: a compass, dried fish, rice, a full water bottle as well as extra ammunition.

Satisfied with his disguise, Fuji set out. He had two missions in mind and within the hour found himself on the outskirts of Keela's village, which stretched out into the sea on stilted wooden houses. Part of the village was on land where mangy dogs and scrawny pigs scrounged amongst the piles of garbage.

The Japanese sailor had been trained well and waited patiently, observing movement to and from the village. Eventually he spotted the track through the bush being used by the villagers to go to the beach where he had met Keela. As for Keela, he could not see any sign of her among the groups of young girls sitting and gossiping under the houses ashore and could only guess that she might be in one of the huts perched over the sea.

Afternoon came and Fuji retrieved from his *bilum* a piece of dried fish. He was also thirsty but ignored the craving for water.

Eventually a young boy sauntered down the track on his own and Fuji risked leaving his hide to confront the startled youth, who was about eight years old. The boy stood petrified at this stranger who had seemingly appeared from nowhere.

'I will not hurt you,' Fuji said in Motu. 'Do you know the woman called Keela?'

The terrified boy nodded.

'I will give you a penny,' Fuji said with a reassuring smile and stretching out his hand with the copper coin, 'if you go to her and tell her that Fuji will be waiting for her just after the sun rises at the place they met.'

The boy hesitated but the sight of the Australian-minted coin overcame his fear. As the stranger looked like his clanspeople and had not tried to hurt him, he accepted the coin, staring wide-eyed at the stranger.

'If you tell anyone that you met me,' Fuji threatened, 'I will come in the night and slit your throat.' He produced the knife he always carried. The boy's mouth gaped at the terrifying blade and he nodded his head vigorously. 'Good, now go and tell Keela the message I have paid you to deliver.'

The boy nodded once again, turned on his heel and ran back towards the village. Fuji prayed that his threat would be enough and made his way back to his hide near the beach, where he slaked his thirst from the water canteen he had brought ashore as part of his survival supplies.

Night came and Fuji slept fitfully with the pistol in his hand. Had he been betrayed he would not be taken alive but would fight to the death, keeping the last bullet for himself.

After what seemed an eternity the sun rose and Fuji stood to gaze down on the beach from his hiding place in the scrub. She was there! He had not expected his message to be delivered but Keela was wading in the shallows, holding up the hem of her long, wrap-around skirt. Her breasts were exposed in the custom of her people and she had a flower behind her ear.

Fuji did not immediately identify himself to her lest she had been followed and he walked into an ambush laid by either her kinfolk or the Australian military. Instead, armed with the pistol, he scouted the area very cautiously to make sure she was alone. Satisfied that she was, he stepped out onto the beach. Her back was to him as she stood in the gentle wash of waves.

'Keela,' he called softly.

She turned and ran to him. 'I have waited for you,' she said and looked down shyly. 'You said you would return for me.'

'I could not immediately return because I am a warrior of the Emperor and had important things to do,' he replied stiffly. 'But I am here now to say that you are still my woman.'

'Our baby grows in me still,' Keela said, looking up at Fuji. 'And you look silly pretending to be one of us,' she added mischievously.

'I must pretend to be of mixed race,' he answered in an indignant tone. 'If I am betrayed I will be killed.'

'Have you come for me?' Keela asked.

'I will come for you when we have defeated the Australian and American barbarians. I will return to Papua and we will build a house here. Then I will take over my father's boat business when the peace comes.'

'I always knew that you would be my man,' Keela responded. 'Our baby will be born a strong warrior like his father.'

Fuji stood uncomfortably in Keela's presence. He knew he was letting his heart overrule his mission. But it had been so opportune that he should be put ashore so close to Keela. Remembering his primary purpose for being there, Fuji asked, 'Do you know what happened to the Chinese trader, Kwong Yu Sen?'

Keela frowned as she had wanted her man to talk more of his feelings for her. 'Who cares,' she answered with a pout, and was startled when Fuji gripped her shoulders.

'Do you know what happened to the Chinese trader?' he repeated fiercely.

'I heard from the market that he was killed by the army men from Port Moresby and that they then burned down his house. The people who worked for the Chinaman have all disappeared, and at the market some say they ran away in fright.'

Fuji released his grip and stepped back.

'You hurt me,' Keela accused. 'I thought that you came back to see me.'

Realising how threatening his manner had been, Fuji shook his head. 'I am sorry,' he apologised. 'I am tense from being in the land occupied by my enemies. I did not mean to harm you.'

Appeased, Keela stepped forward and took his hand. 'I think we should go to the bushes,' she said. 'It has been a long time and I have missed the feel of your body against mine.'

'That will not hurt the baby?' Fuji asked, ignorant of such matters.

'The old ladies say it will not,' Keela replied with a flash of a shy smile, leading him away from the beach.

It was a day that Fuji wished would never end. He half-heartedly hoped that the submarine would never return for him as, spent from their day of lovemaking, they lay on their backs watching the crescent moon rise in the tropical sky. For the moment, the war was a long way away. They whispered to each other as lovers do and the night would become Fuji's most treasured memory for as long as he lived.

Keela protested her lover's insistence that they not meet again as she could not truly comprehend the danger the Japanese sailor was in every minute he remained ashore. For the Motu woman danger was simply a way of life as her village still remained under threat from other clans and tribes. Despite the coming of European law to contain tribal fighting, raids were still made for women and for the payback of grievances.

In the morning Keela returned to her concerned relatives, telling them that she had felt ill and decided to sleep out in the bush. The glowing expression on the young woman's face did not fool the older women who sat around on their grass mats cackling that she had found a lover from another village. Or was it the Japanese man who had once killed the young man Keela was supposed to have married? The latter supposition had more scandal attached to it and was thus accepted as being the fact.

Mounted on a horse, Police Sergeant Ian Groves was on a routine visit to one of his outposts beyond Port Moresby to inspect the contingent of native police under the command of one of his trusted native sergeant majors. He liked the visits because they took him out of the bombed township and into the bush. This journey would take him a day and his saddlebags were filled with the necessities of life camping out. Accompanying him on foot, with his police carbine slung on his shoulder and a bandolier of .303 rounds across his broad chest, was one of his constables, who spoke Motu and could act as an interpreter if required. They were on the track in the vicinity of the Sen residence in the early afternoon when they were hailed down by an old bearded native man who hobbled over to meet them.

'What's he saying?' Sergeant Groves asked.

'He say that he see a Japanese man called Fuji Komine hanging around here,' the constable replied. 'Say he saw him this morning.'

'Komine?' Groves repeated. 'Is he sure he saw the little bastard?'

The constable turned to the old man and asked questions, most of which the police sergeant could follow with his basic knowledge of the language. From what he could understand the old man had worked at Sen's house as a gardener, and when his Chinese employer had mysteriously disappeared the house had been razed to the ground by the army. He had been forced to return to his village on the coast and it had only been because he had returned to his former place of employment to see if anything was worth scrounging from the ruins that he noticed the young Japanese man. Although the Japanese man had attempted to disguise himself, he did not fool the old man, who had known Fuji from when he was a young boy working with his father, the Japanese boat builder. The old native had not approached Fuji because he had heard the Australians were in a big tribal fight against Fuji's relatives from somewhere called Japan. The old man could only think that Japan must have been up in the highlands because he knew of the fierce reputation of the stocky little men from that region.

'Ask him if Komine was with anyone,' Groves

said, convinced that the old man knew what he was talking about.

After a matter of a few seconds the police constable turned to the Australian police sergeant. 'He says he did not see anyone else with him but it has been gossiped by the old native women in his village that the girl, Keela, is going to be the mother of his child,' the constable answered in pidgin.

Ian Groves had a lot more questions at the report of Fuji being sighted in the area. He had been with the party that had gone to Fuji's parents' place on the coast and taken them in for internment somewhere in Australia as enemy aliens. The sergeant had not really believed that the old man and his wife were any real threat to national security, and it had not been a pleasant task at the time to force the two from their home. Sergeant Groves was also aware that their son was a member of the Japanese navy and had read the report of his clash with young Lukas Kelly. He also knew that at the time of the clash Fuji had been operating out of a submarine; and the fact that he had been seen alive in Papua in the last twenty-four hours seemed to contradict the RAAF Beaufighter pilot's report that he believed that he had sunk the submarine now confirmed as the I–47.

Ian Groves pumped the old man for as much information as he could give and leaned down from his horse to pass him a generous twist of dark tobacco. The reward greatly pleased the old man who beamed a betel-stained smile at the police sergeant, showering thanks and praises on the policeman before hobbling away, cackling to himself over his windfall.

Ian Groves took a deep breath. He knew that he must make a decision. The information about the Japanese sailor was of great importance to the military in Port Moresby. The presence of the Japanese sailor ashore could only be to gather intelligence or carry out acts of sabotage. Either way, Komine had to be found. Should he initiate a search for Fuji with his constable or go for help? Ian Groves was a sensible man and considered his options; he would need reinforcements if he was to attempt to locate the Japanese sailor and knew that his visit to the outpost would have to be postponed. He withdrew a notebook from his pocket and scribbled down the necessary facts. 'Constable,' he said. 'You are to take this report to HQ at Port Moresby and tell them where I am.'

He tossed his constable a couple of cans of corned beef from his saddle-bags and wheeled his horse around to ride on to Sen's former residence. The police sergeant was nervous but had to weigh his fear against the search for the Japanese sailor while the trail was still fresh. He was armed with his revolver and had a .303 rifle in the saddle bucket by his knee. He hoped that he also had the element of surprise on his side. He did not underestimate Fuji. Not all the sweat running down his body was from the tropical sun's shimmering heat.

As he waited for the submarine to return for him Fuji was blissfully unaware that his presence on Papuan soil had been noted. Nor was he aware that the Allies had the ability to monitor the naval codes of Japan and that they were also aware of his submarine. What they did not know was its whereabouts.

Fuji had made another visit to inspect the deserted ruins of Sen's house in the hope that he might find some clue as to what had happened. Keela's story did not make sense. The Australians might be the enemy but they played by a strict sense of British justice. No, something was wrong, and Fuji was slowly forming the suspicion that the Chinese man was in all probability a double agent, now working for the Allies.

THIRTY-TWO

The winds were in the *Independence*'s favour. It was sailing under a full canvas to the location designated by military HQ, arriving mid afternoon off the beach south of Sen's house and land.

Lukas reported that he had reached his destination and was informed that a RAN frigate was on its way to assist him. The news made Lukas feel a little easier about the situation. To be allocated the task of searching for any signs of a Japanese submarine armed with nothing heavier than a .50 calibre machine gun and some grenades, which were no real deterrent should a sighting result in the submarine electing to sink him, was worrying. Lukas stood on the deck scanning the jungle-covered shoreline. Iris would be at Sen's home, Lukas thought and felt compelled to go ashore and ensure that all was well at the Chinese trader's place.

'Momis,' he called. 'Make sure the boys are fed.

And I want you to organise a lookout for this afternoon. I am going ashore for a short time but will be back before sunset. If you see a submarine you are to radio Moresby and fire a shot to alert me. You understand?'

'Yes, Masta Lukas,' Momis replied proudly. Lukas had taught him how to use the powerful radio, and the fact that the masta had given him the responsibility of looking after the schooner puffed his ego.

The dinghy was lowered and Lukas rowed ashore, taking a revolver and a water canteen. He knew that he could reach Sen's house along the track from the beach within the half hour on foot and possibly visit Iris before returning to his schooner. Looking back over his shoulder as he rowed away from the schooner, he was struck by just how familiar the *Independence* was to him – maybe like living with a wife, he smiled. There had been bad times and there had been good times.

Sergeant Ian Groves could feel the short bristles of his grey hair rising. He sat astride his police mount, gripping the Lee Enfield rifle. The place was deserted and eerily silent. The blackened timbers and smoke-stained sheets of corrugated iron spread about were a sad reminder of how grand the Chinese trader's residence had once been. Sen had always provided hospitality to him on the occasions that his patrols had brought him to this part of the district.

'Bloody waste,' he muttered, surveying the ruins. 'Bloody army.' His horse shifted under him, snorting, and Ian Groves felt his heart pound in his chest. An instinct born of years patrolling the dangerous tribal areas where warriors still met intruders with long bamboo arrows warned him he was not alone, and he forced himself to very carefully scan the bush at the edge of the ruins. He knew not to fix his attention on the bush as much as force himself to focus through the scrub. Sure enough he saw movement and the rifle came up to his shoulder, his finger slipping to the trigger while he brought his sights to bear on the figure who had emerged from the scrub to stand with an expression of shock fifty yards or so away.

'Bloody hell!' the sergeant muttered, lowering the rifle. 'You almost got yourself shot.'

Lukas was not as surprised to see the police sergeant as he was to see the ruins. He walked towards the man on the horse. 'What in hell happened here? Are you blokes responsible for this, Sergeant Groves?'

'Not us, young Lukas,' Ian Groves said, the rifle against his hip. 'Your mob, the army did this when the Chinaman disappeared.'

'What about the woman who was staying with him?' Lukas asked. 'What has happened to her?'

'If you mean Iris,' Groves replied, 'she was shipped out to Australia a few days ago. That Major Shaw, who used to be in the police back in Australia, was in charge of putting her aboard. I hear she is all right.'

Lukas shook his head in bewilderment. Things happened so fast during war. 'Why did they burn the place down?' he asked.

'Don't know,' Groves replied, allowing himself to roll a cigarette when he had replaced the rifle in the leather rifle bucket. 'If you ask me, the bastards who did this should have been locked up. Army people or not, it makes no sense.' When he had completed licking the edge of the paper and was satisfied it would not fall apart he lit the cigarette and puffed a long snort of smoke into the air. 'What are you doing around these parts anyway?'

'Thought I might pay my respects to Sen,' Lukas answered. 'I don't suppose you know where he is now?'

'About as much clue as you have,' Groves replied. 'But I do know your old mate Fuji Komine was spotted around here only a few hours ago by a native. That's why I am out this way. I hope to have some help by the morning.'

Lukas blanched. Fuji! So he was not dead. 'Then you are going to need a hand right now,' Lukas said. 'I have known Fuji since I was a kid and I know how cunning he is. If he is hanging around here then he may have already seen us.'

'Thought the same thing myself,' Groves said. 'I was just praying to hell that, under the circumstances, he would rather hide than fight. But I also learned that he has knocked up a local *meri* from the village just up the coast from here. Might be that he has dropped in from God knows where to see how she is going.'

Lukas was puzzled why Fuji would be ashore. Last thing he knew of the Japanese sailor was that he was part of a submarine crew. Why was he here? The possible answer chilled him. Submarine! Was it that his sub was even now sitting off the coast with its periscope trained on the *Independence*? Lukas's first reaction was to immediately return to his schooner. However, he also realised that there was nothing he could do right at this moment and it seemed that Fuji was within their grasp. It was an agonising decision to make but Lukas felt that capturing – or killing – the Japanese sailor took precedence.

'You all right, young Kelly?' Groves asked when he noticed how sickly the normally robust young man appeared. 'You look like you have seen a ghost.'

'Nothing I can do anything about right now,' Lukas replied in a dull voice. 'Except help you look for Fuji before he causes any mischief.'

'Got any ideas?' the police sergeant asked.

'You said that Fuji has a local woman around here?'

'Her name is Keela.'

'Maybe she could tell us where he is.'

The police sergeant flicked the stub of his cigarette into the ruins. 'Get on the back,' he said with his hand outstretched. Lukas took the grip and was assisted up onto the horse. 'We will see if we can find her and convince her to tell us where he might be.'

It was not often that the police visited Keela's village as her people enjoyed a reputation of keeping to themselves in a law-abiding manner. So the appearance of the two Europeans doubled on the horse caused quite a commotion amongst the villagers. Men, women and children gathered out of curiosity in the centre of the village to greet the men. Keela was huddled amongst them.

Lukas dismounted but Ian Groves remained astride his mount. 'Anyone here know the woman Keela?' the sergeant asked, and the excited chatter brought on by the visit suddenly evaporated into an uneasy silence. Children received a slap around the back of the head from nervous parents when they continued to talk amongst themselves, oblivious of the change in mood. The fact that the sergeant had singled out a member of their clan bode no good.

There was no response as the villagers remained silent but Lukas noticed several pairs of eyes nervously shift to a pretty young Motu girl standing in the gathered crowd. He strode forward, parting the villagers and confronted the girl. 'You are Keela?' Lukas said in fluent Motu. 'We will not hurt you. All we want to know is the place where Fuji stays.'

She refused to look at Lukas and remained silent. Lukas turned to Ian Groves. 'I am pretty sure this is the girl but she won't talk.'

The police sergeant slid his rifle from the leather bucket. 'This is wartime and the King has given me orders that anyone who does not help me will be considered an enemy. I have his personal permission to take the head man of your village back to Moresby, where he will be tried, found guilty and hanged unless you tell us where the Japanese man known as Fuji Komine is.'

It was a lie but Groves hoped his bluff might scare the information from the villagers.

A rumbling sound of voices protested the

sergeant's demand. They genuinely did not know where the Japanese man was. The village leader, an old man scarred and bent by life, stepped forward. 'If we knew where he was,' he said, 'we would kill him ourselves for the killing of my nephew who was to marry Keela. If she knows where the Japanese man is then she must tell you.'

All eyes seemed to swivel on Keela. They were not friendly eyes and Keela knew that if she did not talk then she would be castigated by her own kinfolk. She also realised that the two men who had come to her village meant to harm her man and to tell them anything would endanger him. 'I do not know,' she said, partially lying as she was not certain that Fuji would be hiding near the beach.

'Then the sergeant will be forced to take away your head man and hang him in Port Moresby,' Lukas threatened. He could see the fear in Keela's face grow stronger and the nearest villagers strained to hear the conversation between the young woman and the white man with the eye patch.

'Fuji is in the bush that way,' Keela blurted, pointing west. 'He is at the place where the track joins from the river.'

Lukas knew the area she identified. 'Good,' he said with a faint smile. 'We will go and meet him.' He turned to Ian Groves. 'The woman has told us what we need to know,' he called in Motu. 'We can leave these people alone and go to fetch the Japanese man but we will be forced to shoot anyone who attempts to follow us to exact payback on him. He will be a prisoner of the King.'

From the mumbled reaction of the gathered villagers Lukas knew his message had got through. 'We have to get out of here now,' he said quietly in English when he had reached the sergeant. 'She lied but I think I know what she is about to do.'

Ian Groves helped Lukas mount behind him. 'So if she lied, what help is that to us?' he asked in a puzzled voice.

'What would you do under the circumstances?' Lukas asked.

'Go and warn Fuji that . . .' The sergeant paused as what Lukas planned sank in. 'Follow her!' he exclaimed. 'You are as cunning as your old man.'

'Not that easy,' Lukas cautioned. 'She may have the same idea and will be extra cautious. You will have to pretend to ride west towards Moresby, drop me off while I sit off the village and cover the trail west. I have a gut feeling Fuji would have to be down near the beach if he has been dropped off by a sub. If I am right she will head straight for the beach to warn him. I will follow. All you have to do is double back to give me support if I need it.'

'You only have a six shooter,' the police sergeant noted. 'What if Fuji is better armed?'

Lukas had thought about this problem should he confront the Japanese sailor again. 'I doubt that he will be better armed. The Japs have put him ashore on a spying mission is my guess. Therefore he would have to travel light. Maybe he has a pistol but I doubt they would have issued him with anything heavier.'

The sergeant nodded and they rode out of the village west towards Moresby while Keela intently watched them leave. From the direction they were riding, it seemed that they had accepted her lie, she thought and returned to her family's hut. But when she thought the excitement of the police visit had died down, she discreetly slipped from the village to take the track to the beach. She was careful and stopped to check occasionally to see if she was being followed. When it did not appear that she was, she continued to seek out the man she loved and warn him that the police were searching for him.

Lukas followed behind off the track in the thick scrub. His guess had been right. The Motu girl was leading him to his old enemy. This time only one of them would walk away from the meeting alive for he knew Fuji would never allow himself to be taken prisoner.

Fuji sat with his back against a palm tree staring at the placid sea in deep thought. It had been a long time since he had felt so lost. He was deep in enemy territory waiting to rejoin his comrades aboard the I–47 and yet, he grudgingly admitted to himself, he was harbouring a reluctance to leave Keela. He had not thought it possible that anything could ever divert him from his divine mission in the Emperor's cause and yet Keela haunted him with her beautiful smile and deep dark eyes of almost pure black. For a moment he even imagined that he could hear her calling to him from the far end of their beach.

Realising that her call was real and sensing the fear in her voice, Fuji snapped from his dreamy thoughts and snatched the pistol at his side. Turning aside, he flattened himself against the hot sands above the beach and sought out the Motu girl. He saw her hurrying along the beach towards his concealed position and knew something was terribly wrong, as she had been instructed not to come to him.

'Fuji,' she called desperately.

Fuji cursed under his breath, every instinct telling him danger lay in wait should he reveal his position to her. But she was upon him before he could warn her off.

'Here,' he hissed. Keela hesitated, then rushed towards him.

'They are looking for you,' she sobbed, falling into his arms.

'Who is they?' Fuji asked, holding her at arm's length.

'A policeman and one other,' she answered, her anguished face reflecting her fear.

'How did they know I am here?' he asked with a trace of anger in his voice for the betrayal he suspected.

'The people of my village know of you,' Keela said, wiping with the back of her hand the tears that splashed her face. 'You must leave here now or they will find you.'

Fuji did not answer. He could not tell Keela about the submarine coming for him. The dramatic turn of events changed everything and if the police or army had any force in the area searching for him, that would jeopardise the safety of the I–47. He had to get out of the area even if he could not contact the submarine and warn them to stay away. At least when it surfaced at night he would not be there to respond to its signal and the captain would immediately leave. Fuji gently pushed Keela away. 'Are you able to get a canoe and some supplies for us to sail a long way from here?' he asked, deciding on his only real option.

Keela looked at him, eyes wide with surprise. 'I think I can return to my village and take a canoe,' she answered. 'It will not be easy but I could do so tonight.'

'You are to meet me beyond this beach at the place of the mangrove swamps in the direction of the rising sun. Do you know the place?' Keela nodded. 'You will have a lantern at the stern of the canoe so that I might find you,' he continued.

'Where will we go?' she asked in a trembling voice.

'Your people trade each year with the people of the islands to the east of Milne Bay,' Fuji said. 'That is close to safety for me. From there I will be able to make my way to New Britain and my superiors.'

'It is a long way,' Keela said softly. 'But I will be with you.'

Fuji thought about that and felt a twinge of guilty sadness. He had only planned to have her accompany him as far as possibly the Trobriand Islands – no further. He would be in fact deserting her to return to his mission for his Emperor, but for the moment what was most important was getting out of the Moresby district and leading his enemies away from the rendezvous point with the sub.

'Go as fast as you can back to the village,' Fuji said. 'My life is in your hands.'

Keela understood. Turning on her heel she walked away from the Japanese sailor and hurried away without looking back.

'I see her,' Lukas said, kneeling by the police sergeant beside him.

'She disappeared into the palm grove and came out the same way,' Ian Groves replied, pushing his rifle forward. 'I bet the little yellow bastard is in there.'

They were concealed in the bushes back from the curving beach, around two hundred yards from where Keela had stepped off the beach into the stand of palms.

'Maybe if you give me a couple of minutes I will circle the bush while you edge forward towards the palms,' Lukas said. 'That way we can take him from two sides.'

The older man looked sideways at Lukas. 'You think that is a real good idea?' he asked. 'He is a cunning bastard and might be better armed than us. What if I go back to Moresby and round up some help from the army?'

'He will get away before you return,' Lukas replied. 'It's going to be dark soon enough and he can use the night to elude any reinforcements you bring back. No, we have him now and it's only a matter of pinning him down to the beach during daylight hours.'

Ian Groves was rightly nervous about him and young Kelly taking on the Japanese sailor with only a rifle and pistol between them. Maybe Komine was armed with grenades or something heavier. But what the younger man proposed made the only sense for the moment. They would lose him if they waited. 'Okay,' he sighed. 'We do it your way.'

Lukas nodded and without another word disappeared into the thick bush adjoining the beach. The police sergeant waited for a short time then carefully pushed his way through the undergrowth running down to the beach. The safety catch of his rifle had been slipped off and his finger was never off the trigger. Every nerve in his body was on edge. He had survived the last war and did not want to die in this one.

Fuji's keen eyes caught the movement. So they had found him, he thought bitterly, gripping the pistol in one hand and his razor-sharp knife in the other. As far as he knew he was only being hunted by two men, and whoever had been clumsy enough to disturb the bush alongside the beach was a dead man. He would not wait for his enemy to come to him. He would take the fight to the enemy.

Crouching, Fuji eased forward without bending a branch or breaking even a twig of the undergrowth. This is how he had been trained to fight in the jungle and this is how he would bring death to the enemy.

THIRTY-THREE

The soft swoop-swoop of the overhead fans and the low murmur of men's voices drifted to Jack Kelly between his fevered dreams. He knew that he was in a hospital in Port Moresby but had little recollection of how he got there. From time to time he would have flashes of stumbling and struggling along trails of clinging mud overshadowed by rainforest. He dreamed of a dank, still world of eerie silence and body-clinging sweat where words of encouragement had come from both natives and Europeans who had helped him to get back to Moresby. At times he was carried in a litter, at others supported as he stumbled over buttress roots. How long it had taken him he did not know but the clean sheets and gentle administrations of the nursing staff in the hospital were far divorced from his journey on the edge of hell.

Dengue fever – he had heard a male voice say at one stage – coupled with malaria was racking his battle-scarred body. Not a good combination for a man his age. But Jack fought the microscopic bodies attacking him from within. He was tough in both body and spirit.

'How are you feeling, Sergeant Kelly?' a woman's voice asked.

Jack tried to focus on the pretty face hovering in a mist over him. 'I'll live,' he croaked with a weak smile. 'But I've been better . . . You look vaguely familiar.'

'It's Sister Megan Cain. We met when I was up around Morohe way, and I have met your son, Lukas. He brought us safely to Moresby on the *Independence*.'

'Ah, the pretty angel,' Jack said, reaching out with his hand. 'I think my son should be taking you to the pictures.'

'I think so too, Sergeant Kelly,' Megan responded.

'Just call me Jack. I'm not used to ladies calling me Sergeant.'

'I will do that, Jack,' Megan said, although she knew she was breaking the strict rule of non-fraternisation with her patients. She saw this man as different – he was the father of Lukas Kelly.

'How long am I going to be here?' Jack asked. 'My unit will be missing me.'

Megan took a thin thermometer, shook it and placed it under Jack's tongue. She measured Jack's pulse whilst waiting for the reading on the ther-mometer. Both tasks completed, she frowned. 'As for your question concerning when we release you, I can tell you that it will not be before the end of this week.'

Jack sighed. He knew he was too weak to rejoin his comrades up the track but felt guilty at leaving them under-manned to face the Japanese.

'I will have to continue my round of the wards,' Megan said. 'If you need anything, just call me.'

'Thank you, Sister.' Jack replied, closing his eyes.

'He is very weak and still has a long way to go before he will be back on his feet,' Megan said to her visitor waiting on the verandah of the hospital. 'I have just spoken to him but he has slipped back into a deep sleep.'

The information about Sergeant Jack Kelly's admittance to the Moresby hospital had come to Ilsa Stahl from her colleague, Gene Fay, who had been at the hospital visiting an American airman shot down near Lae and rescued by an Australian navy ship en route to Port Moresby. Whilst at the hospital, Gene had scanned the list of patients to ascertain whether any other Americans were being treated. When he saw Jack Kelly's name on the list he remembered how Ilsa had shown a great interest in this particular man from the NGVR. Upon his return to their quarters outside Moresby, Gene mentioned that he thought the man she sought might be in hospital. Ilsa immediately hitched a ride there.

Now Ilsa stood in the late afternoon sunlight a mere twenty yards from the man she had discovered, from questioning the nursing sister, must be her father.

'Would you like to come in and see him?' Megan asked gently. 'He will be asleep however, and it would not be wise to wake him. His body needs the rest to fight the dengue.'

'I will do that,' Ilsa answered hesitantly. 'Thank you.'

Megan led the way and the sight of the beautiful young woman in the baggy battle dress of the war correspondent turned many a head in the ward. A few rough compliments were passed but Ilsa ignored them as she followed Megan to Jack Kelly's bed.

Ilsa stood beside the bed, staring down at the face jaundiced by the anti-malarial drugs and was struck by how fragile this man seemed. She tried to find similarities between his face and her own and, now seeing her biological father for the first time, realised how much she resembled her mother. She thought she could see a kindness in her father's face, the same expressions as those of her half-brother when she had been aboard the schooner.

'I think Jack will be allowed to have visitors tomorrow,' Megan said. 'He is recovering well and I think he will be sitting up by then.'

'Thank you,' Ilsa replied, attempting to stifle the tears welling in her eyes. 'I may come tomorrow.'

'I know it is not my business to ask,' Megan said, 'but why do you have such an interest in Sergeant Kelly?'

Ilsa bit her lip. Did it matter that this woman she

had come to know and like should know? 'He is my father,' she said softly.

Megan was stunned by the revelation. So Lukas Kelly must be Ilsa's half-brother, she thought with some relief, as Megan had feared that the beautiful young woman might have been a threat to her own affections for Jack Kelly's son.

'I think I would like to go now,' Ilsa said, turning on her heel and walking away from the bed towards the entrance to the ward.

Megan remained by the bed and watched her leave. Life was so full of surprises. Immediately her thoughts turned to Lukas. Where was he and what was he doing at this very moment? Wherever he was, she prayed that he was safe and that she would see him soon. There was so much to talk about.

At the very time Megan was thinking about Lukas he was warily creeping towards the place he last suspected Fuji was hiding. Every sense was heightened by the hunt – or was he the hunted? Fuji was a highly trained agent and Lukas began to have doubts about his abilities to take on the Japanese sailor.

The crack of a pistol caused Lukas to start with such force that he literally felt his heart thump in his chest. It had come from his right and Lukas swivelled his body to meet the threat. As he did so he suddenly felt weak and experienced a dull pain in his chest. I've been shot, Lukas thought, the revolver slipping from his hand as the pain overcame him. Slowly, he slumped to his hands and knees on the hot earth.

The pistol! I must get my revolver! Fuji had to be close by to have shot him with a pistol. The heavier echo of a rifle shot followed. Sergeant Groves, Lukas thought, searching the undergrowth for his revolver. The single shot was followed by a rapid volley. Lukas could hear the rounds thumping into the trees around him. He also heard Fuji swear in English and the sound of a man scrambling away through the undergrowth.

Lukas found the revolver, snatched it up and lay on his side pointing the gun in the direction he thought the shot that had claimed him came from. If Fuji was about to finish him off he would not go down without a fight. Blood welled in his mouth and he spat a glob. As it trickled down his chin he realised grimly that he was having trouble breathing. Maybe Fuji did not have to come for him, Lukas thought.

Lukas let go of the pistol and rolled on his back to ease the pain. In the blue sky above little powder-puff clouds spotted the heavens. There had been so much to do in his life and now a tiny projectile made in Japan had cut short all plans for the future. Lukas closed his eyes and began to whisper the Lord's Prayer.

The sudden appearance of the figure to his right had taken Fuji unawares. The Japanese sailor knew the limited range of his pistol and also knew that he would have to wait for the rifle-armed man to get close to him before he could fire. The outflanking manoeuvre by the second man, who had almost stumbled over him, had caused Fuji to snap a shot off.

He was not sure if he had been successful and knew that he would have to relocate after having disclosed his position by firing. He would also have to ensure that he had neutralised the man on his right before he could escape. He began to warily creep forward to where he calculated the ambusher had been. A furious crackle of fire from the rifleman chopped twigs, dirt and leaves into a shower around him. Fuji had a great respect for the penetrating power of the Lee Enfield .303 round and clutched the earth on his belly. Whoever the man with the rifle was he appeared to be experienced in what he was doing. Fuji opted to crawl away, leaving the man who had almost ambushed him to his own devices.

The firing ceased momentarily. Changing magazines, Fuji thought as he continued to make his way through the undergrowth to safety. When he felt he was sufficiently concealed by the bush he rose and ran east, putting precious yards between him and the two men who had attempted to pin him down. Night was not far away and he had to make his rendezvous with Keela – presuming she had been able to steal one of the canoes from her village.

Momis was nervous. He sat behind his beloved .50 calibre machine gun on the deck of the schooner watching the sun slide below the horizon. Masta Lukas had not returned and during the late afternoon the Solomon Islander thought that he had heard gunshots on the breeze.

'What should we do?' one of the crew asked.

Momis shook his head. 'We wait for Masta Lukas to return.'

It was halfway to the middle of the night before Momis left his post to go to the galley and make himself a mug of sweet, black tea. His comrades were above deck, sleeping under the stars and oblivious to the tension Momis felt. A single lantern lit the cabin, its feeble light trapped inside by the curtains drawn over the portholes. 'No good,' Momis muttered as he raised the mug to his lips.

They would be the final words he would utter. His world exploded around him as the *Independence* rose out of the water to break its back and slowly sink in two pieces. The torpedo from the I–47 had found its target and there were no survivors left aboard.

THIRTY-FOUR

It had always been Megan's worst nightmare that someone she cherished would be brought in on her shift. Her nightmare came true in the early hours of the morning when Lukas Kelly was delivered to the hospital by an army patrol, which had come across Sergeant Groves attempting to bring the critically wounded young skipper back to Port Moresby. Bent over in the saddle of the horse that the police sergeant led on foot, Lukas was barely conscious, his body fighting desperately to keep him alive.

The army doctor was roused from his quarters whilst Megan prepared Lukas for the operating theatre. Lukas recognised her through his pain and attempted a weak smile when he saw her stricken expression. 'When I get out of here I thought we might go for a picnic down the coast,' he said with great difficulty and coughed up a glob of dark blood.

'Don't speak,' Megan said, unconsciously gripping his hand in hers as two orderlies placed him gently on the operating table. 'The doctor is going to be here soon and he is very good. We will talk when you are in the ward recovering.'

Lukas closed his eyes as if that could block the agony and Megan continued to hold his hand, watching his pain-racked face and forcing back the tears. She was a nurse, and this was no time to break down. Later, in the privacy of her nursing quarters, she would have the opportunity to be human again but for now she was a professional with a job to do.

From what she could ascertain from her preliminary examination Lukas had been shot through the right side of his chest. She guessed that the wound had been caused by a low velocity projectile rather than the devastating higher velocity of a rifle round. From the blood on his mouth and the trouble he had breathing, it was obvious that the bullet had at least penetrated his lung. Like his father though, Lukas was tough, and sheer force of will had kept him breathing. Despite everything that said he should die, Megan entertained a small hope that the wound would not be fatal. Only God knew his fate and Megan prayed silently that this man would not be taken from her life.

The doctor arrived in a dishevelled state, having been woken from a deep sleep. Grumpy but efficient he barked out his orders to those present. 'Sister Cain, you will scrub up and assist me,' he said, peering at the tiny discoloured spot marking the bullet's entry in Luke's side. 'Where's the bloody anaesthetist?' he growled – and as if on cue the anaesthetist arrived, also dragged from his sleep. In a matter of minutes Lukas was ready for theatre, with his fate now in both God's – and the doctor's – hands.

Captain Kenshu had come to rue the day he had sworn to sink the *Independence.* Overhead he could hear the propellers of the Australian frigate on its second run across the submerged submarine. Already the I–47 had taken a terrible concussive pounding from the depth charges bracketing his boat and he suspected that it was the explosion of the torpedo hitting the schooner that had attracted the Australian naval ship to him. Selfish ambition had motivated him to destroy the schooner which he felt was taunting him with its invulnerability against the might of the Japanese navy. Now from its watery grave it seemed that the spirit of the schooner was wreaking revenge against him.

Kenshu stood in the control room, gripping the periscope whilst his crew stared with frightened eyes at him. No matter how much they had been indoctrinated in the ethos of dying for the Emperor, when the time came to face death they were still only human. The captain felt a wave of sympathy for his frightened young crew.

'We will be safe,' he said. 'Soon it will be our turn to go after the Australian ship.' But his words fell on deaf ears as the next barrage of depth charges drifted down into the dark, tropical waters to explode at pre-timed depths.

The blast of concussive air hammered the hull of the Japanese submarine, stationary at its most extreme depth. There was a hiss of water from a tiny crack and then a sudden blackness as the electrical system failed. One of the crew cried out and Kenshu was glad that he did not know who it was, as he would be compelled by the Emperor's naval law to punish the man for cowardice. How could he have done that when every nerve in his own body screamed to be away from this terrible place of death?

'Seaman Horrie,' Kenshu said in the total darkness. 'Get our lights going again.'

A muffled voice acknowledged the order and the boat's electrician flicked on the torch he always carried, casting a ghostly dim light in the control room.

Kenshu's young executive officer stood at his elbow. 'What do we do, sir?' he asked, attempting to keep his fear under control.

'We sit it out,' Kenshu answered. 'The enemy will have no indication of whether he has sunk us.' The lights in the control room flickered on and Kenshu muttered praise for his electrician who had performed well under the difficult circumstances. Kenshu could see that his executive officer had an expression of doubt. 'Either that or we die for the Emperor,' he added matter-of-factly.

The executive officer was only twenty-three years of age and had a wife and baby daughter living in Nagasaki. He was not convinced that dying for the Emperor was all that good an idea – but he had faith in his captain.

On the surface the Australian frigate made two

more passes over the submarine's suspected position, which it had detected on its sonar. All the depth charges had been used and all the frustrated captain of the frigate could do was radio for assistance.

Kenshu noted the change in the ship's pattern and suspected that it was his turn to become the attacker.

'Our torpedo room has sustained too much damage to fire the fish, sir,' his torpedo officer reported from the bow.

Now it was Kenshu's turn to feel the frustration. He could surface and possibly use his deck gun to engage the Australian frigate but knew that he would be matched shell for shell. Besides, the American or Australian air forces may have been called on, and on the surface they could blow him out of the water.

'Prepare to get under way on a course forty-seven degrees east,' he said softly to the men who navigated. 'We will return to Rabaul for repairs.'

Kenshu could see the expressions of relief on the faces of his men. His mission to pick up Leading Seaman Komine had failed, the young spy had not answered the lamplight signal to shore. But whatever Fuji's fate was, it was not as important as the safety of his own boat and crew. They had survived the best the Australian navy could throw at him below the surface of the Papuan Gulf and at least the submarine could be repaired and readied for the great invasion of Port Moresby that he knew must come soon, considering the current naval strategy. It did not take a tactical strategist to understand that the key to denying the Americans their sea routes to Australia lay in the capture of the vital facilities in Port Moresby. When Moresby fell the Australians would be cut off from any American assistance – and that inevitably meant the fall of Australia to Japan.

'Captain, sir!' the young sailor manning the rudder control cried out. 'The boat is not responding. We are diving out of control.'

Kenshu swung on his rudderman. 'What is it?' he demanded, knowing the sailor was not really in a position to answer. 'Get the chief engineer up here now,' Kenshu bellowed, and even as he issued his order he could feel the slope under his feet become more acute.

'The forward quarters are flooded,' someone cried in a panicked voice, and the Japanese submarine commander took a deep breath to steady his taut nerves. The depth charges had caused damage to the hull that had not been immediately recognised. Behind him a tightly strung voice called the depth. 'Two hundred, two fifty, two seventy-five . . .'

'Get the rudders working,' Kenshu said loudly but calmly. His ashen-faced crew crammed around him in the control room. The dim lighting flickered on and off as somewhere water short-circuited the system. Then the lights went out completely, pitching the submarine into a darkness only found in the grave. 'Get a torch going,' Kenshu called in the darkness, and at the same time he heard the creaking, groaning sound that all submariners recognised as the prelude to their deaths: the sound of the metal-skinned hull imploding under the massive weight of water outside. A torch beam illuminated the terrified faces, sweating even in the creeping chill of the control room. The executive officer turned to his captain and bowed from the waist in a last gesture of comradeship. Kenshu knew that they were descending too far and too fast to stop the inevitable. The hiss of water under intense pressure muffled the sound of sailors praying to their ancestors or softly sobbing for those they left behind.

Kenshu returned the salute as the submarine reached a depth guaranteed to crush the boat to twisted metal. His last thought as the hull burst inwards with a rush of cold sea water was that somehow the spirit of the *Independence* had wreaked its awful revenge. He and his crew would join it at the bottom of the sea.

The stars were rapidly being obscured by the dark clouds billowing in from the sea. There would be a storm, Fuji thought, standing at the edge of a small rocky outcrop being sprayed by the rising waters beating against the shore. From where he stood he had a good view of the mangroves and in the distance he could hear the crump of the exploding depth charges coming from the west. He shuddered. Maybe his escape had been in vain. All he had was a hope that Keela would be successful.

Fuji remained at his vigil throughout the night, fighting off a need to sleep by humming songs popular in Japan before he had left a year earlier. But Keela did not come and the Japanese sailor's hopes faded. What were his options now? At least he would get some sleep before he made any decisions.

With the sun's first rays touching the night sky he retreated from the small, rocky promontory to seek a place in the jungle to camp for the day. He knew of a brackish creek behind the mangrove swamp so water was not a problem and he still had a small supply of dried fish and rice. With a sigh, Fuji slipped into the jungle.

Fuji did not know how long he had slept but when he awoke he was not alone. The closely shaved hair of his scalp prickled and very carefully he moved his hand over the pistol under his chest.

'Fuji!'

The Japanese sailor rolled over, his pistol outstretched to meet the threat. 'Keela!' he cried in his utter surprise at seeing the woman he thought he may never see again. 'How . . .?' he did not know what he should ask as she knelt beside him with an expression of utter joy.

'I had to hide when I stole the boat,' she said. 'I knew my people would come looking for me when they found the canoe missing so I pulled it into the trees. Then I saw a ship dropping bombs in the sea and I was afraid to go out again. In the dark I saw my people in their canoes also but they turned back when they saw the big ship dropping bombs in the sea. I walked all night until I came to the place you said we should meet. I could not find you until I began searching the jungle. Then I found you here asleep.'

Fuji sat with the pistol between his legs, shaking his head and grinning at his woman's initiative. 'You would have made a good soldier in the Emperor's army,' he said, looking up at Keela. 'Maybe our son will be a great warrior in the service of the Emperor. Well, I will prepare a meal for us and tonight we shall go back for the canoe.'

Keela slumped to her knees beside him. No matter what the future held she did not care as long as she was with her man. Together they would face the sea and sail to the islands beyond her clan's influence. She would go to Rabaul with Fuji – although he did not know that at the moment. In time she would convince him that they should never be parted again.

THIRTY-FIVE

U nder cover of night Keela led Fuji to the hidden canoe, and the small outrigger was launched into a slowly rising swell. Keela had stolen a good supply of yams, cooked pig meat and water contained in gourds. If used sparingly it was enough for three days.

Both rowed at a steady pace until Fuji was able to catch some wind with the single woven sail. Growing up on the edge of the Gulf of Papua he was an experienced sailor and guided the craft skilfully through the rising roll of the waves. The stars were hidden behind a low, dark blanket of clouds but the Japanese sailor had an uncanny sense of direction, navigating in an easterly direction by keeping in sight the Papuan coast on his portside.

Keela proved to be equally adroit as a sailor and between them they were able to rise with the rolling seas and slide into the troughs without capsizing. Eventually the wind and seas conspired to force the sail down, leaving them with the oars to continue their passage to safety.

Just before dawn Fuji felt that they should make for shore to find a place to hide up for the daylight hours. In this part of the world the Allies had aircraft flying recon missions and at sea – close to the shore – they might be spotted. It was unlikely that a couple of natives in a canoe would attract much interest but he was not about to take any chances. Landing ashore would also give them the opportunity to replenish their store of meagre supplies.

Fuji could not see any lights that might mark a village. Nor could he see what was ahead, so he listened intently for the sound of anything unfamiliar. He knew this part of the coast well and did not expect any trouble landing on the narrow strip of sand. He was tempted to use his torch to see what was ahead but preferred to trust his instincts. The sudden jolt of the canoe coming to a halt, only to be tossed forward on a small wave, told him he had been on the right course.

Fuji leapt from the canoe and began to haul it up the narrow strip of sand to the trees he could vaguely make out in the dark. Keela helped and he marvelled at her strength. But being a native girl she knew what hard labour was.

With the canoe concealed in the underbrush, they slumped exhausted together to sleep. When they awoke in the early hours of the morning Fuji could see that the skies had cleared. It was a good omen and now he would relax with Keela and eat some of their supplies before setting out to find a water source. He knew from past experience that he was on a part of the coast with very few villages and this at least gave him a sense of security.

Megan had Lukas placed in the bed next to his father. He was still unconscious from the effects of the chloroform but looked at peace, Megan thought, pulling up the clean sheet to the young man's chin.

'Sister, how will he be?' Jack asked from the adjoining bed. He had been woken earlier by one of the orderlies, who knew Jack and told him of Lukas' operation to remove a bullet from his lung.

'The doctor thinks Lukas will recover very well,' Megan replied, turning to Jack in the dim light of the ward now filled with the sounds of men snoring or talking in troubled voices to themselves in their sleep. 'There is no reason for you to worry, Jack,' she continued in a soothing voice. 'I am here to make sure of that.'

'God bless you, Meg. I know Lukas and I are in good hands with you.'

Impulsively, Megan leaned over and kissed Jack on the forehead. 'What did I do to deserve that?' Jack said with a gentle smile. 'An old man like me – when my handsome son over there missed out.'

'Lukas will get his kiss when he wakes up,' Megan said, returning the smile. 'For now you must go back to sleep and if you are a good boy, I might let you out of bed in the morning for some exercise in the garden.'

'Does that mean, Sister, if I can get to the edge of the garden I can head down to the pub?' Jack asked with a cheeky grin.

'Not on your bloody life, Sergeant Kelly,' Megan replied with feigned sternness. 'You are restricted to the hospital grounds – until I grant you leave.'

'Ah, women,' Jack sighed. 'You rule our lives with iron wills.'

Megan turned away, pretending not to hear Jack's view of her gender. She had her rounds to do with the other men in her care and although they were all precious to her, the two men in the beds she had just left behind were definitely nearest to her heart. She had once heard a girlfriend in Brisbane comment that if you wanted to see what the son would be like in the future, look to the father in the present. Megan knew that she truly loved Lukas Kelly, and if he turned out like his father she was a fortunate woman.

Captain Karl Mann stood on the verandah of his parents' house in Townsville, his kitbag beside him.

'Karl, oh Karl,' he heard his mother cry, as she rushed to smother him in kisses and hugs as if he were still a little boy. Close behind her was Angelika, tears of joy streaming down her face as she flew to meet her brother. 'Why did you not telephone to say that you would be coming home?' his mother chided between tears and kisses.

'I was not sure if I could get any leave,' Karl mumbled, having the breath squeezed from him. 'I have been posted to Port Moresby and our train is only here for a few hours.'

Karin stepped back to examine her son. It had been almost two years since she had last seen him and her mother's eye immediately noticed the changes. He was leaner, with an air of toughness she had not seen before in her normally easy-going and gentle boy. Behind the eyes she could see the haunted look of a man always on the alert. However she did not care about these differences, and broke down into another fit of sobbing at the joy she felt for the sudden and unexpected appearance of her boy.

Angelika was a little more composed than her mother and set about preparing coffee and biscuits for a morning tea. But she could not hide her pride at seeing her brother standing so tall and handsome in the living room and wearing the uniform of an officer, a small strip of colourful riband on his tunic recognising his courage. Oh how different you look, she thought. You have seen much pain, my dearest brother. Tears came to her and she turned away lest her brother see that they were not of joy but of sorrow, for she had lost the boy who in company with Lukas Kelly would tease her when they were in Papua as children. The man who stood in the living room now was a man who had come from war but would have to return to war – this was just a temporary state of joy, for when he was gone from the house the pain of waiting would return.

'Oh, Karl, I miss your father so much and fear that I might lose you also,' Karin said when they were sitting at the tiny wooden table with the pot of coffee between them. 'He was supposed to join us but he just disappeared to God knows where, and then we were told that he had been killed in action,' she added. 'I have written to your Uncle Jack in Port Moresby but I have heard nothing back from him to date. No one in Townsville is able to help me and I don't even have the consolation of burying my husband.'

'Dad was a tough old bastard,' Karl attempted to soothe. 'I am sure wherever he lies he is at peace.'

As soothing as Karl tried to be, he felt a leaden ball in his stomach at his father's fate. He had learnt just how cheap life was in war, and his only hope was to finally get to Papua where he would be in a better position to solve the mystery of his father's death for his mother's peace of mind.

The time went all too fast. Karl had not wanted his mother and sister to come with him to the railway station to see him off but left them with the promise that he would return on leave before he was shipped out again.

They accepted his request and Karl set out from the old high-set timber house just outside Townsville to walk back to the station. He did not turn back to see his mother and sister standing forlornly watching him depart as he did not want them to see the tears in his eyes. Oh, how he hated war. It only brought pain to those who could not stand and face their enemies as he could.

As Karl took his seat on the train, and as it steamed away from the railway station, he stared at the window, where a vague reflection showed him the face of a man lost in hell. His father had disappeared in mysterious circumstances and Karl suspected that the once-proud German had taken up the cause of the Allies only to die.

Rattling north into the tropical countryside of northern Queensland, Karl knew he was once again going back into action – but this time in the country he called home.

THIRTY-SIX

Even the doctor who had operated on Lukas Kelly marvelled at his rapid recovery from the bullet wound. Within a week Lukas was in his hospital-issue dressing gown sitting in a deck chair under the shade of a tree in the ward grounds. He gazed at the bright splash of bougainvillea flowers and brooded about his future now that he had received the news of the sinking of his schooner with the complete loss of life of his crew.

'I thought that we might make our escape to the pub tonight,' a voice cut across Lukas's melancholy thoughts. 'Just you and me.'

Lukas glanced up to see his father standing over him with his hands in the pockets of his gown. 'That would be nice, Dad,' Lukas replied evasively. 'Except I don't think I am well enough yet.'

Jack took a seat in a deck chair beside his son's. 'It

just so happens that Sister Megan Cain also has the night off – or so I heard in the ward.'

Lukas shifted in his deck chair with what Jack knew was guilt. It was obvious that his son had already made plans and was torn by the choice.

'Ah, is that right,' Lukas commented lamely. 'Maybe I will get the opportunity to sit out in the garden and talk to her then.'

Jack grinned. He sometimes enjoyed gently teasing his son. 'You could do worse than Meg,' he finally said to let his son off the hook. 'She has a beautiful soul and I can see how much she is in love with you every time she is around you, cobber.'

'You think so?' Lukas blurted. 'Meg has never really said anything to me. Not even when . . .' He checked himself. He was not about to confess to his father how he and Meg had spent their time at the plantation.

Jack burst into a rolling laugh. 'The loss of your bloody eye was worse than I thought. You must be the only bloke here who has not seen how she acts around you.'

'I think I did ask her out when they brought me in,' Lukas replied. 'I think I asked her to go on a picnic with me when I was better.'

'Then you should think about seeing Megan tonight.'

Lukas gazed at his father and felt a swell of love, yet at the same time an unfathomable depth of sorrow. What would happen after they were both cleared to return to service? For his father it probably meant rejoining the NGVR and returning to their front lines in the jungles west of Lae. As for himself? There was no immediate answer. He had lost his schooner but still remained a rifleman with the NGVR. Maybe he could join his father when he returned to his unit. At least that way he could keep an eye out for him.

'What's funny?' Jack asked when he heard his son burst into laughter.

'Nothing, Dad, just something I was thinking.' Keeping an eye out for him would make me completely blind, Lukas thought and was glad the unspoken joke at himself had helped clear the terrible sadness. The way the war was going for the Allies against the Axis powers made the future bleak enough.

'You know, when I get out of here I am heading down to Sydney,' Jack said. 'I have some unfinished business concerning the last will and testament of an old friend.'

Lukas glanced sharply at his father. 'You mean that?' he asked.

'I have to,' Jack answered. 'How else am I going to be able to replace the *Independence* unless I have some money? I think my old cobber, Lord Spencer, would have approved of that idea. And under the conditions of his will my appearance in the offices of Sullivan, Levi & Duffy will ensure that Iris and her daughter are well taken care of.'

Lukas was elated at his father's proposal to journey to Sydney. To do so meant taking him out of the front lines and away from danger.

The idea of another schooner had not entered

Lukas' mind. But it had Jack's. The schooner had been the soul of Victoria after she had been killed and to Jack another boat would show the Japanese that they could not destroy his life so easily. It was as much an act of defiance as it was a practical way of keeping his son out of the jungle hell he had come to know so well. Jack Kelly was not optimistic about the chances of the vital port of Moresby withstanding a full naval assault by the seemingly unstoppable Japanese navy. At the back of his mind was the thought that at least his son would have a guaranteed means of escaping the impending invasion. The new schooner would be his ticket out of Papua – and hopefully also for Megan and others. It was a long shot but better than nothing.

Weeks had passed for Keela and Fuji in their slow but cautious sea voyage to the most eastern tip of Papua. Fuji knew the area as Milne Bay and also knew that he would now have to tack a course north-east through to the Trobriand Islands if he wanted to reach the safety of the waters controlled by his navy.

In the weeks of paddling, sailing and going ashore each night Fuji's knowledge of the coast from his boyhood voyaging with his father had kept them away from known European outposts and native villages. Occasionally they had been buzzed by aircraft from the RAAF or the American air force but left alone when the observers above realised it was just a couple of natives out at sea.

Sustained only by the fish they caught and the coconut flesh they were able to obtain when they went ashore, both had lost weight and Fuji worried about Keela's condition, but she proved as durable as he in the voyage. She did not complain and appeared to be content in his arms each night they lay and watched the stars overhead.

With Milne Bay on his portside, Fuji began to believe that they would make it to Rabaul or be lucky enough to be picked up by one of his own naval ships patrolling the Solomon Sea. If that was to happen, what would become of Keela, he thought, watching her as he sat in the narrow hull of the wooden canoe. He was still a sailor and subject to the discipline of his superiors, who had little time for relationships between their men and the native girls.

Keela turned her head to glance at him and her long dark hair fell over her face in a heart-wrenching manner. She smiled briefly and turned back to fix a point ahead to navigate. It was a part of her ancestral seagoing instincts, Fuji thought, that she could keep a course as he directed from his hand-held compass. If only his people could see just how worthy this woman was, the Japanese sailor brooded morosely, they could not consider her a mere animal. For once in his military life Fuji had doubts about the rightness of his own people. Was it that he was thinking more like a Papuan native than a Japanese man?

Soon, the tropical coast rose and fell below the horizon and the tiny sea craft was alone with its occupants upon the expanse of the Solomon Sea.

• • •

Megan paraded her two patients in her office. 'The doctor has given his approval to discharge you both,' she said from behind her desk. 'Like me, he thinks any longer in hospital and we would have to recruit you to the staff – or have you both locked up for being awol from the wards at night, only to return with the strong smell of alcohol on your breaths.'

Megan tried to sound cheerful and joke about Jack and Lukas' release from her care but felt differently. She had seen the orders from the NGVR HQ posting Lukas somewhere in the mountains overlooking Lae. That meant coming into direct contact with the Japanese in their stealthy war of information gathering and fooling them into holding their ground on the coast rather than pushing forward through the rugged jungle passes towards Port Moresby. She was at least pleased that Jack had been granted leave to return to Australia on urgent family matters. At least he would be safe for the moment.

'Aye, aye, ma'am,' Lukas saluted. 'Permission to ask you out tonight, before I ship out, Sister Cain.'

Megan crossed in front of her desk, taking Lukas's hand and kissing him on the cheek. 'Do you mind if I speak to your father alone?'

Lukas frowned, but shrugged and stepped outside.

'What is it Meg?' Jack asked, and could see that she appeared to be struggling with something of great concern.

'I heard that you have been able to hitch a ride out with the RAAF to Australia,' Megan said. 'That means you will be going out to the Seven Mile strip.'

'That's right,' Jack replied. 'This afternoon, for a flight to Cairns.'

Megan took a deep breath before saying, 'Some weeks ago when you were in the grips of the fever you had a visitor.'

'Yeah, one of the other blokes in here mentioned something about a Yank journalist coming to the ward,' Jack said. 'He said that she was a real looker.'

'Her name is Ilsa Stahl and she is quartered out at Seven Mile,' Megan explained. 'I think you should make every attempt to find her before you leave for home.'

'Why, Meg? If I remember rightly she was the Yank Lukas brought back with you, wasn't she?'

Megan could not look Jack in the eye. She stared out the window of her office at Lukas standing in the garden patiently waiting for his father. 'Miss Stahl is that same woman,' she answered.

A thought dawned on Jack. 'Is my son somehow involved with her?' he asked in a protective tone.

'No, no,' Megan hurried to counter Jack's unfounded suspicions. 'I would like to say more but I do not feel that it is my place to explain why it is important that you find Miss Stahl and speak with her. If you do, I know you will understand why I have not been able to tell you more than I have. All I can say is, just find Miss Stahl and all will be revealed.'

'Not even a hint?' Jack frowned.

'I'm sorry, Jack, but you must find out for yourself.'

Jack sighed. Why was it that women tended to be so mysterious about even the simplest of events in their lives? What could be so important to warrant all this mystery and intrigue? 'Well, okay,' he shrugged.

'Jack, you promise?' Megan asked.

'I promise,' he replied. 'So long as it does not disturb my plans to fly out of here this afternoon.'

Megan leaned forward and reached up to kiss Jack on the forehead, gently brushing his face with her hand. 'You take care, Sergeant Kelly,' she said as she stepped back. 'I would like you to be at your son's wedding.'

'Does he know yet?' Jack asked with a broad grin.

'Not yet,' Megan replied with a gentle shrug of her own. 'He is not quite as bright as his father.'

'You know I would be honoured to give my son into your care,' Jack said, taking her hands in his. 'He could do no better if he searched the world ten times over.'

Megan gave his hands a quick squeeze of pleasure. 'Well, I should not hold you two up as I suspect your first stop will be the pub.'

Jack's grin confirmed her assumption. 'See ya, lassie,' he said, plonking his battered slouch hat on his head before leaving the room to join his son in the garden.

'What was that all about?' Lukas asked.

'Nothing much,' Jack answered as they fell into step to head towards the busy hotel. 'Just something about wedding plans.'

'Whose?' Lukas asked suspiciously.

'No one in particular,' his father replied.

But Lukas frowned. It was just like his father to tease him.

THIRTY-SEVEN

At the Seven Mile airstrip Jack found the quarters of the American war correspondents. 'I'm looking for Miss Ilsa Stahl,' he told the man who introduced himself as Gene Fay.

'You just missed her but she should be back in about an hour,' Gene said. 'Any message I can take for her?'

Jack was not sure what to say. He did not even know why he was supposed to introduce himself to the Yankee woman but at least he had satisfied his promise to Megan. 'Just say Jack Kelly dropped by to make himself known,' Jack said.

'I don't know if that will make any sense to Miss Stahl because it sure as hell doesn't make any sense to me,' Gene said. 'But I will make sure Miss Stahl gets the message. I don't know why, but I think you are the man she has a hankering to meet for reasons she has not revealed to me.'

'That leaves us both mystified,' Jack said in parting.

Jack sat in the shade of a bulldozer out of the blazing sun and watched as men stripped to their waists and tanned black by the sun went about the business of repairing the airstrip which had been damaged by Japanese air raids. The C47 Dakota that was to take him south to Australia was being refuelled and Jack waited for the signal to board. He had used one of his innumerable contacts in the administration to obtain the precious passage aboard the plane after being granted leave from his unit. An hour passed and Jack noticed the twin engines of the transport plane cough into action. He hefted himself to his feet and swung his kitbag over his shoulder. From the corner of his eye he noticed a car driving at top speed towards the strip from the direction of the correspondents' quarters at the far end of the Seven Mile encampment.

The pilot of the Dakota was leaning out of the window and signalling urgently for Jack to board, having just received word that a flight of Japanese bombers escorted by fighters was reported on its way to Port Moresby. The pilot was eager to be out of the area before they arrived. Already fighter pilots were scrambling to the cockpits of waiting aircraft and the transport pilot knew he only had a minute or two to get his plane off the runway before the fighters needed to be airborne.

Jack sprinted to the doorway in the fuselage and hauled himself aboard with the help of a crewman just as the car skidded to a halt and a young woman leapt from the driver's side, frantically waving. From a distance Jack could see that she was young and pretty but he was not in a position to do anything except wave back. Her urgency surprised Jack but whatever she had wanted to see him for would have to wait.

The pilot revved his engines to roll the plane onto the airstrip ready for take-off. Jack stared out the window and watched the girl standing alone below until the plane banked and took a course south over the Gulf of Papua and away from the war. Jack wondered about the American girl. There was something familiar about her, he puzzled as the plane droned upwards into the rolling bank of clouds which would help hide the transport until it was clear of the area of operations. Buffeted by turbulence, Jack tightened the seat belt across his waist. Stahl, he thought. She was related to the Mann family through marriage, he vaguely remembered. And then he stiffened. Ilsa Stahl! She was possibly Erika's daughter and now wanted to make contact with him. But why, considering the circumstances of his stormy relationship with her mother? Jack frowned. It could wait until he returned to Moresby, he concluded, and attempted to get some sleep before they put down at Cairns.

Fuji had cleared the China Strait and within five days of relatively easy sailing reached the southern end of the D'Entrecasteaux Islands. Keela had worked hard with him to paddle when the wind was not in their favour. Although the critical shortage of food was an ongoing problem, the occasional squally weather provided enough fresh water to keep them alive. Their attempts at fishing were not successful however and the sight of land on the horizon was welcome and spurred them on to navigate north-east.

Fuji was worried for Keela. The rigorous demands of the voyage were taking a toll on her health and she was becoming listless.

'It won't be long and we will be eating fresh pork,' he said reassuringly, stroking her cheek with a tenderness he rarely displayed. Keela smiled, taking his hand in her own but not replying. She simply stared with tired eyes and sighed.

Within a half day the little outrigger canoe slid onto a deserted beach. Fuji helped Keela from the boat and up the beach to a stand of tall coconut trees. He left her to rest in the shade while he struggled with the canoe. He did not know how he would find them fresh supplies but at least he was in a part of the world he knew. He also knew that it could be under Allied control. Slipping the pistol from the bag where he carried his most essential supplies, Fuji checked its action but as it had been cleaned religiously each day, it was in good working order. For now he would let his woman rest whilst he went into the bush to scout out something to eat.

Fuji hunted all afternoon and was fortunate enough to come across a cuscus in the trees. A well-aimed shot brought down the creature. He had never eaten cuscus meat but he was so hungry he would try anything. With it over his shoulder he made his way back to where he had left Keela and was shocked to find her sitting under the tree, happily chatting to a young native boy of about ten years old.

Fuji dropped the dead animal and pulled the pistol from the waistband of his lap-lap.

'I have been told that there is a village not far from here,' Keela said, looking up at Fuji striding towards her with a grim expression on his face. 'Loko has said that we can go with him to meet his family.'

Fuji stared at the young boy, who stared back with big brown curious eyes. He had hoped to avoid all contact with the natives in these islands as they may be dealing with the Australian coast watchers.

'Ask him if there are any Japanese soldiers or sailors close by,' Fuji said, with the pistol at his side.

Keela asked the boy in his language. Her people had contact with the people in this part of the world and she knew some of their words – enough to ask simple questions.

'He says that there are none of your people near his village, as far as he knows.'

'What about Europeans?'

Keela asked again and the boy nodded. Yes, there was an Australian coast watcher but he did not know where.

Fuji signalled to the boy to come to him and the boy understood. He approached warily, eyeing the gun at Fuji's side.

'What are you doing?' Keela asked.

'The boy and I are going into the jungle so that

he can show me the path to his village,' Fuji replied, placing his hand on the boy's shoulder and smiling down at him reassuringly.

Satisfied, Keela did not ask any more questions and watched as Fuji and the boy turned to disappear into the thick undergrowth. She sat back against a tree to rest further and was dozing when she heard the single shot. Starting awake, Keela glanced around to locate Fuji. He was not to be seen, but within the half hour returned.

'Where is the boy? Did he show you the way to his village?'

Fuji did not answer but walked back to the carcass of the cuscus. 'We will cook this animal and eat,' he said without looking her in the eye.

With dawning horror Keela realised that her man was being evasive. 'Did you shoot the boy?' she asked.

'He might have told his people about us and the Australian coast watcher might have been told that we were here,' Fuji said, slicing open the now stiffening cuscus to remove the entrails.

'He was only a boy,' Keela gasped accusingly. 'His mother will miss him. You did not have to kill him.'

'If we are to survive I must do everything to ensure that we reach Rabaul,' Fuji snarled, continuing to gut the creature. 'This is war and I am a warrior of the Emperor. I cannot allow my personal feelings to interfere with my sacred mission.'

Keela rose to her feet. 'He would not have betrayed us,' she said, standing unsteadily on her feet facing him. 'He was my friend.'

'You do not have any friends amongst those who have contact with the Australians,' Fuji snapped. 'Now, gather wood for a fire so that we may eat.'

Keela glared at the man she had considered strong and gentle. Now she only saw a ruthless man, devoid of feelings for those who were helpless. She hated herself for loving the Japanese man whose child she carried but knew – despite what he had done – she would remain with him and so, without a word, turned and went in search of kindling.

Although the meat gave her strength they both remained silent in the tiny glow of the fire that night. When it came time to sleep, Keela lay beside Fuji without touching him. Fuji stared up at the stars. Killing the boy had given him no pleasure but he could not risk the chance of the boy disclosing their presence on the beach. It had been necessary but Fuji could not help consider how he might have felt if the young boy had been his son and someone had dealt with him so cold-bloodedly. He tried to justify his misgivings with the consideration that he had too long been exposed to the weak European ideals concerning the sanctity of life. At least when Japan had conquered the Pacific such notions of compassion would be eliminated. The Japanese were, after all, the master race.

Jack Kelly found Sydney had not changed much with the advent of war. He stood yawning on Central Station with his kitbag slung over his shoulder after sitting up all night on the train from

Brisbane. He was sick of trains, having spent days travelling down from Cairns. It had been a slow trip as his train had often been side-tracked as trains travelling north with war supplies and troops had priority on the tracks.

'You got here, old chap,' the man said, hobbling his way down the concrete railway platform with his hand extended. 'It's been a bloody long time between drinks.'

Jack broke into a broad smile and they shook hands with a firm grip. 'Good to see you, Tom,' Jack said to the friend he had known for over twenty years. 'See you still haven't grown a new leg.'

'You still haven't grown up,' he retorted. 'What bloody madness made you enlist for a second go when you could be back at home in Australia running the canteens?'

'Home for me, Tom, is Papua, and right now it's under threat from the Japs.'

Tom Sullivan nodded. He knew his friend's great love for that rugged country of head-hunters, cannibals, mountains and impenetrable jungles full of fever. 'I have a car outside and feel that our first stop should be for a cold beer,' he said as they made their way to the ticket stand at the exit to the platform.

To Jack the most discernible change to Sydney was its people. There were so many uniformed men and women in the streets it really seemed as if the city was involved in a war. Also noticeable was the number of smartly dressed American soldiers in their flasher, well-fitting uniforms.

Tom showed Jack to a shiny black Dodge sedan where an older man sat in the driver's seat.

'Doing well,' Jack commented, getting in the back seat with Tom. 'Got yourself staff.'

'Have been making a bit of money out of the real estate market,' Tom replied, taking off his hat and fanning himself. Unseasonably sultry hot weather had struck at the end of the Sydney autumn. 'A lot of good properties have been going for a song since the outbreak of the war with the Japs. Lot of people living on the Harbour are selling up, fearing the Japs are going to come storming through their lounge rooms any day now.'

'The way things are going up north they might be smarter than you for buying them out.'

'A few of my clients have as much faith as I do, in us holding off the Japs now that the Yanks are arriving in force,' Tom said. 'So I have been able to turn over the properties at a good profit. You know there is always a job working in my companies if you get any sense and get yourself out of military service. You are getting too old to go running around with the young lads up there.'

Jack appreciated his old friend's offer as he too was beginning to recognise that his age was beginning to show in the front lines of such unforgiving country as the Papuan mountains. War was for younger men. His thoughts turned to his own son. Where was Lukas at this moment? Was he safe with the NGVR?

The driver dropped them at Tom's favourite pub. He had already told his partners that he was taking the day off and not expecting to return to the office. The two men made their way into the hotel packed with American servicemen, and pushed their way up to the bar where Tom ordered a couple of beers. 'To the old battalion,' they muttered and swigged the cold beers, leaving frothy moustaches on their upper lips.

'Tomorrow, Iris will attend my office to sign the papers with you,' Tom said, wiping the froth from his lip with the back of his coat sleeve. 'Then both of you will be very rich people judging from the last estimation on Lord Spencer's estates in England, despite the Poms taxing the hell out of everything for the war effort over there.'

Jack nodded, sipped his beer and gazed around at the bright young faces of the American servicemen drinking in the cool confines of the hotel. 'How is Iris?' he asked, wondering at how young the Americans looked.

'She is good,' Tom answered. 'I extended a bit of money from the estate on loan to her at your suggestion so she could secure some decent accommodation. She had nothing else to support them when they arrived in Sydney.'

'Thanks, Tom,' Jack said. 'I owed that to my old mate, George Spencer.'

'What are you going to do with your share of the money?' Tom asked.

'The first thing I am going to do is buy a boat,' Jack replied. 'Preferably a schooner – or even a lugger. Then I am going to sail back to Papua and hand it over to Lukas.'

Tom raised his eyebrows. 'You are mad. Why

would you head back to a place we both know is going to fall to the Japs sooner rather than later?'

'For that very reason,' Jack answered quietly. 'It is the only guaranteed ticket I can buy for my son to get out of the place if the proverbial hits the fan.'

Tom understood now and admired his friend's logic. He had a daughter who he doted on and knew that he would have done the same had she been in the same situation.

The two men drank the afternoon away and when it was time to leave, Tom had his driver pick them up and take them to Tom's fashionable mansion overlooking Sydney Harbour.

War was profitable for some, Jack thought as he carefully exited the car, ensuring that he did not fall flat on his face.

'Home, old chap,' Tom said, waving at his newly acquired property. 'Home is where the heart is – or what a lot of money can buy.'

At the mention of money Jack realised that within hours he also would be a very wealthy man. His heart though was still in the jungles with his comrades facing the Japs in the hills around Lae. It was strange but he knew that when he returned he would probably die in those same rugged mountains. Whether from disease or enemy action, he would die and all the wealth in the world would mean nothing to him. At least he had made out his will, leaving his half of the fortune to his only heir. Nothing else mattered except that Lukas lived to see out the war and enjoy the fruits of peace.

• • •

The following day Jack met Iris in the waiting room of the offices of Tom's legal practice in the heart of Sydney. She was dressed smartly and wore a small hat and gloves, the style of her hat seeming to highlight her delicate cheekbones.

Tom Sullivan ushered them into his office. It had changed since the years when Jack had spent many hours there discussing his legal affairs after becoming wealthy in his own right from the gold he had mined from his claims in New Guinea's Morobe fields. Once an office of organised chaos, it was now neat without a file in sight: just a shiny desk and expensive cabinets of exotic polished timbers.

Tom gestured for them to take a chair, each in front of his desk, and retrieved a manila folder crammed with an assortment of papers. He droned through the terms and conditions of the will until finally it was time to sign the most important paper of all – the one transferring the late Lord Spencer's estate and finances to Iris and Jack.

'It's only been twenty years,' Tom said lightly, holding out his hand to Iris and Jack. 'But you are now both very wealthy people.'

Wealthy and soon probably dead, Jack thought sadly, taking his friend's hand. Now it was time for him to return to the war.

THIRTY-EIGHT

Fuji was sure he could hear the distant throbbing of an engine out to sea and instinctively grabbed his pistol, signalling for Keela to move deeper into the trees adjoining the beach, while he moved forward in an attempt to identify the craft now appearing around the corner of land jutting out to sea. It was a landing barge, flying the ensign of the rising sun and filled with Japanese troops.

'Keela,' he called. 'We are saved – it's one of ours!'

Fuji stepped onto the beach when the barge was only a few hundred yards from him and waved his hands above his head. He was immediately seen by those on the barge and a machine gun was swung on him. 'I am Japanese,' he called at the top of his voice, looking nervously at the weapon trained on him. 'I need help.'

The barge altered course but the machine gun

remained trained on him. The craft chugged into the beach and ten fully kitted Japanese marines spilled out to surround him with a ring of bayonets. Fuji guessed that as he was dressed in nothing more than a native lap-lap he must have cut a suspicious figure to his countrymen.

A junior officer strode up to him. He wore glasses and at his side was a samurai sword. 'Who are you?' he asked and Fuji came to attention to answer.

'I am Leading Seaman Fuji Komine with His Imperial Majesty's submarine I–47 under the command of Lieutenant Kenshu.'

The officer was young and from his accent Fuji guessed he was from a noble family.

'Can you prove your identity?' the young officer asked, and Fuji realised that he did not have any papers.

'I am sorry, sir, but I cannot prove who I am at this very moment. I am sure if you have any means of contacting Lieutenant Kenshu he can verify who I say I am.'

'That will be very difficult, Komine,' the officer answered in an icy tone, causing Fuji to feel a rising fear that something was wrong. 'The I–47 is missing, presumed sunk by the enemy and, if that is so, how is it that you are alive and here? My only guess is that you are a deserter since no others have been located. It is therefore my duty to place you under arrest and take you back with us under guard.'

Fuji felt sick. He and Keela had sailed over three hundred miles through waters heavily patrolled by Allied shipping and aircraft. They had weathered storms, thirst and near starvation in search of his own countrymen, only to be arrested for desertion. It was at that moment that Keela appeared from the bush, thinking that all was well.

The officer noticed her. 'Seize that woman,' he commanded, and two of the soldiers immediately broke from the ring to physically grab hold of the confused pregnant native girl, dragging her struggling towards the officer in command, where they dumped her beside Fuji who still remained at attention.

'Who is this native woman?' the officer asked Fuji.

'She is my woman, sir. She helped me escape from the Port Moresby district many weeks ago.' The soldiers were ogling Keela and Fuji's fear for himself was forgotten. 'I would beg that she not come to any harm, sir,' he added, his mouth suddenly dry with fear.

'You are a deserter, Komine, and thus a coward. You have no rights to ask anything,' the officer said, his voice rising in his anger. With a sudden movement that Fuji did not see coming, the officer lashed out with his fist, smashing into Fuji's face and knocking him back on his heel to fall beside Keela, who was cowering in fear. Fuji reached out to take her hand in reassurance that all would be well.

'Take this cur of a coward away,' the officer bawled and Fuji felt hands grab him under the arms to haul him to his feet. He knew that there was no sense in attempting to fight. As a sailor in the Emperor's navy he was subject to all its laws, although back in Rabaul he might have a chance to clear his name when his part in the I–47's mission to the Moresby district was revealed.

The two soldiers forced him to his feet and marched him at the end of bayonets down to the ramp of the barge whilst the officer and the rest of the section remained with Keela. Fuji did not know what they would do with her but presumed that they would just simply leave her stranded on the island. At least her people had trading contacts with the peoples of this part of the world and he knew that she would be cared for until she could return to her own people near Port Moresby.

He was stood with a soldier either side of him and stared up the beach at Keela, wanting to cry out that everything would be all right in the future and that he would one day return for her. But to his horror he saw that she had been forced to her knees while a soldier holding her long, lustrous hair forced her head forward. What came next seared Fuji's soul forever. He saw the officer slide his slightly curved, long sword from its scabbard and with both hands raise the sword above his head where the sun caught the razor-sharp edge with a shiver of silver fire. The cry of 'Banzai!' went up in a roar as Keela's head came away from her torso and a jet of blood stained the white coral sands black.

The soldier holding the head fell backwards and his misfortune was greeted with rollicking laughter from his comrades. Fuji buckled and retched into the shallow water at the edge of the beach.

Smiling smugly, the young officer wiped the blade of his sword with a white silk handkerchief without giving Fuji a glance. He slid the sword back into the scabbard, turned his back on the dead girl and walked away from the execution ground. She was after all, nothing more than a sub-species of humanity, and to take her with them would have necessitated extra work. Leaving her behind alive might have meant a serious breach of security should she have reported their presence at the southern end of the island. The officer had done what was required by all the Japanese ethics of war.

Grief-stricken, Fuji was taken aboard the barge with his hands tied behind his back with wire. It was hardly necessary as he was numbed into a state of emotional shock. The worst part was that he was powerless to contest the actions of a superior officer, he brooded, huddled in the corner of the barge. One day, he swore to himself, he would kill the man who had so brutally taken his woman and future child from him. Maybe the Papuan idea of 'payback' had rubbed off on him. Perhaps he was more Papuan than Japanese, but one day he would kill the officer. For now all he had to do was get back to naval head-quarters at Rabaul and prove that he was not a coward and a deserter.

Jack Kelly dozed fitfully in the railway carriage bumping its way north to Townsville. In the dark he could hear the soft murmur of soldiers' voices, or the occasional laughter from an unheard joke told by one of the young men unable to sleep on the cramped and hard seats. His business was done in

Sydney and it was time to go home. He would go as far as Townsville and then hitch a flight through one of his contacts in the RAAF stationed in the big rural town of Queensland's north.

Jack found getting to sleep hard and hefted himself upright in his seat to rifle through his kitbag, which he had been using as a pillow. From the kitbag Jack retrieved his pipe and tobacco. He formed the tobacco into a plug in the bowl of the battered old briar pipe and automatically cupped the lit match in his hand. It was something he even did in peacetime from years being careful in the trenches of France. How strange that his old habit was once again in vogue with this new war, he thought as he puffed contentedly on the thick sweet smoke.

What a surprise Lukas would receive when he was told of the purchase of the new schooner, he contemplated, staring out the window at the dark countryside passing by. He would get Lukas discharged from the NGVR the same way he had enlisted his son. The NGVR were an entity unto themselves and fought their own war according to their rules although they were a part of the Australian army overall. Maybe it was because the men of the NGVR were a peculiar breed – the last real adventurers of the twentieth century.

Jack turned away from the window to stare ahead at the interior of the dark carriage. If nothing else he was ensuring that his son would be looked after. His own death had come to him in his dreams many times and Jack knew that he would not survive a second war. Since the death of Victoria he had remained alive only long enough to protect his son's future. He was no longer a young man and age would only slow him down whereas a Japanese bullet would be faster.

The train clanged to a halt at a tiny railway station and the mail bags were offloaded while a platoon of soldiers boarded. 'Hear the news?' he heard one of the soldiers declare to anyone still awake. 'Our navy and the Yanks have stopped the Japs in the Coral Sea.'

Jack grabbed the young man as he made his way down the aisle. 'What's this about the Coral Sea?' he asked.

'Bloody Nips were going to try and take Port Moresby with a sea invasion but our boys turned them around in some big battle out in the Coral Sea. It looks as if the Japs will have to find some other way of capturing Moresby.'

'Thanks, cobber,' Jack said, and let the soldier stumble on down the aisle as the train pulled out from the station.

Jack had an old mate on the HMAS *Hobart* and had a gut feeling that his ship had been in the thick of action. So the Japs had thrown their powerful navy at Port Moresby and failed. No doubt there would be some celebrating in the Moresby pubs, Jack thought with a relieved smile. The immediate danger to the frontier town was gone and Lukas' life was guaranteed for a bit longer.

THIRTY-NINE

Fear pervaded the very air in the room and sweat rolled down Fuji's body as he stood to attention before the commanding officer of the dreaded *Kemptai* police in the former Australian government office in Rabaul. He still only wore the lap-lap he had been wearing when he had been taken prisoner, and his body was showing the ravages of beatings from the hands of the Japanese military police whilst he awaited the investigation to be completed. It had been three weeks since the death of Keela, and Fuji did not care if they executed him, for his world was now a bleak place of dishonour and emptiness.

The officer sitting behind the desk was immaculately dressed and standing to one side was the toad-like senior NCO Fuji had known from months earlier when he had helped round up the Australian soldiers who had fought against them in New

Britain. It had been this same man who had beaten Fuji here in Rabaul, in an attempt to force him to confess to desertion, but the young Japanese sailor had resisted and after a time the NCO beat him for the sheer pleasure of inflicting pain. It had only been Fuji's desire to remain alive long enough to hunt down and kill the marine officer who had beheaded Keela that kept him alive. Meanwhile, the NCO was careful that he did not go too far and kill his helpless prisoner as the man was still under the protection of strict Japanese military law.

The silence of the room was ominous. Two extra guards were posted at the door and Fuji continued to stare straight ahead at a point just above the officer's head, which was bowed in examination of the papers before him. With a delicate movement the officer turned each page and peered at the report. Fuji could hear the laughter of native children penetrating the walls of the building and envied them their innocence in a time of war.

'Leading Seaman Komine,' the officer said, looking up from the papers before him. 'After a thorough examination of the findings conducted by the navy and interrogations carried out by my staff I am under the impression that you carried out your duties as directed by your superior officer, Lieutenant Kenshu in April. Evidence has come to our attention that you were to be put ashore near Port Moresby to carry out espionage activities and that you were unable to return to the I–47.'

Fuji could hardly believe his ears – the findings had found him innocent!

The officer ceased speaking and stared belligerently at Fuji on the other side of the desk. 'I am not satisfied that you are a fit sailor to wear the rank you now have. It is the way of Bushido to die with your comrades rather than live to run for safety.' This sudden turn of events in the dialogue caused Fuji to relive his misgivings about his fate. 'I am therefore recommending that you be stripped of your rank and any awards or decorations that you may have received for your past services to the Emperor. You are to report immediately to naval headquarters where you will be reassigned at their discretion. That is all, Seaman Komine.'

So he was to live – but in a state of dishonour for having the instinct to survive rather than die the honourable way with his comrades. Even Fuji could see how ridiculous the finding was but remained silent. With a deep bow from the waist he saluted the officer behind the desk.

'March out,' the NCO bawled and when Fuji turned to do so he felt the broad hand of the police sergeant push him through the door. 'You are a disgrace to the Emperor and your dead comrades,' the NCO snarled. 'If I had my way I would have had you executed for cowardice.'

Fuji stumbled into the light and continued walking away from the dreaded headquarters of the *Kemptai*. He was alive and would prove his worthiness to the Emperor. But he would also keep his blood oath to Keela and one day he would hunt down her executioner and kill him.

• • •

Even as Fuji was making his way to naval headquarters in Rabaul, Jack Kelly was standing in the gardens of the Port Moresby hospital clutching a brown paper wrapped parcel. The hospital had been his first stop upon his return from Australia after landing at Seven Mile airfield.

'Sister Cain will be out soon to see you,' a cheery-faced nurse said, popping her head out the door.

Within a couple of minutes Megan appeared in the garden.

'Well, Sister Cain, I have brought you a little present from my trip to Australia,' Jack said, beaming a broad smile which began to fade at the stricken expression on the pretty young woman's face. Her eyes were puffy and red as if she had been crying for a long time. 'What is it?' Jack asked placing the parcel on a garden seat.

Megan burst into tears and Jack put his arms around her. 'What is it?' he asked again.

'They haven't told you yet?' Megan sobbed against his shoulder.

'Told me what?'

'About Lukas. Oh God, you don't know . . .'

'I only arrived back a few hours ago,' Jack said with a frown. 'What about Lukas?'

'He has been reported missing in action in the fighting around Lae a week ago. I only found out last night.'

The blood drained from Jack's face and he thought that he might be physically sick as he fought to stay on his feet. Only Megan clinging to him in her own desperation kept him upright. 'He can't be MIA,' Jack whispered. 'He is my only reason to live.'

'Don't say that, Jack,' Megan implored when she recognised the total despair in his voice. 'Don't do anything stupid. You must cope, for a man we both love. I refuse to believe Lukas is dead.'

'It can't be,' Jack mumbled, knowing that to be listed as MIA was as good as being dead. 'I wasn't away that long. I should have been with him. It's my bloody fault. He was the first and last of my body and soul.'

Megan detached herself from the arms of the man who might have been her father-in-law. 'Don't think that. He is missing – not dead – and he loved you more than anyone. I know that he would have wanted you to go on despite everything.'

'I think I need time to be alone,' Jack said softly, and sat down on the garden seat beside the parcel.

'Promise me that you will do nothing stupid,' Megan demanded gently. 'Promise me.'

Jack glanced up at her blankly and did not answer. Tears rolled down his cheeks but there was no sound of sobbing. The tough soldier of two wars had lost so many from his life. What was it that a friend had once said when philosophising on the nature of war and peace? *In peace, sons bury fathers. In war, fathers bury sons.*

So it was for Jack Kelly except that he did not even have the privilege of burying Lukas and saying some words of closure over his grave.

Megan respected Jack's wish, leaving him alone

in the garden, a tiny sea of tranquillity in a town otherwise ravaged by war.

'Sister Johnson,' Megan said re-entering the hospital ward. 'I want you to take over for my rounds. I have something that I must do, and please inform Matron Cary that I will be away for a couple of hours.'

Sister Johnson did not ask why Megan was taking her sudden leave but she was aware that her friend had lost a man she loved.

'Take all the time you want, Meg,' Sister Johnson said, placing her hand gently on Megan's shoulder. 'I can cover for you.'

Megan thanked her and hurried away, praying that the one she sought would still be in Port Moresby. Her mission could not bring back Lukas but it might save his father. From what Megan could see, Jack had all the signs of a man who had given up on life. Megan knew such men well, having nursed their war-broken bodies and minds day in and day out. Alone and in despair it would be so easy for them to end the pain.

'Mr Kelly?' a voice asked and Jack took his hands from his face to look up at the young woman standing over him. Where Megan was pretty this young woman was strikingly beautiful.

'We should have met earlier but events seem to have conspired to keep us apart until now,' she said uncertainly.

'Erika?' Jack half-whispered as he took in the full

effect of the woman standing before him in her fatigue trousers and jacket. It was as if he was seeing a ghost from his past.

'My name is not Erika,' she replied. 'My name is Ilsa and my stepfather was Gerhardt Stahl. My mother is Erika Mann, who you knew.' Ilsa appeared to hesitate and looked away before returning her attention to Jack once again. 'I have learned some time ago that you are in fact my real father. Both my mother and my stepfather, before he died, have confirmed this to be true.'

Jack looked beyond Ilsa to see Megan standing at the doorway to the hospital. Her arms were crossed across her breasts and she nodded to Jack. Her gesture said so many things and one of them was to go ahead and speak with this, his daughter, who was the result of the union with the woman Jack had once loved so much and yet had hurt him with her betrayal. 'You look so much like how I remember your mother,' Jack said in an awed voice, rising to his feet and attempting to take in the stunning revelation.

'When I was a little girl, and my mother was angry at me, she would say I was just like my father,' Ilsa said softly. 'She did not mean my stepfather, who I loved – and still continue to love very much. It was from my stepfather that I was told of the man my mother would make references to. She was talking about you.'

Jack continued to stare into Ilsa's face, searching. 'Your eyes,' he said. 'They are so much like Lukas'.'

Ilsa bowed her head. 'I have been told of your . . .

my half-brother being listed as missing in action,' Ilsa said quietly. 'I was fortunate enough to have met him briefly.'

'How is it that you are my daughter?' Jack queried in a stunned voice. 'I . . .' he faltered and noticed Megan step forward.

'Ilsa is your daughter, Jack,' she said. 'I have known for a while and hoped that you two would meet before you flew out for Australia but I think now is a good time. Maybe it is God's way of attempting to give you something for what you think that you have lost.'

'I . . .' Jack continued and faltered again. He was lost for words.

Ilsa felt a sudden wave of sympathy for this man who was in fact almost a total stranger to her, and felt guilty for not revealing her identity to him when she visited the hospital earlier. 'Mr Kelly, please forgive me,' she said bursting into tears.

'Forgive you for what?' Jack asked gently when he saw his daughter's distress.

'I don't know,' Ilsa said, tugging at a handkerchief from her pocket.

Jack placed his arms protectively around the young woman. 'Forgive you for being a beautiful young woman any man would be proud to call his daughter?' he asked.

Megan smiled sadly and sighed. The hand of man takes and the grace of God gives, she thought, turning to return to the young men of her ward who now needed her hand to nurse them back to health. Why was it necessary for men to resort to war when nothing good came from its consequences, she thought angrily. It was a question to which no man could give her an adequate answer.

When Jack left, Megan opened the parcel he had brought to her. She held up the exquisitely stitched silk wedding dress with its accompanying veil and burst into tears. 'Oh Lukas, I will wear this for you one day,' she sobbed softly, crushing the dress to her breast. 'You are not dead,' she said fiercely. 'I know that you are somewhere out there alive and will return to me.'

FORTY

The waiting was always the worst. Captain Karl Mann of the Independent Commando Company had deployed his team of eight men into their ambush positions alongside the winding dirt track that led up to the jungle-covered hills west of Lae. He had chosen the ambush location after a careful reconnaissance of the area earlier. It was a mere two miles from a Japanese encampment, which was virtually right under their very noses. Now it was only a matter of waiting for the Japanese truck that had been reported by local intelligence sources as being due this day. The truck was taking a section of soldiers to reinforce the outpost the enemy had established as a jumping-off point in their search for Australian troops operating in the mountains.

This was not Karl's first operation against the Japanese. He had worked alongside the NGVR in small raids and ambushes for three months now with great success. Hitting hard and fast, in places the enemy had become complacent in, and thus forcing them to deploy greater numbers of troops simply to guard against interdiction of their supply lines into the Markham Valley, was causing a blow to the enemy's morale. Karl understood the strategy of guerrilla warfare and its delaying tactics, which caused the enemy to tie up large numbers of their forces in a hit-and-run war, thereby frustrating the Japanese high command who would rather deploy soldiers to fight the Americans in the Solomon Islands.

'I heard that you were a patrol officer up here before the war,' the NGVR corporal who had acted as a guide to their present location said in a whisper, to break the monotony of waiting.

'That's right,' Karl answered, watching the road and straining to hear the sound of a truck engine while laying on his stomach in the thick undergrowth. 'I worked mostly out of Mount Hagen in the highlands.'

The corporal was a young man in his late twenties and spoke with an educated accent.

'I was wondering why I hadn't seen you around,' he said. 'I was with Burns Philp in Moresby.'

'You might have known my parents, then,' Karl said. 'Paul and Karin Mann.'

'I should have known from your name!' the corporal replied, shifting on his stomach to make himself a little more comfortable. 'I knew your father when he had dealings with us. Good bloke for a

Germ–' the corporal cut himself short, realising that he might be construed as casting aspersions on the German race, but Karl only grinned at his obvious embarrassment.

'And here I am,' he said with a slight chuckle. 'A good German fighting the Japs.'

'Sorry, sir,' the corporal hurried. 'It wasn't meant that way.'

'No offence taken, Corporal,' Karl said. 'As a matter of fact, you might know of a bloke by the name of Jack Kelly – I believe he is with your mob somewhere up here.'

'Sergeant Jack Kelly?'

'That sounds like one and the same,' Karl answered. 'Do you know where he is now?'

'The last I heard, Sergeant Kelly died of a bad bout of malaria about two weeks ago. He was a bloody good soldier and liked by us all.'

Karl closed his eyes. Not Jack, he thought. The bloody war had taken just about everyone Karl had loved. First Victoria, then his own father, then Lukas had been reported MIA and now, apparently, Jack had been taken by the war. Karl could no longer feel the sorrow but simply a feeling of emptiness.

The thin rope trailing off into the jungle moved, yanked by one of Karl's sentries located down the road to give early warning of anything entering the ambush killing ground. Karl opened his eyes, forgetting for the moment the loss of Jack Kelly. Raising his hand, he caught the attention of his Bren gunner and the gunner's second in command a few feet away. They acknowledged with a grim nod of the head, the Bren gunner tucking the stock of his magazine-fed machine gun into his shoulder and swivelling the barrel to cover a bend in the road. Karl could almost feel the tension in his men scattered along the track as they strained to hear the sound of the truck. Beside him, the corporal was alert as a hunting dog sniffing for prey. The high, whining sound came to them of an engine straining to climb the steep gradient of the rutted road. Karl slipped the safety catch off his Thompson sub machine gun and curled his finger around the trigger.

Within minutes the truck appeared over a rise and into the designated killing ground fifty yards from the ambushers. Karl was pleased to see that their intelligence had been spot on and the open tray of the Japanese army truck was crammed with a dozen or so soldiers, rifles upright between their legs, sitting unsuspectingly in the back. The pre-arranged order to initiate the ambush would be a burst from the Bren. Karl raised his hand and the Bren exploded into action, raking the truck and its occupants with a deadly burst of .303 rounds.

Karl could see the windshield shatter under the sustained burst and the truck slewed off the road into a dirt embankment. Men spilled from the truck, desperately seeking cover. The Bren's fire was joined by that of the rest of Karl's fighting patrol. Rifles and Tommy guns poured death into the body of men who had only moments before been chatting about their families at home or of good places to go on leave in Lae. There was little cover for them as Karl had planned his ambush well. He levelled his sights on one Japanese soldier attempting to duck behind the shelter of the truck. Squeezing the trigger Karl could see dirt spurt up around the man on the embankment behind him. He cursed the weapon's inaccuracy at such a long range. Suddenly the Japanese soldier dropped his rifle and fell to the ground. At least one of his men had shot him, Karl thought with grim satisfaction. The cry of 'Grenade!' came from Karl's right and a Mills bomb arched through the air to fall near the truck. It exploded amongst a group of three soldiers attempting to fire back at Karl's men. Shrapnel ripped through them and they fell from the effects of the blast. Two appeared to be dead but a third sat on his rump holding his hands to his face. Karl could see blood pouring through the Japanese soldier's fingers.

The ambushed men had little hope in the cleverly laid-out killing ground and when Karl was satisfied that they had neutralised any resistance he raised a whistle to his lips to signal the cease fire. The shrill blast reached all of his section and the highly disciplined combat unit held their fire. The silence that followed the deafening crash of small arms was always disconcerting for Karl. It felt as if they were waiting to see what would happen next. All that reached Karl was the ringing in his ears and the moans of the wounded below. Scanning the bodies that littered the road by the truck, Karl could still see the Japanese soldier sitting beside his dead comrades, holding his face and crying in his despair. Karl nodded to his Bren gunner who took a sight on the wounded man. With a gentle squeeze of the trigger he let a burst of rounds go, hitting the soldier with the full impact of nine bullets. The wounded Japanese was flung on his back, his legs kicking in his death throes. Karl waited only minutes, knowing the local Japanese garrison would by now be aware of either the gunfire or the overdue truck bringing them reinforcements. He had achieved his aim and now it was time to get out before the enemy reacted with overwhelming forces against his small patrol. On signal, his men gathered at a pre-arranged rendezvous point well behind the ambush site, picked up their heavier supplies and moved in a fighting formation quickly and silently away from the scene of the killing.

Over the next couple of days, Karl led his weary but jubilant men back to a jungle base camp where he made his report. So far he had not lost one man to the enemy, Karl thought, standing in the sullen jungle by the tiny tent used to house their radio. Once the written report was submitted to the signaller for transmission in code back to Port Moresby, Karl thought bitterly about the vagaries of war. He may be capable of keeping his own men alive but those beyond his reach, such as his father, Jack and Lukas Kelly, he could not protect.

The signaller bent intently over his keyboard tapping the Morse code signal away and waited with Captain Karl Mann for a response. The dot-dash response came and the signaller scribbled down the code, then deciphered it into English.

'They say, well done, sir,' the signaller said, holding up the message to Karl.

'Thanks, Sparkie,' Karl said. He read the full message and was surprised to see that he had been recalled to an assembly point in the Moresby district. Ordered back to rejoin his old battalion, on its arrival in Papua Karl could only guess that they required his knowledge and skills before they went into action against an enemy far more ruthless than any they had encountered to date. Karl had mixed feelings about the recall. Out here he was virtually his own boss with his small army of tough, battle-hardened men with attitudes not unlike his own. That the army deemed he should return was up to them. Karl had once been known as an easy-going young man with a bright smile and infectious laughter, but the war had taken that from him. He was now becoming the warrior Featherstone had always wanted, a pawn in the grand plan for the intelligence man's envisaged post-war world.

'Yer got some mail, sir,' the signaller said, rummaging in an ammunition box and producing three jungle-stained envelopes. 'They came in the last resupply from Moresby.'

Karl took the letters, recognising one from his mother and one from his sister. But the third puzzled him. Any mail was more valuable than bullets to the men so far from home. He turned the envelope over in his grimy hand and broke into a broad smile.

'Got a lady back home, sir?' the signaller asked.

'I think so,' Karl replied and walked away to sit down in privacy and carefully open the fragile letter from Marie. It was dated a month earlier.

'*Mon cheri*,' she addressed him and the very first

two words made Karl feel for a moment that he was no longer in the jungle surrounded by men who would kill him. Karl continued to avidly read the neat, precise words.

> I have many times wished that we had more time together. You are a man who I feel that I was fated to meet although I do not know why or truly understand my feelings in this matter. I hope that you will write to me and we may be able to share our thoughts. I am thinking of you and hope to see you returned to me safely.
> Marie.

Karl read Marie's words three times, hanging on to every word. Then he carefully folded the letter, placing it in the top pocket of his shirt above his heart. Although the letter was brief it had been unexpected and its existence meant more to Karl than anything else in the world. He felt that with all the sorrow that had occurred in this war he had at least found a tiny piece of happiness.

Karl scrounged some sheets of paper from the signaller and wrote his own letter.

In the months ahead Marie's letters would find him in isolated outposts, and growing out of the words on the pages slowly emerged a yearning for each other.

FORTY-ONE

Captain Karl Mann slid down the last part of muddy track. He gripped the buttress roots of the forest trees to break his falls and cursed when the narrow, winding trail of crudely cut steps threatened to give way under the heavy tropical rains. It was the end of August of 1942 and Karl had been in the front lines of the jungle war for the last five months. His Thompson machine gun was slung over his shoulder, and around his waist hung a belt of the tools of war: spare Mills bombs, a razor-sharp commando knife and a keenly honed machete. He was alone and from his heavily bearded face shone the staring eyes of a man who had seen hell in the green jungles and ridges he had left behind him. He knew that soon he should break into the base area known as McDonald's Corner.

Eventually he broke out into a clearing, passing

tin-helmeted guards with .303 rifles, bayonets fixed. They greeted him with respect; the staring eyes told them that he was a soldier who had been in contact with the fierce and unforgiving enemy somewhere up the track.

Karl unslung his machine gun and trailed it in his left hand. The clearing was busy with the signs of a unit preparing to head up what was being called the Kokoda Track. Tents serving as quarters, mess halls and cover for military supplies covered the clearing. It was almost a peaceful place compared to where he had been. His independent company of com mandoes had struck at the Japanese, who could seemingly come out of nowhere to inflict heavy casualties before melting back into the jungle.

As Karl marched stiffly in search of the head-quarters tent to report in, his eye was attracted to a lone figure sitting with his back to a tree and an American .30 calibre Garand rifle across his knees. The man was much older than most of the troops around him and under his battered slouch hat his face was clean shaven.

Karl stopped, peered at the man and broke into a broad smile. He picked up his step and walked across to the tree. 'Uncle Jack?' he said and the man looked up at him.

'Karl!' Jack said with an equal burst of pleasure across his face. 'Where the hell have you been?'

Karl hurried the last steps to Jack, who rose to embrace the commando officer with a gesture of love. 'God almighty, young Karl, it is good to see that you are still alive.' The quick embrace done, Jack stepped back to examine the man who was more like a son to him than simply the son of his best friend now months missing in the jungles of New Britain. 'The last I heard of you was in a letter from your mum. Must have been at least three months ago. She said you were being posted back to Papua but could not tell anymore than that.'

'I was told you were with the NGVR and had been posted to the commandoes working up around your area but seemed to keep missing you. Someone from your old unit said they thought you might have copped it but unless I actually saw your body or grave I was not about to accept anyone could kill my Uncle Jack.' Tears brimmed in Karl's eyes and he forced them back with the wipe of a tattered sleeve of his jungle fatigues. 'It's bloody good to see you, Uncle Jack.'

Jack was also desperately fighting the almost overwhelming desire to break down but such behaviour was not befitting two seasoned warriors. They fell into an awkward silence for a brief moment as the terrible months came flooding back. Finally Jack spoke. 'What are you doing down here?'

'I have been reposted from my unit to return to my original battalion. The army felt that my experience would be of great help to share with my old cobbers who are going up the track fairly soon. They got me back with a promise of a company command. What about you?'

'I think I am being posted to a Papuan infantry battalion to train a bunch of native troops, but you know the bloody army. I have been sitting around here for a week and they cannot confirm anything.'

'I heard about Lukas and Megan,' Karl said, slumping to the ground and using the butt of his Tommy gun as a support. Jack also sat down. 'I am going to miss my old mate. I only wish I'd had the chance to see him when he came home from America.'

Jack nodded. 'You two were as close as any brothers could be. I guess I always considered you my other son anyway. When I last saw Megan she confided that she was pregnant. She is planning to leave the baby with her parents in Australia. She does not believe Lukas is dead and wants to return to nursing in Papua. Guess I will be a grandfather. I only wish Victoria had lived to see the day.'

Karl looked away lest Jack see the pain in his face. With his own father dead, Jack Kelly was now his adopted father – in spirit at least. 'I also heard about Ilsa,' Karl said to distract the conversation from memories too hard to bear.

'Kind of strange how life takes one thing and gives you another,' Jack said, staring at the new troops disembarking from trucks being driven by American Negroes. 'I was fortunate enough to get to know Ilsa in Moresby. She is a remarkable young lady and during the short time we had together I started to think of her as my daughter. It was a really strange feeling I can tell you.'

'Is she still in Moresby?' Karl asked.

Jack shook his head. 'No, she was recalled back to America for reassignment. I just wish she would stay there out of harm's way but she tells me that she was unlucky enough to inherit my nature and hopes to go to Europe to cover the war.'

Karl smiled for the second time. 'What else could you expect from the daughter of the infamous Jack Kelly?'

Jack glanced up at the bearded face smiling at him. 'Yeah, well, you have to promise me that you have no intentions of going out and doing something stupid. Not just for your old Uncle Jack but also for your mum and Angelika. I suspect that your mum still holds me responsible for your life in the absence of your dad.'

'Promise, Uncle Jack,' Karl said, holding out his broad hand to seal the bargain.

Jack took the extended hand and the handshake was strong. 'So when is Ilsa returning?' he asked.

'She said she would like to be with me after all this is over,' Jack replied in a wistful tone. 'She reckons we have a lot of catching up to do.'

'After all this is over,' echoed in Karl's mind. The Japanese had landed strong forces in northern New Guinea to march across the Owen Stanley mountains in an attempt to take Port Moresby by land after failing in the Battle of the Coral Sea. Karl had heard others refer to this battle as the first naval action in history where the opposing naval forces had not seen each other. It had been a war of carrier-based aircraft striking from the sky whilst the two fleets remained out of sight of each other. And now it was up to the soldiers in some of the most rugged country on earth to fight each other. The enemy had been temporarily halted but far from beaten.

'Thank God for the Yanks,' Karl muttered, reflecting his thoughts.

'Yeah,' Jack agreed. 'Thank God for the Yanks. I got this rifle off a Yank supply sergeant for a samurai sword,' Jack said, holding up the semi-automatic, thirty calibre rifle. 'Had a mate down in Moresby make the sword from an axle spring of a truck.' Both men grinned at the duplicity. The convict blood was still strong in some Australian families. 'At least the Yank will have something to hang on his wall and tell his grand-kids how he got it off a dead Nip officer.'

'Well,' Karl said, easing himself to his feet. 'I had better report in to HQ and get myself refitted. You and I will have to catch up over a bottle of beer or two – if it is possible to find one around here – and tell a few yarns, true and false, of our time at the front.'

Jack also rose and again took Karl's offered hand. 'Remember your promise to me,' he reiterated but in a more serious tone. 'No bloody heroics. That's how I lost a lot of mates in the last war.'

'You shouldn't be in this one, Uncle Jack,' Karl said. 'You should be home enjoying that fortune I heard you finally inherited.'

'Not much good to an old hand from Papua,' Jack answered. 'Unless he has someone to share it with.'

'Maybe one day,' Karl said, turning on his heel to walk away. 'When this bloody war is over.'

Jack watched the young man walk away, trailing his well-used Tommy gun. 'Maybe one day when the war is over' echoed in the distance between them.

Jack sat down and continued cleaning his rifle. How much more would the war take from him before it was over one way or the other? he wondered sadly. A giant butterfly flitted across the clearing to land on the edge of an empty ammunition box. Jack stared at it. His thoughts were not looking back but forward as he stripped down his newly acquired weapon. Somewhere in one of Sydney Harbour's little bays sat his new schooner at anchor. She still had no name.

Ilsa would learn to sail as had Lukas, and the boat would be hers to own, Jack thought. He watched the butterfly flit upwards from the empty ammo box and fly towards the jungle at the edge of the clearing. Before the war came to this land Victoria called it her Eden, he reflected, putting together the last parts of his well-oiled rifle. When he and Ilsa finally got to step aboard the new schooner she would have a name. A name befitting the memory of all those he had loved – and lost. The new schooner would be called the *Eden*.

EPILOGUE

IORA CREEK

August 1942

The jungle was thick and dank. The forward scout slowly lowered himself to the ground, simultaneously giving the hand signal to the man following him that he had spotted something.

Lieutenant Ian Barnes crept cautiously forward to confer with his scout.

'Hear it?' he whispered into the officer's ear, keeping his gaze fixed forward scanning the heavy rainforest ahead for any movement.

'Piston, barrel, butt body and bipod,' came the

distinct chant from a thicket of downed trees ahead on the narrow ridge patrolled by the infantry platoon. Ian Barnes knew the litany well. It was the sequence of stripping a Bren light machine gun.

'Sounds like one of ours,' he hissed back to the forward scout. 'Try and get closer. I will make sure you get covering fire from the machine gun section.'

With a nod, the forward scout proceeded to edge forward on his belly, his old Thompson held forward and ready to use. Behind him, the platoon waited in absolute silence and stillness. In this jungle war, battles were often fought from a mere few yards apart, by an almost invisible enemy waiting in ambush.

The forward scout wriggled to the edge of the fallen timber and, through a space between the logs, could see the man talking to himself. He wore nothing but a pair of shorts and an old floppy broad-brimmed hat. In his lap was a fully assembled Bren gun with two full magazines laying beside him. The man was terribly gaunt from the obvious effects of malnutrition. His face was bearded but the scout could see that whoever this madman was, he was at least European.

'Hey, digger, are you all right?' the scout asked quietly from behind the safety of the logs. The man looked up sharply and swung the loaded Bren in the direction of the voice.

'Who the bloody hell is that?' he rasped. 'Show yourself.'

'Aussie, cobber,' the scout replied. 'Go easy with the Bren.'

The scout slowly raised his head above the logs to reveal himself and the man under the canopy of the rainforest squinted in the semi dark of the day.

'Rifleman Lukas Kelly of the NGVR,' he finally said slowly, lowering the Bren at the sight of the scout's sweating face. 'You are a sight for sore eyes, and you don't have to worry about any Japs for another couple of miles up the track,' he added. 'I know, because I have been wandering around this part of the woods for the last few weeks. At least I think it has been weeks. Maybe it was months, I don't know. But I do know that I would like to get back to Moresby for a cold beer as soon as possible.'

'You and me both, cobber,' the forward scout grinned and guessed that this half-mad soldier, whose body was marked by the ulcers of leech bites, had a courageous story of survival to tell.

AUTHOR'S NOTE

If any one year was to be nominated as the most critical in Australia's short history since the First Fleet arrived in 1788 it would have to be 1942. In that year Australians saw large northern towns such as Darwin, Broome, Derby and others bombed with serious loss of life and property. Not only was Australian soil being attacked as off our coasts German U boats and Japanese submarines sank shipping, but the Japanese navy also infiltrated Sydney Harbour. The tourist walk at Point Danger on the Queensland–New South Wales border provides a plaque describing each sinking in our coastal waters for this generation to view.

That year, 1942, it seemed nothing could stop the Japanese onslaught and many Australians considered it was only a matter of time before Australia was absorbed into the rapidly expanding Japanese Empire.

Eden, although a fictional novel, attempts to describe the role played by the handful of unsung heroes – men who held the gate shut long enough to frustrate Japanese plans and thwart the possibility of invasion on Australian soil while we rallied enough troops to fight the Owen Stanleys campaign.

I realised that these brave men had been mostly forgotten, overshadowed by the subsequent fierce fighting by Australian and American troops to push the Japanese back along the Kokoda Track to the northern ports of Buna and Gona. Such military units I identified as operating before the Kokoda Track battles included the New Guinea Volunteer Rifles, the Coast Watchers, and the men of the doomed 2/22 Battalion stationed in Rabaul. None of them should be forgotten for the sacrifice they made against overwhelming odds in the opening days of the war in the Pacific.

For Jack and Lukas Kelly's military background in the NGVR I am indebted to Ian Down, OBE. His book *The New Guinea Volunteer Rifles NGVR 1939–1943: A History* provided more stories than could be covered in this novel. I only hope that I have honoured the memory of those little-known diggers within the pages of *Eden* in a way that ensures they will not be forgotten in the future.

Although the I–47 is fictional, the experiences of Leading Seaman Fuji Komine are based on fact. Prior to the outbreak of war in the Pacific, the Japanese navy was already actively carrying out espionage in various forms, including the deployment of supplies into the areas around Papua and the nearby

Pacific islands. Their activities were being monitored by the Americans, who had cracked the naval codes and quietly passed on the information to the British Admiralty, who sent a warship to locate and destroy the military dumps before 7 December 1941.

Real names appear within this novel. These are mostly men connected to the NGVR. All the rest is fiction.

The occasional references to the HMAS *Vampire* and HMAS *Hobart* are the result of the author's indulgence; as my Uncle John Payne from Tweed Heads served on both ships during the actions referred to. He was on the *Vampire* when it was escort to the *Prince of Wales* and *Repulse* when those two ships were sent to the bottom, and was himself on the *Vampire* when it was sunk in the Bay of Bengal. He later served on the *Hobart* at the Battle of the Coral Sea and was aboard when it was torpedoed during the Battle of Savu Island. These actions are but two historical events in the experiences of a sailor who also saw action in the Mediterranean Sea and who after the war continued his service off the Indonesian coast and into Mao's China in 1948.

Peter Watt
Papua

'Papua is a rousing historical adventure'
GOLD COAST BULLETIN

Two men, bitter enemies, come face to face on the
battlefields of France. Jack Kelly, a captain in the
Australian army, shows unexpected compassion towards
his prisoner Paul Mann, a high-ranking German officer.
Neither expect to ever see each other again.

With the Great War finally over, both soldiers return home.
But war has changed everything. In Australia, Jack is alone
with a son he does not know and in Germany, Paul is
alarmed by the growing influence of an ambitious young
man named Adolf Hitler . . .

A new beginning beckons them both in a beautiful but
dangerous land – Papua.

A powerful novel with 'plenty of plot twists and sweaty
jungle intrigue'
SUN-HERALD

Peter Watt
To Chase the Storm

Major Patrick Duffy is torn by conflicting duties: his oath to
the Queen is unwavering as she gathers her armies
together to march on the Boers of southern Africa, but his
duty to his family is equally clear. But when his beautiful
wife Catherine leaves him for another, returning to her
native Ireland, Patrick's broken heart propels him out of the
Sydney Macintosh home and into yet another bloody war.
However the battlefields of Africa hold more than
nightmarish terrors and unspeakable conditions for Patrick
– they bring him in contact with one he thought long dead
and lost to him.

Back in Australia, the mysterious Michael O'Flynn mentors
Patrick's youngest son, Alex, and at his grandmother's
request takes him on a journey to their Queensland
property, Glen View. But will the terrible curse that has
inextricably linked the Duffys and Macintoshes for
generations ensure that no true happiness can ever come
to them? So much seems to depend on Wallarie, the last
warrior of the Nerambura tribe, whose mere name evokes
a legend approaching myth.

Through the dawn of a new century in a now federated
nation, *To Chase the Storm* charts an explosive tale of love
and loss, from South Africa to Palestine, from Townsville to
the green hills of Ireland, and to the
more sinister politics that lurk behind
them. By public demand, master
storyteller Peter Watt returns to this
much-loved series following on from the
bestselling *Cry of the Curlew*, *Shadow
of the Osprey* and *Flight of the Eagle*.

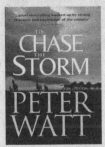

PHOTO: DEAN MARTIN